Bean, Greg.

Grave victory /

GRAVE VICTORY

Other books by Gregory Bean

No Comfort in Victory
Long Shadows in Victory
A Death in Victory

GRAVE VICTORY

GREGORY BEAN

ST. MARTIN'S PRESS ♊ NEW YORK

A THOMAS DUNNE BOOK.
An imprint of St. Martin's Press.

GRAVE VICTORY. Copyright © 1998 by Gregory Bean. All rights reserved. Printed in the United States of America. No part of this book
may be used or reproduced in any manner whatsoever without written permission except in the case of brief quotations embodied in
critical articles or reviews. For information, address St. Martin's
Press, 175 Fifth Avenue, New York, N.Y. 10010.

Library of Congress Cataloging-in-Publication Data

Bean, Greg.
      Grave victory : a Harry Starbranch novel / by Gregory Bean.—
1st ed.
        p.   cm.
      ISBN 0-312-18590-1
      I. Title
PS3552.E1525G7   1998
813'.54—dc21   98-2825
                                                        CIP

First Edition: May 1998

10   9   8   7   6   5   4   3   2   1

For Linda

Truth never comes into the world but like a bastard, to the ignominy of him that brought her forth.

—John Milton

It's silly to go on pretending that under the skin we are all brothers. The truth is more likely that under the skin we are all cannibals, assassins, traitors, liars, hypocrites, poltroons.

—Henry Miller

ONE

I rolled my Jeep to a stop at the bottom of Cassie Buchanan's driveway behind an aging Volvo sedan with a faded "Wyoming Native" bumper sticker. In front of it was a new Toyota four-wheel-drive with a temporary permit in the back window and a newer sticker on its shiny chrome bumper: "God, just give me one more boom, and I promise not to piss it away."

Above us, on the wooden deck of Cassie's tidy split-level home—just at the point where the city limits of Victory, Wyoming, end and the piny foothills of the Snowy Range begin—a lethargic-looking golden lab with a floral-print bandana around its neck stood up and peered between the boards of the railing to see if we were anyone worth eating.

"Mornin', Buttercup," I called out.

The dog recognized my voice, gave a desultory wag of its tail and lay down at the top of the steps, tongue lolling in the warm August sun, huge paws hanging over the edge of the top step, tail thumping the wooden planks of the deck. Quite a watchdog, Buttercup.

I turned off the engine but didn't get out, just listened morosely to the ticking of the hot motor as it began to cool. The bright sunlight coming through the windshield burned my knuckles as I drummed my fingers on the steering wheel.

"I don't know exactly why she wants to see you this time, but it won't hurt you to find out," said my passenger, Frankie Tall Bull.

Bull, a six-foot-four-inch Teton Sioux who tips the scales on the far side of three hundred pounds is the only officer on the Victory police force, a proud unit of which I am chief. Dressed in his unofficial uniform—black jeans, black leather motorcycle vest over a long-sleeved white shirt, mirrored sunglasses, eagle feathers in his braided black hair, a bone-handled bowie knife on one hip, and a .44 magnum on the other—Bull's menacing appearance belied his talents as a sculptor, gourmet cook, and aficionado of tawdry romance fiction. He can also be a nag, not my favorite character trait.

"It might not hurt, but I can almost guarantee it won't be pleasant," I told him. "And you know why she wants to see me as well as I do. Same reason as always. Hasn't changed for the last ten months, and it's not gonna change today."

He smiled indulgently. "Well, even if it's the same old song and dance, can it hurt to listen to it one more time?" he asked. "She really believes Carl's innocent."

I blew air through my cheeks, pulled off my sunglasses, and tucked them in my shirt pocket. Frankie and I had gone over this ground for a week, ever since Cassie called to request yet another meeting, and I was fairly sick of it. I regretted allowing him to cajole me into driving by her house in the first place. Now that I was there, having second and third thoughts, what I really wanted to do was turn around and do something pleasant *and* productive, like head to Ginny Larsen's Country Kitchen for lunch.

"I was a homicide detective for a long time, Frankie," I told him. "And mothers never want to believe their own kids are capable of murder, not even in a case like this where the evidence was strong enough to get him the death sentence. She still won't believe it after all of his appeals have run out and they strap him down on the gurney, give him the needle, and send his miserable soul where it belongs. There's nothing I can do or say that's gonna change that, and to tell the truth, I'm not even sure I want to waste my breath."

I quit drumming my fingers and grabbed the wheel hard. "I think he killed that girl, Frankie. Murdered her in cold blood. He's getting exactly what he has coming."

Frankie reached over and laid a big hand on my shoulder.

2

"Maybe so, Harry," he said softly. "But whether or not Carl Buchanan is a stone killer, Cassie is your friend. You need to hear her out. You owe her that much, at least."

Of course he was right. I just didn't want to admit it, and had been using any excuse to put the visit off. "I could listen to her from now 'til sundown, and it wouldn't make a bit of difference," I said unhappily. "There's nothing I can do for her kid, even if I wanted to. The girl wasn't murdered in our jurisdiction. It wasn't our case."

Frankie sighed. He was as sick of the ongoing dispute as I was. "Then we've got nothing to lose but a half-hour of our precious time," he said. He opened the passenger door and folded his long legs out. He's so tall, it seemed to take him forever to stand up.

I cursed under my breath, pulled the keys from the ignition, and tucked them under the seat. "I can't believe you, Frankie," I snapped. "For a week now you've been pestering me to come over here and listen to Cassie Buchanan tell me one more time that Ken Keegan and the State Department of Criminal Investigation got the wrong man and beg me to do something about it. You don't think Carl's innocent, do you?"

He shook his head no. "What I *think* is beside the point," he said impatiently. "What I *know* is that Cassie Buchanan has always been there for you, defended you when almost everyone else in town wanted your hide nailed to a barn door. Now she thinks you're her last hope, the only chance she has of keeping her son alive. You can disabuse her of that notion if you want to, but now that I've finally gotten you this far, by God, you're gonna listen to her, even if I have to carry you in there myself."

"You could try," I muttered halfheartedly, but I was getting out of the Jeep when I said it. Sometimes, arguing with Frankie Bull is like debating a force of nature. I figured I might as well do what he wanted and get the visit over with. Not that I had much choice. I knew him well enough to know he wasn't joking when he said he'd carry me in if he had to.

Cassie Buchanan met us at the screen door and ushered us into her darkened kitchen. Dirty dishes filled both sides of the double sink, and the counters were covered with bread wrappers, jelly jars, used tea bags, empty baked-bean cans, and plenty of other stuff I didn't want to think about. The plastic garbage can was full, and a black trash bag sealed with a twist-tie sat in a cranny near the front door. The mahogany table was littered with cups, newspapers, and magazines. The air smelled faintly of rotten potatoes and cooked bacon.

Cassie, muttering an apology about the mess, waved us toward the table, where I had to move a stack of back issues of the *Laramie Boomerang* off a chair before I could sit down. I laid my hands on the tabletop, but removed them when I felt something sticky.

I'm no perfectionist when it comes to housework, but the disarray took me by surprise and spoke volumes about Cassie's mental state. I'd been in her home on a number of occasions, and it had always been spotless. She'd never greeted me in her housecoat and slippers before, either. Usually, she dressed for every occasion, even a visit to the beautician, like she was on her way to high tea at the Waldorf. Now, she had other things on her mind.

Cassie didn't sit down, but stood with her hip resting against the countertop. Her iron-gray hair was disheveled, and she brushed a strand of it away from her eyes. She looked tired. "Thanks for coming, Harry," she said, not even trying to hide the rebuke in her voice. "I was beginning to think you wouldn't bother. Lord knows you wouldn't be the only person in town who's made it his mission to avoid me since this thing happened."

I spread my hands in apology. "I haven't been avoiding you, Cassie," I lied. "It's just that we've been . . ."

"Busy," she broke in. "I know how busy you've been. Hell, between the two of you, you've probably had to write at least a half-dozen speeding tickets in the last week, to say nothing of all the time you've put in sitting on that bench outside your office in case a tourist gets lost on the only main road through town."

I felt my face flushing with embarrassment, but I didn't answer because, of course, there was no answer. I stared at the toes of my boots, took my punishment, and waited for Cassie to go on. She was silent for several long seconds, and when she spoke again, her biting anger had been replaced with sadness.

"Of all the people in Victory, I expected better of you, Harry Starbranch," she said. "I thought we were friends."

I rubbed my knuckles over my eyes and sighed. "We are friends, Cassie," I said. "But we've gone over it and gone over it. I can't do a solitary thing to get Carl out of this trouble."

"And you wouldn't even if you could," she said, poking the air with a knobby finger to drive home her point. "Because you think he's guilty."

I shrugged. She was my friend, and I wanted to protect and comfort her, but I couldn't lie. I did think Carl was guilty. He'd even confessed. And for what he'd done, I agreed with the twelve jurors who recommended he pay for the crime with his life.

Ten months before, a couple of antelope hunters working the high plains near Bosler in Albany County noticed a trio of coyotes hanging around the opening of a drainage pipe used to keep the rocky jeep trail that provided access to their hunting area from washing away in a flash flood. The coyotes ran off as the hunters approached, and the men soon discovered what had piqued the animals' interest. The body of a young woman with ligature marks around her neck lay near the entrance of the pipe, half-submerged in water. From the looks of things—her color, the bloating, and the fact that scavengers had already consumed a lot of her flesh—she'd probably been there a while.

After the hunters reported their grisly discovery and the authorities brought the body back to town, it was only a matter of minutes until Tony Baldi, the county sheriff and my personal nemesis, pulled the only missing-person report filed with his department in the last three months and identified the victim. He said she was Victoria Austin, a twenty-four-year-old grad student from Port Arthur, Texas, who'd ten days earlier been reported absent from her position as a research assistant at the University of Wyoming's agricultural college in Laramie. Austin had begun an important lab experiment late one afternoon and failed to show up to finish it the next morning.

Due to an apparent lack of physical evidence and Tony's own general ineptitude, that's about as far as his investigation went. Inside of a week, he threw up his hands and requested the assistance of the State Department of Criminal Investigation, which assigned my friend, Ken Keegan, one of the best criminologists in the state, to the case. It didn't take Keegan long to start putting it together.

Twenty-eight-year-old Carl Buchanan, a heroin addict who'd taken two falls for drug offenses and one for grand theft auto, had an older brother, Trace, who was a professor in the agricultural college. When Keegan spoke to Trace and to Austin's adviser, a professor by the name of Annie Quinn, he quickly learned that Victoria Austin had been the victim of several harassing phone calls during the previous six weeks. And she had complained several times that she believed she was being followed. Trace even confided that he suspected Carl, who on a visit to his older brother at the university had met Austin and had seemed smitten with her, might have been the caller. Although he didn't want to get Carl in trouble, Trace told Keegan that Carl had a history of developing obsessive crushes on women he barely knew and on more than one occasion had been visited by the police for harassing the women on the telephone.

Keegan confirmed through phone records that Carl had indeed called Austin on his cellular phone no less than ninety-three times in the six weeks before her death.

Armed with the only decent physical evidence recovered from the site where Austin's body had been found—a partial tire print in the soft earth about fifteen yards from the drainage pipe and a few strands of long, sandy-colored hair the state crime lab technicians found caught in the murdered woman's clothing that didn't match her dark brown locks—Keegan got a warrant to search Carl's apartment in Laramie and brought him in for questioning.

Forensics eventually determined that the tire print was an exact match with a tire on Carl's Ford pickup and that the hair came from Carl's own scalp. But Keegan didn't need that circumstantial evidence to make his case because after about eight hours of questioning, Carl broke down and confessed.

Although Carl recanted his written confession during the trial, he told Keegan that he had been stalking Austin and had become increasingly angry at her spirited rebuffs of his advances. On the evening she disappeared, he said, he'd followed her from the university to the darkened parking lot of her apartment building. When she rejected him again and threatened to call the police, he said he held her in a sleeper hold until she was unconscious, and then he put her in his pickup and headed out of town. On a deserted side road, he tried to have sexual intercourse with his victim, an effort that failed because the heroin in his veins prevented him from gaining an erection.

He strangled her with a length of clothesline he found in the back of the pickup, he said, because he was afraid she would tell the cops, even though she promised she wouldn't if he'd only let her live. After that, he threw her body in the back of the truck, drove to the prairie near Bosler, and dumped her. The rope was never found. In his statement, Carl claimed he must have lost it.

Carl Buchanan's confession matched what Keegan had learned from forensic and autopsy reports. And hair, fingerprints, and minute blood traces matching the victim's and found inside Buchanan's pickup suggested that she had been a passenger in the vehicle.

Three months later, in late January, a twelve-person jury sitting in the district court in Laramie found Carl Buchanan guilty of premeditated murder. Even though he and the expensive attorney Cassie hired to defend him claimed the evidence had been planted and his confession coerced, the jury recommended the death penalty, and the judge enthusiastically agreed.

Cassie, a divorced woman who'd raised her two sons on the money she made as a landscape artist and free-lance writer for women's magazines, had been fighting like a wildcat to get him off death row ever since. At this point, we all knew she was grasping at straws.

"I apologize, Cassie," I said, "but I can't help what I think. You're a good woman, and I see what this has done to you, but you have to know I think Carl did just what they said."

Cassie scoffed. "That evidence was bullshit. Every bit of it. If they'd only done their jobs and investigated instead of jumping to absurd conclusions, they'd have found that . . ."

"Ken Keegan is also my friend," I broke in, "and one of the best investigators I've ever known. I've got to believe that if he . . ."

"Ken Keegan is a no-good son of a bitch," she spat. "He made my son confess to a murder he didn't commit, and now they want to *kill him!* What kind of man would do something like that, Harry? Is that the kind of person you call a friend? Because if it is, I don't want to be on your list."

She shuddered violently then, her frail body racked by choking sobs. I stood and put my arms around her shoulders, held her close, felt her heart hammering beneath her robe. "I'm sorry," I said gently. "If there were a way for me to take away your pain, I'd do it. But I can't do that, Cassie; you've got to do it for yourself. And the first step is taking a realistic look at the facts and admitting that . . ."

She pushed me away angrily, and when she spoke, I could see it took every ounce of self-control she possessed to form the words. "There's only one fact that's important here, and it's that Carl is innocent, damn you!" she hissed between clenched teeth. I didn't see her hand coming up to slap the side of my face until it was too late. Her palm connected with my cheek forcefully enough to leave an angry red mark. While it didn't hurt that much, it did render me speechless with surprise.

Cassie's anger was almost immediately replaced by a look of horror when she realized what she'd done. She shook her head as if to clear it, and tears gathered in her eyes. She reached out and touched my cheek gently with her fingertips. "I didn't mean that, Harry," she whispered. "I don't know what . . ."

"Don't worry about it," I told her brusquely. I turned away and started for the door. Behind me, I heard Frankie's chair scraping the wooden floor of the kitchen as he stood up. Despite the slap, I was almost happy. This was turning out to be the shortest conversation I'd had with Cassie in months.

"Harry?" she asked plaintively.

I stopped reluctantly and turned around. Frankie was watching my face, with a sheepish expression on his own. He knew exactly what I was thinking, that I'd make him pay for dragging me into this against my better judgment. "What is it, Cassie?" I asked. "What do you want from me? What do you think I can do? Do you know something that might help Carl? Have you come across some new evidence? Anything?"

"No," she said quietly.

"Then what do you want?" I asked again, more forcefully.

"You're all I have left—even those private investigators in Cheyenne turned me down," she said simply. "I need your help."

She looked so hopeless and pitiful, I felt my resolve weakening. I fought it off, tried to put some steel in my voice. "What can I do?" I asked, the same question I'd posed to her a hundred times before. "This was never my case, and even if it were . . ."

"I know exactly how you feel, so I'm not asking you to try to get him off," she broke in. Her statement stopped me in my tracks.

"Then what . . ."

"All I'm asking is that you find something, *anything*. Anything that will mitigate Carl's sentence, get it reduced from a death penalty to life imprisonment. If you can do that, it will be more than enough."

Oh, is that all? I wondered. Might as well ask me to heal a leper, turn water into wine. "Cassie, I don't see any point in . . ."

"Harry," Frankie broke in, his wide face clouded with emotion, his tone telling me to shut up and give the poor woman a break. I gave him a look that said I thought he was crazy, and completely out of line for butting in. He shrugged his wide shoulders. What could it hurt?

How do I get myself into these situations, I wondered ruefully. I shuffled my feet and fumed for a couple of minutes, then decided to throw my tormentors a bone—something to get the pair of them off my back long enough to escape from Cassie's kitchen. I'd deal with Frankie later. "All right, Cassie, I'll make a couple of calls," I grumbled. "But don't expect anything to come of it." Then I slammed out the screen door and almost tripped over the sleeping Buttercup as I hurried down the stairs.

If I had known then where my desperate promise would lead, I would have driven away and not looked in the rearview mirror until I hit Bolivia.

I was so angry I didn't speak to Frankie until we got back to the office. Instead, I kept my hands on the wheel and my eyes on the road, glancing from side to side as I checked the midday pulse of my adopted hometown. For a town of only 650 full-time residents, Main Street in Victory was crackling with activity.

Nestled in the foothills of the Snowy Range on Highway 130, the only paved road that crosses the mountains to the other side in Saratoga, Victory is quiet for most of the year except the summer. Then, we are invaded by hordes of Bermuda shorts–wearing, Winnebago-driving tourists from places like Ohio and New Jersey, every harried one of them anxious to soak up a little local color before they head back to the mall-infested, traffic-congested flatlands they are trying so desperately to escape. Their harsh accents and hurried manners try our patience, but we tolerate them because they spend money, enough of it in fact, to keep our municipal coffers and the pockets of most local businesspeople full through the lean months between September and June.

Aside from the occasional missing toddler, case of heatstroke, or overindulgence in too many margaritas at the Trail's End or Gus Alzonakis's—the two competing steak houses that sit across from each other on the highway into town—the tourists don't cause Frankie and me much trouble. At the city limits coming into town from Laramie, we park a decrepit old sedan painted black and white and festooned with a red coffee can on the roof. Known affectionately as the Starbranch Unmanned Traffic Control Device, the dummy cop car looks enough like the real thing to cause most speeding tourists to take their foot off the gas. By the time they realize the scam, they're almost to the other side of town, where they have to goose it again in hopes of gaining enough momentum to nurse their RVs over the 10,847-foot pass at the top of the Snowy Range.

Once in a while, one of the tourists fails to notice the Unmanned Traffic Control Device in time, and also fails to notice that our municipal speed limit plummets from fifty-five to fifteen miles per hour at the exact point where Highway 130 crosses the Victory city limits. In those cases, we get out our citation books and write our hasty guests a $25 ticket. Once in a while, we're called to break up a scuffle between tourists and locals at one of the steak houses or gas stations. And occasionally, the county sheriff calls us in to assist in the search and rescue of a greenhorn who has wandered away from his campsite and can't find the way back.

Other than that, we have plenty of time to devote to keeping the full-time residents of Victory on an even moral keel and to taking care of the other consuming passions in our lives—fly-fishing, hand-tying trout flies, and reading trashy mysteries for me; sculpting, cooking, and being a decent husband to wife Frieda for Frankie.

That day, it seemed as if every one of the town's parking places was taken by a vehicle with out-of-state plates, and the sidewalks were crowded with families of wide-eyed kids and parents who looked like they'd been too long in a cramped space with their offspring and were grateful for a chance to stretch their muscles and get a breath of air that didn't smell like bubble gum or orange soda.

I noticed a handful of locals mixed in with the throng, but there were probably two hundred package-laden people on the three-block length of Main Street I didn't recognize. It was the kind of free-spending summer crowd Victory merchants live for. Three young boys rushed out of Shapiro's Hardware happily clutching new Zebco fishing reels and poles, followed by a man I took to be their father, chasing after them as he tried to stuff his wallet back in his pocket. Down the block, a sixty-something couple admired the new outfits I imagined they'd purchased at the dry goods store. I figured his new lizard-skin boots set the man back at least two hundred bucks, the Stetson he was wearing tilted back on his head about a hundred more. His wife's new boots and Western dress were probably less expensive, but she was wearing enough turquoise jewelry to have set them back five hundred easy. By the time they were thirty miles out of town, his tight new pointy boots would be hurting his toes, and so would hers; the hat would be constricting the blood flow to his brain, and the clunky jewelry would be causing a crick in her neck. They'd regret their rash purchases immensely, but by that time it would be too late to turn around and return them without going all the way back over the mountain. Score another win for free enterprise, capitalism, and the great American way.

It even looked like my boss, Mayor J. B. "Curly" Ahearn, was having a good day at his bar, the Silver Dollar Saloon. Curly and his assistant manager, a Dolly Parton look-alike named Lou McGrew, had set up a huge barbecue beside the front door, which had attracted a crowd of tourists waiting for Polish sausages, ribs, and fresh corn on the cob.

I whipped the Jeep into the reserved space in front of the police department and killed the engine. Frankie, whose long legs make it difficult for him to get comfortable in almost any vehicle, was scrunched in the bucket seat on the passenger side, peering at the street carnival and humming a Garth Brooks tune. I think it might have been "The Beaches of Cheyenne," but because he even hums off-key, I wouldn't bet the rent.

After all we've been through together, it's hard for me to stay mad at Frankie, and I figured I'd given him enough of the silent treatment. "Are you happy now?" I asked.

I couldn't see the look in his eyes behind the sunglasses, but he was smiling. He quit humming and slapped the knees of his black jeans like he was knocking out the dust. "*Happy* is a relative term," he said. "If you're asking, am I generally happy with my life, I suppose I'd have to say yes. If you're asking, am I happy at this particular moment, I'd have to say no. Right now, I'm too hungry to be happy in the strictest sense." He rubbed the hard muscles of his stomach. "You suppose we could go over to Ginny's and get some chili-cheeseburgers before we go back to work?"

12

All I needed in my life was another smart ass. "You know exactly what I meant, Frankie," I grumbled. "Are you happy about that scene at Cassie's?"

"Oh, that," he chuckled. He opened the door and got out. "That I'm very happy about."

"I don't know why," I muttered. "All we did was get her hopes up for nothing. It's not gonna change a thing."

"You don't have to change anything," he said. "That's not important."

"What do you mean?"

Frankie had the look of a patient fourth-grade teacher explaining long division to an especially dense student. "Let me ask you a question, Harry," he said. "When you were running for re-election as county sheriff a few years ago and Tony Baldi was doing his best to assassinate your character, who in Victory wrote at least ten letters to the editor of the *Boomerang* attesting to your sterling moral fiber and fitness for office?"

Oh, oh. Here we go again. "Cassie," I said, "but this is much different, this is . . ."

He waved me off impatiently and held up two fingers, counting off his questions. "And the next year, when Kit Duerr put that bullet in your shoulder and smashed up your leg, who was it who brought you Sunday dinner and the latest hardback mystery every week for two months while you were recuperating? It wasn't me, Harry, because for a good part of that time, I was out of commission too. It wasn't Curly, either."

"You know who it was," I snapped.

He smiled, happy I was finally getting it. He held up a third finger. "And the next year, when Curly was in jail on that phony murder rap and the town council fired you, who was it who organized the petition drive to get you reinstated?"

"Curly gave me my job back, Frankie," I snapped, "as soon as the prosecutor dropped the charges against him."

He shook his head. "That's a technicality, Harry," he said. "If Curly hadn't given you your job back when he did, Cassie Buchanan would have stirred things up on your behalf around here so thoroughly every person on that council would have had to sneak out of town in the dead of night."

"You're right," I said, "but this is something else. Carl Buchanan is a gutter-crawling piece of slime, Frankie, a stinking hunk of human excrement. There's no way in hell I want to do anything that would help . . ."

"But his mother's your friend, and she's a good woman," he broke in. "It's not important what her son did; you owe her. So what if you don't turn anything up? At least she'll know you tried. *That's* what's important."

I hung my head and stared at my feet, kicked up a little dust storm with the toe of my boot. "I don't know," I said. "I just don't feel . . ."

"Listen, Harry," he said, more serious now. "I know how you feel, but you know I'm right, whether you want to admit it or not. And if I thought you didn't know, I couldn't respect you as much as I do. I'm just encouraging you to quit stalling and do the right thing."

"And what's that, Frankie?" I groused.

"Make the calls like you promised," he said brightly. "I'll handle things around here, so you can start right after you eat."

Then he steamed off toward Ginny's, leaving me to hobble after him as fast as my bum leg would allow.

TWO

In a murder investigation, you always start with the victim and work from there. But this wasn't a murder investigation, and since I already knew Carl Buchanan killed Victoria Austin, I decided I'd start with him if possible.

Unfortunately, even a cop can't just drop in unannounced on a death row inmate, even in a small and usually informal state like Wyoming. When Frankie and I finished our lunch at Ginny Larsen's, Frankie skulked off to discourage speeders, and I lumbered back to the office, where I propped my boots on the desk and dialed the number of the Wyoming State Penitentiary in Rawlins.

Both the warden and his assistant were in a staff meeting, but I explained my desire to an administrative aide, who said she'd pass the request for an interview along to Carl Buchanan's counselor, who'd run it by Carl. If the condemned man agreed, they'd set up an appointment for a visit at the penitentiary. "I wouldn't get my hopes up, though," she said. "He's had about a thousand requests for interviews since the sentence, and he's turned them all down."

I knew the media had been drooling for a chance to go one on one with Buchanan in a jailhouse interview, not only because of the brutality of his crime, but because he was unique. For all its reputation as a wild and woolly bastion of frontier justice, Wyoming doesn't hand out death sentences lightly, and had only put one person to death in the last two decades. At the moment, Buchanan was the lone inmate on death row, and the only one who was likely to be in residence for the foreseeable future. Quite a story. Might even knock a story about wolves or some other liberal environmental think piece off page one of the *Casper Star-Tribune,* Wyoming's statewide newspaper.

"I'm not looking to get him in the papers," I said. "I'm talking to him at his mother's request. Tell him that, would you? It might make a difference."

I sat there in the chilly silence that followed, listening to the static on the ancient telephone lines that link Victory to the outside world. "You're helping Carl Buchanan?" she finally asked. "Are you working for his lawyer?"

"I thought I told you I'm a cop. I'm not working for him or his lawyer," I said defensively. I was embarrassed that this woman I'd never even met thought I was working for someone like Buchanan, and a little angry, I felt the need to explain myself. "I'm a friend of his mother's, doing her a favor."

"I'm sure they'll want to check that out," she said icily. She didn't clarify who "they" were, and I didn't want to ask. I didn't want our conversation to go on any longer than was absolutely necessary.

"That shouldn't be difficult," I said. "You have any idea when someone might get back to me on this?"

"None whatsoever, Mr. Starbranch," she said. "But we've got your number." The way she emphasized the word *number* told me she meant it both literally and figuratively. She hung up without another word.

I cursed the receiver and slammed it back in its cradle. Then I sat and stewed for about five minutes, listening to the hum and rattle of our window-box air conditioner and the ticking of the windup grandfather clock.

On Main Street outside my office window, I could see Frankie down the block writing a ticket to a balding man in sandals, baggy shorts with tropical flowers, and a bright pink T-shirt. The man's face was flushed, and he was gesturing angrily with his bony arms. Frankie was unflappable, and waved good-naturedly at the perpetrator's kids, whose eyes were wide as saucers and who had their noses pressed against the glass of their minivan. I doubted they'd seen many cops back home wearing a bowie knife and eagle feathers.

I watched the drama until Frankie finished writing the summons. Then I picked up the phone again and dialed Ken Keegan's number at the State Department of Criminal Investigation.

Despite the reason for my call, I was looking forward to speaking with my friend. In the years since I quit my job as a homicide investigator for the Denver Police Department and moved to Victory in search of a quieter life and a shot at avoiding a mid-life psychological meltdown, Keegan and I had worked a number of difficult and dangerous cases together, and we'd developed a strong personal relationship based on mutual respect and trust. A black Irishman in his late forties with a nineteen-fifties brush cut, a stocky, square frame, and perpetually rumpled suits, Keegan is one of the most competent and honorable law enforcement professionals I've ever had the honor of working with.

He's also a pretty decent fly-fisherman, and I figured that after we finished talking business, I'd try to coerce him into driving over the mountain to Victory that weekend for a bit of late-summer trout fishing on the Little Laramie. I had a half-dozen Royal Coachmen I thought he was going to love—so realistic, even he could catch a fish with one on the end of his line. Afterward, I'd treat him to a prime rib dinner at the Trails End. As I recalled, it was my turn to buy.

Keegan answered on the third ring, his cigarette-scarred voice as rough as pea gravel in a Highway Department crusher. "Keegan here, speak to me," he croaked. He sounded like one of the half-human creatures in *The Island of Dr. Moreau.*

"Jesus, you sound awful," I said. "You sure you shouldn't be home in bed?"

"Fuck you too, Hollywood," he laughed. "What's the matter? You get tired of basking in the celebrity limelight? Decide it was time to touch base with the common folk?"

That was his standard opening these days, but I didn't rise to the bait. A year and a half before, a murder investigation had culminated in a showdown with a cold-blooded killer named Kit Duerr, who in addition to being a racist, dry-gulching coward was a nationally known professional football player.

I crawled away from the shootout with a ruined leg and a bullet in my shoulder, but Duerr didn't, and the story made international headlines. I sold my side of the tale to one of those real-life cop programs for an embarrassing amount of cash. There was even talk of a movie, but that died as soon as the next tragedy came along to capture the media's attention.

My fifteen minutes of fame was over in exactly fifteen minutes and two seconds, but people in the law enforcement community around here started calling me "Hollywood," and it stuck. For a while, I tried to discourage them, which only made it worse. Now I just bite my tongue.

"As I remember, you've got a full complement of fingers," I said. "The phone line goes both ways, pardner. You can push the buttons as well as I can."

He laughed again, deep in his chest. "You're right, Harry. I've been remiss," he said. "But it's always good to hear your charming voice. Are you calling for a professional reason or a personal one?"

"A little of both," I admitted. Unlike the woman at the penitentiary, I figured Keegan wouldn't be angry I was making calls about Carl Buchanan on Cassie's behalf, particularly once I explained how I'd been dragged into the endeavor by the short hairs.

He listened quietly while I told him my story, and clucked his tongue in sympathy when I got to the part about Frankie laying a guilt trip on me the size of Nebraska. "Well, I guess it can't hurt to go through the motions, make her feel better," he said. "And if you're looking for information, you've come to the right place. I'll tell you whatever I can, although you're not gonna find anything to get this skell off."

"I'm not looking to get him off," I assured him. "Cassie just hopes I can find something to get his death sentence commuted to life."

"Good luck," Keegan said. "As far as the jury, the state of Wyoming, and myself are concerned, anything less than death in this case would be a miscarriage of justice. He did it, Harry, pure and simple. He stalked Victoria Austin, tried to rape her, violated her body, strangled her, and dumped her body. It was premeditated murder, and he admitted to it.

"You aren't gonna find much to mitigate that. About the only thing that boy can do is get some religion. Hope Jesus feels a little more forgiving than we do when they meet up."

"You feel pretty strongly about this," I observed.

"That I do," he said. "How much do you know about this case, Harry?"

"Not all that much," I admitted. Then I floated a halfhearted theory. "I followed it fairly closely in the papers, but from what little I know, I figure he might have abducted her without intending to kill her. It sounds like a bad situation that escalated, like he might have panicked when she resisted and strangled her because he didn't know what else to do. From what I've heard about Carl Buchanan, he isn't the sort who would have planned something like this in advance."

"How about the sexual assault? You know the details?"

"The newspaper stories said he tried to rape her, but couldn't get it up," I said. "Maybe that's what pushed him over the edge."

"He was over the edge all right," Keegan said. "Here's a little something that came out in the trial that the papers didn't report because it was too gory, even for them. Before Carl strangled Victoria, he raped and sodomized her with a shovel handle. Tore her up bad. The coroner found wood splinters in her uterus, which was completely ruptured by the force of the thrusts. We never found that shovel. Too bad, too. Would've been evidence."

Keegan paused for a second, letting that gruesome image sink in. "Knowing that, Harry, how do *you* feel?" he asked tersely. "You think Carl Buchanan deserves to spend the next forty or fifty years of his life living at the state's expense, taking correspondence courses from the university, working out at the gym, and filing inmate lawsuits over the cruel and inhuman conditions we're forcing him to suffer?"

He knew me too well to expect an answer. Until I moved to Victory to escape the slaughter—and the toll it took on my mental health—I'd spent almost all of my professional career doing everything in my power to put people like Carl Buchanan on death row, and I'd been fairly successful. So far, three killers had been put to death as a direct result of my investigations, and two more were still waiting on the row in Colorado's Canyon State Prison while their painfully slow appeals process ground to a close. Although I still see their faces most nights before I go to sleep, I maintain a sometimes tenuous hold on sanity by telling myself, over and over, that these were—and are—men who needed killing.

I didn't always feel that way, of course. When I went into law enforcement, I went in idealistic. Like so many young cops, I believed that most criminals could be rehabilitated. I believed it was better for ten guilty people to go free than for one innocent person to be killed by the state's hand. I believed that exercising the death penalty only brings us to the same moral level as the killer, so that when the state takes a life, it harms itself almost as much as the killer's crime did. And I believed that the death penalty wasn't much of a deterrent to crime.

In that much, at least, I was right. The murder rate in death-penalty states is just as high as it is in non–death penalty states, and I've never heard of a single case where a felon refrained from taking a life because the action might eventually cost him his own.

What changed, over time, was my own belief in the righteousness, even the necessity, of the death penalty. Like most people who are honest about their rationalization for supporting capital punishment, I came to realize it's not about deterrence; it never was. It's really about revenge. The only short-coming of the death sentence, I came to believe, is the unfortunate fact that you can kill the bastards only once. It would be better if you could do it six or seven times.

20

I know that sounds harsh, but I'm a product of my environment and experience, so I stand by every word. Show me a person who opposes the death penalty, and I'll show you a person who has never seen a fourteen-year-old high school girl's naked, disemboweled, and sexually mutilated body hanging by the feet from the branches of a tree while her head lies six feet away, staring at her violated, bloody corpse with sightless eyes.

See something like that, and you want the animal who did it to *die*. You want him to die hard. You want to stare into his eyes when his heart stops and he looks beyond the white light at the gates of hell.

I was disgusted with myself for making the call in the first place. "Forget it, Ken" I told him. "I don't even know why I'm doing this. I told her I'd make a call or two, and I've done it. That's good enough."

Keegan didn't speak for several seconds, but when he finally did, his voice was soft, as comforting as someone who sounds like a woodchipper can be. "I'm sorry, Harry," he said. "I know you're not sticking up for Carl Buchanan. You just let your good nature put you in a bad position." He paused briefly. "Tell you what," he said. "Why don't you drive over here to Cheyenne in the next day or so and go through the case files? Take a look at the reports and crime scene photos? At least then you'll know what you're talking about when you tell Cassie there's nothing you can do for her kid."

"Nah," I said. "That's not necess . . ."

"Trust me, you'll fell better," he broke in. "I'll let you buy me lunch afterward at the Hitching Post, and I'll tell you all about all the new gizmos I got for my boat—a new gadget that shows me the contours of the bottom, a doodad that bounces a beam off a satellite and tells me my exact location, a fish finder so sensitive it can show me if the lunker I'm watching is a boy fish or a girl fish."

The tension broken, I chuckled and agreed to his offer. I didn't make a specific appointment, though, because I wanted to keep my schedule flexible in case Carl agreed to an in-person interview at the penitentiary in Rawlins. After that, I might go over the files.

In a murder investigation, I would have done it the other way around. First, I would have thoroughly acquainted myself with the nitty-gritty details of the crime; then I'd interview the suspect. That way, he couldn't lie about what he did or try to confuse me by omitting significant facts. But as I kept telling myself, this wasn't a murder investigation. Unless Buchanan could tell me something that would convince me to take the next step, there was no good reason to make a hundred-and-fifty-mile round-trip to go through the case files, even though I'd enjoy seeing Ken.

"No problem, Harry," he said. "The files will be here when you want them—if you ever decide you do."

When we rang off, I spent the next couple of hours at the Victory branch of the Albany County Library, going through back issues of the *Laramie Boomerang* and the *Casper Star-Tribune* from the time of Austin's murder through Buchanan's subsequent trial.

The trial itself had lasted six days, and held few surprises. Despite his lawyer's best advice, Buchanan had taken the stand in his own defense to claim innocence and swear the confession had been beaten out of him by Ken Keegan. All in all, the news stories made it sound like Carl's attorney had almost allowed him to convict himself. Carl didn't know who killed Austin, he told the jury, because he didn't remember anything about the night of the abduction and murder. He'd consumed so much whiskey and heroin, he'd blacked out around five o'clock in the afternoon and had remained in a drug- and alcohol-induced stupor for the next five days. When he finally came back to earth, he was in a flea-bag motel on the outskirts of Fort Collins, Colorado, his clothing crusted with vomit and less than a dollar in change in his pants pocket.

Although Carl reluctantly admitted he'd harassed young women in the past, had even been arrested for it twice, he promised that wasn't the case with Victoria Austin because he barely knew her and what little he knew told him she "wasn't my type." He'd only seen her a couple of times, he said, when he went to visit his brother at the university, and they hadn't spoken beyond pleasantries.

Needless to say, the county prosecutor chewed him up on cross-examination, made sure nobody believed him. Buchanan had no explanation for the dozens of calls made to Austin from his cell phone, no alibi for the night police believed the abduction had taken place, no explanation for how tire tracks from his pickup came to be yards from the spot where the body was dumped, and no clue as to how hairs from his head ended up on the body. He certainly couldn't account for the victim's blood in the front seat and bed of his truck. When the prosecutor challenged Carl to give the jury one shred of hard evidence to show he was innocent, Carl became hysterical, crying, moaning, and hyperventilating. He eventually had to be carried out of the courtroom by the bailiffs and taken to the hospital emergency room. They pumped him full of antidepressants and sent him back.

There was no mention in any of the news reports about the actual brutality of the sexual assault, but I could imagine how those details played with the jury.

The second surprise was the number of character witnesses who turned up to speak on Carl's behalf, including the former principal of Laramie High School and the daughter of a Laramie city councilman who claimed to be Carl's childhood sweetheart and current girlfriend. The testimony of the character witnesses, in fact, took up two of the six days of the trial—two-thirds of the total time Carl's attorney spent on his defense.

Out of habit, I jotted down the names of the character witnesses, although I doubted I'd ever need them. Then I tucked the list in my pocket, restacked the papers, and spent a few minutes thumbing through the new crop of hardback mysteries the librarian brings in from the main branch just for me. I was halfway through the liner notes for the latest Elvis Cole adventure from Robert Crais when I caught a delightful whiff of perfume I knew very well, since I was the one who bought it.

"I'm always happy to find a municipal employee using his time so productively," Cindy Thompson whispered in my ear. Her breath was warm and moist and smelled of cinnamon. "Although if you have so much time to kill during business hours, I can think of a better way to do it than hanging around the public library." She gave me a kiss on the cheek that undoubtedly left a lipstick impression visible for miles. I'd have to remember to wipe it off before I went back out in public.

"I'll just bet you could," I said. I turned to give her a regulation kiss on the lips, then held her out at arm's length so I could get a better look. As usual, I liked what I saw so much my heart fluttered.

At thirty-seven, Cindy Thompson is still the kind of woman who makes the local cowboys put a little extra swagger in their step when they meet her coming down the street. Five-seven and a hundred-twenty-five pounds, her strawberry-blond hair falls to her shoulders in the kind of luxurious natural curls most women pay a fortune for, framing a lightly freckled face that looks hauntingly familiar when you first meet her—like maybe you've seen her before in an ad for expensive foreign cars. For my money, she's the best-looking woman in Victory, which is fortuitous, since she's also my girlfriend.

A member of the city council (which makes her one of my bosses) and the ex-wife of my banker, Harv Thompson, Cindy and I had been dating exclusively for nearly a year since her divorce was final and my latest attempt at reconciliation with my ex-wife, Nicole, went down in flames. Although neither of us had mentioned marriage, or even living together, ours was a comfortable, supportive relationship enlivened by fairly incredible sex.

Unlike Nicole, who always felt I'd sold myself and my family short by giving up a promising career in the Denver Police Department and moving to Victory for about half the salary, Cindy understood that for me, life in smalltown Wyoming is the realization of an ideal, my two-person police department a destination stop instead of a rung on the journey up the career ladder. Perhaps because she inherited enough money from her family so that she doesn't really have to work at the real estate business she owns, she accepted me for what I am, not for what I might become or what she thought I should be. Our expectations of each other don't go much beyond tomorrow, and so far, we've lived up to them very well.

We hadn't seen as much of each other as either one of us would have liked in recent weeks, however. At the start of the summer, my twenty-year-old son Robert had made two major announcements. First, the kid who never made life plans beyond next Friday night, said he planned to join the Navy. Second, because he absolutely detested his mother's new boyfriend—a balding, fifty-something attorney named Howard Stokes whose vanity plate on his black Mercedes read TORT ACE—he planned to spend his last summer as a civilian with me. Since Robert had barely spoken to me since Nicole and I divorced, I was surprised by his decision, but I agreed readily. I figured it would be good for us to spend some time together mending fences, and besides, I needed his help putting the finishing touches on the new house I'd been building for the better part of a year.

For the past six weeks, we'd spent nearly every evening after work watching baseball or puttering around the house. There were still a host of unresolved issues between us, and more than a little anger on Robert's part, but we were making progress, becoming more accepting, learning a little more about each other every day. Among other things I didn't know about him, I'd discovered Robert had a knack for plumbing and electrical work, which he certainly didn't inherit from me. He was also pretty good with a paintbrush, and best of all, he worked for free, as long as there was plenty of food in the cupboard.

So far, Cindy had accepted my absences without complaint—had in fact encouraged me to spend as much time with Robert as possible—but I could tell it was time for a little preventive maintenance. I gave her another peck on the lips and what I hoped was a seductively devilish smile. "If that was a genuine offer, I'll take you up on it," I said. "Why don't we take the afternoon off? We'll

25

go to your house and find out exactly how a woman like you kills time."

She laughed and took me by the hand. "Sorry, Harry. I'm afraid my mouth was writing checks my body can't cash. I've got an appointment to show the Bauer estate to a stockbroker from Manhattan in about thirty minutes."

"Break it."

"No can do," she said. "It's listed for a million-two. I could use the sale."

What's a million bucks compared to a nice roll in the hay? "Postpone it," I suggested hopefully.

"Can't do that either," she said wistfully. "He's driving back to Laramie to catch a plane immediately afterward. I think this will be my only chance, and I don't want to blow it."

I tried not to let my disappointment show, but I don't think it worked. A frustrated libido always makes me sulky.

"Come on," she chided. "I've got another suggestion."

I perked up immediately.

She took me by the arm and began leading me to the front door of the library, where she waited while I stopped by the desk to check out the book. "What have you and Robert been eating lately?" she asked when I was finished.

"Oh the usual," I shrugged. "Fried bologna sandwiches, canned stew, chili, the occasional steak." I wasn't going for pity, just telling the truth.

"Garbage in other words," she chuckled. "Why don't I come out tomorrow evening and make you two happy bachelors dinner? How does seafood jambalaya, homemade bread, and fresh peach pie sound?"

I smacked my lips in approval. "Wonderful."

We walked slowly down Main Street in the general direction of the office where she'd parked her car. As we strolled, she filled me in on the details of her day, and I told her about mine. There was a hitch in her step when I mentioned I'd agreed to make some calls about Carl Buchanan, but she didn't say anything right away. She was still mulling when we got to the corner, so I stopped and leaned against the wall of Shapiro's Hardware to wait her out. I half-expected she'd be angry I'd agreed to do anything that might help the brutal murderer of a young woman, so I was surprised when she finally spoke her mind.

"I'm glad you're doing this," she said.

"It's the least I can do for Cassie," I stumbled.

She shook her head. "Not just Cassie," she said. "For Carl."

"What?"

"I've known him since he was a toddler, Harry," she explained. "It broke my heart when I read they'd given him the death sentence."

"Yeah, well, he changed from how you remember him," I said, more forcefully than I intended. "Heroin is a real effective behavior modification device."

"Maybe so," she admitted. "But the Carl Buchanan I remember would have been incapable of doing what he's accused of."

"Convicted of," I reminded her.

She reached up and gently stroked my cheek. "I know your opinion on this subject and how you came by it, Harry," she said softly. "I can't even argue with you because I know what drug addiction can do to a person and I didn't sit on the jury. But there's a part of me that just can't believe it, and I'll feel better knowing you've checked things out. The crime they've sentenced him for is horrible, but it will be just as horrible if he dies for something he didn't do."

After I saw Cindy off, I spent a couple of hours involved in the sort of high-level police business that occupies a good portion of my normal working day. In other words, I reviewed the dozen or so call sheets and citations filed since Frankie started his morning shift, took a leisurely walk around town to show the flag, then came back to the office, made a pot of coffee, put my feet on the desk, and dove into the Elvis Cole novel. I've got plenty of bad habits, and I figure any one of them could kill me before my time—but if I drop dead at fifty, at least it won't be from job-related stress.

The only crisis of the afternoon came about four-thirty, when Essie Rock called in a tizzy to report that her Pomeranian, Lucky, had been chasing a squirrel in the backyard and gotten his head stuck in her chain-link fence. Although I didn't think that Lucky, a little drop-kick dog that looked more like an overgrown rat, was in much danger of strangling, I grabbed a pair of wirecutters, raced to the scene, and released the ungrateful mutt. He showed his appreciation by sinking his pointy fangs into my ankle. Fortunately, he couldn't bite hard enough to poke his teeth through the leather of my cowboy boots, but the glare in his tiny, hateful eyes let me know that if he only weighed forty more pounds, he'd cheerfully have had a bite of my ass for lunch.

Frankie had plans to attend an art show and dinner over the mountains in Saratoga that evening, so I sent him home to his wife, Frieda, about six. I was just locking the office door when the phone jangled. I cursed under my breath, trudged back inside, and picked it up. "Starbranch," I answered.

On the other end of the line, I could hear an unpleasant cacophony of noise—banging metal, the loud voices of many men, someone talking on a loudspeaker. In other words, I heard the sounds of a jail. "This is Luther Barnes," the caller said. His voice was harsh, with a trace of an Oklahoma accent. "Carl Buchanan's counselor."

"What can I do for you, Mr. Barnes?"

"It's not what you can do for me," he said. "It's what I can do for you. I hear you requested an interview with Carl Buchanan."

"That's right."

"You got it," Barnes said. "Tomorrow morning, nine o'clock at the penitentiary. He'll give you a half-hour."

I did some quick mental calculation. It was over a hundred miles from Victory to the state pen at Rawlins. A four-hour round-trip, not counting the interview. And unless I could catch Frankie at home that evening, I couldn't make arrangements for him to cover the office while I was away. "This is kind of short notice," I said reasonably. "You think we might reschedule for noon?"

Barnes snorted derisively. "You come at noon if you want to,

Starbranch," he said. "But by that time, your interview with Buchanan will have been over for two-and-a-half hours."

Then he hung up, leaving me listening to nothing but the wind whistling through the long-distance wire.

THREE

The parking lot of the Wyoming State Penitentiary lurks at the end of Higley Boulevard on the outskirts of Rawlins, a dusty town that serves as a fueling stop for motorists setting out across the Red Desert on Interstate 80. It was nearly full when I pulled in at about eight-thirty the next morning.

Guards coming off shift loosened their ties as they ambled down the long sidewalk to their vehicles, and a row of delivery trucks were lined up at the service entrance. I felt the same sense of free-floating anxiety and nonspecific foreboding I feel every time I come near one of those places. Just a bad reaction to guard towers and razor wire, I suppose. Either that, or I was the Count of Monte Cristo in a previous life.

I pulled my Jeep into a visitor's space and followed the signs to the administration building. There, a burly guard met me at the sign-in station, studied several forms of identification, took my .357 Blackhawk, and waited around while I filled out the paperwork required by the prison before anyone can visit a death-row inmate. The exact procedure is supposed to be a big secret, but I can tell you this. One of the forms visitors must sign is one absolving the prison of responsibility if the inmate takes them hostage. If that happens, according to the form, the officials won't bargain for their release. No wonder most visitors leave looking over their shoulder to make sure they're not being followed, some of them making the sign of the cross so frantically it looks like they're giving the Pledge of Allegiance in sign language.

Before he led me down the long hallway to the visitation area, the guard eyed the blackthorn walking stick I've used off and on since Kit Duerr ruined my leg, perhaps debating whether Buchanan could snatch it and use it as a weapon. I'm sure some of the Scots who fought with Bonnie Prince Charlie carried weapons that were not half as effective or deadly, but in the end the guard let me keep it. Maybe it was just professional courtesy. Then again, maybe he hoped I'd have the chance to use it.

The visitors' room was large and sterile, the color scheme institutional green. A row of couches lined the wall on the visitors' side of the glass wall that divided the room in two. The wall itself was partitioned into cubicles, each with a plastic and metal chair you sit on while you talk to the prisoner on the other side. A pall of cigarette smoke hung just below the ceiling, but even that couldn't kill the scent of the dozen competing perfumes of the female visitors or the body odor of some of the prisoners.

About half of the cubicles were already occupied when the guard let me in and pointed to an empty one near the end. When I was seated, he picked up the telephone beside the door and spoke for a few seconds. "They're bringing Buchanan down," he said when he hung up. "When you get ready to leave, one of the guards outside the visitors' room will escort you back to the administration office."

Soon two guards led Buchanan in through the prisoners' entrance, shuffling slowly because of the restraints that bound his ankles and wrists. The buzz of conversation between the other prisoners and visitors dropped to a whisper when Buchanan came through the door, the presence of the lone death-row inmate drawing their morbid attention. A dead man walking, they watched him closely, the way children watch a caged lion or a shark behind the glass wall of a saltwater aquarium.

I watched too, waiting for some glimpse of the violence and unspeakable evil that brought him to this desperate end.

I don't know how I expected this young killer to look, but I was surprised by the man I saw. About five-nine, Buchanan was rail thin and would only break one-hundred-forty-five pounds after a full-course Thanksgiving dinner, and only then if he had plenty of marshmallows on his sweet potatoes. His jailhouse clothes were baggy, and the scrawny arms that poked out of the short sleeves were so insubstantial that I imagined I could circle his entire bicep with my hand. Thin, dirty blond hair hung to his shoulders, and there was a tattoo of Tweetie Bird on his forearm. His face was sallow and gaunt, he had dark circles under his eyes, and his lips were dry and cracked. There was a yellowing bruise on the right side of his forehead around a scrape that had scabbed over and begun to peel. His cheekbones were so pronounced his face looked skeletal, except for his eyes, wide and warm brown, darting around the room like a cornered fox.

I'd seen plenty of hard men in my day, but Carl Buchanan didn't look like one of them. He was just a sack of bones in a skin pouch. I'm no Charles Atlas, but I imagined I could grab Carl by the scruff of the neck and shake him one-handed until he fell apart and died. Unless appearances were very deceiving, I guessed I didn't have to worry about being taken hostage.

I soon discovered, however, that any physical shortcomings were more than compensated for by a surprisingly bad attitude.

He sat down in the chair and fumbled around in his shirt pocket until he came up with a nearly empty pack of menthol cigarettes. He pulled out one that was badly bent, straightened it carefully, and lit it with a paper match. He sucked the smoke deep into his lungs, coughed most of it out, and spent a few seconds picking a piece of stray tobacco out of his teeth. He looked me in the eye to make sure I'd noticed. Mr. Tough Guy. "You must be Harry Starbranch," he said in a voice that was high-pitched and breathy, girlish. "Glad you could finally make it. My mother's been tellin' me you were comin' for so long, I didn't believe her any more."

Two seconds, and he was already coming at me with accusations. I didn't care for it one bit. "Yeah, well, I'm here now," I growled. I'd gotten up with the meadowlarks and driven over a hundred miles to see this killer. I wasn't about to take a bunch of shit from him in the bargain. I went at him hard and fast, my words like bullets. "I'll tell you something else, as long as I have your attention. I came here as a favor to your mother, but I truthfully don't give one rat's ass about you or your problems. I don't appreciate being ordered here like some schoolboy, and I don't appreciate your punk insolence. You get your head on right, Carl, and do it in one damned hurry, or I'll turn around and walk out of here so fast you'll be talkin' to my shadow."

Emotions warred on Buchanan's skinny face as he struggled for a response—outrage, anger, and behind it all, an unmistakable trace of fear. In the end, fear won out. Carl was a drowning man grabbing for a life preserver, even though that life preserver might be held together by barbed wire. He sat back in his hard chair and almost seemed to deflate. His bony shoulders sagged, and his hands, which had been gripping the edge of the table, dropped into his lap. His words came at a high personal cost. "I'm sorry," he said softly. "I know why you're here, and I know who asked you to come." He shrugged his shoulders. "It's just that livin' here is making me crazy. Can you get me out?"

The question, his transparent attempt to narrow the wide gulf between us, almost made me laugh. "I wouldn't count on it," I told him.

His gaze was level, taking my measure. "You wouldn't do it even if you could, would you, Mr. Starbranch?" he asked, letting me know he read me as well as I thought I read him. When I didn't answer, he smiled thinly. "Then what can you do?"

I gave him a shrug of my own, told him the brutal truth. "Probably nothing," I said. "It depends on what you tell me. Maybe, if it's good enough, your mother can convince the governor to commute your sentence to life."

He crushed his cigarette in the overflowing tray, but it stayed lit. Tendrils of foul-smelling smoke drifted up to his face. He brushed them away with a chopping wave of his hand. "Life?" he asked sarcastically. "For a murder I didn't do? Sounds like a hell of a deal to me." His cheeks colored, and some of his old attitude reappeared. "I don't want to spend my life here, damn it. I'm innocent." He pulled another smoke from his pack and flicked a match to life.

Screw this.

I closed the notebook I'd brought along to record the highlights of our conversation, capped my pen, and put it in my shirt pocket. "Come on, Carl." I swept my arm in the general direction of the main prison. "Everyone here is innocent, at least if you ask them. I'm not here to listen to that story. Over the last twenty years, I've heard it ten thousand times, and life's too short to hear it again." I stood up, adjusted my Stetson, and turned for the door. I only made it a couple of steps.

"Don't go," he called, a note of panic in his voice. I turned back and saw him standing, with his palms against the glass that separated us. "You don't believe me, you don't have to," he said. "Just tell me what you want."

I shook my head and turned back reluctantly. As far as I was concerned, the whole thing was a waste of time. Still, I might as well get what I came for. "I want you to tell me the story, with no bullshit, right from the beginning. If I catch you lying, or even have a suspicion you're lying, I'm out of here. Do we understand each other?"

Buchanan nodded and sat back down, waited until I'd seated myself. "I didn't even know Victoria Austin," he said. "How's that for a start?"

Pitiful, I thought, and just what I expected. "Not very good," I said. "If I remember, there was plenty of evidence . . ."

"It's the truth," he broke in. "They say I'd been stalking her, but when the police picked me up for questioning, I didn't even remember her. I guess I met her once when I went to visit my brother Trace, and we maybe talked a little, but I was so high I forgot all about it. I couldn't remember what she looked like until they showed me the pictures."

I wondered if he could remember raping Austin with a shovel handle, but I swallowed my disgust and didn't ask. I'd save that question for later. "What about the phone calls, Carl?" I asked

34

skeptically. "Ninety-three calls to her from your cell phone in six weeks? That doesn't sound like someone who barely made an impression on you."

"Somebody else must have made those calls," he told me straight-faced. "I lost my cell phone three months before that girl's body was found."

"Don't bullshit me, Carl," I said. "They found the damned thing at your house. You telling me someone else used it to make all those calls, and then returned it?"

He shook his head, almost sadly. "I don't know," he said. "All I know is I didn't make them."

I was beginning to understand why the jury hadn't believed him. The man's story was as thin as gossamer. "What about the rest of it?" I prodded. "What about the tire tracks? What about the victim's blood in your pickup? What about your hair on her body? Was some other guy responsible for those things too?"

He thought about his answer for thirty seconds, but when he gave it, it wasn't the one I expected. "I'm a heroin addict," he said. "And if that doesn't get me high enough, I drink and take any other kind of pills I can find. You know what that means, Mr. Starbranch? You know anything about junkies, you should."

"I've been around plenty of drugs and too goddamned many junkies," I told him. "But I don't know what they have to do with anything."

"They've got everything to do with it," he said, leaning forward in frustration. "I've been an addict for over five years, and at this point, drugs are my life. I'm interested in drugs, Mr. Starbranch, not women. I've been through detox now, but even so, a fix is still the last thing I'm thinking about when I fall asleep at night and the first thing I'm thinking about when I wake up. And when I'm high and drunk, I'm impotent. I haven't been able to have sex with my girlfriend for over two years."

By that point, his bottom lip was trembling. "I'm not interested in sex, so why in God's name would I try to rape someone? I have no idea how the blood got in my pickup, or any of the rest of it. I just know it wasn't me. It couldn't have been."

I'd heard more than enough. "That is the single most ignorant thing I've ever heard," I snorted. "Rape isn't about sex, Carl; it's about power, it's about control. I'll tell you what I believe. I believe you when you say you couldn't get it up, and I also believe that's why you used a shovel handle. How did that make you feel, Carl. Did it make you feel strong? Did it make you feel like a real he-man? Really put that bitch in her place, didn't you, pardner?"

He flinched as if he'd been slapped. "I didn't . . ."

I held my hand up to stop him. "Spare me the denial," I said. "I've heard too many fairy tales for one day."

I stood up and took a step toward the door. At the last second, I stopped and turned back toward him. "Where were you the night Victoria Austin was abducted?" I demanded.

He hung his head so low his chin touched his chest. "I don't know," he said. "I went home to fix that afternoon and ended up taking a few pills someone had left behind to get a better buzz going. I blacked out, didn't pull it together for several days. That happens sometimes."

"So you *could* have killed her," I said. "You could have killed her and just not remembered it, right? That's what you're telling me, isn't it?"

"No!" he protested. "I'm telling you I passed out! I'm telling you I didn't do it!"

"Then why did you confess?" I spat. "Seems like you remembered that night well enough to write it all down."

"I didn't write a confession," he said. "I only signed it. That son-of-a-bitch Keegan kept me locked in a room until I broke down. I was coming down, going through withdrawal. I was sick, Mr. Starbranch. He beat me. Stuck a confession he'd written in my face. Told me if I signed it, he'd stop. Told me if I signed it, he'd get me a fix. At that point, I would have signed anything. I would have confessed to killing Nicole Brown Simpson if he wanted. At that point, it just didn't fucking matter."

I laughed out loud. "That's your story?" I asked. "That's all of it?"

He nodded, leaned back in his chair.

36

"You know, Carl, I used to be a murder investigator," I told him. "And one time, I arrested a lowlife name of Dieter Haas, and in his wallet he just happened to have the credit cards of a man whose body we'd found stuffed in a dumpster."

Buchanan looked confused, but I went on with my story. "There was so much blood in the back of Dieter's truck, it looked like he'd been butchering hogs," I said. "And when we got to his house, there was blood all over there too."

I pulled out my sunglasses, put them on. "But the kicker . . . the kicker was the little hunk of skullbone I found between the cushions of his couch. That bit of skull, it turned out, was a perfect match for a chunk of bone missing from the victim's head." I paused, gave him a wicked smile. "I had old Dieter cold, Carl, but you know what he said?"

Buchanan shook his head no.

"He said that piece of bone didn't prove a thing, because he'd bought that couch *used.*" I chuckled at the memory. Dieter standing before me triumphantly, chin forward, red eyes glowing like coals in a bed of slag. Smug, like he'd just discovered the theory of relativity. Daring me to find fault in his outlandish explanation.

"I don't understand," Buchanan stammered.

"It's very simple," I said. "Dieter was lyin' out his ass, but he was tellin' a good story." I pointed the copper tip of my blackthorn in his direction. "Yours, on the other hand, needs a lot of work."

Then I spun on my heels and walked toward the exit.

"Mr. Starbranch!" he yelled, his voice high, pleading.

I didn't turn around, but rapped on the glass to get the attention of the guard stationed on the other side of the door.

"You call me if your memory miraculously improves," I called over my shoulder.

The guard opened the door, held it for me to pass through. I left Buchanan with a bit of cruel counsel. "But don't wait too long, Slick," I warned him. "There aren't many days left on your calendar." The door closed behind me with a metallic thud, and I stalked away, my blackthorn tapping on the tiled floor like a metronome.

Would he take my advice? Did I care? As far as I was concerned, I'd already done as much as I could for Cassie Buchanan's son, which was more than the murdering son of a bitch deserved. I left the prison as fast as my aching legs would carry me, and watched with satisfaction as the grim fortress disappeared in my rearview mirror.

My resolve to wash my hands of Carl Buchanan lasted for most of the ride back to Victory, but it began to fade as I passed the jutting peaks of Elk Mountain. My interview with Buchanan had taken less than thirty minutes, but playing it over in my mind, I gradually came to the guilty realization that its tenor and duration stemmed from my attitude toward Carl and his crime more than from anything he'd said or done.

I was a trained interrogator, but that day I'd behaved like an emotional rookie. I'd told myself my reaction was brought on by his appearance and his attitude, but that wasn't the truth.

I went in believing Buchanan was guilty. I wanted to keep believing it, and I don't know if there was anything he could have said to change my mind. He'd told me the same thing he'd been saying since his trial, and I shouldn't have been surprised that he was sticking to it.

Instead of listening, coaxing the real story out of him bit by bit, prodding here, poking there, taking him through it time after time until I got close to the truth, I'd gotten in his face immediately, willing him to make me mad enough to storm out in a huff. Then I felt righteously angry when he obliged.

Not a textbook example of detached, professional police work. As a matter of fact, it was fairly shameful behavior. If a green detective working for me had acted the same way when I was in Denver homicide, I'd have fired him on the spot. Or at least had him reassigned to traffic.

I couldn't fire myself, however. So what was I going to do now?

I was still mulling over that question when I coasted down the long hill into Laramie and stopped at the light at the intersection of Third Street and Highway 130, which would take me home to

Victory. Instead of going home, however, I knew how I'd be spending the rest of the afternoon.

"Oh shit," I muttered as the light turned green. Instead of turning right on 130, I followed Third to Grand Avenue, turned left, and headed out of town on Interstate 80, which would take me over the mountain to Cheyenne.

An hour later, with my belly rumbling because I'd missed both breakfast and lunch, I pulled into the parking lot of the Wyoming Department of Criminal Investigation, a sprawling, utilitarian structure on the outskirts of Cheyenne with all the personality of a brick-and-glass refrigerator box. I waited in the lobby while the long-legged receptionist buzzed Ken Keegan.

Five minutes later, my square friend emerged from the elevator, looking like he'd wrestled a badger. He was in his shirtsleeves, and his outdated paisley tie was pulled down at the collar. His black suit pants, wrinkled at the back of the knees, rode low beneath a gut that overhung his belt by a couple of inches. There were sweat stains at his armpits, and the straps of his shoulder holster bunched the fabric of his shirt on both shoulders. The ever-present Camel dangled from the corner of his mouth. When he saw me, his face broke into a huge grin. "Harry, good to see you!" he boomed. "You rescued me from The Meeting That Time Forgot."

"Big case?"

"Budgets," he grimaced. "I've been spending so much time on them lately, I might as well be working for the IRS. Sometimes I envy you, Harry. Around here, it's always close more cases, close 'em faster, and do it with fewer resources. God, I miss the oil boom. In those days, we couldn't hire investigators fast enough." He chuckled, clapped me on the shoulder. "They can do without me for a while, though. I'll tell 'em it was pressing police business."

Keegan punched the elevator, and we rode it to the third floor, where his office was located. We shuffled down the hall, made small talk while he scrambled up two coffees, black foul-smelling sludge the consistency of molasses and as bitter as quinine. Cop coffee—it's the same the world over.

I waited until he had his coffee sugared to taste, with the precise amount of powdered creamer floating in gelatinous clumps on top; waited until he'd fired a fresh Camel. And then, because being around Keegan always encourages my own indulgence in bad habits, I pulled a slim cigar from my pocket and lit it with his battered Zippo. I puffed contentedly while I told him how I'd spent my morning.

"So what did you think?" he asked when I'd finished.

"I think we're lucky most killers are as dumb as Carl Buchanan," I said. "It makes 'em so much easier to catch. He still swears you beat his confession out of him by the way. Says you just made up something for him to sign."

"That's his standard song and dance," Keegan snorted. "But he's telling you at least part of the truth. He didn't write that confession. Hell, he was so fucked up it took him a half-hour to sign his name. I just took it orally and had it transcribed." He looked at me thoughtfully. "You don't believe him, do you?"

"Nah," I said. "Between you and me, Ken, I'm just going through the motions for Cassie. Thought I'd come over here and look through the case files, make a couple more calls, and call it good."

"I understand," he said. He stood and walked to a gray metal filing cabinet in the corner of the office, rummaged through the bottom drawer until he came up with a thick manila envelope. He threw it on top of his desk. "I've got to get back to my meeting, but you stay here and take all the time you need," he said. "Afterward, I'll let you buy me an early dinner."

"Sorry, pardner," I said. "Cindy is cooking for Robert and me tonight. Wouldn't be wise to stand the woman up."

"You're a lucky man. When you been married as long as I have, you mostly eat meals that come from the microwave," he said. "How does Robert feel about your girlfriend?"

"Sometimes, I think he likes her better than he likes me."

"A man with extraordinary common sense," he laughed. He pitched his empty Styrofoam cup in the trash, smashed out his latest butt. "If you finish before my meeting lets out, just leave that

40

on the desk," he said, pointing to the folder. "Give me a call tomorrow, and tell me how it's going."

I spent the next hour poring through the investigation reports, Victoria Austin's autopsy report, Buchanan's confession, and the transcripts of his trial. I found no surprises in any of it, nothing that would lead me to suspect Buchanan might be telling the truth. It was an easy case, open and shut. In their effort to put the killer on death row, the good guys didn't have to break a sweat.

The photos of the crime scene, about four dozen eight-by-ten color glossies, were the final items in the pile, and I saved those for last. They were standard evidence photos, some of the general area taken in daylight, and others snapped the night police recovered Austin's body, taken by the harsh light of a strobe.

I glanced through the photos of Buchanan's tire prints, the blood evidence in his truck, the drainage pipe where Austin's body had been dumped. I slowed down when I came to the macabre photos of her corpse. A human body in an advanced state of decomposition is a sobering thing to see, particularly if the body has been further damaged by the effects of water and predators. Definitely not for the squeamish.

Austin was barefoot, but still wearing a pair of faded blue jeans. Her short-sleeved summer shirt had been ripped by the coyotes, and they had opened her body cavity and feasted on her internal organs, which spilled from a ragged wound in her abdomen. The skin of her chest was ghostly white, painted with darkened swaths of gore. Her arms were bloated almost to the point of bursting, the skin of her hands swollen and grotesque.

I could not see her face, however, because her head was tightly wrapped in a jacket that matched her pants. Whoever put it there had held the jacket in place with a knot tied in the sleeves, a double knot so secure even the scavengers had not been able to undo it.

I stared at that awful tableau, absorbing every detail, until my eyes burned and lost focus. My experience told me something in that picture was very wrong.

* * *

Keegan was still in his meeting when I finished with the files, so I left them on his desk and made my way outside to the Jeep. Before I left town, however, I stopped at a convenience store for a large soda, a microwaved burrito, and a handful of quarters. I took the coins outside to the pay phone and thumbed through my black book until I found Aaron Cohen's number in Chicago.

A special agent for the Federal Bureau of Investigation, Cohen had been involved with me in the Kit Duerr investigation a little over a year before. We'd disliked each other on sight, but had come to a grudging mutual respect as the affair came to a close. He was the only person in the bureau who would take my calls on a moment's notice, and certainly the only person who owed me a favor. I was deeply troubled by the crime scene photos, and needed a second opinion. Aaron Cohen was the man to provide it.

After the usual battle with the switchboard, Cohen answered on the second ring. "What can I do for you, Harry?" he asked when we'd dispensed with the pleasantries.

"I need your impressions," I told him. "I'm going to describe a murder and a crime scene to you. I want you to tell me what the details suggest about the killer."

There was a long pause. "I'm not a profiler," he said. "If you want, I'll put you in touch with someone in the Behavioral Sciences Unit. They're much better at this sort of thing than I am."

"That's not necessary, Aaron," I said. "You've gone to their seminars, haven't you? You've got a working knowledge of this stuff. That's all I'm looking for."

"Then shoot," he said reluctantly.

I gave him the details of the initial crime scene reports and the autopsy. Finally, I told him about the jacket tied securely around Victoria Austin's head. "What kind of person killed her, Aaron? Based on what little you know."

He did not hesitate to answer. "Someone very organized."

"Why?"

"Several reasons," he said. "First, they dressed her after the sexual attack. Second, the remote location where the body was discovered suggests whoever killed her didn't want her found, at least not right away. If you'll just let me call one of the guys in Behavioral, I'm sure they'll be able to tell you whether your killer is a man or a woman, how old he or she is, even what kind of car the perpetrator drives. But I can tell you this, it doesn't sound like a crime of opportunity. It sounds like it was fairly well planned."

"What else can you tell me?" I asked.

"Whoever killed her felt bad about it," he said.

"Why?"

"They covered her face," he said. "They didn't want to have to look in her eyes and see what they'd done. Someone who felt no guilt wouldn't have bothered. Look for a planner, Harry. Someone with a clear head."

"The killer's already been caught and convicted," I said. "I'm just doing a little follow-up."

"Oh," he said, surprised. "Does what I've told you describe the murderer?"

"Not in the least. He's a junkie who could barely concentrate on breathing. Here's the rub though. He confessed. Recanted it later, but it was still a solid confession."

Cohen whistled through his teeth. "Then maybe I'm wrong." There was an edge in his voice. He was annoyed I'd held out on him. Men like Cohen do not like to play games. "I'm just talking off the top of my head here, Harry. Like I said, if you want a more thorough interpretation and a lot of detail, you'll have to talk to someone who profiles these bastards for a living. Don't hold me to anything."

"I won't," I said. "But how often are your guys wrong?"

"Their methods are based on hundreds of interviews with convicted killers, and they've been proven time and again," he said. "How often are we wrong? On the small details, fairly frequently. We might get the guy's age wrong. Kind of car he drives. What he does for a living. On the big things? Hardly ever."

"Best guess, Aaron," I said. "What do you think?"

Cohen waited a beat. "I don't like to be put on the spot, Harry," he groused. "But based on what little you told me, if the guy who was convicted is as disorganized as you say, if it wasn't for the confession I'd think it's possible, just possible, they convicted the wrong person," he said. "He doesn't fit the profile for this crime."

FOUR

My girlfriend and my son were in the kitchen when I got to my house about seven-thirty, both of them wearing aprons and using long knives to chop vegetables on a cutting board. The air was thick with the spicy smell of seafood jambalaya and baking pies, a combination that is infinitely more inviting than the odor of scorched bologna, which had been standard fare for Robert and me recently.

I sat the two bottles of wine I'd purchased in Laramie on the way home—a sporty merlot at twenty bucks a pop—on the counter, and gave Cindy a kiss on the back of the neck. She scooted away. "Don't you know better than to disturb a couple of culinary artists at work?" she asked. Then, with mock accusation. "I hope you brought the wine."

"Hi, Pop," Robert said, without looking up. At six-two-and-a-half, my son is just a half-inch taller than me, with the same full head of sandy-colored hair, broad shoulders, and a face too much like mine, one women would call "interesting," but never handsome in the traditional sense. His nose is a bit too sharp, his gray-blue eyes are a little too close together, his forehead a tad too pronounced, and his chin looks like it was carved from a cinder block. Coupled with the earrings he wears, and the scraggly goatee, he looks more than a little intimidating. In fact, if you met him in a dark alley, you'd probably just give him your wallet to save yourself the trouble of being mugged.

He's a courteous and gentle young man though, so I try to curb my opinion of his taste in bodily ornamentation. I figure I'll leave that for the Navy. "Don't call me Pop, you ungrateful puppy, or I'll box your damned ears," I growled good-naturedly. I reached between them to grab a carrot from the cutting board, but Cindy swatted my hand away. Unlike some women I have known, she used the hand without the knife.

"Get yourself a beer, and get out of my kitchen," she said. She wiped a smudge of flour off her nose. "Dinner won't be ready for another twenty minutes. Take a look at what Robert did in the hot tub room. It took him all day, but he seems to have it working—which is more than you could accomplish after . . . What was it Robert? . . . Three weeks?"

Robert, caught up in the good-natured conspiracy, laughed happily. "Pop thinks you do every household job with a hammer," he said. "His motto is: If you can't fix it with a hammer, get a bigger hammer."

"I know," Cindy chuckled. "You ought to see what he did to the tile in my bathroom. All it needed was a little caulk, but Harry tried to hammer the loose tiles back in place. In the end, his 'help' cost me over six hundred bucks."

"It was cheap tile," I grumbled. Man, I hate it when they gang up on me. "Couldn't even take a few love taps without falling apart."

"Bam! Bam! DAMN!" Robert howled. That's the imitation of my home improvement technique he and his brothers have been doing for the last fifteen years, every time I try to explain one of my disasters.

I grabbed a cold Coors from the refrigerator, left Cindy and Robert to their labors, and strolled through my new living room with its cathedral ceiling and two stone fireplaces into the adjoining, redwood-paneled hot tub room. Like the rest of the house, the room smelled of pitch from the pine logs the house is built with and fresh paint, but there was also a faint chemical tang from the chlorine in the water.

For weeks, I'd been trying to get the pumps and jets of the tub

46

to work properly, but my efforts had been a balls-up failure. That day, I flicked the switch at the side of the tub, and the contraption bubbled happily to life, the result of Robert's handiwork. I dipped my hand in the warm water and then dried it on my pants leg.

That evening, it would be nice to open all of the windows to the cool air coming down from the mountains, soak in the warm water, and sip a glass of wine. I thought it would be fun if I could talk Cindy into sipping and soaking with me *au naturel,* but there was no chance that would happen. She's very shy about physical intimacy when Robert's in the house, and hadn't stayed with me a single night since he came. Most likely, Robert and I would pull on our swimsuits and soak our weary bones after she went home. Maybe we'd even drag in a television set and watch a baseball game. That night, the Yankees were playing the Boston Red Sox in a doubleheader. Ought to be a good game, I thought with anticipation.

I left the tub burbling and took my beer outside onto the wrap-around deck to watch the sun beginning to set over Victory Valley. From the location of the house atop Coyote Butte, I could look down from the deck and see the blackened ruins of the farmhouse I had rented from my friend Edna Cook. Edna had been murdered the year before by a thug named Junior Stone, whom she surprised in the act of torching my old house. She went after Junior with a shovel. He took it away and used it to beat her to death.

Her family buried her a half-mile from her house on the willow-covered banks of Antelope Creek. I missed the funeral, but I'd watched over her final resting place, which I could see from where I was standing, every day since. I had even adopted the three geriatric horses Edna had treated better than she had her many husbands.

I had nearly finished the beer and was thinking about another when Cindy called me to dinner. I included a formal dining room when I built the house, but we usually eat in the huge kitchen, gathered around a chunky butcher-block table. Cindy served the steaming jambalaya in a large crockery bowl, and we mopped it up with hunks of crusty homemade bread. Robert and I were too happy to have a home-cooked meal to talk much during the main course—we were too busy eating. But during dessert, over huge slices of warm peach pie, Cindy told us about her progress in selling the Bauer estate (she'd gotten a twenty-thousand-dollar deposit), and I filled them in on how I'd spent the day.

Robert and Cindy listened quietly while I described my visit with Carl Buchanan and my perusal of the case files in Cheyenne. I didn't mention the doubts that had been gnawing at me since I looked at the crime scene photos.

"So what are you going to do now?" Cindy asked when I finished.

I shrugged my shoulders, loaded a fork with pie. "I don't know," I said. "I've got to talk to some more people who knew Carl, and I suppose I've got to go and see the people at the university's agriculture department where Victoria Austin worked. Carl's brother is a professor there, and that's where Carl met the victim. I'll just go look around a little. Maybe I'll turn up something useful."

"That should be interesting," Robert said thoughtfully. "I wouldn't mind visiting there myself."

"Why?" I asked. "Why would you be interested in this case?"

Robert shook his head. "I'm not particularly interested in the case," he explained, "but I am interested in the agriculture department. They're doing some cool things there. I read about it on the Internet."

"You get the Internet on that computer in your room?" I asked. "I thought you just used it for games. What's that thing you're always playing? Doom Warriors?"

I could tell Robert didn't like my teasing much, because he glared and a little of the old anger flashed across his face.

"What cool things are they doing, Robert?" Cindy interjected. Miss Peacemaker.

For some reason, I couldn't give it up. "They're learning how to grow corn without a cob," I winked at Cindy. "They figure they'll make a mint from the Geritol set."

"No, Dad, really," Robert said impatiently. "They're doing some incredible research. Genetic engineering, that sort of thing. A while back, some of the professors there came up with a potato that's resistant to the Colorado potato beetle. They took a gene from a bacteria that's toxic to the beetles and implanted it into the potato. When the insects eat the leaves, they drop dead."

"Amazing," Cindy said.

"It sure is," Robert agreed. "And that's not all they're doing. They also used genetics to modify the leaf structure of the plant so that when a bug crawls on it, it gets stuck. They're working on things to make plants more resistant to frost. All kinds of neat stuff."

I couldn't believe what I was hearing. "I didn't know you were interested in this, Robert," I said.

"Well, I am. After I get out of the Navy, I may use the education money they give me to get a degree in agriculture. I can't think of a better way to spend my life than finding ways to help feed people." He gave me a meaningful look. "Do something really useful, you know?"

His subtext was clear, at least to me. He was saying he'd like to do something useful, in comparison with my own wasted life. "I didn't even know you wanted to go to college," I said peevishly. "The last I heard you wanted to move to California and start a punk band. Maybe work in a tattoo parlor."

"That was five years ago, Dad," he said, like he was talking to a moron. "And no, I guess you wouldn't have known I want to go to college, because you've never asked. Maybe you don't think I'm capable of college." With that he got up from the table and started clearing the pots and pans from the stove, making a lot more noise than was necessary. The kid had gone from zero to pissed in five seconds flat.

I looked helplessly at Cindy. What did I do?

She held a finger to her lips and shook her head no, telling me to drop the whole thing, for now.

I finished my coffee in a gulp, and she took me by the arm and led me outside. We walked down the driveway, then followed the bank of Antelope Creek in the bright moonlight. A small herd of mule deer, three does and a couple of spike-horn bucks feeding in the alfalfa outside the corral, bounded off when we approached, their white rumps bouncing through the darkness like cotton balls in a sea of gray. Overhead, bats zipped through the light from the mercury-vapor lamps lighting the driveway. A hoot owl called from the prairie.

"I'm sorry we ruined your dinner," I told her. "I don't know what gets into him sometimes. If he was seven years younger, I'd write it off to puberty."

"You guys didn't ruin anything," she said. "And I understand perfectly well why he's angry. It would've made me angry, too."

I stopped in my tracks. "What are you talking about?" I asked. "You think that was my fault? What did I do?"

Cindy stood on her tiptoes and kissed my cheek. "You were treating him like he's three years old, Harry," she said. "He's an adult now, or close enough. You can't do that anymore."

"Come on, Cindy, I was just teasing him," I protested. "I didn't say anything that should have chapped his ass like that. He was teasing me too, for cryin' out loud."

"That's different, and you know it," she said. "He was teasing you to make you laugh. You were teasing him to put him in his place."

I didn't respond because there was nothing to say. She was right, of course, and I suddenly felt like a fool.

She put her arms around me and held me close—letting me know it was all right—then pulled us backward in a shuffling walk until she was leaning against the trunk of a mature aspen, our bodies hidden in shadow. She took my face in her hands, brought my lips to hers, and kissed me deep, her tongue darting across the tip of my own. She tasted like peach nectar.

I ran my hands down the muscles of her back, across the swell of her full hips, cupped her buttocks, and held tight. She ran her fingers across the front of my jeans, murmured happily when she found I was already beginning to respond. She fumbled with my belt buckle and the button-fly of my pants, took me in her hand. I felt full and hard, straining against her caress.

50

I lifted her gauzy skirt to her waist, caught the elastic of her panties in my thumbs and began to slide them down. She stepped out of them in one fluid motion, wrapped her arms around my neck and her legs around my waist. I held her against me with her back to the tree, and she seemed light, almost a part of myself. She gasped softly when I entered her, her breath warm against my neck, then began to buck eagerly, pushing me deeper with each thrust, in a hurry.

She came almost immediately, and I was only a nanosecond behind. The whole thing had lasted less than two minutes. Drag-race love. She kissed me again, and I held her for a minute before I let her down. She found her panties on the ground and put them on, then smoothed her skirt and my hair with the tips of her fingers. "Thanks for the quickie, cowboy," she giggled. She rubbed her fanny. "Next time we fool around in the forest though, remind me to watch out for splinters."

I kissed her forehead. "You planned that, Cindy, didn't you?"

"Yep," she smiled. "I've been thinking about it all day. You got peach pie for dessert, and I got the best of you. I'd say it's a fair trade."

I tucked my shirt in, buttoned my pants. "I believe it was," I said. I took her small hands in my own. "Why don't you stay with me tonight?" I asked. My voice sounded thick in my throat. "We can expand on the theme."

She shook her head no.

"It's all right," I told her. "As you said, Robert's a big boy. He can deal with it."

"Maybe he could, Harry," she said. "But the two of you still have enough problems to work through as it is, without throwing me into the mix. Trust me on this, okay?"

I nodded dejectedly. "Then at least come back in for another glass of wine," I said. "We've still got a whole bottle of the good stuff. I'll make sure you're out of here by midnight."

She began walking in the direction of her car, her skirt billowing gently in the slight breeze. "Thanks anyway, but I got what I came for. I think I'll head on home," she said. She motioned toward the yellow light coming from the kitchen windows. "Now that we've stabilized your testosterone level, you need to go back in there and apologize to your son."

The young woman waiting for me at the office when I arrived at eight-thirty the next morning looked like she'd jump up and bolt at a loud noise like a yearling colt. She was dressed in a white blouse, blue blazer, matching skirt, and sensible pumps, and her eyes darted behind a pair of eyeglasses with tortoise-shell frames. Pretty in an understated, high-school debate club kind of way, her shoulder-length dark brown hair was held back with barrettes that matched her glasses, and her hands were folded tightly in her lap, as if to keep them from fluttering away.

She was seated in a metal chair in front of Frankie Bull's desk, watching him use an orange stick to detail the clay of his latest sculpture, a thirty-six-inch-tall Lakota medicine man inspired by Henry Farney's famous oil painting, *The Sorcerer.*

Frankie looked up when I came in the door, wiped the excess clay from his stick with a tissue. "You're early today," he said. "Which is just as well." He nodded at the young woman. "Someone's waiting to see you."

I hung my Stetson on a peg by the door and waited while the woman stood and extended a tentative hand. She was small, about five-four. Twenty years old, maybe twenty-two, with a slightly pinched face and worry lines already forming in her forehead. "Mr. Starbranch?" she asked. "I'm Susan Walker." Her hand was dry and warm. "Cassie said you're looking into Carl's case?"

I recognized her name from the news stories written at the time of Buchanan's trial. Susan Walker was the daughter of Laramie City councilman Stanley Walker. She was also Carl Buchanan's childhood sweetheart and claimed to be his current girlfriend. It was she who had testified on his behalf at the trial.

"I'm looking a little," I told her. I motioned her back to the chair, and she took it almost gratefully. "What can I do for you, Miss Walker?" I asked.

"I was talking to Cassie last night, and she mentioned what

you're doing. I asked her if there was anything I could do to help—whether I should come and talk to you. She said it couldn't hurt."

"And here you are," I said. I filled my coffee mug and stirred in a packet of sweetener, took it back to my desk, and made myself comfortable. Susan Walker looked so prim and clean-cut, I wondered how she'd gotten herself mixed up with a world-class loser like Carl Buchanan. I'll bet her daddy was tickled to death about her taste in men. Still, she'd driven thirty miles from Laramie to see me. The least I could do was hear her out. "Do you have some information about the crime that can help me?" I asked. "If you do, I could surely use it."

She shook her head sadly. "I don't know anything about the murder," she said. "I hadn't seen Carl for at least three weeks before it happened, and I didn't see him afterward until he was already in jail. Even then, he wouldn't talk to me about it much, because he said he didn't know anything."

I took a sip of coffee and grimaced. Frankie Bull is a gourmet chef, but he can't make coffee for spit. Always tastes like paint thinner. "Then what would you like to talk about?" I asked. "If you can't tell me about the murder, what *can* you tell me?"

I could almost see her gathering resolve. "I can tell you about Carl," she said.

I'm sure my disappointment was written on my face, because she leaned forward earnestly. "I can tell you why he couldn't have done it," she said.

"No disrespect, Miss Walker," I said. "But if you don't know anything about the murder, and you hadn't seen Carl for weeks, what can you tell me that will help? Have you come across some new evidence?"

She shook her head. "No, I haven't."

Perfect, I thought. I glanced at Frankie, who gave me an almost imperceptible shrug. I don't know what to make of her either, his look said.

I leaned back in my chair, crossed my legs, balanced my coffee cup on my knee, and waited for her to go on.

"Cassie told me what you think," she began tentatively, "and if

53

all I knew about Carl was what they said at the trial, I'd think he did it, too. But the man the prosecutor talked about wasn't the real Carl Buchanan, Mr. Starbranch."

I flashed a mental picture of the man I'd interviewed at the state pen. He seemed pretty real to me. "Then enlighten me, Miss Walker," I said. I tried to keep my tone neutral, but the fact that I was already growing impatient came through anyway.

She leaned forward and clasped her hands together on the front of my desk. "Did you know Carl's a hero?" she asked, making her best point.

I was too surprised to answer, so I just shook my head dumbly. She might as well have asked if I knew Carl was a quantum mathematician.

"Well, he is," she said. "Two summers ago, we'd gone out to Pathfinder Reservoir for a picnic. An old man and his grandson came paddling by in a canoe, about a hundred yards offshore. Somehow, they tipped over, and the old man hit his head. He was unconscious in the water, and the little boy couldn't swim. Carl's not much of a swimmer either, and I can't swim at all, but he went out there and brought that little boy in, and then went back out for the old man.

"He was face down in the water, but Carl got him to shore and started mouth-to-mouth, kept it up for nearly half an hour before the man could breathe on his own. He saved their lives and risked his own to do it without a moment's thought." She paused for emphasis. "*That's* the kind of man Carl is. He's a gentle, caring man who would give his life to save a total stranger's. I know he got caught up in drugs, and some other bad things too, but underneath all that, he's still the same boy who saved those people's lives. He couldn't take a life, even now; it's just not in his nature."

Her bottom lip was quivering, and tears were forming behind the lenses of her glasses. "Now it's Carl who needs saving, Mr. Starbranch, and I just want you to know that despite everything you've heard and everything you believe, he's worth it."

Her loyalty and obvious love for Buchanan were touching,

and I didn't want to make light of her honest emotion, but there were hard facts to face. "He confessed to the crime, Miss Walker," I told her.

She waved her hand angrily. "Come on, Mr. Starbranch," she said, "you know how that confession was obtained as well as I do. He was going through withdrawal, and that Keegan beat him and wouldn't let him talk to a lawyer, even though he asked for one. That confession isn't worth the paper it was written on, and if Carl's lawyer had been worth a damn, it wouldn't have been allowed as evidence."

"As I recall, his lawyer tried to keep it out," I said, "but the judge denied the motion."

"He didn't try hard enough," she said. "That man should be behind bars."

I knew the man she was referring to was Ken Keegan, and my first impulse was to jump to his defense. Instead, I bit my tongue. I knew I couldn't change her mind if I argued all day, so there was no point in trying. "So what do you think, Miss Walker?" I asked. "You think Carl was set up?"

She nodded eagerly. "That's the only thing it could be," she said. "Nothing else makes sense."

"But why would someone want to set him up?" I asked.

"I don't know," she said. "I've been racking my brain, and I can't figure it out. I just know it happened. I can feel it."

"If you don't know why, I suppose you don't know who," I said, just because I needed to say something. Again, her response surprised me.

"That's easy," she said. "There's only one person who hates Carl enough to do something like this. Trace Buchanan."

I almost spilled my coffee. "Carl's brother? The professor?" I sputtered. At this statement, Frankie rolled his eyes and looked at the ceiling. I knew exactly what he was thinking, because those were my sentiments exactly. Another nutcase.

She sensed our reaction and didn't like it. "Yes, that's right, his brother," she said. "If you want to find out who hated Carl enough to do this to him, that's where you have to look. If Carl dies, Trace will be getting just what he's always wanted, his embarrassing little brother out of the way permanently."

"Miss Walker, I . . ."

She wasn't about to be interrupted. "Ask Carl if you don't believe it," she said. "He'll tell you Trace has always hated him. He'll tell you how cruel he can be. Unlike Carl, he has no morality, none whatsoever."

I'd heard about enough. "Miss Walker, we've all got a few embarrassing relatives, but there aren't many of us who go to such lengths to get them out of the way. If you want me to believe Trace was involved in the murder of Victoria Austin, you've got to give me a better reason than that. You'll have to admit, it's pretty far-fetched."

"I don't care how it sounds," she said, standing up. "Trace Buchanan was involved in this somehow. You find out what else he had to gain from Austin's death and Carl's conviction, and you'll have the key to everything."

My frustration bubbled over. "And how am I supposed to do that, Miss Walker?" I asked. "Just march into his office and ask him?"

"You're the trained investigator, Mr. Starbranch," she said, with surprising steel in her voice. "You tell me."

Then she spun around and marched to the door, slamming the screen in accusation on her way out. The heels of her sensible shoes clacked angrily on the concrete sidewalk. She did not look back.

After Susan Walker's departure, I stared out the window after her, gathering wool, and Frankie went back to his sculpture. He was detailing the lines on the medicine man's face, his hand as sure and steady as a surgeon's. "I guess the case is solved now," he said, without looking up. "You've got the real culprit, and all you have to do is prove it."

"Right," I laughed. "I wish they were all this easy."

He used a magnifying glass to study his work. "How's it going, really?"

I refilled my coffee, picked up the morning mail, and poked idly through the bills and fliers. "It's not," I said. "So far, everyone I've talked to with the exception of Keegan swears Carl is innocent, but they can't tell me why except for vague assertions that murder is out of character for him. That's what Carl says, too, by the way."

Frankie squinted down the length of the orange stick, concentrating like a man trying to thread a needle. He made a swift furrow in the clay a fraction of an inch long. "But you think there's more to it, right?" he asked.

I hate it when he starts reading my mind, gets all mystic on me. "Why would you say that?" I asked.

Frankie smiled. "Because I know you, Harry," he said. "I can tell by the look on your ugly Anglo mug. You want to talk about it?"

I sat on the edge of my desk to watch him work. "There's not much to talk about," I said. "There's just something that doesn't fit. Something that bothers me."

He raised his thick, black eyebrows and listened intently while I told him about visiting the Department of Criminal Investigation and the crime scene photos. I also told him about my conversation with Aaron Cohen and about my own doubts.

Frankie chewed the end of the orange stick thoughtfully for several seconds. "I don't know, Harry," he said. "Covering her head and all that other stuff after killing her might have been out of character for a disorganized killer, but it still seems pretty thin. And what did Cohen say wrapping her up that way indicated? That the murderer felt guilty about what he'd done?"

"Yeah, that's his theory," I said.

"Well, if Susan Walker is right about Carl's belief in the sanctity of life, that would fit, wouldn't it? If he killed someone, he might feel pretty bad about it afterward? Bad enough to cover her face?"

"Yeah, you may be right," I said. "But I don't like this case, Frankie, and I don't like the feeling I have about it."

"Then trust your instincts, Harry," he said. "Do what feels right. But if you continue, you know where your next stop has to be, don't you?"

"Of course," I said. I stood up from my desk, wiped out my coffee mug with a paper towel, and jammed my hat on my head. "I'm going over to Ginny Larsen's for a couple of scrambled eggs and some biscuits and gravy. Top it all off with a good cigar."

He rolled his eyes again. "Jesus, Harry, that's not quite what I had in mind when I . . ."

I cut him off before he could finish. "Then, if you can cover the office for a few hours, I'm going to do what I was planning before Susan Walker even suggested it," I said.

I checked the grip of my .357 Blackhawk to make sure the weapon was firmly seated in the holster. "I'm going to meet Trace Buchanan."

FIVE

The University of Wyoming's College of Agriculture, built from the same native sandstone as most of the other college buildings, is tucked between the the College of Engineering and the College of Education on the university's main campus.

I parked behind the college on Lewis Street and walked around the building to the main entrance, where I was treated to a nice view of Prexy's Pasture and a half-dozen willowy coeds lounging on the grass in the morning sunshine. I went through the front door and found Trace Buchanan's name listed on the directory in the lobby. A professor in the Department of Plant, Soil, and Insect Sciences, his office was on the third floor, so I trudged up the long staircase and wandered the halls until I found it.

Buchanan was talking on the phone, with his beat-up Red Wing workboots resting on the top of his desk. A couple of computers, one of them dark and the other one's screensaver blinking the message, "Some days, it's not worth the effort of gnawing through the leather straps," shared space on the desk with a stack of papers six inches deep and a number of textbooks that looked heavy enough to serve as ballast on a battleship. I rapped on the door, and when Buchanan saw me, he scowled and held up two fingers to indicate how many minutes he'd be. I nodded and stepped away from the door to where I could watch him without seeming to intrude on his conversation.

A robust-looking man in his early thirties, Buchanan had a full

59

head of carefully trimmed brown hair and a sculpted beard that was starting to gray. Very distinguished, the kind that gives beards a good name. In deference to the relaxed dress standards of the summer term, he was wearing jeans and a black polo shirt that didn't do much to hide the fact that he was beginning to thicken around the middle. Despite the extra pounds, he looked strong enough, kind of like a not-so-gracefully aging rugby player. His cheeks were full and a little pudgy, with the pinkish tinge that sometimes indicates a man who likes his whiskey. If he smiled, he'd look like one of those happy Irishmen you imagine hanging around the village pub, but Trace Buchanan didn't seem the type who smiled much at all. His dour countenance, however, was about the only familial resemblance he had to his brother, Carl.

I cooled my heels politely until he finished his conversation and waved me into his office. The only other seat was covered with books and papers, but he didn't offer to move them. Instead, he just waited until I moved them myself and then frowned disapprovingly when I put them on the floor. His mood didn't improve any when I introduced myself and told him the reason for my visit.

"I know my mother has been talking about bringing you into this, because she's convinced Carl's innocent," he said. "But I'm afraid I'm going to have to tell you the same thing I've told her. This is all a waste of time." To emphasize his point, he glanced meaningfully at the expensive gold watch he was wearing, letting me know that even if I didn't have something better to do, he did.

"You think your brother's guilty then?" I asked.

"Well, the jury certainly thought so," he said. "And knowing Carl, I guess I do too. This doesn't sound like a very brotherly thing to say, Mr. Starbranch, but Carl and I never got along, and I always figured he'd come to a bad end. It's just too bad he had to take someone like Vicky Austin with him."

I had the notion my welcome would be worn out before long, so I got right to the point. "Carl says he didn't even know Victoria Austin," I said. "Is he telling the truth?"

Trace shook his head as if he couldn't believe what he was hearing. "Of course not," he said. "He met her right here, and he came up here to hang around and moon over her whenever he could think up some half-assed excuse to stop by. I knew what he was really coming here for, though, and it sure as hell wasn't to see me."

"Did she encourage him?" I asked.

His smile was not at all pleasant. "No, she didn't encourage him," Buchanan said. "Why would she? Smart, beautiful girl like that, you think she's going to encourage some junkie? She didn't lead him on. She was afraid of him."

"Did she talk to anyone about it?"

"Did you read the police reports? The trial transcripts?" he asked.

I agreed that I had.

"Then you know what I told both the cops and the jury," he said. "She talked to her adviser, Annie Quinn, about it, and Annie came to me. Carl had a history of harassment, so I did what I could."

"And what was that?" I asked.

"I went to his house and beat the crap out of him," Buchanan said calmly. "Told him that if he didn't knock it off, I'd come back and do it again."

"Did it work?"

"Apparently not," Buchanan said sarcastically. He looked at his watch again. "Is there anything else I can help you with, Mr. Starbranch?" he asked. "I was due in a faculty meeting five minutes ago."

I didn't care much about his faculty meeting, so I made no move to get up, which only seemed to perturb him more. "How long before Austin's murder did you go to your brother's house for that little talk?" I asked.

He shrugged his shoulders. "A week, maybe ten days."

"Did you see him again after that?"

"No. I went by a couple of times when I heard Vicky was still getting phone calls and thought she was being followed, but he was never there."

"Did you report him to the police?" I asked.

Buchanan shook his head no. "I should have," he said sadly. "I don't know why I didn't, except that Vicky didn't want to. Until the day he kidnapped her, he hadn't done anything that could really be proven anyway, and she figured sooner or later he'd just get bored and give up. That's what I thought too, I suppose. Carl is a weak, pitiful person, but I never thought he was capable of anything like this." He rolled his shoulders. Just one of the tragic mysteries of the universe, his gesture said.

"Now," he said, standing up, "if you've got no further questions, I really do have to be going."

I stood up, capped my pen, and closed my notebook. I reached out to shake his hand, and we shook cordially. His grip was firm, but unlike some men, he didn't turn a simple handshake into a macho test of strength. "Thanks, Professor Buchanan," I said. "I appreciate the time you've given me, and I appreciate your candor."

"Whatever I can do," he said grandly, gesturing toward the door.

I took a couple of steps, then stopped and turned around. "Well, there is one thing," I said. "As long as I'm here, I may as well drop in on Austin's adviser. Can you point me in Professor Quinn's direction?"

His face seemed to tense momentarily, but I figured it was just annoyance at being delayed again. He pointed a finger at the ceiling. "Next floor up," he said. "I don't know whether you'll find her in, though. She's probably out in the field."

With that, he took my elbow, gently guided me the rest of the way out of his office, and pulled the door closed behind him. Before he marched off toward the department conference room at the end of the hall, he gave the door an extra jiggle to make sure it was locked.

Annie Quinn was not in her office, but with the help of a department secretary, I finally tracked her down in the Department of Molecular Biology's laboratory, perched on a high stool with her eye glued to a microscope. A couple of young people, a man and a woman who I assumed were students, flanked her on either side, taking notes as she talked.

On the way in, I'd noticed on the directory that Annie Quinn was one of fourteen full professors in the department. Because of my preconceived notion of what full professors look like, I'd half-expected her to be fiftyish and slightly dowdy, probably wearing a pair of Birkenstocks and glasses on a chain.

The woman who looked up from her work when I knocked gently on the door was a long way from fifty, and she most assuredly was not dowdy. Dressed in a pair of sharply pleated black pants, heels, and a white blouse scooped low enough to reveal some serious, freckle-sprayed cleavage, Quinn looked enough like the actress Annie Potts to be her twin sister. In her early to mid-thirties, she shared not only the actress's first name, but she also had the same burnished red hair and dark eyes, even the same slender but invitingly lush body.

She smiled pleasantly, and when she spoke, her voice had a trace of Southern accent—maybe Oklahoman or northern Texan. "May I help you?" she asked.

Her smile faded when I told her who I was and that I was interested in talking to her about Carl Buchanan and Victoria Austin. The two students noticed her discomfort, and the young man glared at me protectively. He obviously thought the subject caused her pain and wanted to make sure she didn't suffer unnecessarily.

"It will only take a few minutes," I said hopefully. "But if you're busy, I can come back later."

She thought it over for ten long seconds, and then seemed to gather some internal strength. "No, that won't be necessary," she said. She put a hand on the male student's shoulder. "Will you two finish up here while I talk to Mr. Starbranch?" she asked.

Quinn hopped off the stool and smoothed her trousers. "Why don't we talk in my office?" she asked. "It's a bit more private."

I followed her halfway down the hall to a spacious office overlooking the heart of the campus. Unlike Buchanan's study in cramped academic clutter, Quinn's office was clean and tidy, with several hanging plants, two soft black leather chairs facing her large oak desk, and a matching couch along one wall. The adjoining wall was jammed with computers and assorted paraphernalia.

I don't know too much about computer systems, but it looked to me like you could have purchased your own Third World country for what she must have spent on hardware alone. There were three separate personal computers, a CD-ROM with its own video display screen, a photo and copy scanner, and a whole bunch of other gadgets and gizmos I couldn't identify. Some nice classical music was coming from a couple of small speakers hooked to one of the terminals. I'd heard that you could play music on some of the newer computers, but I'd never met anyone who actually had one with that capability.

If you were measuring status by office size and technological capability alone, it looked like Annie Quinn was a lot higher up the academic food chain than was Trace Buchanan. No wonder he was cranky.

Quinn motioned me to one of the leather chairs and waited until I was comfortable. She made a little steeple of her index fingers and rested her chin at the top. Cute. Studied, but cute. If she was married, she didn't wear a ring. "Now, what can I tell you about poor Victoria?" she asked.

I crossed my legs and balanced my Stetson on one knee. "I'm just kind of banging around in the dark here, Professor Quinn, and I . . ."

She held up a hand. "Call me Annie, please," she said. "I'm only Professor Quinn to my students."

"All right," I said, a bit flustered. "Annie it is. Anyway, I know a few things about the crime itself and the trial, but I don't know much about Victoria Austin the person. Maybe you could help me out there, tell me a little about her."

Quinn nodded soberly and thought about the question for a full thirty seconds before she answered. "Vicky was born and raised in Port Arthur, Texas, and she was a very bright and talented young woman," Quinn said. "After high school, she got a full-ride academic scholarship to Stanford University, where she took a bachelor of science degree with a straight A average. She applied to several universities for scholarships when she was ready to go for her master's, and we were lucky enough to talk her into coming here. She'd just finished up her first full year when all this happened."

"She was a research assistant?" I asked.

"Yes," Quinn said, "she worked under me. In addition to money for tuition and books, research assistants get a stipend to live on, so we save those positions for the best and the brightest."

"Can you tell me what she did for you?" I asked. "What was she working on at the time of her disappearance?"

Quinn's brow furrowed. "Is that relevant, Mr. Starbranch?"

I shrugged my shoulders. "I don't know whether it's relevant or not, Annie," I said. "It probably isn't, but you never know."

Quinn bit her lip and shook her head no. "A lot of our research projects here are funded by grant money from the corporate world, Mr. Starbranch, so the subject matter is often confidential. If a corporation gives us a million dollars to study a certain topic, they don't always want their competitors to know about it while it's still in the research phase."

I looked around her office. "This place is fairly opulent by university standards," I said. "I take it you're working on a few of those top secret private-sector projects?"

She laughed, and it lit up her pretty face. "This isn't the Central Intelligence Agency, Mr. Starbranch, and we check our cloaks and daggers at the door. But yes, I guess I'm involved in a few confidential projects, and my research assistants are totally involved. Vicky had been working on the same project for the entire year she'd been in Laramie, but I don't want to discuss the specifics of what it was about unless I have to. I do hope you understand."

I didn't understand, as a matter of fact, but I kept that to myself. "I can't force you to tell me anything, Annie," I said. "But how about enlightening me in general terms? I promise I won't tell a soul."

Quinn smiled again. "You look trustworthy enough," she said.

"So I guess it won't hurt to tell you that our primary focus is on cell research. In this department, most of our research deals with some form of genetic engineering. How to make a better and stronger plant, and ultimately, how to take what we are able to do with plants and apply it to humans. That's what Vicky was doing, working with plants and their genes. If it sounds like I'm deliberately being vague, then I suppose I am."

"Vague or not, you must be very good at what you do."

"That's why they pay us the big bucks, Mr. Starbranch," she said. "Is there anything else I can tell you about Vicky, or is that all you wanted to know?"

"Did she have a steady boyfriend?" I asked.

Quinn seemed happy to change the subject. "She went out with other students once in a while for a pizza and some beer, maybe to a football game or a movie," she said. "But, no, she didn't have a steady boyfriend. She said she didn't have time for one."

"How about girlfriends?" I asked. "Anyone who could tell me a little more about her personal life?"

"She spent a lot of time with Marsha Jackson," Quinn said. "The other research assistant. The one you saw a few minutes ago in my lab."

"Do you think she'd speak with me?"

"I don't know," Quinn said. "She's busy now, and it's against policy for me to give out a student's home number, but if you leave yours with me, I'll ask her to call you."

"Fair enough," I said. "I don't have much more right now. Can you tell me . . . when Victoria was receiving those harassing phone calls, did she ever tell you she thought Carl was making them?"

"No," Quinn said. "She just told us she was being harassed and followed, and Trace figured out who was behind it. It made sense, I suppose. That boy had been mooning over her for months."

"After Victoria came to you and told you about the calls, why did you go to Trace?" I asked. "Did *you* suspect Carl?"

"I went to Trace Buchanan because he's my friend and my colleague. I wanted his advice."

"You say Carl was mooning over Victoria Austin," I said. "Did he ever cause a scene around here? Do anything that was untoward?"

Quinn thought about that one for a while before answering. "Not really," she said tentatively. "He was just here more than he had good reason to be. One minute we'd be working together in the lab, and the next you'd look up and there he'd be, looking at us through the window in the door. It was creepy, Mr. Starbranch, and it happened six or eight times. As soon as we spotted him, he'd always hurry away. I followed him once to ask him what he wanted, but he just got flustered and said he was looking for his brother."

"When was that?" I asked.

Quinn shrugged her shoulders. "Two days before Vicky disappeared," she said.

"Did you believe him?"

She scowled. "Of course not, but there was nothing I could do. Maybe he did come to see his brother, because I saw them leaving together just a few minutes later."

I leaned forward, suddenly more interested in the conversation. "Are you sure about the time?" I asked. "Sure it was two days?"

"Absolutely," she said. "It was a Monday, and we'd just finished our weekly staff meeting. We had a big presentation coming up, and I wanted to make sure everyone was prepared."

"Thank you for your time, Annie," I said, standing up. She took the hand I offered and held it for a half a beat longer than was absolutely necessary, treating me to a full smile while she looked into my eyes. The simple flirtation seemed to come as easily to her as breath. "Only one more thing before I go. Besides Carl, do you know of anyone else who might have had something against Victoria Austin? Was there anything else going on in her life that might have led to her death?"

Her face hardened, and she let go of my hand. "Victoria Austin didn't have an enemy in the world," she said. "She was a sweet and talented young woman with a fabulous future ahead of her. Trace

Buchanan and I are close, so God forgive me for saying this, but his brother stole that future away from her.

"For that, Mr. Starbranch, Carl Buchanan deserves to die."

I left Annie Quinn in her office, then sat at the top of the stairway for a few minutes, trying to figure out what to do next. I hadn't learned much in my visits with Trace Buchanan and Annie Quinn, and the only item of any interest at all was that Trace said he hadn't seen Carl for a week or ten days before Austin's disappearance, while Quinn's statement put them together only two days before the crime.

There were several possible explanations for the discrepancy. Buchanan might have been lying. Quinn might have been lying. They both might have been lying. Or they both might have just been confused.

I decided to ask Buchanan about it before I left, but when I rapped on his office door, which was still locked, nobody answered. Nor could I find him on a quick walking tour through the halls of the Plant, Soil, and Insect Sciences Department. When I popped my head in the door of the department head's office, however, the secretary told me Buchanan had left as soon as his faculty meeting ended and wasn't expected back for at least two days. She wouldn't give me his home number, but she did let me borrow the phone book to look it up myself. It was unlisted. I left a message for Trace Buchanan to call me at his convenience, and walked back to where I had parked the Jeep. It was just about noon. If I hurried, I could get to Ginny Larsen's before she ran out of her Tuesday lunch special, meatloaf sandwiches on thick slabs of homemade bread, mashed potatoes, and cream gravy. A little bit of heaven on earth.

With my stomach rumbling on the thirty-mile drive back to Victory, I thought about my interviews. I tried to figure out how I was going to find out what Victoria Austin had been working on at the time of her death, or if the inquiry was even worth the effort. An idea came to me just as I passed the Starbranch Unmanned Traffic Control Device on the outskirts of town, so I passed Ginny's without slowing down and drove to my house. Robert was in the corral, brushing the old and cantankerous mare I'd adopted after Edna Cook's death. He looked up from his efforts when he heard the tires of the Jeep crunching gravel in the driveway and waved happily. The mare, peeved at the interruption, nipped Robert on the butt, and he jumped away, swatting at her nose. "Hey, Pop," he called, "I didn't expect to see you this afternoon."

"I thought I'd come and take you to lunch," I told him. I leaned against the fender until he had finished with the mare and turned her loose in the pasture. Then we walked together into the house so he could wash up at the kitchen sink.

Detecting is thirsty work. I poured myself a glass of iced tea from the pitcher in the fridge, and drank the whole glass in a single long gulp. "Before we go, do you think we could look up something on that computer of yours?" I asked. "It shouldn't take more than a few minutes."

He dried his hands on a paper towel. "Sure, Pop. What do you want to see?"

I told him a bit about my conversation with Annie Quinn and my desire to learn more about her research projects. "You think that information might be in cyberspace somewhere?" I asked.

He shrugged his shoulders. "Can't tell until we look," he said. He grabbed me by the elbow and pulled me in the direction of his room. "Why don't we fire the puppy up, and see if she sings?"

Robert's room was, is, and probably always will be a dump of such epic proportions as to constitute an immediate environmental hazard. However, I learned a long time ago that it's best if parents just keep the door closed and try to ignore it. Since he was doing me a favor, I cleared a small space at the foot of his bed and sat down, trying to effect a Zen-like trance that would keep me from being aware of my immediate surroundings.

Robert booted up his computer and logged on to the Internet. Five minutes later, he had called up the University of Wyoming's home page and then clicked on the link to the page maintained by the College of Agriculture. Two minutes later, he had gone a level deeper to the Department of Molecular Biology page.

"There's a lot of stuff in here," he said, concentrating on the screen. "There are staff résumés, course requirements, class schedules. You have any idea where you want to start?"

"Nope," I said helplessly. "Not a clue."

"Then we'll just surf for a while," he said. "See what turns up."

It was a full forty minutes before he hit pay dirt. He whistled through his teeth and clapped his hands victoriously. "Here we go," he said. "Here's what you're after."

"What did you find?"

"The department's internal newsletter," he said. "I'm sure it's not given out to the public, but they post it on their Web page for some reason. The one from the start of last year's fall semester is the one you're after." He pointed at the text filling the screen. "Look here," he said.

I sat down in his chair and began to scroll through the newsletter, which listed new faculty, upcoming seminars, alumni information, retirements, promotions, and donations to the department. At the end was a section dealing with current research being conducted by department faculty.

The short paragraph devoted to Annie Quinn was about halfway down the list.

"What the hell does this mean?" I asked, reading aloud. "Dr. Annie Quinn is working in applied research with the goal of developing cell-specific cytotoxic agents which have a large variety of potential uses. Feasible applications include the preparation of anticancer agents, antiviral agents, therapeutics for autoimmune diseases such as multiple sclerosis, noninvasive neutering agents for pets and farm animals, and selective fat-cell killing for obesity or cosmetic purposes. She is also studying apoptosis, programmed cell death, with a view of using viral agents to retard or stop the process."

Robert was reading over my shoulder. "It means she's using plant research to find a cure for autoimmune disease, maybe even AIDS and cancer," he said. "But she's doing more than that. It sounds to me like she's looking for the fountain of youth."

"What?"

Robert was too preoccupied to answer my question. "You mind if I sit down for a minute?" he asked. "Let's check something out."

I relinquished control of the computer to Robert, who spent twenty minutes playing the keyboard like a concert pianist. Several times, his face wrinkled in frustration, but he only redoubled his efforts. "Bingo!" he shouted when he found what he was looking for.

"What is it?" I asked.

"Loveladies Pharmaceuticals," he said, as if that explained everything.

"What is Loveladies Pharmaceuticals?"

"It's a drug company headquartered in North Brunswick, New Jersey," he said. "They make a lot of over-the-counter and prescription drugs, but they specialize in cosmetics. Their cosmetics arm made almost three hundred million dollars last year in profit."

I couldn't have been more confused. "Would you mind telling me what a New Jersey cosmetics company has to do with anything?" I asked sharply.

"It has to do with *everything,*" he said, pointing a finger at the screen. "The university has to report to the government where private-sector research money comes from, and I just tapped into their report. Loveladies Pharmaceuticals gave Annie Quinn a million dollars last year to support her research—and I have an idea that while the medical applications of that research might be important, Loveladies is more interested in the cosmetic applications."

"That fat-cell mumbo jumbo?" I asked.

"Absolutely," he said. "Can you imagine the position a company would have in the market if it came up with a pill that would not only burn away your fat, but would retard aging? Jesus Christ! Every man and woman in the world would be lining up to buy it."

I laughed in spite of myself. "Come on, Robert, that sounds like science fiction."

"It's not science fiction!" he said hotly. "This is reality, Pop. This is where genetic research and engineering have been heading all along. And if Loveladies Pharmaceuticals is shelling out that kind of money to some professor at a backwoods, podunk school like the University of Wyoming, instead of giving it to the really prestigious genetic researchers at places like Princeton or Harvard, they must think Annie Quinn is onto something pretty phenomenal."

I turned away from the screen and navigated the clutter on the floor until I reached the window. I stood there, looking out over Victory Valley at the thin clouds scudding over the top of the mountain range to the north, the contrail of a jet winging its way toward Denver. The topic of Quinn's research sounded pretty far out to me, but I've learned in my lifetime never to underestimate the potential of scientific research. No one ever thought they'd find a way to prevent polio, either, and that's been all but eradicated. Why not a way to prevent aging, or keep you perpetually skinny? "You think you could find out some more about this?" I asked him.

"Like what?"

"Like the projects Annie Quinn is working on, and which one Victoria Austin was involved in," I said. "And when you get through with that, everything you can learn about Loveladies Pharmaceuticals."

"You think it relates to your case?"

"I don't know," I said. "But it is interesting."

"Very," he said. He turned back to his computer and began clacking away on the keys.

I watched him type for a few minutes. "You know, Robert, if Annie Quinn is successful in any part of her research, particularly that fountain of youth business, it might be worth a million dollars after all," I said.

"Yeah," Robert chuckled, without looking up. "A million dollars a *minute.*"

SIX

Carl Buchanan killed himself at four o'clock that afternoon by lashing one end of a strip of torn sheet to the bars of his cell, then knotting the other around his throat. After that, he knelt and leaned forward against the restraint until he strangled to death. Because he weighed so little, I imagine it must have taken him a long time to die.

It was an act of will and remorse, explained in the note Buchanan left behind, written on a length of toilet paper. In his last communication, he said that since our conversation at the prison, he'd become more and more unsure of his innocence. Because he had no memory of his actions at the time of Victoria Austin's death, he'd come to believe it was entirely possible he was guilty. If that was the case, he could no longer bear the thought of living and would save the state the trouble of a lengthy and expensive appeals process.

He apologized to his mother, his girlfriend, and Victoria Austin's family. He asked that his body be cremated and his ashes scattered across the base of Elk Mountain, where he'd enjoyed camping and fishing as a child. He did not mention his brother.

I didn't hear about his suicide when it happened, of course. I got the news about three hours later, after I had gone home for the day and found Cassie Buchanan seated at my kitchen table, her eyes swollen and red-rimmed from crying, a jelly glass half-full of Rebel Yell bourbon in her hand.

When I came through the door, Robert, who had obviously been trying to console her, put the whiskey bottle he'd been pouring from on the counter beside me and hightailed it out of the kitchen toward his bedroom. This was obviously beyond his ken.

Cassie stood as soon as we were alone, and was so shaky I thought her knees might give out and send her tumbling in a heap. Instead, she gathered her strength, took two steps toward me, and threw her whiskey in my face.

"You son of a bitch!" she hissed.

Since I had no idea what was going on, the bourbon spritzer came as a surprise. I wiped at it madly with the sleeve of my shirt, tried to get the stinging liquid out of my eyes. "What was that for?" I asked dumbly.

She threw the empty glass to the floor, where it shattered in a zillion splintery shards.

"You killed him!" she said. "I asked you to help him, but instead, you went over there and talked him into killing himself!" She hit me on the chest, and before long, I was holding her in my arms while she pounded on me with all her failing strength. "God damn you, Harry!" she said, over and over. "Damn you to hell!"

I held her until the worst of her rage was spent, and then I took her wretched face in my hands and forced her to look into my eyes. "I don't know what you're talking about, Cassie," I said. "How could I have killed Carl?"

Haltingly, between sobs, she told me the story of Carl's death and about his final note. She'd gotten the news herself about an hour and a half earlier from the assistant warden, who'd called to let her know there'd be an autopsy and then she was free to make her own arrangements. She'd come directly to my house because she didn't know where else to go.

When she was finished with her story, she collapsed in a kitchen chair and held her head in her hands.

I took two glasses from the cupboard and sat down beside her, pulled my chair close. I poured two fingers of bourbon into her glass, poured the same for myself, drank deeply. It burned the back of my throat all the way to my belly. I put my arm around her shoulders. "I'm so sorry, Cassie," I said. "I had no idea. But it's important for you to understand this . . . I did not talk Carl into killing himself."

She pulled away from me. "He told me all about your conversation, Harry!" she said. "Don't lie to me now."

"I'm not lying," I said. "I might not have been as understanding as I should have been, and I'll admit that wasn't very professional. But what passed between us wasn't enough to cause him to take his own life."

"Then what was it?" she asked. "That boy wanted to live! If it wasn't you, then what was it?"

"I don't know," I said honestly, "but we'll find out. I'll help you make whatever arrangements you want. As a matter of fact, I'll take you to the prison tomorrow. After that, we'll get to the bottom of this. That's my promise."

Cassie drank her bourbon in a single gulp, wincing as it went down. Then she put her hands on the table and pushed herself shakily to her feet. There were sparks in her eyes when she spoke. "Fuck you and your promises," she said. "I came to you for help, and now my son is dead because of it. Your job is over. What more could you possibly accomplish?"

She paused, the muscles of her jaw tense, her hands balling into fists. "I hate you, Harry," she said. "I'll hate you until I die."

Then she slammed out of the kitchen and down the steps of the deck.

When she pulled out of the driveway, the tires on her new Toyota four-by-four threw a rooster tail of gravel into the air. She swerved to avoid hitting the mailbox and fought to gain control of her vehicle as she roared away. She floored it as soon as the nose of her car straightened out, the torqued-up Japanese engine screaming like a scalded cat.

I stood at the kitchen door and watched until she hit the highway. Racing down the blacktop, her car grew smaller and smaller until it disappeared into the harsh red and yellow glare of sunset.

I was still standing there five minutes later when I heard Robert behind me in the kitchen. I turned to find him with a broom in his hands, sweeping up the broken glass from Cassie's visit.

"I'm sorry, Dad," he said. "You didn't deserve that."

I shook my head sadly. The fact was, perhaps I had deserved everything Cassie gave me, and more. "Thanks," I told him. I sat down and watched him work and thought about pouring myself another bourbon. Instead, I capped the bottle and put it away. "She was very upset, Robert," I said. "I appreciate your staying with her until I came home."

He shrugged his shoulders. No problem. "It's over then?" he asked.

"I don't know," I said. "I suppose so. With Carl dead, there's not much point in going forward. Not that I was getting very far, anyway."

Robert swept the glass shards into a dustpan and dumped them in the trash. Then he got out a mop to clean up the spilled whiskey. "That's too bad," he said. "This was getting to be fun."

"What was?"

"The research I've been doing," he said. "After you left this afternoon, I searched the web for more information about Loveladies Pharmaceuticals, and I turned up some pretty cool stuff. I thought it might help your investigation, but now it may be moot."

I couldn't help being interested. "What'd you find?"

He finished cleaning up and propped the mop in the closet. "You're really interested?" he asked.

"Of course I am," I told him.

A huge smile cracked his face. "Then hold on for just a second," he said. "I made some printouts that might help explain things."

I sat for a couple of minutes until he returned with a stack of perhaps twenty pages of computer paper. He sat across from me at the table and thumbed through the pages until he found a starting point.

"Annie Quinn's research project certainly isn't the only one

Loveladies has funded in the last couple of years, but it sure is the sexiest one," he said. "And it's the one that's generated the most interest in the business community. The whole thing raised havoc with the company's stock last summer, but it's back to normal now."

"What do you mean, raised havoc?" I asked. "And where did you get this information, anyway?"

"From the Dow Jones business wire," he said, shuffling the papers. "I ran a search on Loveladies, and came up with all this. It's only a start though; I'm sure there's more."

"Tell me about it," I said, leaning toward him.

"You know anything about the stock market, Pop?" he asked.

"A little, but not as much as I'd like," I admitted. "I suppose I understand it as well as I understand the electronic fuel injection that replaced my old-fashioned carburetor. When it works, everything's fine, but when it breaks down, nobody but a computer technician knows how to fix it."

Robert laughed. "That's true, I guess. But here's something you have to remember. The stock market responds to fact, but it also responds just as readily to rumor, and as in real life, rumor can be very damaging sometimes and there's no way to go after it."

I nodded like I knew what he was talking about.

"That's what happened to Loveladies Pharmaceuticals last year," he said. "They almost got wiped out by a rumor. It could have cost them millions and millions of dollars if they hadn't stopped it."

"And this has something to do with Carl Buchanan and Victoria Austin?" I asked.

He laid out the first few printouts on the table, and even reading upside down, I could see they were copies of a couple of Associated Press stories. The headline across the first was, "Investors Eager to Cash In on Loveladies' Fountain of Youth." The story, datelined New York, was published in June, almost four months before Austin's murder.

"It's an open secret in this industry what research projects people are working on, but once word leaked out early last year that Annie Quinn's research with cell-specific cytotoxic agents was showing remarkable progress, investors started buying Loveladies stock on the come," Robert said.

"Companies don't like it when there's too much activity, either purchases or sales, all at once, because that usually gets the attention of the regulators. But in this case, that didn't happen. The stock rose steadily all summer, from about $28.25 a share in June to a high of $38.50 by the third week in September."

"And this was all due to that fat reduction business you were telling me about?" I asked. "These investors figured that if her research panned out, they'd have enough Loveladies stock to make them rich?"

"Sure," he said, "but there's more to it than that. The fat-cell reduction and programmed cell-death part of her research was important enough, but if you remember, that's not all she's working on. Even if those things didn't pan out, it looked like she might be on the trail of a new cancer treatment, maybe even something with implications for AIDS. If any part of her research was successful and could be applied to humans, the economic rewards for Loveladies and its stockholders would be enormous. If she hit on more than one front, those rewards are unimaginable. These projects could change the entire course of human history, and people who get in on the ground floor will be zillionaires. Think about what would have happened if you'd bought a hundred thousand shares of stock in American Telephone and Telegraph's parent company at fifty cents apiece just a few weeks before Alexander Graham Bell invented the telephone."

I blew through my teeth. "I get your point," I said. "So when did the havoc start?"

He shuffled through his stack of papers until he found the one that would answer my question—another Associated Press story, headlined "Dead Potatoes May Cast Doubt on Fountain of Youth Research."

"The last week of September," he said. "Somewhere, the rumor got started that a lot of the plants in Quinn's test plot, the potato plants in her programmed cell-death experiment, were dying. That's not supposed to happen, and by itself that rumor would have been enough to cause real problems for Loveladies. But the rumor mill also said that her cytoxic work was going down the tubes as well. Nobody knows where those rumors got started, but by September twenty-seventh, Loveladies stock was starting to drop. By the thirtieth, it was sinking like a stone. Went from $34.50 a share to $16 in the course of one morning's trading. It bottomed out at $14.75 on October third. Loveladies is a solid company, even without this fountain of youth stuff, so the drop was due to a huge panic reaction completely out of proportion to what would have happened had Quinn's research actually flopped. It threatened the whole company is what it did. Another week of that, and Loveladies might as well have put a 'for sale' sign in the window and turned out the lights."

"What happened?" I asked. "Did the regulators come in to investigate? Did they suspend trading?"

"They didn't have to," Robert said. "On the third of October, Quinn took a bunch of reporters and scientists out to the field research site so they could see her plants for themselves."

He rifled through his pile again until he came up with another story, this one headlined, "Quinn's Potatoes Alive and Well," with a subhead reading "Rumors of Their Death Greatly Exaggerated."

I scanned the story and looked up. "So it worked?" I said.

"Sure did," he said. "That story appeared in the next day's edition of the *Wall Street Journal,* squelching the rumors, and stock prices went back to their previous high almost immediately. There was a real flurry of buying, and the value of that stock has been going up steadily ever since, even though Quinn still hasn't announced the results of her research and isn't expected to do so for at least another year."

I sat back to absorb what I'd just learned. It didn't take me long to see the troubling association between the timing of the stock plunge, the remarkable recovery, and Victoria Austin's murder. The stock began to drop September twenty-seventh. Victoria disappeared October second and was probably murdered that day, even though her body wasn't discovered for more than a week, after hunting season was well under way. Annie Quinn had saved Loveladies from financial disaster, and her own research projects from extinction, on October third.

"Those were the projects Victoria Austin was working on, weren't they?" I asked. "The projects that caused all the trouble?"

"Yep," Robert said, "she was up to her elbows in them. When she disappeared and was later found dead, they gave her responsibilities to another one of the graduate assistants."

"You think there's a connection?" I asked rhetorically, my mind racing.

"I don't know, Pop," he chuckled, gathering his papers. "I'm just the computer geek. You're the cop. What do *you* think?"

I thought I was too damned old to believe in this kind of serendipity, but I didn't say so. I wondered why Ken Keegan hadn't discovered any of this. Maybe he would have if Carl hadn't confessed so quickly. As it went down, Keegan didn't have to dig more than an inch below the surface. "Here's what I think," I said. "I think I'm gonna buy a computer of my own. It's time your old man embraced the twentieth century semi-wholeheartedly."

"Better late than never," Robert mumbled. "I don't know what your hurry is, though. You still got a couple years' grace before the millennium."

I got my hat from the rack, held the door open, and waved him outside. "Shut up while you're ahead, junior," I said. "While I'm at it, I'm gonna take you to the Trails End and buy you a steak as big as your head—unless you keep yappin' and piss me off. You do that, it's Spam and fried eggs again."

My son was out the door and in the Jeep before I could even close the screen. Flash Gordon. With a fifty-dollar appetite.

Robert and I shared a blood-rare, high-protein dinner, which should have put me to sleep twenty minutes after we finished eating. It would have, too, if I hadn't noticed Cindy Thompson's car parked outside the Silver Dollar Saloon as we passed through Victory on the way home. Not that I'm the jealous type, worried Cindy might meet another man, but I certainly didn't want her to spend the night as a pitiful, neglected wallflower, sitting all by her lonesome with no one to talk to or buy her a drink. I'm too much of a gentleman for that.

I dropped Robert off at the house and hotfooted it back to Victory as fast as I could. I probably broke the speed limit, but there wasn't much chance I'd write myself a ticket for it.

The Silver Dollar had a good weeknight crowd going, lots of cowboys and cowgirls and lumberjacks drinking beer, eating cheeseburgers, and watching a baseball game on one of the three large-screen televisions Curly supplies to entertain those customers not interested in shooting pool or buckle-polishing on the dance floor to the country music coming from his antique Wurlitzer jukebox. I stopped when I walked through the door and took a moment to savor the atmosphere. As wild West saloons go, the Silver Dollar is as good as it gets, the kind of place I feel comfortable in the minute I sit down. Not that it's much in the way of ambience, mind you. The place reeks of smoke, stale beer, cheap perfume, and cooking meat. The booths are held together by duct tape that doesn't match the upholstery, the tables are unsteady, and the decor is strictly redneck chic—posters provided by beer companies of women in bikinis, clocks with whiskey logos, stuffed animal heads on the walls, and sawdust on the floor.

That night, the jukebox was dark and the pool tables were empty, as nearly every eye in the place was glued to the final innings of the game—Yankees against the Texas Rangers.

In Wyoming, we usually root for Denver's major-league baseball team, the Colorado Rockies, but that year the Rockies were doing poorly and we needed somebody with potential to root for. The Braves were burning up the National League, but since nearly everyone in conservative Victory hates Ted Turner on account of his wife's liberal past, most of Victory's sports nuts were pulling for the Yankees to take the American League pennant. It was the consensus around town that if it came down to the Yanks and the Braves in the World Series, the Yankees would clean those Southerners' clocks and send them packing back across the Mason-Dixon line, where they belong—and send Jane Fonda with them.

I waved to Curly Ahearn, Victory mayor and owner of the Silver Dollar, as soon as I caught his eye. He was behind the bar, drawing fresh beers and loading them on a tray held by Lou Mc-Grew, his assistant manager, chief barmaid, and spiritual adviser. In honor of the game, he'd traded his favorite Boston Red Sox baseball cap for a Yankee cap tilted back on his bald head and a "Bronx Bombers" T-shirt. I happen to know that he personally hates the Yankees, so his outfit was nothing short of heresy. Just shows how far a smalltown businessman has to go to keep his customers happy.

Curly smiled when he saw me and pointed to the end of the bar, where Cindy was nursing a tall drink with plenty of crushed ice and a wedge of lime. Dressed in a black skirt, hose, heels, white blouse, and burgundy blazer, she looked like she might have just come from an appointment. I wondered if she'd made a sale, which always puts her in a good mood. I made my way through the crowd and hiked myself onto the empty stool beside her, motioning to Curly to bring me the usual, a draft Coors and a shot of Jack Daniel's neat.

"Hey, good lookin'," I said happily, kissing the back of her neck. "You come here often?"

She jumped a little because the kiss tickled, but she smiled and gave me a smacker on the cheek. "Only when I'm hopin' to get lucky," she said. "What brings you down here so late at night, cowboy? You meeting someone I don't know about?"

"Nah," I grinned, "just kinda hopin' for a little luck myself."

She finished her cocktail and sat the empty on the bar. "Buy me another one of those, and we'll see if we can't work something out," she said.

When our drinks came, we sipped them slowly, talking quietly so we wouldn't bother the people around us watching the game. Cindy filled me in on her day—she'd gotten a purchase contract on a summer home a few miles outside of Victory that was selling for a hundred-fifty-thousand—and I told her about mine. Her face fell when I got to the part about Carl Buchanan. Apparently she hadn't heard it yet, which was unusual. Usually, news like that travels through Victory's rumor mill faster than a nervous mackerel through a school of hungry sharks.

"My God, Harry," she said. "That is so terrible. Cassie must be devastated."

"She is." I told her about Cassie's visit to my house, of her promise to hate me until her dying day.

"She didn't mean it, Harry," Cindy said, her face softening. "Cassie doesn't have that in her. When she has time to get over the initial pain, she'll realize it wasn't your fault."

"I know," I said. "But it still hurt, Cindy. It hurt because I know I could have handled the situation differently. For all I know, maybe I did have something to do with Carl's decision to kill himself."

Cindy put her arms around my neck and held me close, kissed me warmly. When she pulled away, her eyes were beginning to tear. I was touched by her concern. "So what will you do now?" she asked.

I shrugged my shoulders. "I don't have the faintest idea," I said. "I've got a feeling there's something fishy about this case, and it even looked like I was making a little progress. But now that Carl's dead, I don't know if there's much point in going forward."

She arched her eyebrows. "What kind of progress?"

I described my conversation with Trace Buchanan, and my feeling that he might have been lying about when he saw his brother last. I mentioned Robert's research concerning Annie Quinn and Loveladies Pharmaceuticals. And I told her about my own feeling after I'd looked at the crime scene photos that something was out of place.

None of that was enough to prove Carl's innocence, I said, and none of it might mean a thing. But it was more than enough to pique my curiosity. I had a hunch I'd learn a lot more if I just poked under the right rocks.

"Then keep poking," Cindy said.

"What?"

"Keep poking," she said again. "I've known you long enough to know your gut is often a better indicator of reality than your brain, Harry. Listen to what it's saying. What have you got to lose?"

I almost laughed out loud. "What have I got to lose? Well, darlin', let's start with a lot of my time and my professional reputation. I've known a lot of cops who went chasing after wild geese and became obsessed with cases that went nowhere for years and that never would go anywhere. Other cops felt sorry for them, Cindy, but they didn't respect them. I'm not the kind of man who tilts at windmills, and even if I were, I don't feel that strongly about this case."

"Bullshit," she said. "You wrote the book on windmill tilting, Harry. And if you gave a damn what other people thought of your methods, you never would have closed all the cases you did."

"She's right, pardner," Curly said, wiping the bar in front of us with a clean rag. I don't know how long he'd been listening to our conversation, but it was apparently long enough to form an opinion. "And as your boss, I feel free to observe that you've got plenty of time on your hands. For the life of me, I can't see you're so busy lookin' over Victory you don't have time to help a loyal constituent like Cassie Buchanan. As a matter of fact, you've been doin' so damned little around here, you ought to feel guilty taking a paycheck."

"Screw you, Curly," I said, smiling. "You got so many complaints, find yourself some new chump who'll work for thirty thousand a year."

I pushed my shot glass forward for a refill, and as he poured, I noticed again the awful toll the last year had taken on his face. He seemed to have aged ten years in the last six months alone. Losing a child will do that to you.

The year before, Curly's daughter, Faith, had gotten herself mixed up with a bad seed named Liam O'Bannion, whose apparent murder had taken place just a few miles outside of Victory. O'Bannion was not only involved in drugs and the poaching of black bears, whose organs he sold on the Chinese medicinal market in San Francisco, but he also had the bad sense to slap Faith in front of her father. Curly went ballistic. He made enough public threats in the heat of anger that when O'Bannion turned up dead, my friend the mayor was charged with the murder.

It took me a while to clear him. Meanwhile, Faith was so distraught by the whole affair she took an overdose of drugs that put her in a coma from which she never recovered. She'd died about four months before, and although Curly was putting on a good front, he was my best friend, and I knew better than anyone how much he was really hurting.

"I may just do that," he said, sliding me the fresh shot. "Find myself a new chief of police with a little sand. Somebody who won't give up just because the confessed killer does himself in and everyone says the case is as dead as he is."

"Seriously, Curly, you really don't mind me working on this?" I asked. I shot the bourbon back, and it burned my throat. I washed it down with a deep drink of Coors.

"Of course not," he said. "Cassie Buchanan has been a good friend to us, Harry. I can't think of a better use of your time." He pointed at Cindy, who as a member of the town council is another of my bosses. "I think you ought to think about what your employers are tryin' to tell you before you wash your hands of this."

"You think Carl was innocent?" I asked.

"I don't know, Harry," he said. He put the bar rag over his shoulder and bent one ear toward Lou, who was waiting at the waitress station with a new round of drink orders. "But as someone who was accused of a crime he didn't commit, I know better than anyone in this room that sometimes even the best legal minds in the state can make a mistake. You keep lookin' as long as your instincts tell you there's the slightest chance Carl wasn't the murderer. You're a cop, Harry, that's what you do. You dig through all the shit until you come up with that little gem of truth. If that boy was innocent, then somebody's gotta pay."

With that, he trundled off to fill his orders, and Cindy and I sipped the remainder of our drinks and cheered with everyone else when the Yankees took the game three to two.

I'd been thinking about what my girlfriend and Curly had said as I watched the end of the game, but despite their opinions, I'd all but convinced myself that there was no point in doing another thing on Carl's behalf, or on behalf of his memory. Next day, I'd just pick up my life where it was when Cassie first shamed me into looking into her son's case. Maybe, if things weren't too busy, I'd even have time for a little late summer trout fishing on the Little Laramie. Take Robert out and help him perfect his fly casting before he gave himself over to Uncle Sam.

My intentions were about to be shattered, although I didn't know it at the time. Cindy and I were just walking out the door, arm in arm, on the way to her house for a nightcap and a friendly roll in the hay, when Lou called my name. I turned back to see her standing at the phone, with the receiver cradled between her chin and her shoulder. "For you, Harry," she said. "Says it's important."

I made my way back through the crowd and picked up the phone, expecting to hear Robert or Frankie Bull on the other end. I was surprised by the small and tentative female voice that responded when I said hello. "Mr. Starbranch, this is Marsha Jackson. Annie Quinn's graduate assistant?" She made it sound like a question.

I turned away from the din in the saloon so I could hear better. "Thanks for calling, Marsha," I said. "How did you happen to find me here?"

"I called your house," she said. "Your son gave me this number."

"I appreciate your getting back to me so soon," I said. "Annie Quinn must have told you why I wanted to talk to you."

Jackson hesitated for a second before she answered. "No, Mr. Starbranch, Annie didn't mention it."

"Then what . . ." I began, confused.

"I heard around the department you're looking into Vicky Austin's murder," she broke in. "I decided I might want to talk to you, and then I was visiting with Katie O'Neill in the student union this evening, and she helped me make up my mind. I'm a little afraid and I don't know enough to go to the police, but she says you can be trusted."

Katie O'Neill is the wife of Mike, one of my closest friends in Victory. She also teaches grade school at the university preparatory facility in Laramie, but I didn't have a clue why she would have been talking about me to Marsha Jackson. "How do you know Katie?" I asked.

"We met each other at the union toward the end of last fall's semester, right after I took over Vicky's assistantship," Jackson said. "We have lunch or coffee together two or three times a week. She says she knows you pretty well, and to tell you hello."

"Tell her hello back," I said. I waited a second or two for her to go on, but she didn't. "Why do you want to talk to me, Marsha?" I asked. "What are you afraid of?"

"I can't tell you about it now," she said. "I'd rather do it in person, if you don't mind. Are you doing anything tomorrow morning around ten?"

"No."

"Then how about meeting me at the Village Inn?" she asked.

"Of course I'll meet you," I said. "But at least give me an idea what you want to discuss. I hate surprises, Miss Jackson."

She started to speak, but stopped short. When she spoke again, her words came in an insistent rush. "There are some very strange things going on in the Molecular Biology Department," she said. "I need to tell someone about them, and it looks like you're as safe a person as I can hope for. That's all I can say right now, Mr. Starbranch. But please come. I need to get this off my chest."

I was straining to hear her over the noise in the bar. I put a hand over my free ear to drown out the racket. "I wouldn't miss it for the world," I tried to tell her, but by that time, she'd already hung up. The phone line crackled like heat lightning in the summer air.

SEVEN

A grown man shouldn't have to tiptoe into his own home at four in the morning, but that's what I did after I stayed at Cindy's for the better part of the night. Robert was still asleep when the alarm clock went off at seven-thirty, so I showered, filled myself full of black coffee, left him a note, and was on the road to Laramie by eight-thirty, feeling fuzzy-headed and sleep deprived.

I wasn't to meet Marsha Jackson until ten, so when I arrived in Laramie a few minutes after nine, I used the extra time to stop in at the offices of Pacific Power and Light. Trace Buchanan's home phone number was unlisted, and that meant I couldn't pull his address out of the phone book, but when I flashed the office manager my badge, it only took her a couple of seconds to look Buchanan's address up in her service records.

I thanked her, hopped back in the Jeep, and less than five minutes later was prowling past the split-level ranch on Reynolds Street where he lived. I wanted to give him my condolences on Carl's death and offer him whatever help I could. And I also wanted to find out when he really last saw his brother before Austin's disappearance.

The grass in Buchanan's front yard was long and slightly shaggy looking, as if it was about five days overdue for a mowing. From a distance, the house looked nice enough, gray with some kind of fake rock fronting, but when I pulled into the driveway, I noticed the place needed a coat of paint. One of the windows on the second floor was broken, and the flowers in the planters on the front porch were scraggly and dying. There was an old Ford pickup with last year's license plates parked on the grass at the side of the driveway, and an even older Yahama dirt bike with two flat tires leaning against the side of the garage. There were a couple of well-used kids' bikes at the side of the garage as well, and a tricycle with one of the wheels missing.

There was no car in the driveway and the front door was closed, so unless Buchanan had pulled his car into the garage and was sleeping late, it looked like everyone was away from home. I killed the engine and made my way up the sidewalk. There were three editions of the *Laramie Boomerang* on the porch, all of them still bound by rubber bands. Either Buchanan had been gone for a few days, or he wasn't much of a reader.

Just to make sure he wasn't home, I knocked on the door, rang the bell three or four times, and then waited until I was positive no one was going to answer. Then I took my notepad from my pocket and left him a message with my name and phone number and a request to call me as soon as possible.

I stuck the note in the screen door and was just climbing into the Jeep when I saw an elderly woman staring at me over the fence that separated Buchanan's home from the one next door. Still in her housecoat and slippers, she was also wearing a pair of soiled work gloves, and her hands were full of the weeds she'd obviously been plucking from her lawn. I gave her a friendly wave, but she didn't wave back. Instead, she just gave me one of those suspicious old-lady stares that let me know she figured I was up to no good.

"Just dropped by to see Trace," I called out cheerfully.

"Hasn't been home in a couple of days," she said, and as she spoke I realized her suspicious stare was caused more by the fact that she wasn't wearing her glasses and was squinting to see who I was.

I took a shot in the dark. "How about his wife and kids?" I asked. "They around today?"

"You a friend of theirs?" she asked.

"Not really," I admitted.

"That's what I thought," she said. "Wife and kids been gone all summer, out to her parents' place in Kansas. Ought to be back any time, though. School starts before too long."

"How about Trace?" I asked.

She clucked her tongue disapprovingly. "Seems like he hasn't been around much this summer either," she said. She gestured at the Buchanan yard with a bony finger. "If Helen saw the way he's treated her flowers and grass, she'd have his head on a biscuit."

I shook my head knowingly. "Well, I hope she doesn't have to do that," I said. "But if Trace comes home and you happen to see him, would you please tell him Harry Starbranch stopped by? I left a note in the door, but . . ."

"Sure, I'll pass it along," she said, and I had no doubt she'd do just that. If Trace held still long enough, I was sure she'd also be happy to give him a piece of her mind, let him know just how lazy she thought he was for letting his property run down the way he had. Might just put his head on a biscuit and save poor Helen the trouble.

I left her looking out across her yard in search of more weeds to assassinate and drove to my appointment with Marsha Jackson at the Village Inn. The restaurant is a popular place on Third Street in downtown Laramie, a regular of the local businessmen and the fraternity boys who bring their girlfriends in for brunch after Sunday services. That morning it was crowded, the air thick with the smell of fresh coffee and pancakes and sausages.

I told the hostess who I was looking for, and she led me to a table for two at the back of the restaurant. Jackson was already there, sipping a tall glass of orange juice and reading the morning edition of the *Denver Post*.

She recognized me from my visit to Quinn's lab, and I recognized her as well, although that morning she looked much more fatigued than she had the last time. About twenty-three or twenty-four with shoulder-length, mouse-brown hair, she was dressed in sweatpants, running shoes, and a T-shirt from the Boston marathon. Her hair was held away from her face by a lavender sweatband, and there was a matching windbreaker draped across the back of her chair. Her eyes looked a bit bloodshot, puffy, like she hadn't had a good night's sleep in a month, and her skin had a pallor that contrasted sharply with her athletic attire.

I sat down, and we made small talk while the waitress filled my cup with coffee and took our orders. Marsha ordered a full breakfast of a bacon waffle, sausage, eggs, and hash browns. I went easy with a lightly buttered English muffin and a poached egg. Marsha thanked me for coming and gabbed about the weather and her friendship with Katie O'Neill until our orders came, and then she was quiet while she picked at her huge breakfast. Maybe she wasn't hungry after all, because after a few bites, she pushed the loaded plate away and covered it with a napkin.

She sighed and stared at her fingers, which were folded around her warm cup. I got the distinct impression she was having second thoughts about talking to me.

I reached over to give her hands a pat. "Marsha, why don't you tell me what you're afraid of?" I said softly, so the diners at the tables near us wouldn't overhear.

She rubbed her forehead with her fingers and shook her head. "It's probably nothing," she said. "I don't know why I even called you."

"Why don't you let me decide whether it's important or not?" I told her encouragingly. "It might be nothing, but I'll bet it's interesting. Am I right?"

She looked into my eyes for a second, still unsure of herself and me. She must have seen something there to give her courage. "Where should I start?"

I shrugged my shoulders. "Wherever you'd like," I said. Then I gave her a suggestion. "Did you know Victoria Austin?"

She shook her head yes.

"Then why don't you start with her?" I said. "Did you work together? Were you friends?"

Jackson picked up a napkin and began picking bits of paper off the corner, a nervous habit, something to do while she talked. "Not really good friends," she said. "She was the department's star pupil, the one the rest of us looked up to. I talked to her often enough, and we studied together. Sometimes, we'd even go out to a movie on Friday nights and stop off at the Buckhorn for a few beers afterward. I suppose I knew her as well as anyone else in the department, but that all started changing in the six weeks before she disappeared."

"How so?"

"*She* changed," Jackson said. "When I met her she was very open, always eager to talk about what she was working on. If you didn't know her, you might have thought she was bragging a little, letting us know she was working on the kind of projects the rest of us only dream about. But she wasn't bragging. I honestly don't think she knew how jealous we all were of her.

"In the weeks before she died, though, she withdrew. Got very secretive about what she was doing. Walked around all the time like someone was after her."

"The jury said Carl Buchanan was after her," I said.

Jackson shook her head almost angrily. "No, that wasn't it," she said. "She didn't talk much, but she did tell me about Buchanan, and I got the impression that even though she was annoyed about the phone calls and all, she wasn't frightened about it. She told me she could handle a guy like Carl. In fact, she said she'd been handling them all her life, and the way she looked, I believed her. It was something else, Mr. Starbranch. She was frightened about something else."

"Did you ever try to talk to her about it?" I asked.

"Yeah, once or twice I tried to bring it up, but she just brushed me off," Jackson said sadly. "The way she looked at me, I knew it was because she didn't trust me anymore. She looked at everyone like that, Mr. Starbranch. I felt sorry for her, but I didn't know what to do."

"Were you on campus when she disappeared?" I asked.

"No," Jackson said. "I'd gone back home to Wisconsin for my grandmother's funeral. I was back in Laramie by the time they found Vicky's body, but I didn't see her for at least a week before she was abducted."

"Do you have any idea who killed her? Or why?" I asked.

She ripped the napkin in half, and in half again. "No, of course not," she said. "I thought it was Carl Buchanan, like everyone else. All the papers said so, and he was convicted. He even confessed, didn't he?"

She stopped, trying to find the words to continue.

"But you don't think that anymore?" I asked.

"I don't know," she said, and she seemed almost pained to admit it. "But I know that things aren't right in the department, and I think I'm beginning to feel the same way Vicky did before she died."

I took her hands and held them between my own. They were warm and damp and felt as small and fragile as bird's wings. "Nothing's going to happen to you if I can help it, Marsha," I promised. "But you've got to tell me everything you know so I can protect you."

She almost cried then. "That's just it, Mr. Starbranch," she said. "I can't put my finger on exactly what's wrong. It's just a feeling I have that something awful is going to happen, and it's terrifying me. I think I may be going crazy."

I held her hands tighter. "When did this start, Marsha?" I asked quietly, my voice almost to a whisper. A woman and a man who ignored her enough to be her husband were at the table next to us, and she scowled when she saw Marsha's hands in mine. No doubt she thought a man my age had no business touching such a young and vulnerable woman. I gave her a dirty look of my own that told her it was none of her business, and she went back to her omelette. She kept stealing quick glances at us, though, apparently to make sure I was maintaining public decorum. Some days, the world is just full of people who can't mind their own business.

I leaned closer to Marsha, so the eavesdropping biddy couldn't pick up our conversation. "Don't worry, I've got plenty of time," I said. "Just tell me in your own words and at your own pace."

Marsha nodded as if she understood, and then stared out the window for a few minutes to watch cars coming and going in the parking lot. She smiled when one young mother extracted a toddler from its car seat and then had to paw through the junk on the floorboard until she found the child's teddy bear. The child was absolutely refusing to go anywhere without it, especially not to someplace as scary as a pancake house.

When Marsha looked back at me, her lips were tight, and when she spoke her voice was so soft I had to strain to hear. "For this to make sense, I have to start with Vicky and her role in the department," she said. "It's a longer story that way. Do you mind?"

I shook my head no.

"Good," she said. "The first thing you have to understand is that when Vicky was the graduate assistant in charge of the field trials for the programmed cell-death research and some of the ancillary research that goes along with it, she was really in charge," Marsha said. "She was responsible for checking the plants on a daily basis and for keeping her own logbooks and notes. She planned to use the information later on when it came time to write her thesis. All that changed after she died and I took over her responsibilities."

"What do you mean, changed?" I asked.

Jackson smiled ruefully. "What I mean is, the job responsibilities changed. I go to the field every day, just like Vicky did, but I'm not allowed to keep the logbooks or the notes I make. I have to turn them over to Annie Quinn at the end of every day, and she uses them to keep track of the research results and to report her progress to the people funding the studies—although God only knows what she's been telling them. They haven't pulled her grants, so she must be telling them what they want to hear, or at least what she wants them to hear."

"You don't have anything?" I asked. "Nothing on paper?"

"No," Jackson said. "As a matter of fact, Professor Quinn made it clear that if I held out and didn't turn everything over to her, I'd lose my position."

"When I was visiting your department, I noticed another grad student with Quinn, a young man," I said. "Does he turn his notes over as well?"

She nodded yes. "But the thing is, he just started this term, and that's the only way he's ever done it. He doesn't think there's anything strange about it at all, because he doesn't know we used to operate in a different fashion. Besides, he's not responsible for any of the most important projects. He's mostly a lab assistant."

I remembered Robert's description of the rumors that had almost bankrupted Loveladies Pharmaceuticals in the weeks before Victoria Austin died, rumors that the research was going badly. "Is Annie Quinn really going to find the fountain of youth?" I asked. "From what you said a couple of seconds ago, it sounds like you have your doubts."

Marsha shrugged her shoulders and gave me a thin-lipped and very sardonic smile. "Who knows if she'll eventually find it, Mr. Starbranch?" she asked. "But if we're judging by the number of dead potato plants I find out there every day, I'd say it's been a total failure so far."

Now Marsha had my undivided attention. I leaned forward so I wouldn't miss anything she said. "Then Quinn hasn't been able to stop this programmed cell death?" I asked.

"No," Marsha said. "As a matter of fact, it appears that in some cases, the genetic engineering has done the exact opposite of what we wanted. In some cases, I think the aging process has actually speeded up exponentially. Plants are dying of old age far in advance of what you'd expect in normal circumstances."

"Have you asked Quinn about her theories?" I asked.

"Yes, and she tells me that everything that is happening is within normal parameters. But here's a really odd thing. Whenever I go back at the end of the day and report a fresh bunch of dead plants, they're always replaced with healthy ones when I come back in the morning."

"And who's doing that?" I asked. "Quinn?"

"I don't know," she said. "I've never stayed at the field research station all night to find out."

"Did you keep any of these dead plants?" I asked hopefully.

"I'm afraid not," she said. "We're supposed to leave them in situ for Professor Quinn to examine. That's been one of the cardinal rules since Vicky's death."

I sat back in my chair, wishing I could light a cigar to help me think. I settled for the dregs of my coffee and poured myself a fresh cup. When I held the carafe over Marsha's cup, she put her hand over it to indicate she'd had enough. "What are you afraid of, Marsha?" I asked. "Have you been threatened in some way?"

She held her hands over her eyes for a few seconds and sighed deeply. "No, I haven't been threatened," she said. "As a matter of fact, everyone is as nice to me as can be. But something's going on, Mr. Starbranch. I just know it. A couple of times I've come back to my dorm room, and things have been changed, moved just enough so I noticed. I know someone was in there while I was gone. Same with my interdepartment mail."

"Someone's been opening interdepartment mail sent to you?" I asked. "How do you know?"

"No, mail I send to other people in the department," she said. "Whenever I send something that way, I always seal it with clear tape. A couple of times, I've seen envelopes I've sent on the recipient's desk a day or so later, and another type of tape is on top of the clear tape. Someone opened that mail, Mr. Starbranch, and then used another type of tape to reseal it. If I hadn't noticed the different tape, I would have never known."

"Have you said anything about this?" I asked. "Have you told anyone about your suspicions? Did you tell anyone outside your department about the dead plants?"

"Who would I have told?" she asked plaintively. "I don't know who to trust. That's why I'm talking to you."

I looked into her eyes for a few seconds and then put my fist under my chin and looked away, deep in thought. She interpreted my silence as doubt.

"I know this sounds paranoid," she said. "But I even think there's someone listening to my phone calls. They never say anything or make a sound, but I can sense them there all the same. Do you know what I'm talking about, Mr. Starbranch? Or do you think I'm crazy."

I smiled my most benign smile and took her hand again to reassure her. "I don't think you're crazy, Marsha," I said. "You seem like a very rational and sane young woman to me. I'm just think-ing about what we can do about all this."

"Maybe I should just quit," she said. "I don't want to wind up like Vicky Austin."

"I don't think that's going to happen," I told her. "I think you're safe enough, if you just keep your head down and go about your business as you normally would. I don't think you should talk to anyone else about any of this, though. At least not yet."

"Then you'll help me?" she asked. Her eyes looked brighter, and I saw another trace of that pretty smile.

"I'm on the job," I told her. "I intend to find out what's going on—but I might need your help."

"Anything," she said eagerly.

I slipped a twenty-dollar bill under my saucer to cover our check and finished the last gulp of my coffee. Then I took a pen and my notebook out of my pocket so she could give me her phone number. "Just keep your eyes and ears open," I said. "And if you think of anything else that might be important, call me as soon as you can. I won't call you at your dorm unless it's an emergency, just in case you're right about someone listening in on your calls. When you call me, it might be wise to do it from a pay phone."

"I can't believe this," she said sadly.

I shrugged and stood up, then walked Marsha outside to the parking lot. She was driving an old Volkswagen Rabbit with a bent coat hanger where the radio antenna should have been and a set of tires as bald as Telly Savalas. There was a dent in the driver's side door that made it difficult to open. She gave it a yank, and the door came open with a searing groan of metal that made the hair on the back of my neck stand up. She had to slam it three times before it closed properly. I waited until she'd adjusted her seat belt and was fitting her key in the ignition. Then I leaned down so I could see her face through the open window. "Did you ever see Carl Buchanan around the department?" I asked.

"Sure, lots of times," she said.

"With Vicky?"

"Once or twice I saw them talking, but that's about it," she said. "Usually when I saw him, he was with his brother, Trace."

"How did Carl and his brother get along?" I asked.

Jackson turned the key, and the ancient Volkswagen diesel engine sputtered to life. Sounded to me as if it was missing on at least half the cylinders. A noxious cloud of poorly burned diesel chugged out the exhaust pipe.

"If you saw them at a distance, they almost looked friendly," she said. "But I always had the feeling Carl was trying to please his brother without much luck. Whenever I was close enough to overhear them, Trace was usually talking to Carl in a very cutting and condescending way, but either Carl was too stoned to understand him, or was just ignoring it."

"Did you ever pay attention to what they were talking about?"

"Not really," she said. "It was mostly brother stuff. You know, Trace ragging on Carl to clean up his act. Giving him hell for coming to the department with liquor on his breath, that sort of thing. About two weeks before Vicky disappeared, I heard him say that if Carl ever did something again—I don't know what that something was—he'd kick his butt so hard he'd be looking out his asshole."

Her face colored at the harsh language she'd used. "I'm sorry," she said. "I . . ."

"No problem, Marsha," I said. "How did Carl respond?"

She eased her tired transmission into reverse, and the gears ground mournfully before they engaged. "The things Trace said usually rolled off him like water, but they weren't that day. That day he was crying, Mr. Starbranch," she said. "Crying like a baby."

After I watched Marsha Jackson putt-putting away in her rumbly old car, I hopped in the Jeep and took another swing by Trace Buchanan's house. My note was still in the door, so I figured he hadn't been home. I thought for a minute about stopping by the university to speak again with Annie Quinn, but I talked myself out of that because I didn't know for sure what I'd say, or even the right questions to ask. I knew I'd be talking to her again, but when it happened I wanted to be prepared.

98

The sun was high and the late summer heat baked the asphalt on the thirty-mile drive back to Victory. Since Laramie is 7,200 feet above sea level and Victory higher still, it seldom gets uncomfortably hot here, except for the occasional scorcher in August.

That day, the temperature was well into the nineties, and the wind blowing through the open windows was dry and oppressive. The heat rose from the pavement in shimmering waves, and the air smelled of dust and alkali. In the distance, the blue flanks of the Snowy Range looked cool and inviting, and it would have been nice to keep driving into the mountains and not stop until I came to the first patch of glacial ice at the 12,000-foot level near Medicine Bow Peak. I'd strip off my clothes and make snow angels like a five-year-old kid.

Near the place where Highway 130 crosses the Little Laramie River, I stopped to help a family driving a minivan with Alabama plates change a tire. I gabbed with the driver—a hard-bitten man with pudgy arms, a sunburned forehead, and a wad of tobacco in his cheek the size of a grapefruit—about campgrounds in the national forest where he and his family could pitch their tents.

When the van was repaired and rolling again, I leaned against the fender of the Jeep and took a few minutes to enjoy the view. The slender ribbon of the river twisted gently through the broken hill country, a single, pure blue thread in a rich tapestry of browns and greens. In the sky to the west, a lone golden eagle rode the strong air currents above the rich hunting grounds, wing tips barely moving in its majestic, perpetual glide. To the east, a family of pronghorns watched me warily from their daytime hiding places in the bitter sage. A meadowlark sang a midday serenade, and from further in the distance came the sound of cattle lowing as they ambled across the hard-packed ground toward water.

Sometimes, I can spend hours that way, just standing still while the prairie life ebbs and flows around me, but that day I couldn't afford the luxury. I got back in the vehicle and was in Victory ten minutes later, my shirt sticking to my back from sweat and a headache beginning to build right behind my eyes from the blinding glare.

Frankie Bull looked up from his paperwork when I came through the door and almost winced.

"Jesus, boss, you look like fifty miles of dirt road," he chuckled. "What happened? You stay up all night cattin' around like a teenager? Older fella like yourself ought to know better than that."

I sailed my hat, and it landed in a perfect ringer on the peg. "Thanks for the compliment on my good looks," I said with mock severity. "But it's none of your concern whether I stay up all night or not, Mr. Bull. For your information, I was in bed by midnight last night. I just didn't sleep well, that's all."

He was really smiling now. "You know, that's the same exact story Cindy told me when she stopped by earlier this morning, and I didn't believe her, either," he said. "Why don't you go on home and take a nap? It looks like you could use one."

"Why don't you mind your own business?" I groused. "When I need you to tell me it's time for a nap, I'll rattle your goddamned cage." I sat down at my desk, put on my reading glasses, and rifled through the morning's calls and incident reports and copies of the three or four traffic tickets Frankie had written.

When I was done, I looked at him over the rim of my spectacles. "Don't you have something you should be doing?" I asked. "Or were you planning to spend your whole shift here in the office while lawlessness rules our quiet streets?"

He stood up, pulled his Stetson from the peg beside mine, and jammed it low on his forehead. "Now that you mention it, it is time to walk the beat," he said laughing. "Maybe by the time I get back, you'll be in a better mood."

"You keep making cracks about my appearance and my sex life, I wouldn't count on it," I said, but I was smiling.

I watched his broad back through the window as he ambled up Main, and when he was out of sight, I leaned back in my squeaky chair and propped my old boots on top of the desk. I held the phone receiver between my cheek and shoulder as I punched in Cassie Buchanan's number. I listened to it ring twenty times before I gave up.

I needed to talk to her for a variety of reasons, and I needed to do it soon. Naturally, I wanted to soothe the hard feelings between us and make her understand that my offer to help with Carl's arrangements was genuine. But I also wanted to talk to her about the relationship between Carl and Trace. I wanted to understand the dynamics of their sibling behavior and the background that caused it. I didn't believe Cassie could tell me the whole story; mothers never can. But I did think her perspective would be informative.

It occurred to me that she might have gone to Rawlins that morning to start making the burial arrangements on her own, so I dialed the penitentiary on the off-chance I'd catch her there. The receptionist wouldn't give me any information, but when I finally talked my way through to the assistant warden, he told me Cassie had already been there and left. She had hoped the body would be ready for release, and had apparently been upset when she learned she couldn't claim it for at least another twenty-four hours.

"Did she tell you whether she was coming back to Victory today, or whether she's staying over tonight?" I asked.

"She didn't mention anything specific," he said. "But I got the impression they were staying over. You might try the Holiday Inn."

"They?" I asked.

"Yeah," he said. "Cassie and her other son. What's his name? Trace?"

"That's the one," I said. "I'm surprised he's with her though. I got the impression he didn't have much use for his brother, dead or alive."

"What would make you think that, Mr. Starbranch?" he asked.

"I don't know," I said. "When I talked to him just a couple of days ago, it sounded like he thought Carl was getting exactly what he deserved."

"That may be," he said. "But let me tell you something. While Carl was here on death row, it was the older Buchanan boy who visited him more than anyone else, even his own mother. He was here at least once, sometimes twice a week. Carl didn't always want

101

to see him, but the brother insisted. I think he was helping his little brother make peace with what he'd done, helping him take responsibility."

A cold chill ran the length of my spine. "Could you tell me the last time Trace visited before Carl's death?" I asked.

"Is it significant?"

"I don't know," I said. "I'm just trying to understand what happened, like everyone else."

The assistant warden sighed and put me on hold for thirty seconds while he tracked down the visitors' log. When he came back, I heard the rustle of the papers he was reading. "Here it is," he said. "Trace saw him yesterday—just a few hours before the boy killed himself, in fact."

Which meant Trace had driven to see Carl shortly after I'd finished talking to him in Laramie. That's where he'd been going in such a rush after his department meeting ended. Why the hurry? I sure as hell didn't know.

My mind was racing so fast I forgot I was on the phone until the assistant warden brought me back to earth. "Mr. Starbranch, are you still there?"

"Oh, sorry," I said. "You wouldn't happen to know how Carl was acting immediately after their conversation, would you? His state of mind?"

"I'm afraid I don't," he said, and his tone implied he thought it was a stupid question. "I can ask the duty guard, if it's important."

I knew he wouldn't follow up, not even if I begged. "No," I said, "it's not important."

And in truth it wasn't, because I already knew the answer. Very shortly after his final conversation with his brother, Carl Buchanan was dead at his own hand.

In the state-of-mind sweepstakes, that's as bad as the sucker gets.

EIGHT

I had a whole afternoon to kill, but no good way to kill it, no idea of how to move my investigation forward. I felt as if I'd just walked into a dark room and was moving slowly with hands outstretched, hoping I didn't trip over an ottoman and break my fool neck.

For lack of a better idea, I dropped by the house and made a batch of egg salad for lunch, which Robert and I heaped on thick slices of fresh bread. We munched on our sandwiches while we talked about the possibility that additional useful information might be available on the Internet or through direct access to Love-ladies Pharmaceuticals computer system. Robert didn't know if the company's computer system was an open or closed network, but if it was open and accessible by outside modem, he thought it possible he could hack his way inside, root around for a while, and see what turned up about Quinn or her cell research.

I'd been pleasantly surprised by his efforts so far, so I told him to go ahead. I also urged him to be careful, since what he had in mind was probably illegal.

When we were finished, Robert went off happily to his computer, and I tidied up the kitchen. Then, because I do my best thinking on a trout stream, I called Frankie to let him know I'd be out off the office for the better part of the afternoon. I put my graphite fly rod and fishing vest in the backseat of the Jeep and headed back toward the Little Laramie River.

Twenty minutes later, I was standing on the bank at the top of a small run of fast-moving water from which I'd probably pulled a hundred trout in the years since I first moved to Victory. As any trout fisherman knows, the early afternoon isn't the best time of day to coax trout out of the water, since their normal surface-feeding times are the cool of the morning and in the evening after the sun begins to sink. On a hot day like the one we were suffering, the fish are even more lethargic. If they're eating at all, they're doing it well below the surface, and only then if the bait is so appealing they simply can't resist.

I'll admit to being a snob when it comes to trout fishing. I never use live bait like worms, and as a general rule, I don't associate with worm fishermen. They're lazy people, to my way of thinking, more interested in bringing home a fish than in the spiritual act of *fishing*. Bait fishermen also use barbed hooks, which injure the fish so badly that they can never be released live back into the stream. I'm a dedicated dry-fly fisherman because it's the most difficult and pure form of the sport. I usually release the fish I catch, except for the rare occasion when I decide I'd like one or two for breakfast.

That day, however, the only thing I had a chance to catch on a dry fly was the seat of my own pants. It was wet flies or nothing, so I rifled through my fly box until I came up with a good representation of a grasshopper on a barbless hook and tied it carefully to the end of my two-pound leader.

When you cast dry flies, your presentation must be nearly perfect. Otherwise, you'll frighten the fish because the delivery won't look like a bug lighting naturally on the surface of the water. When you fish with wet flies that float below the surface, the presentation isn't as big a deal. I snaked out thirty feet of line and made a decent cast into the top of the run, letting the line slip through my hand as the current carried the grasshopper through the fast water and into a pool at the end.

Nothing.

And there was nothing on the next cast, or the next one, or the twenty I made after that.

I spooled my line and replaced the hopper with a bumblebee, which had exactly the same result. Next, I tried a stonefly nymph, even though it was too late in the season for that particular bug to have much chance of success. To my surprise, the stonefly attracted a small brook trout on the third cast, and I played him gently, brought him to the bank, slipped the hook from his jaw, and held him in the water until he swam away.

That was the only fish I caught as I worked more than two hundred yards of river, but I wasn't disappointed, since trout fishing isn't really about catching fish anyway. The sun was warm on my forehead, and the burbling of the river was as peaceful and comforting as an old pair of slippers. I just let my mind wander, hoping that if I didn't concentrate too hard, my subconscious would mull the problem on its own and come up with a stroke of genius.

Unfortunately, even my subconscious was on holiday, and the best I could come up with was Carl's girlfriend, Susan Walker. When she'd visited my office to swear Buchanan's innocence, I truthfully hadn't paid much attention to what she said. But now, her description of Carl's abysmal relationship with his brother, Trace, was becoming more interesting.

I made my way off the river and back to the Jeep, broke down my rod and reel, and threw them in the backseat. Twenty minutes later, I was crossing the city limits of Laramie for the second time that day.

I hadn't even gotten Walker's phone number before she stormed out of my office at the end of her visit, and I didn't know where she lived. I figured it was likely she still lived with her parents, however, so I stopped at the West Laramie Fly Store and used the pay phone to dial Councilman Stanley Walker's number. The woman who answered was decidedly chilly when I identified myself and told her who I wanted, but she agreed to call Susan to the phone.

When the young woman picked up a couple of minutes later, her voice was so soft and shaky I could barely hear her. She loved Carl and was obviously taking his death hard. In the background,

I could hear the woman who answered the phone telling her she didn't have to talk with me if she didn't want to. I think Susan must have put her hand over the mouthpiece so I couldn't hear, but I was still able to understand her when she told her mother to butt out.

When she came back on the line, she listened quietly while I gave her my condolences on Carl's death and told her I'd like to talk with her about Carl and Trace.

"You weren't interested in that before," she said. "What's changed, Mr. Starbranch?"

"What's changed is that I've been doing what I promised Cassie I would do," I said. "I've been looking into Carl's case, and I have some questions I didn't have before. Maybe you can help me answer some of them."

"You're a little late, aren't you?" she asked. The note of accusation in her voice was unmistakable.

"I suppose I am," I told her truthfully. "Nothing I can do now will bring Carl back, but if he was innocent, maybe I can help clear his name. Knowing Carl as you did, don't you think that would help him rest easier?"

"Are you really worried about Carl, or are you looking for a way to help yourself rest easier?" she asked.

"Miss Walker, I . . ."

"Save it, Mr. Starbranch," she snapped. "For Carl's sake, I'll talk to you, but not here. I live on Ninth and Ord Streets. There's a little park a couple of blocks from here on Seventh. Do you know it?"

I told her I did, and we made arrangements to meet there in ten minutes.

The park was busy that morning, with lots of moms and young kids playing on the grass and the playground equipment, children running through one of the lawn sprinklers, and a couple of boys playing a desultory game of catch with a baseball. The usual assortment of birds and squirrels and dogs were looking for a quiet place to dump.

Susan Walker was already waiting for me when I arrived, sitting atop a picnic table and wearing a pair of open-toed sandals, khaki shorts, and a white halter top that hung loosely on her slender torso. With her brown hair held back in a ponytail, no makeup on her face, her thick eyeglasses, and a pair of skinny, coltish legs peeking out from the shorts, she looked even more childlike and vulnerable than she had at our last meeting. She gave me a half-hearted wave when she saw me coming and didn't bother to speak again until I'd gotten myself situated on the splintery table. The wooden planks of the table were spattered with white bird droppings, but there was no way to avoid them. I just hoped none of them were particularly fresh.

"So you've decided to look into what I told you about Trace Buchanan after all?" she asked.

I picked at a large glob of bird shit with my fingernail, then brushed it away disgustedly. "As I recall, you didn't tell me much," I reminded her. "You said that Trace was the only one who hated Carl enough to set him up for the blame in Austin's murder, but you didn't give me any specifics."

She glared at me then, and the effect was not pretty. The expression pinched her thin face and lips, and gave me a good idea how she'd look in another fifteen or twenty years—like a dyspeptic librarian. "As I recall, you weren't interested in hearing any details," she said tightly. "As a matter of fact, you seemed to think I was crazy, and you couldn't wait until I left."

There was nothing to say to that, because of course she was right. I shrugged my shoulders and put on my best hangdog expression. "I'm sorry for the way I acted, Miss Walker," I told her. "But I'm ready to listen now."

If she was buying my sincerity, it didn't show on her face. She looked away from me and spent a few minutes watching the kids running through the sprinkler. I couldn't imagine her doing the same thing at their age. She was just too serious for that kind of frivolity. I wondered if Carl had ever made her laugh. "What do you want to know?" she finally asked.

I shrugged my shoulders again. "I don't know for sure," I told her honestly. "Whatever you can tell me that will help me understand their relationship. Whatever you think is important."

She frowned and scraped the toe of her sandal across the wooden bench, spent a few moments in contemplation. "There's only one thing that's important," she said. "Carl spent his whole life looking up to his brother and trying to gain his love, and he never got it. All Trace could do was criticize and yell at him, and whenever Carl would try to get himself together and put his life on track, Trace was right there to knock him back down. Trace took everything that was good in Carl and spoiled it. He left him with nothing, no self-respect, no dignity, no faith in himself. My God, Mr. Starbranch, aren't brothers supposed to love each other, look out for each other?

"Carl would have done anything Trace asked, and would have wanted nothing in return but a smile and a hug. But Trace isn't that kind of man. He never gives anything in return; he only takes."

"What did he take?" I asked.

She pursed her lips. "It'd be better to ask what he didn't take," she said. "You know that Cassie and her husband divorced a long time ago, don't you?"

I shook my head yes.

"Well, when the boys' father died three or four years ago, he left about a hundred thousand dollars to Carl and Trace, but he named Trace executor of that part of his estate. Carl wanted to use his share to go to college, but how much of that money do you think he saw, Mr. Starbranch?"

It was a rhetorical question.

"Not one penny!" she spat. "Trace took it all and spent it to buy himself a new house. He even kept most of their father's personal effects. The only mementos Carl had of his dad were an old pocketknife and some Korean War medals."

"Why didn't Carl fight Trace?" I asked. "Surely he could have forced Trace to give him what was rightfully his."

"He didn't fight because he loved his brother and he believed Trace when he told him that he couldn't be trusted with that much money, that he'd be better off letting Trace invest it for him, and that he could have it if he ever really needed it. He gave in, just like he always did, just like he was going to do with the ranch."

That was a new one, and my ears perked up. "What ranch?"

"It was the only thing Carl owned that he cared about," she said sadly. "It's nothing but 1,600 acres of sagebrush and prickly pear and cactus up by Pumpkin Buttes. It was where the Buchanan family homesteaded when they first came to Wyoming, but it isn't worth much now because there's no water and it was overgrazed so badly you can't even run a few sheep on it. Nobody else in the family was interested in the place, but Carl's father willed it to him outright because Carl was the only one who ever wanted to spend time there. He had this wild dream of moving up there someday, building a house, and raising horses. I believed him when he said he'd do it, too."

"You said he was going to give in," I said gently, keeping her on track. "Give in on what?"

"To Trace's demands," she said. "Trace wanted the ranch, too, just like he wanted everything else, although I can't imagine why. Carl said Trace hadn't even visited there for more than fifteen years. Still, he wanted Carl to sign the title over to him, probably so he could sell it for next to nothing. He promised he'd share the proceeds, but neither of us believed him. He couldn't stand the thought of Carl having even that little bit of a dream."

"Carl didn't sign over the deed, did he?" I asked. "He held out?"

"He would have signed it over eventually, because he could never refuse Trace," she said. "But to my knowledge, he hadn't given in before he died. I suppose it doesn't matter either way now, does it? With no other family, Trace and Cassie will get everything Carl had, unless he made a will of his own and left it to someone else."

"They might," I said. "I'll ask around about a will, but from what I've been told about Carl, I doubt he had one."

"Me too," she said. She looked down at her toes again, and I noticed there were tears forming in the corners of her eyes. "I miss him so much, Mr. Starbranch. I can't believe he killed himself without telling me goodbye."

I put my arm around her thin shoulder and pulled her close. She stiffened initially, but then she gave in and leaned against me. When she'd had her cry, she took her glasses off, dabbed her eyes, and blew her nose in a tissue she pulled from her front pocket.

"When was the last time you talked to him?" I asked. "Did you ever visit him in prison?"

She shook her head no. "He wouldn't let me visit," she said. "I saw him in jail when they were holding him here in Laramie, but when he was moved to the penitentiary he didn't want me there. He said he couldn't bear the thought of having me see him like that."

"But you talked to him?"

"Not often," she said. "I wrote him letters almost every day, but I couldn't call him. He could call me collect once in a while, and I suppose we did that three or four times. The last time was the day before you visited him. He was excited that maybe you'd find something that would get him off. I was happy to hear that hope in his voice. He'd been so depressed for months . . ."

"But he didn't tell you anything about the murder?"

"Only that he didn't do it," she said.

"Did he say anything about Trace's visits?" I asked. "Despite what you tell me about their relationship, it sounds like Trace was his most frequent visitor."

"He told me Trace went to see him a lot," she said, "but he didn't tell me what they talked about. All I know is that he always felt worse after Trace left than he had before. Maybe Trace thought Carl wasn't miserable enough already. Maybe he thought he needed to drive over as often as possible to rub salt in the wounds, make Carl feel even more worthless and despicable than he already felt. I know this though: Whatever Trace was visiting for, it wasn't to help Carl. Trace had some self-serving motive, just like always. He wanted something from Carl, Mr. Starbranch, and all I can do now is hope to hell he didn't get it."

*　　*　　*

Susan and I spent another half-hour talking, but it was apparent she had nothing more to tell me.

When we finished, I drove her home and then headed to the County Courthouse Building, parked in the employee lot, and trudged up to the second floor of the old granite building, which houses the offices of the Albany County assessor and the county clerk.

I kept my head down, hoping to avoid being recognized by anyone from the sheriff's department, which has its offices in the basement of the building. I didn't want to be seen by anyone who worked there, particularly not by Anthony Baldi, the county sheriff. The bad blood between us went back several years, to the short period when I held his job, and we're like a couple of old pit bulls in each other's company. When we see one another, the hairs stand up on our necks, our lips curl back to bare our fangs, and we start circling, looking for an opening so we can jump in for the kill. If you put us together in a locked room for twenty-four hours, when you finally opened the door, all you'd find would be hair and bones and gristle. I make it my personal policy to evade him at all costs.

I made it to the second floor unnoticed, but I was disappointed to find Larry Calhoun out of the office when I got there. Despite his vow to leave the assessor's job to some other nincompoop who doesn't mind having abuse heaped on his head every working day, Calhoun has been the popularly elected assessor for as long as I've been in Victory. As the man who assigns a formal tax valuation on everyone's property, he can be the most unpopular man in the county, but because he has a reputation for fairness, he keeps getting elected by huge margins. Even the people who curse the very ground he walks on for most of the year turn out in droves to vote him back into office for yet another term.

Larry Calhoun's also one of my best friends, and even served as my campaign manager during my aborted campaign for county sheriff a few years ago. I always look forward to our visits, because he catches me up on all the latest political gossip, including the latest peccadilloes of Tony Baldi and his evil master, Albany County prosecutor Walker Tisdale, a man so slimy even his mother asks for identification when he writes a check.

That day, Larry's desk was empty, and the only person in the office was his strange daughter, Tina, a morose young woman who's always reminded me of a cross between Wednesday Addams and Ricki Lake before she lost all the weight. As usual, Tina was on the phone, popping her gum into the mouthpiece and directly into the ear of whomever she was speaking to. Dressed in her standard uniform of Doc Martens, a pair of blue jeans blown out at the knees, and a Nine Inch Nails T-shirt, she'd changed her hair color since the last time I saw her, from an eye-popping red the color of a cherry Tootsie Pop to a nice hue just a tad lighter than the pea green used in hospital bathrooms. And instead of black polish on her clawlike fingernails, she was now into variety, every nail painted a different color, like an LSD hallucination of a neon rainbow. She looked like the Rocky Mountain distributor for the herpes virus, but I'm nothing if not tolerant of youthful expression, so I tried not to wince.

Tina looked up and wiggled her claws at me when I walked through the door, but she didn't hang up the phone. From the way she was laughing and joking, I knew it was one of her many personal calls and it might be a while before she was finished. Because Tina figures business can always wait for pleasure and she becomes very surly when a visitor to the office suggests otherwise—but mostly because I was in no great hurry—I got the previous month's *Playboy* out of Larry's top desk drawer and settled in to wait. By the time Tina finally finished her conversation, I had studied the playmate's vital statistics, admired her delicate tattoos, absorbed her views on life and love, looked at all of the other pictorials, breezed through the joke page and the advice column, and in desperation began reading a long interview with Ross Perot. Luckily for me, Tina interrupted that painful endeavor before I had to choke down any of the jug-eared old windbag's pontification. Even by Texas standards, he's unbearable.

112

"Long time no see, Harry," she said happily. She nodded at the magazine, which I had placed still open and faceup on the desk. "You may be the only man in America who can honestly say he paws through that sexist garbage for the stories."

I smiled sheepishly. "I looked at the pictures first," I confessed.

"I know, I saw you," she laughed. "What brings you here today? Pop's out for the afternoon. Said he had an appointment at the proctologist, but I think he has a girlfriend." She smiled wickedly. "Wouldn't it be cool if we could catch him in the sack with some bimbo during working hours? You wanna help me do it?"

I chuckled and shook my head no.

"Come on, Harry," she said. "It'll be fun. Imagine the look on his face."

"And the gun in his hand, Tina. I can imagine that, too," I said. "You, I suppose he'd only wound, but me he'd shoot to kill."

"You owe him any money?" she asked.

"Not much, maybe twenty bucks."

"Then he wouldn't kill you either," she giggled. "He's too damned cheap to forgo collecting on a double-sawbuck if he can help it. He might kneecap you, though, if you stand still long enough for him to aim."

"Thanks anyway, darlin', but my knees are screwed up enough as it is," I said. I closed the magazine and put it back in the drawer. Then I found a yellow legal pad on Larry's desk and wrote out what little I knew about Carl's inherited ranch. I handed it to Tina, and her brow wrinkled as she read it.

"What's this, Harry?" she asked. "You thinking of buying some property?"

"It's a favor I need from your old man," I told her. "I need him to find out whatever he can about this piece of ground. How much it's valued at, what it's really worth, whether it's got a clear title."

"This ranch is in Campbell County," she said, as if I didn't already know. "Pop only has the paperwork for Albany."

"I know that, Tina," I said patiently. "But I was hoping he could call some of his colleagues up there, the assessor and the county clerk, and get them to give him the information over the phone as a professional courtesy. If it's too much trouble, I suppose I can do it myself, but I was hoping that since he knows those folks, he might also be able to pick up whatever buzz is going around about this land, if there is any."

She tucked the paper away in a manila folder. "Nah, it's no trouble," she said. "It'll give him something to do tomorrow. Lord knows he'll do anything to avoid work."

I could have pointed out that compared to her, Larry Calhoun is as industrious as one of those little ants who carry entire bird carcasses for miles back to their nests, but I held my tongue. Tina was in rare good humor for some reason, and I didn't want to spoil it. Maybe her doctor had upped her dosage of Prozac. Maybe she'd dumped her old head-banger boyfriend and found a new one who was actually smart enough to spell *cat* the same way twice. Whatever the reason, it was a nice change.

"Thanks a lot, Tina," I said. I pointed to Larry's desk. "Mind if I use the phone before I go?"

"Of course not," she said. "And if it's long distance, make sure you dial direct. The county's paying." Then she went back to her telephone and punched out numbers, her long nails clacking on the buttons like a duck eating dominoes.

Once she was immersed in conversation, I picked up the receiver and dialed Ken Keegan's extension at the State Department of Criminal Investigation. He answered on the second ring, his voice as slow and scratchy as an old-time phonograph record playing at 45 rpm instead of 78. "Keegan here," he growled. He sounded as if he was drowning in molasses.

When I identified myself and he realized I wasn't one of his supervisors calling to check up on the state of his budget paperwork or expense reports, he became a bit more friendly, but not much. He sounded harried and stressed and not in the mood for small talk. "What can I do for you today?"

"Did I catch you at a bad time?" I asked.

114

"There's never a good time, Harry," he sighed. I heard the scratch of his old Zippo lighter, heard him suck in a lungful of smoke. "Too bad about Carl Buchanan, huh? Guess that gets you off the hook."

"Well, it might," I admitted.

There was a long silence on the other end of the line while Ken chewed that over. "What do you mean, it might?" he asked cautiously. "Not only did the bum confess before his trial, he left a suicide note saying he couldn't deal with the guilt for what he'd done. This thing is over, Harry. Dead as Ted Bundy. Officially and irrevocably deceased."

It wasn't exactly true that Carl's note said he couldn't deal with the guilt, only that he was no longer sure of his innocence, but I didn't point that out. I wanted to talk to Keegan about all of this at some length, but I wasn't ready to do it then. When I spoke to him, I wanted to do it face to face, so I could look into his eyes as we talked. At that moment, all I wanted was a bit of information.

"Well, Ken," I told him, "as Miracle Max said in *The Princess Bride,* 'there's all dead and there's mostly dead.' This case is only mostly dead."

He swore, snorted through his nose. "You come up with some information I ought to know about?" he asked.

"Nothing I can take to court," I said.

"Then what is it?"

"It's just a feeling, Ken," I said. "I've come up with a few things that don't add up, and I just want to see where they lead."

"Another one of your hunches," he said. "I don't suppose I have to point out that your hunches are usually about as accurate as that old lady who reads chicken entrails down on Grand Avenue?"

"Usually, not always," I said peevishly. "It might be a waste of time, but that's the one commodity I seem to have in abundance these days."

"Suit yourself, pardner," he said. I thought I could sense a trace of anger in his voice, but maybe it was just impatience. Maybe he was just in a bad mood. Wouldn't be the first time. "Then I'll ask you again, what can I do for you? I'm pretty sure you didn't call to discuss the weather."

"The evidence you collected from Carl Buchanan's house . . . what happened to it?" I asked.

"It's downstairs from where you're sitting right now," he said, "in the evidence locker at the sheriff's department. Carl was tried in Laramie, so it was kept there for the trial."

"How about his other possessions?" I asked. "The things from his house."

"Cassie and his brother cleaned all that out after Carl went to jail," Keegan said. "The landlord wanted to rent the apartment, so they had to get his junk out. I don't know what they did with it."

"Any chance I could look at the things that were collected for evidence?" I asked.

"You looking for anything in particular?"

"Nope, just fishing," I said. "I don't know what else to do, to tell you the truth."

"Then knock yourself out," he said. "Just let me know if you find anything interesting."

"That I will," I promised him. "I may drive over and talk to you later in the week."

"I'm counting the hours, Harry, and that's the absolute truth."

"One more thing, Ken," I said before he could hang up.

"What?"

"Do you think you could call Tony Baldi right now and tell him you said it's okay for me to go through that stuff?" I asked. "If I go down there on my own, he'll just tell me to fuck off."

I cooled my jets in Calhoun's office for ten minutes in order to give Ken time to make the call to Tony Baldi. Then I trudged down the stairs to the sheriff's department in the basement, dreading it every bit as badly as I dread my annual visit to the oral hygienist.

When I was sheriff for that brief and thoroughly unpleasant time a few years back, the best thing I did for the department was to hire a new crop of deputies who were actually trained to do their job and had them take as many classes at the state police academy as I could afford to give them. Because he doesn't trust anyone who is smarter than he is, however, Tony fired almost all of my people within two months of taking office and replaced them with a motley collection of loyal sycophants, cretins, and steroid-jumpy bullies whose collective brainpower might score 50 on a standard IQ test if they used crib sheets.

Maybe I'm overly harsh and bitter, but I can't help it. The people in his department might be saints and philanthropists for all I know, but every time I walk through the door, I feel like I ought to be matching the faces I see at the desks with the photos of wanted felons at the post office.

They don't like me, either, of course, and a hush fell over the bullpen as soon as the half-dozen deputies, the dispatcher, and the two women on the clerical staff saw me come in. I ignored them, looked through the door of Tony's office, and saw him sitting at my old desk with his feet up, smoking a stubby, vile-smelling black cigar in direct violation of the county's "no smoking in public buildings" policy.

I gave him a tight smile that I'm pretty sure looked like a snarl, but he didn't smile back. He had a telephone receiver jammed between his chin and shoulder, and although I couldn't tell for sure what he was saying, I'm pretty sure the word *cocksucker* was in there somewhere. He made a point of slamming the receiver into its cradle, standing up, strutting over to his office door, and slamming it in my face.

"Fine, you prick," I muttered. "I didn't want to talk to you, anyway."

"He knew that," said a lanky, gap-tooth deputy with greasy, slicked-back brown hair who was sprawled out at the gray metal desk closest to me. His name tag said he was William Goggins, but I knew that in Albany County he went by the nickname Pups. I'd arrested his older brother, Wesley, known as Dogs, about a dozen times in the last three years for drunk and disorderly conduct, but he'd died about six months before from alcohol poisoning after he bet someone he could drink a whole fifth of vodka in a single chug.

His younger sister, Stella, was a hooker who worked conventions and the political crowd at the Hitching Post motel in Cheyenne. Real nice family. "Boss says you're here to look at evidence. You wanna follow me?"

I knew where we were going and didn't need an escort, but I nodded and followed him out of the bullpen and down a short hall to the evidence room, which he opened with a key attached to a wooden dowel. He flipped on the lights, motioned me inside, and indicated I should wait by the door while he pulled a box with Buchanan's evidence from the top of a metal shelving unit. He carried the box to a dilapidated table in the middle of the room and slammed it down. "Knock yourself out, Starbranch," he said. "Tony says you've got ten minutes."

I bit back the urge to tell him that if Tony wanted me out in ten minutes, he could shag his fat ass in there and try to throw me out himself. No point in being confrontational, and besides, I had no desire to spend the night in jail.

I pulled the top off the box and picked up the first of the clear labeled evidence bags inside. It held Carl's cellular phone. The bags I pulled next contained pretty much what you'd expect—hair samples, clothing, photographs, a plaster cast of the impression made by Buchanan's truck, his wallet, Austin's phone number and address scribbled on the back of a business card from a local florist. In one large bag was a battered Ruger .22-caliber pistol and, in another, a nice folding Case pocketknife, the kind designed for fishermen, with a long and sharp main blade and another blade with a little fork at the end for removing hooks from fish jaws.

At the bottom of the box seemed to be Carl's drug paraphernalia and the entire contents of his medicine cabinet. He had a couple of packages of cigarette papers for rolling joints, and a hash pipe made out of tinfoil and the round cardboard tubing from a coat hanger. There was maybe an ounce of pot, and a dozen of those little orange vials that cocaine comes in. A couple of them were full, but the rest were empty. His heroin works were in a nice leather case that had once done duty as a day planner, and in another bag were three dime bags of what I assumed was smack.

There was also plenty of over-the-counter medications. He had cold pills and some laxatives, a couple of boxes of sinus medication, some aspirin, and Sominex.

The last evidence bag contained Carl's prescription medications, perhaps a dozen orange plastic pill containers with child-proof caps. I held the bag up so Pups Goggins could see what I was doing. "Mind if I open this up and look?" I asked.

"Don't take anything," he warned.

Each of the containers was labeled with an evidence number, but they still had their prescription tags attached as well. I took the first one from the bag and held it to the light. Antibiotics. The next three bottles, all empty, were prescriptions for Tagamet, which Carl must have gotten before that antiacid medication became available over the counter. He also had a prescription for Restoril, which I recognized as a light sleeping aid.

The rest of the containers appeared to have been taken, maybe even stolen, from other people. One, prescribed for a woman named Candace Boller, was for diet pills, and so were two more for a woman called Beatrice Sloane. Two of those bottles were empty, but the third had perhaps a dozen pills remaining. Three containers with Robert Baxter's name on the label were for antidepressants, and two more were for painkillers prescribed by local dentists for men named Charles Martinez and Michael Salinger. All of the prescriptions had been written in Laramie, but I didn't recognize any of the names.

"Where'd he get all this crap?" I asked Goggins, who only shrugged and went back to the intense study of his fingernails.

The last container in the bag had no prescription label, only a tag with an evidence number attached. I opened the bottle and shook a few of the pills into my hand. They were white, chalky looking. Nothing I'd ever seen before.

I held them out toward Goggins. "What are these?" I asked.

"How the hell should I know?" he asked. "I look like a pharmacist?"

"Not even remotely," I said. "But I was hoping you could look on your evidence list and tell me. I trust they were analyzed before the trial."

I read the numbers off the evidence tag, and waited while he laboriously worked his way down the evidence list, his expression letting me know he was doing me a big favor. When he came to the evidence number in question, his ugly face cracked in what must have passed on it for a smile. "Now those are interesting," he said. "We're seein' more and more of those around here with the college kids. Goddamned degenerates."

"So what are they, Pups?" I asked impatiently when it became obvious he wasn't prepared to volunteer the information.

"Roofies," he said. "Rohypnol . . . date rape pills. College boys use 'em to knock women out so they can take advantage of them. They're illegal, though. Get caught with those, and you can go to the can for twenty years. They found that bottle in the glove compartment of Carl's pickup."

I'd heard of the pills, naturally. Among other nasty effects, I knew they practically obviate short-term memory. The unsuspecting women drugged with roofies remember bits and pieces of their attack, but nothing coherent, nothing they can testify to with certainty in court. They know they were raped, but it was like it happened in a dream. Still, I didn't think the drug played a part in Austin's disappearance. I tried to remember the autopsy report and trial transcript, but couldn't recall any reference to roofies.

"Do you know if they found any of this garbage in Austin's system when they did the autopsy?" I asked. I figured Goggins would have read the report out of morbid curiosity. Probably memorized it.

"Nah, they didn't find anything like that," he said. "The roofies were Buchanan's, but maybe he just didn't need to use them. Maybe they were just a backup in case she was too strong to rape and choke otherwise."

"Was the bottle tested for prints?" I asked, although I'm not sure why. Like I told Keegan, I was fishing.

"Why would it have been?" he asked. He grabbed his tie and pantomimed hanging himself with it—his impression of Carl killing himself. "We knew who it belonged to. Your little pervert buddy."

NINE

I picked up Mel Gibson's *Lethal Weapon* trilogy at the video store in Laramie before I headed out of town for the thirty-mile hop back to Victory, my intention being to invite Cindy over, make a pot of chili, and settle in with her and Robert for a blood-and-guts action marathon. Sadly, that plan evaporated as soon as I pulled into Victory and stopped by the police station, where I learned that all hell had broken loose in my absence. Frankie needed me to help pick up the pieces.

My first clue that something was amiss were the two tattered and bruised men handcuffed to the wooden bench in front of the office. I recognized them both as loggers for the Pacific Northern Timber Company, which had been working the country around Ryan's Park for most of the summer. The men—Steve Kiley and George Crisp, if I remembered correctly—looked like they'd been in a fight with a wildcat and come out on the losing end.

I nodded at them when I got out of the Jeep, but they looked down at their shoes and didn't answer, as if they were embarrassed by their circumstances. Since we usually confine prisoners in our single jail cell and not shackle them to the bench, I wondered briefly why Frankie had chosen that particular restraint option. My question was answered as soon as I walked through the door and saw four more prisoners in similar states of disarray. All of the men were handcuffed, and although none of them seemed to be in need of emergency medical attention, they all looked like they'd been in a nasty scrap. Lots of bruises, contusions, scrapes, and blood. Maybe even one or two broken noses.

Two of the walking wounded I'd seen around the Silver Dollar and recognized as loggers who worked with Crisp and Kiley. The other two were strangers, both young men in their early twenties, both of them considerably smaller than the puniest of the lumbermen. One, who maybe weighed one-forty, had a goatee and shaggy dark brown hair that came to his collar. The other, a bit heavier, had a mop of curly blond hair and a Fu Manchu mustache. Both were wearing Greenpeace T-shirts, blue jeans, and hiking boots. Both were eyeing the loggers and Frankie Bull warily, as if someone might take a notion to start waling on them again at any second.

Frankie, sitting at his desk filling out paperwork, appeared as if he'd taken a few good licks himself. His hair, which he usually keeps in neat braids, was loose and wild looking, and there was a red patch right above his hairline where it looked as if a handful of hair had been yanked out. The knuckles on both of his hands were scraped and bleeding, there was crusted blood on both of his nostrils, and he had the makings of a real disgusting fat lip.

When he saw me come through the door, Frankie looked up from his writing and glared.

"Quasimodo?" I asked.

"Real funny, Harry," he said, although coming through his swollen lip, the words didn't sound quite right. "I suppose I could tell you that as bad as I look, the other guy looks worse." He indicated the prisoners with a dismissive wave. "But you can see the other guys for yourself."

"You did all this?" I asked, meaning the damage to flesh and bone.

He gave me a no-big-deal shrug, but the blond kid in the Greenpeace T-shirt was truly impressed. "You should have seen it," he told me. "It was like a *Street Fighter* cartoon. Mr. Bull flat kicked ass."

"Including yours, loudmouth," Frankie growled. "Now shut the hell up until I tell you to talk."

The kid's Adam's apple jiggled, he swallowed hard, and his eyes seemed to bug out, but he did as he was told. As big and as mean looking as he is, Frankie is intimidating even when he's doing something as innocuous as reading one of his wife's romance novels. When the storm clouds gather on his face and his fur stands up, he's mad-dog scary. When he tells you to shut up, you do it.

I wanted to hear what had happened to ruffle his dander, but I didn't want to talk in front of our guests. Since the office is so small, however, there's no place to hold a private conversation except the bathroom. It's a tiny one-holer, so that was out. "Take a walk with me," I told him.

Frankie nodded and stood up, giving the assorted prisoners a look that let them know they'd better not try any funny business while he had his back turned. They got the message, believe me. I figured they'd be as quiet as mice. If we never came back, they'd probably just sit there without speaking until they starved.

We walked out the door, past the two prisoners handcuffed to the bench and down the cracked sidewalk toward Main. I waited until we were out of earshot before I spoke. "Maybe you'd better tell me what this is all about," I said. "What was it, some kind of riot?"

"A short one," he said. "They were rioting until I showed up, and then I convinced 'em to calm down quick enough. Curly's furious though. He's pressing charges against the whole bunch."

"Why don't you start at the beginning," I said. "Before you conked them on the heads and restored order."

With a tentative finger, Frankie explored the place where his hair was missing, winced, and studied his finger carefully after he took it away from his scalp. He was apparently relieved at the lack of fresh blood. "You know those monkey wrenchers been screwing up the logging operations around Ryan Park all summer?" he asked.

I nodded that I did. The logging operation was a big bone of contention between the lumber companies, who think the only good tree is a tree made into toothpicks, and conservationists who believe clear-cutting is every bit as bad as clubbing little baby seals. The debate had been played out in the newspapers and the legislature and the courts, but when it appeared there was no way to stop the timber companies from cutting, the battle of words attracted a group of eco-terrorists who took matters into their own hands with a little guerrilla warfare.

In this part of the country, those idealistic goofballs are known as monkey wrenchers after Edward Abbey's book *The Monkey Wrench Gang,* and they do everything in their power to make life miserable for the loggers, timber haulers, strip miners, and other greed-headed despoilers of the environment. Ripping survey stakes out of the ground and pulling the colored cut ribbons off trees are the least drastic of their measures. They also sabotage the timber companys' heavy equipment and the loggers' trucks, and lately had been driving ten-inch nails into trees marked for cutting. A long metal nail plays hell with a chain-saw blade, and at least one logger had received minor injuries when his saw hit a nail and the blade bucked back. It might have cut his head off if he hadn't been wearing a hard hat.

Needless to say, the loggers hate the monkey wrenchers every bit as badly as the eco-terrorists hate them. To date though, none of the skirmishes between the warring factions had taken place within the Victory city limits.

"You didn't catch them in the act did you?" I asked.

"No," he said dismissively. "But it seems those young wrenchers stopped off after work at the Silver Dollar this afternoon and got to laughing about what havoc they'd been causing. Unfortunately for them, the dumb shits didn't realize that Crisp and Kiley were sitting at the table behind them with their buddies and could overhear everything they said."

"Which led, I take it, to a confrontation," I said.

"A humdinger," Frankie agreed. "I think the loggers would have killed those boys on the spot, if Curly and Lou McGrew hadn't jumped in to stop them. That's when one of the monkey-wrench kids socked Curly in the stomach and one of the loggers threw a wild punch that blackened Lou's eye. From there, it was pretty much a free-for-all until I walked in about two minutes later and cleaned it up."

"Somebody call you?" I asked.

"Nah, I saw 'em fighting through the window when I was driving by," he said.

"Who hit you?" I asked.

"All of 'em probably," he said. "It was a little crazy. I think even Curly might have swung at me at one point." He touched his fat lip gingerly. "I know for a fact that Lou did. Woman's got a real pretty right jab."

I figured I could probably get some mileage out of the fact that Frankie had taken a good shot from a woman who looks a lot more like Dolly Parton than George Foreman, but it wasn't the time to start teasing him. I'd wait until he calmed down some, maybe a month or so, then make him suffer. "Curly and Lou okay?" I asked.

"Cuts and bruises," he said. "But they tore hell out of the Silver Dollar, even broke Curly's old Wurlitzer jukebox. He's really mad about that, Harry . . . wants to press charges against all of them for destruction of property, causing a disturbance, assault with intent to do bodily injury, creating a public nuisance, the whole enchilada. I'm throwing in assault on a police officer, just for good measure."

Besides having the advantage of his impressive size, Frankie is an accomplished boxer and studies several varieties of kung fu and other martial-arts mumbo jumbo. But even with those macho skills, I was impressed he'd been able to take on six grown men at the same time and come out of the fracas on top. I would have asked him how he managed that trick, but I knew his modesty would prevent him from giving an honest answer. Frankie hates to brag, but I had the feeling the incident would go down in local legend. Maybe later, I'd stop off at the Silver Dollar and have Curly and Lou give me a blow-by-blow.

I clapped Frankie on the shoulder and started walking back toward the office. "I guess we'd better get finished with the paperwork," I said. "You have any suggestions where we ought to put all those guys? Our jail only holds two."

"No clue," he said. "But I'll tell you this, Harry. I'm not takin' any of 'em home with me. Last time I did that was when those rodeo cowboys started breakin' chairs over each other's heads at the Trails End, and Frieda was none too happy about having surprise guests. She told me no more prisoners sleeping it off on her couch, and I'm pretty sure she meant it."

There wasn't enough space in the jail for all the prisoners, so we packed everyone in two cars and I made yet another trip to Laramie to check the assorted miscreants in at the county jail, where they would await their arraignments in the morning.

It was nearly ten o'clock when I finally got home. When I pulled into the driveway, the lights in the main part of the house were dark, and I figured Robert was already in bed. I kicked my boots off on the front porch, poured myself a double Jack Daniel's neat, and tiptoed through the living room into the spa room, where I stripped out of my clothes and crawled into the hot tub. I suppose I sat there in the dark for twenty or thirty minutes, sipping my bourbon, looking out the window at the moonlit mountainside and letting the water jets beat my sore muscles into shape before I noticed a shadow in the doorway that was darker than the surrounding space.

"If you're a burglar, you'll be unhappy to know I've got a gun somewhere and I'm not afraid to use it," I said. "But if you're my son, why don't you grab a cigar for me, a beer for yourself, and come in here and say hello."

"Don't mind if I do, Pop," he chuckled. "I've been sitting at that damned computer all day. I could use a break."

"Don't call me Pop," I growled, but by that time he was already off on his errand.

I soaked happily until Robert came back with a cigar and his beer and, because he's a young man who thinks ahead, the whole bottle of Black Jack in case I wanted a refill. He stripped out of his own clothes and climbed into the tub across from me, waited until the cigar was going and I'd topped off my drink before he spoke. "You're home late," he observed. "Tough day?"

I sipped and smoked and told him about the showdown at the Silver Dollar, and he cackled when I got to the part about Lou poking Frankie in the kisser. "I imagine he was pretty embarrassed about that," he said.

"If he wasn't, he will be by the time I get finished with him," I promised. "Curly's trying to make Frankie seem like the second coming of Wyatt Earp, so I figure it's my job to teach my titanic Sioux friend a little humility, just to keep him from getting a big head."

"No mercy?" Robert asked.

"Would he show mercy if the tables were turned?" I asked. "Has he ever? Not Frankie Bull, once he smells blood in the water. Whenever he finds something he thinks might embarrass me, that sadist doesn't just rub salt in the wound, he grinds it in, sprinkles on a little lemon juice, and hauls Polaroids of my humiliation all over town."

"Guess you're right, Pop," he said. "Time to hoist the black flag."

I splashed water at his face. "Don't call me Pop, goddamn it, or I'll hold your smart mouth under water 'til you drown."

"Suit yourself," he said. "But if you kill me I'll take this information to the grave."

"What information?"

"What did I tell you I'd been doing all day, Dad?" he asked.

"Working at the computer?"

"Right," he said. "And as you might or might not know, it's a real good source of information. Some of it might even be helpful to your investigation."

"I take it your hacking was successful?" I asked.

"So-so," he said. "But I think I'm making progress."

"You broke into their system?" I asked, impressed.

"Not much problem there," he said. "It isn't a closed system, so I got in through the modem. It took me most of the day to work my way though their servers and find the files relating to Quinn's project. There's a huge amount of information about her and her research. The trouble is, almost all of it is encrypted."

I had no clue what he was talking about, and told him so.

"Encrypted," he said. "You know, scrambled. It's a pretty standard practice in corporate America for sensitive files to be encrypted. That way, they can't be opened unless you have the password for a particular file. The people at Loveladies use an encryption program called Norton Encrypt, which isn't the most sophisticated available, but it usually does the job."

"You can't hack through the password protection?" I asked.

"Somebody who knows more than I do about hacking might be able to," he said, "but that's beyond my level of expertise. The only thing I can do is to start typing in possible passwords at random and hope I eventually hit on the right one."

"In other words, you're talking about a project that could take years," I said dejectedly.

"Maybe several thousand," he said. "I'll call a friend of mine and see if there's a way to get around the password, but I wouldn't hold my breath if I were you. Unless we get incredibly lucky, most of the Loveladies files are out of reach."

Robert's emphasis on the word *most* piqued my interest. I sat forward in the hot tub and leaned toward him. "Most, but not all?" I asked hopefully.

"Not all," he said, and even in the dark I could sense the smile on his face. "I found a couple of memos to Quinn from a Loveladies vice-president named David Sims, one of them written about six weeks before Austin disappeared and the other written three weeks ago. Both files were saved in the wrong folder and because of that, it looks like nobody thought to encrypt them. They popped right open when I clicked on 'em. They were interesting, Pop, but I'm not sure how important they are."

"Tell me about the first one," I said.

"Real short and to the point," he said. "The memo said Sims had heard rumors Quinn was involved with a married man, and he was urging her to either terminate the relationship or use incredible discretion. Because she was in the public eye, he warned her not to do anything that could possibly tarnish her image or the project."

"Is that standard procedure?" I asked. "Why would Loveladies care who Quinn was screwing?"

"Maybe they didn't," he said. "Maybe this vice-president was just throwing his weight around, being a jerk."

I wondered how Sims had come to hear that rumor, and I wondered who Quinn might have been involved with. "What about the second memo?" I asked.

"The second was very businesslike," he said. "Sims told Quinn that because there was great competitive interest in the progress of her research, it was imperative that information about the research be guarded at the university and passed along to the company on a need-to-know basis. He directed Quinn against talking about the project or her results with anyone but him or his direct superiors, and he reminded her that failure to control information had caused them real problems in the past. If she learned about leaks or rumors, she was supposed to contact the company at once, so they could prepare a damage control plan."

He stopped talking long enough to take a long sip of his beer. "They're really paranoid about this, Pop," he said.

"Well, after what happened last time, I guess they would be," I said. "They don't want their stock crashing again." I took a reflective puff of my stogie, blew a couple of smoke rings. "So you're gonna keep trying to get more out of the Loveladies system?" I asked.

"I'll give it a go," he said, "but unless I can get some help with the password, I might have more luck looking elsewhere."

"Like where?"

"The university," he said. "I thought tomorrow I'd see if I can't find a way into Quinn's personal files through the main system. When you were in her office, did you happen to notice whether any of her personal computers were networked? If they're not on a network and her personal files are stored on one of her own hard drives, there's no way I can get to her files from my computer, but if they're networked and her files are saved on a server, I might have a shot."

The kid might as well been speaking Russian, for all I understood. Last I heard, networking was something yuppies did at cocktail parties and involved trading business cards. "And how would I have been able to tell that?" I asked sarcastically. "Do networked computer systems have some kind of sign or something?"

"No, Dad," he said, frustrated. "There's a network connection at the back of the computer terminal and a network cable leading off that."

"Damn, Robert," I said, "there were so many cables in that office it looked like gray spaghetti, but I didn't pay 'em the slightest attention. I didn't even notice whether her computers were plugged in, to be perfectly honest."

"Then tell me, Mr. Trained Observer, what *did* you notice?" he asked, tweaking my ignorance, rubbing it in.

Besides Annie Quinn's perky breasts and her cute little smile? Not much apparently. Next time, I'd have to do better.

After we finished our soak, Robert trundled off to make himself a sandwich and then back to his room to surf the Net. I dried myself off, pulled on my favorite sweats, and crawled into bed with the latest Andrew Vachss novel. I don't know much about the underbelly of New York City, but I've always liked his hero, Burke, and his sidekick, a huge Mongolian karate expert named Max the Silent. I also respect the way Vachss has boiled his prose style down to the bare essentials. His words are like hard punches to the belly, straight, swift, and often painful. I'd finished the first thirty pages when the jangling phone pulled my mind out of the New York gutters and back to Victory. "Starbranch here," I grumbled.

The voice on the other end belonged to Marsha Jackson, and in the background I could hear classical music going full volume. The piece sounded familiar. Bach, maybe Beethoven. One of those dead Germans, at any rate. "Hello, Mr. Starbranch," she said tentatively. "I hope I didn't wake you."

"As a matter of fact I was still up reading. Is everything all right, Marsha?"

The long pause on the other end of the line answered that question for me. "I don't know," she said. "It's probably all in my imagination, but when I got to the school today after our meeting, I had the feeling I was being watched. I don't know why that would be. I'm pretty sure nobody knew that you and I talked."

"Did anything unusual happen?" I asked.

"Not really," she said. "Professor Quinn came to me this afternoon and asked for my notes, just like she always does, but today she asked if I was sure I'd given her all of my material . . . like she thought I might be holding out. She seemed to accept it when I told her I'd given her everything, though, and she just nodded and went on with her business. But I still feel like something's wrong, and it's making me afraid."

"You're not calling from your dorm, are you?" I asked.

"No," she said, "a pay phone."

I looked at the clock by the bed. If I hurried, I imagined I could make it to Laramie in a half-hour. "Listen, Marsha," I said, "my son and I have plenty of room here. Would you like me to drive in and pick you up? It's no imposition, really, and at least you'd feel safe."

She hesitated for a second before answering. "No, that's not a good idea," she said. "If Professor Quinn learned I'd been there, it would raise more questions than I want to answer. I'll just stay where I am for the time being."

"You're a brave girl, Marsha," I said. "But I don't think there's anything to worry about. So far you haven't done anything that would draw attention . . ."

"That's not entirely true," she said before I could finish. "Do you remember when I told you about those dead plants? The ones that are always replaced with healthy ones the next morning?"

"Yeah," I said cautiously. "What about 'em?"

"Well, today I broke the rules, Mr. Starbranch," she said. "We're supposed to leave them in situ. Professor Quinn has been very clear about that."

"But you took some of them?" I asked, although I already knew the answer.

"Yeah," she said. "I've got a half-dozen of them in my freezer, and now I don't know what to do with them. I thought you might be interested, that maybe they could be important, and I guess that's why I'm calling so late. I'm afraid someone will notice they're gone, and I don't want to be found with them. Like I told you, I think somebody has been in my apartment, so they're probably not safe here."

I had no idea what I'd do with a half-dozen frozen dead potato plants, either, but they seemed important to Marsha Jackson and I didn't want to upset her. "Tell you what," I said. "How about meeting me for breakfast in Laramie again tomorrow morning? You can bring them then."

"No," she said without hesitation. "I don't even want to keep them that long. If it's all the same to you, I'll drive them to Victory and have them at your office first thing in the morning. After that, you can do whatever you want with them."

"For the time being, I imagine I'll just put them in my freezer," I said.

"Fine," she said, obviously relieved, "at least they won't be in mine."

TEN

By the time I arrived at the office at eight-thirty the next morning, Marsha Jackson had already come and gone. A sticky-note from Frankie reading "Plants???" are in the freezer" was waiting on my desk, along with another saying he was out on rounds and would be back by midmorning.

Out of curiosity, I opened the freezer compartment of the refrigerator we keep in the back room and saw the plants, packaged in one of those plastic freezer bags, stuffed in among the ice cube trays and microwave dinners we keep around for the occasional inmates of our lone jail cell. Then I closed the fridge and promptly forgot about the plants, since my mind was on more pressing matters, breakfast at Ginny Larsen's being at the top of the list. So that's where I went, to fill my grumbling belly with a Denver omelette and home fries and about a half-gallon of strong black coffee.

It was pleasant sitting there at Ginny's counter with the sun shining through the window and the mouth-watering smells of bacon, sausage, and baking bread coming from her kitchen and all the locals gossiping and passing the time of day. I dawdled for almost an hour before I paid my tab and wandered back to the office, where I found that Frankie had returned and was leaning back in his chair, holding that morning's edition of the *Boomerang* at arm's length as he read the box scores. He needed glasses, but he'd never admit it. Too much vanity, I suppose.

He looked at me over the top of the paper when I came

through the door and nodded at my phone. "Mornin', Harry," he said. "Larry Calhoun is looking for you. I told him I'd have you call as soon as you got in."

I nodded absentmindedly, picked up the news section of his paper, and started reading a story about a company that wanted to drill oil wells on the border of Yellowstone National Park. The ecologists in opposition to that plan were concerned about the possible adverse impact on geothermal activity in the geyser basins, and a few members of an especially vocal group had chained themselves to the fence at the oil company's headquarters in Casper. One of the protesters in the front-page photo carried a sign that said, "Don't Trade Old Faithful for a Barrel of Crude," and was waving a middle-finger salute in the general direction of the main office building. The cop who was cutting the kid's chains loose from the fence with a pair of bolt-cutters had a look on his face like he'd just taken a bite of raw squid. Maybe he thought environmental activism was a communicable disease, like herpes.

"Not for nothin', Harry," Frankie said, before I'd read more than a few paragraphs, "but Larry sounded like it was important, and he said he'd only be in the office for a little while. If you don't catch him now, you might not get him for the rest of the day."

I glared at him in halfhearted rebuke for his nagging, but it didn't make an impression, so I folded the paper and dialed Larry's office number in Laramie. It rang six times before he finally answered.

"Sorry I missed you when you dropped by," he said. "Tina tells me you were on your best behavior."

"I usually am when I want a favor," I said. "She explained what I wanted? Do you think you can help me out?"

"Already done," he chuckled. "This one turned out to be a no-brainer. The assessor in Campbell County is a pal of mine, so I called her first thing this morning, and she gave me everything she had. Turns out the Buchanan property has been quite a topic of conversation around there lately . . . what with the kid killing himself on death row, and all."

I could tell from the tone of his voice that he was fishing for information, but he wouldn't come right out and ask why I was interested in Carl Buchanan's ranch, or what it might have to do with the young man's case. Since I didn't know the answer to that question myself, however, I had nothing to give him, at least not yet. "What did you learn?" I asked.

I could hear the disappointment in his voice when he answered. In politics, information is a commodity, and Larry likes having a little something exclusive in the bank. "Rumors mostly," he said. "But first, I'll tell you what I know for fact. The ranch is a big hunk of sagebrush and rattlesnake-infested alkali flatland, twenty miles southwest of Pumpkin Buttes. Carl's great-granddaddy homesteaded the original hundred-sixty-acre spread during the very late eighteen-hundreds, and gradually bought out his neighbors until he owned sixteen hundred acres. He ranched a little, raised some sheep and cattle, and overgrazed the shit out of it, right down to the nubs.

"When he died, he passed the place on to Carl's grandfather, Benjamin Buchanan, who more or less eked out a living there until he died. He passed it on to Carl's father, who eventually willed it over to Carl . . . who's been doing nothing with the property at all. As far as I know, he's leased out a little of the better acreage for grazing, but that hasn't even brought in enough to cover the taxes. Everybody up there wondered what he had planned, since the ground is so dry and eroded it isn't any good for ranching anymore. Most of them figured he'd probably sell it off if he could find a buyer."

"Assuming someone wanted to buy it, how much would it bring?" I asked.

"Next to nothing," Calhoun said. "Right now, land in that area is going for fifty to seventy-five dollars an acre, which would bring him a hundred twenty thousand for the entire sixteen hundred acres if he could get top dollar, which he wouldn't. All the buildings on the place are falling down, so my guess is he'd have been doing good to get seventy-five, eighty thousand for the whole kit and caboodle. He'd still owe about twenty-five grand in taxes, though, so he wouldn't see the whole nut."

Fifty thousand was more money than most people see at one time, and I figured it was certainly enough to arouse Trace Buchanan's greed, but based on what I'd learned from Susan Walker, convincing Carl to sign the deed over to him had nearly become an obsession. I guess I shouldn't have been surprised. Families have torn them themselves apart over much less than fifty thousand dollars.

"So if those are the facts, Larry, what are the rumors?" I asked.

"That's where it gets a bit more interesting," he said. "My friend in the assessor's office tells me the coffee-shop gossip has it that one of the big oil companies in Casper has been doing some seismic and geological work in that area, and thinks there might be enough oil in the underlying formation to be very profitable. According to the gossip, it's likely they'll start making offers to some of the landowners before too long."

I leaned forward, feeling a little zap of psychic electricity. "What kind of offers?" I asked.

"I don't know the specific details," he said. "But if they turn out to be interested in drilling on Buchanan's sixteen hundred acres, they might be willing to pay a couple of million dollars for the right."

"That sounds like hitting the lottery," I said.

"It's better, in almost every way," Calhoun laughed. "For one thing, you get your money all at once, instead of having it doled out a little at a time. And that two million ends up in your pocket whether they find oil or not. If they strike crude, the money comes in by the truckload."

"How much are we talking about?" I asked.

"Depends," he said. "But say you owned sixteen hundred acres of land and the mineral rights that go along with it, which Carl owned, by the way. If that oil company discovered oil on your property, you'd get a royalty of twelve-and-a-half percent on every barrel that's taken. Right now, crude oil's going for about twenty-three bucks a barrel, but that fluctuates a lot. Even so, if your well pumps a hundred barrels a day, that's almost three hundred bucks a day for the owner in mineral rights."

I whistled through my teeth. "That's money," I said.

"Damned right it is," Calhoun said. "Think how much you'd get if your well pumped three hundred barrels a day? Or a thousand? At that point, you're talking almost three thousand a day in royalties. And that's not the end of it, Harry. On eighty-acre spacing, that oil company could drill ten oil wells on eight hundred acres. On the sixteen hundred Buchanan owned, they could drill twenty. If they got lucky and hit oil in a quarter of them, that would make the landowner a very rich man."

My mind was reeling with the implications of what I was hearing. If the rumors were accurate and Carl hadn't died in prison, it's possible he could have wound up one of Wyoming's richest citizens. No wonder Trace wanted the place for himself, assuming he'd heard the same rumors, which I suspected he had. "Did the local gossip pipeline tell your friend which oil company was involved, or whether they were definitely interested in the Buchanan homestead?" I asked.

"Yes and no," he chuckled. "Word is that the oil company is Black Mesa Petroleum. You ever heard of them?"

I had indeed. As a matter of fact, Black Mesa was the firm involved in the controversy over drilling near Yellowstone National Park, the same company singled out by the ecological protesters in that morning's paper. "Who hasn't?" I asked. "But are they interested in the Buchanan place?"

"That I don't know," he said. "Oil companies hold information like that pretty close to the vest. You know anybody works there?"

"Nobody but a couple of roughnecks who got themselves arrested in Victory last spring for brawling at the Trails End," I said. "I know Black Mesa's owned by Jules Black, but that's about the extent of my knowledge."

"Interesting old man," Calhoun said. "Owns the company all by himself, no stockholders. Legend is he started out as a wildcatter and hocked his wife's wedding ring to pay the freight on his first well. Now he's almost as rich as Bill Gates, but you'd never know it to look at him. All he wears is faded jeans and boots, and he drives a twenty-year-old Chevy with a dented front quarter-panel.

I hear he doesn't even have a full-time secretary. Usually answers his own phone."

"Then maybe I'll just call him up and ask him," I said. "Hey Jules, you think there's any oil on the old Buchanan place?"

"You do that, Harry," he laughed. "But if he's gone completely crazy and gives you an answer, you call me right back, pardner. I might want to call up a real estate broker in Campbell County and invest in some worthless land while it's still worthless."

I did exactly what I threatened, and to my surprise Black lived up to his reputation by answering himself. He was suspicious when I identified myself, and insisted on getting the number for the Victory Police Department through directory assistance and calling me back to make sure I was who I claimed to be.

"Can't be too careful," he apologized after I answered his return call. "Yesterday, some character called me claiming to be an accountant for one of our royalty holders, but it turned out he was a reporter looking for some inside information on a story."

"I'm not a reporter," I promised him. "I'm a cop, and we don't have much voluntary congress with people from the Fourth Estate. Judging from this morning's paper, though, you've had more truck with them than you wanted."

"That's puttin' it mildly," Black said. "Twelve protestors were out here yesterday, and there were twenty reporters and camera crews recording their every move. Looked like a goddamned love-in out there."

"Except for the people wearing chains," I noted.

"You never can tell," he chuckled. "I hear those liberals are into that kinda thing."

We talked for a couple of minutes about the trials and tribulations of dealing with the press and being in the public eye, but I could tell he was only making small talk. He cut it off after a polite interval, his tone letting me know he was too busy to chat. "What can I do for you today, Mr. Starbranch?" he asked.

Black listened while I launched into a bare-bones outline of my investigation into Carl Buchanan's case. I started to explain that I was trying to answer some questions that had arisen in the course of my inquiries.

"You're doing this for Cassie Buchanan?" he asked before I could finish.

"I was," I told him. "But since Carl committed suicide, I'm doing it for myself."

"Well, her sons turned out to be disappointments, I hear, but Cassie Buchanan is a hell of a woman," he said. "I've known her for over thirty years. Knew her family and her husband's family, too. I don't see how I know anything that could help you out, but I'd be happy to try if it's in my power."

I decided to take him at his word. "Then maybe you can tell me if you're planning to look for oil on the old Buchanan homestead," I said. "Did you offer Carl, or anyone in his family, money for the rights to drill there?"

At the question, Black laughed out loud, a hearty belly laugh that sounded like St. Nick. "Well, hell, Mr. Starbranch, why don't I just tell you all my business secrets?" he asked, with more than a trace of good-natured sarcasm. "You're a nice fella, I imagine you'd keep 'em to yourself." Meaning that—no offense—he didn't trust me at all.

"I don't want to know all your business secrets, Mr. Black," I said. "Just this particular one."

"I look for oil in a lot of places," he said. "I hire geologists, and they tell me where there might be oil. If my intuition and experience agree with their science, I make arrangements to drill. I don't end up with any crude in my pipeline, however, if I run off at the mouth about my plans beforehand. If my competition knows what I'm up to, it tends to screw things up beyond belief."

The friendly note was still in Black's voice, but I could tell the man was as hard as tungsten steel. He was not about to part with sensitive information without a damned good reason, and maybe even not then. I didn't know how to convince him to give me what I needed, but whatever I did, I knew it had to be soon. I figured I had his attention for another sixty seconds, tops. "I'm a former homicide investigator and a full-time cop, not an oilman," I told him. "I'm only interested in your business plans as they relate to Carl Buchanan. I think there's an outside chance that boy was innocent, Mr. Black, and one way or another I'm going to find out whether the state convicted the wrong man. I can't make you help me do that, but I'd truly appreciate it. You have my word that whatever you tell me is confidential. You can check me out if you want to, sir, so you'll know my promise is worth something."

"I know who you are, Harry," he said softly. "I've followed your cases over the last few years, and I've got a good idea exactly what kind of fella you are. We get newspapers up here in Casper, you know, and sometimes, I even have time to read 'em. But I can't for the life of me understand why Carl's ranch is so darned interesting to the likes of you. Do you really think this is important?"

"I don't know," I told him truthfully. "At this point, I'm looking at everything. I suppose it might be important. Otherwise, I wouldn't have asked."

He thought about that for a few seconds, and came to a personal decision. It wasn't the one I'd hoped for, but it was better than nothing. "Just theoretically, let's say that my company had been doing some preliminary studies on the land in the general area of Carl Buchanan's ranch," he said. "If we thought it looked promising, and we wanted to drill a few exploration wells, we probably wouldn't contact anyone about it until we were a little more ready to drill, say maybe next spring."

"So you never made Carl Buchanan an offer?" I asked.

"I didn't say that," he said. "I said that if we were interested, in theory, we probably wouldn't have gotten to the point of a formal offer for several months yet, maybe not even until next spring."

"So Carl didn't know what was in the offing? He had no idea he might be a few million dollars richer if he just held onto the land?"

"I suppose he could have heard the same rumors that are going all around Campbell County," Black said. "It's no secret we've been doing seismic work in that area, and he would have known if we were doing it on his land, since we would have had to get his permission in advance. But he wouldn't have known the results of our preliminary work because we keep that to ourselves. And he wouldn't have known for certain whether we were willing to pay him for drilling rights."

"Would anyone beyond your own employees have known the results of your seismic and geological studies?" I asked. "Or whether you were planning to make Buchanan an offer, if—theoretically—you were planning to make one?"

Black pondered that question for thirty seconds before he answered. "Maybe," he said. "I lost a geologist to the university early this year, and he might have seen our material before he moved to Laramie. With that exception, I can't think of another person."

"Did this geologist have a name?"

"Sure," Black said. "He's teaching geology on campus. Name is William Schultz. Nice fella; I hated to lose 'im."

I scribbled the information on my notepad and was trying to think of my next question when Black broke my concentration. "You know Trace is gonna end up with that ranch, don't you?" he asked.

"What?" I sputtered, off guard.

I could tell Black was amused to know something I'd only speculated about. I had the feeling he'd made a career of being underestimated. "Carl didn't leave a will, and Cassie, who's Carl's next of kin, doesn't want it," he said matter-of-factly. "She doesn't feel like she's entitled to it, since she and her husband had been divorced for a long time. With Carl gone, she thinks anything from his father should go to Trace."

"That doesn't surprise me, knowing Cassie," I said. "But how did you hear about this?"

Black laughed again, then said something that confirmed the depth of his interest in Buchanan's ranch, how far he'd go for his own information. It wasn't a slip of the tongue—he was doing me a left-handed favor, telling me something that might be helpful without coming right out and saying it. "Unlike you, apparently, I tracked Cassie down in Rawlins and *asked,*" he said.

142

*   *   *

When I got off the horn with Jules Black, I sat around the office for an hour gathering wool, watching Frankie work on a sculpture, and trying to make sense out of what I'd learned so far.

When I became a homicide investigator, a gray-bearded old warhorse at the state police academy told me that one of the first questions you have to answer in any mystery is *qui bono?* Who benefits?

Although there were elements of the murder itself that bothered me, knowing as much as I knew about Carl—the "organized" nature of the abduction and the fact that Victoria's face had been covered by someone Aaron Cohen said felt guilty for his or her actions—the inescapable fact was that the young man had not only initially confessed to the crime, he had taken his own life because he could no longer be sure of his own innocence. Those acts were the proverbial six-hundred-pound gorillas of the case, hulking in the corner and refusing to be overlooked.

But playing a mental game of "What if?" I knew that even if he had been guilty as charged, Carl didn't benefit in any concrete way from Victoria Austin's death, unless it fulfilled some perverted need, which was entirely possible. Was the fact that she had rebuffed his advances motive enough for her murder? Of course it was. Was it possible, as had been charged, that Carl was so frustrated by his inability to achieve an erection during the rape attempt that he had become enraged, assaulted Victoria with a shovel handle, and choked her to death? Certainly. Was Carl capable of the crime? That was absolutely possible, despite his girlfriend's claims to the contrary. He wouldn't have been the first junkie who killed someone while under the influence. Heroin is not known for bringing out the best side of its abusers . . . and our nation's morgues are filled with bodies sent there by junkies whose sense of morality, of right and wrong, has gone green and withered to the size of a pea.

Was Carl the killer? There was a strong possibility that he was, and my experience told me not to ignore it.

I wouldn't ignore it, but if I threw my experience and my common sense out the window, if I took a major leap of faith and dis-

143

counted Carl's confession, if I accepted for the sake of argument his claims that he was innocent, then I had to come up with another workable theory. And based on what I'd learned in the last few days, I thought I had enough grounds to brew up the beginnings of some pretty good ones.

I had been bothered from the start by the timing of Victoria Austin's death, right in the middle of the crash of Loveladies Pharmaceuticals stock due to rumors of trouble with Annie Quinn's research. That could have been coincidence, of course, but as I've said before, a good cop doesn't believe in coincidence.

Based on my conversation with Marsha Jackson, I knew that Austin's behavior had changed dramatically in the weeks prior to her death, and that change was not necessarily related to Carl Buchanan's unwanted attentions. She seemed distant, constantly afraid.

I knew that Quinn's research had not been as successful as Loveladies wanted its stockholders to believe, and according to Marsha, Austin would have had direct access to, and possession of, enough information to send the company into bankruptcy.

Was it possible Victoria Austin was into something that was beyond her ability to control, or that she knew too much about the project for her own safety? Was it possible that she was the source of the rumors that started the stock panic? Was it possible she had become disenchanted with Quinn's project and decided to expose it to the light of day?

Yes, it was. She might have even been getting ready to go public with her information.

And if that was the case, Annie Quinn could certainly have benefited from her disappearance and death. Austin was already dead and out of the picture by the time Quinn invited the gaggle of reporters and scientists to inspect her research station, a tactic that quelled the investors' fears and put her project back on track. In the intervening months, she and the suits at Loveladies had kept it on track by putting a tight lid on the flow of information about the cell-death research project, some of which I knew would have caused Quinn and the investors plenty of heartache if it got out.

The outcome might have been very different had Victoria Austin been around to tell the "real" story. In fact, it was more than possible her death had saved the company millions and millions of dollars and salvaged Quinn's professional career in the bargain.

So, according to that theory, Quinn had plenty of motive for killing Austin. So did the people at Loveladies Pharmaceuticals, for that matter.

And what about Trace Buchanan? Even though I could see no direct way for him to gain from Austin's death, it was beginning to look like he had a lot to gain by having his brother out of the way.

I had to assume that Trace knew there'd been seismic exploration on the family's homestead, and it was also reasonable to assume he'd learned the results. Not only is the U.W. Department of Geology building just one building away from the Department of Agriculture, but there are also lots of hangouts in Laramie where professors and students gather to drink beer and talk about their lives. It was entirely possible that Trace had bumped into William Schultz, the former Black Mesa geologist, either on campus or off, and discovered what the company planned for the Buchanan homestead.

That would explain Trace's obsession with getting Carl to sign over the deed, both before and after he entered prison. If that failed, all Trace had to do was wait until the state carried out its death sentence, and then he would inherit. As it turned out, he wasn't going to have to wait long, since his brother had saved everyone a lot of time and trouble by killing himself.

Was a chance at several million dollars in oil money enough motive to cause someone as acquisitive and greedy as Trace to set his brother up for a murder conviction? A murder heinous enough to warrant the death penalty? During my days as a Denver homicide investigator, I'd seen men and women murdered for pocket change. Two million dollars—and maybe a lot more down the line—was a motive in spades. Line up all the people in America who'd commit that crime for two million dollars, and they would stretch around the world at the equator.

Which all meant that both Annie Quinn and Trace Buchanan came out ahead when Victoria Austin's body was lowered into the ground, and in my book, that made both of them suspects. Hell, maybe they were in it together.

I remembered the note Robert had pulled from the guts of the Loveladies computer system urging Quinn to either terminate her rumored affair with a married man or exercise incredible discretion. That note was written six weeks before Austin's disappearance.

Could the married man in question have been Trace Buchanan? Of course. I knew for a fact that Quinn and Trace were colleagues and close personal friends. Quinn was a good-looking woman, and Trace was a handsome enough man. I could see why they'd be attracted to each other, and affairs of that sort are about as rare as the common cold.

If they were sleeping together before Austin was abducted and killed, it was entirely possible they'd cooked the whole thing up as a way to get what they both wanted. Either one of them could have committed the actual murder, or it could have been done by both of them. Maybe they even contracted it out, paid a third party to get his hands dirty so they'd have plausible deniability

It was a good enough theory, as theories go—but there were some big, gaping holes, which brought me right back to the place I'd started.

First, if Carl didn't kill Victoria Austin, if it was done by someone else, someone like his brother or Annie Quinn, then why had he confessed? Why had he killed himself? He obviously believed he *could* have been the killer. And what about the physical evidence linking him to the murder? In addition to the phone records, his hair was found on her body. They also found Victoria's blood in his pickup and a tire print at the place where her body was dumped, proving that whoever left her there had been driving Carl Buchanan's vehicle. If Victoria Austin wasn't slaughtered by Carl

Buchanan, then how could that physical evidence be explained away? I couldn't explain it, that was for sure.

Second, although my leaky theory held some water, I had not one shred of hard evidence to lend it credibility. If I took what I had so far to Walker Tisdale, the Albany County prosecutor, or Sheriff Tony Baldi, or even Ken Keegan, I'd sound like a total crackpot. If they didn't call the men with butterfly nets and white jackets, they'd laugh me right out of the room, and I wouldn't blame them a bit. Until I had something concrete, I had to keep my theories to myself. A quiet man will never be thought a fool, unless he opens his mouth and removes all doubt.

At least I knew how I had to proceed. I had to find that evidence, if it existed.

I was still trying to come up with a place to start when the ringing phone brought my mind out of the clouds. Frankie put down the orange stick he was using to detail the clay of his sculpture, answered on the second ring, and held the phone to his ear while he listened to whoever was on the other end, mumbling an occasional affirmative response to let the caller know he was still there.

When he hung up, I looked at him curiously.

"That was your friend at the penitentiary," he said.

"I didn't know I had any friends over there," I said.

"Maybe you don't. But at least the assistant warden thinks enough of you to keep you in the loop. He says he heard you were interested in when the prison was going to release Carl's body, and that's why he called. They released it to Cassie and Trace Buchanan this morning."

"Did he say where they are now?"

"Yeah," Frankie said. "They apparently made arrangements with a local funeral home to take the body down to a crematorium in Colorado. The service isn't scheduled for a few days, but he says Cassie and Trace ought to be home by early afternoon. When they left town, he says they were heading for Trace's house in Laramie."

ELEVEN

I puttered around the office until a little after noon. Then I left Frankie in charge of Victory's safekeeping and took off down Highway 130 toward Laramie and Trace Buchanan's house.

Even at over seven thousand feet above sea level, it was a scorcher of a day on the high plains, with the temperature in the low nineties, the air dry as moon dust. The sun was so bright it hurt my eyes, and the shimmering waves of heat rising from the asphalt roadbed looked like the watery mirages you see in old-time movies about French Legionnaires crossing the desert. The traffic was light, but I got stuck behind an exhaust-belching semi hauling lumber near the Big Hollow oil field. Because the Jeep was cutting out and the engine was stuttering, I didn't work up the courage to scoot around him until we were passing the old Wyoming Territorial Prison on the outskirts of town.

When I stopped at the traffic light on Third Street, I was feeling lightheaded from breathing the trucker's exhaust and from the stifling heat, so I stopped off at a convenience store for a package of aspirin and a cold soda. Then I hopped back in and drove directly to Trace Buchanan's house, hoping to catch him and Cassie as soon as they got back from Rawlins.

I was half a block away when I saw something I didn't expect. There was a Jeep Wagoneer, which I assumed belonged to Trace, parked at the curb outside the house, but in the driveway was a large U-Haul moving van with the double doors open in back and a loading ramp in place. A woman and a man were standing beside the moving van, and even from a distance, I could tell they were having a fierce argument. The man had his fists balled on his hips, and the woman was poking him in the chest with her finger. At one point, she even tried to slap him in the face, but he blocked the blow and held her wrist until she wrenched it loose from his grip.

I pulled my binoculars from the glove box and focused on the irate lovebirds, one of whom was Trace Buchanan. I figured the other must be his wife, home from her extended vacation and, from the looks of things, planning to extend it a little longer, maybe even permanently.

As the marital fracas continued, a second man came out the front door pushing a dolly loaded with boxes and eased it down the steps of the front porch. He said something to the woman, and the woman gestured toward the back of the truck. The second man nodded and pushed the dolly up the loading ramp into the truck. A couple of minutes later, he walked back down the ramp without the dolly, stored the ramp in its slide-in compartment, and slammed the doors of the truck closed. Then he walked back to Trace and the woman, said something that caused Trace to back off a step, took the woman by the arm, and walked her around the back of the truck to the passenger door. He held the door open for her while she got inside, then he walked back around to the driver's door, folded his thick body into the cab, and fired the engine up with a roar. Five seconds later, he was already out of the driveway, heading down the street while Trace stood alone at the edge of his driveway, looking mad enough to bite the head off a live chicken.

I wanted to talk to Trace and Cassie, but I also wanted to talk to Trace's wife, and I figured I might lose that opportunity if I dawdled. I started the Jeep and took off after the U-Haul with a squeal of tires. Trace looked up as I raced past, but I don't know if he recognized me.

I caught them several blocks later at the intersection of Reynolds and Third Street and honked my horn until I got the driver's attention. I held my badge out the window where he could see it in his rearview and motioned to the parking lot of a lumber store across the street, indicating that I wanted him to pull in there. He nodded that he understood, and crossed the street and drove into the lot, where the tired U-Haul rattled to a stop.

I got out and walked to the driver's door, looked in through the open window. Both of them were hot and sweaty, frazzled-looking. The cab of the vehicle smelled like a million cigarettes, and there were plenty of empty fast-food bags and burger wrappers on the floor.

The man, in his early forties and as sturdily built as a beer keg, had a John Deere cap pulled low on his forehead, a two-day growth of dark brown beard, and thick, muscular arms I didn't think he'd gotten in a gym. There was a wad of tobacco in his cheek the size of a plum and a tattoo of the Marine Corps insignia on his hairy forearm.

The woman was dressed in sturdy boots, faded jeans, and a short-sleeved cotton blouse with a scooped neck. In her early to mid-thirties, she was pretty in a world-worn sort of way, with dark brown hair that came to her shoulders and beautiful green eyes. She wore no makeup and the blouse was wrinkled, as if she might have worn it for more than one day. She had a cigarette going and a large bottle of cola held between her legs. She looked as if she hadn't smiled in a very long time.

"What's wrong, officer?" the man asked. "I don't think this old beast could break the speed limit if I pushed the pedal to the metal on a downhill slope. What did I do, run a stop sign?"

"Nah," I smiled. "I just wanted to talk to you for a minute." I held my badge and identification through the window so they could get a better look. They both read it carefully, and their brows furrowed because they didn't understand what was going on. "I saw you back there at Trace Buchanan's house and decided I'd better grab you before you left town. My name's Harry Starbranch, by the way." I held my hand through the window, and the man shook it. His fist was the size of a ham and as rough as a gnarled tree stump.

"Jack Staub," the man said by way of introduction. He cocked a thumb at the woman. "This is my sister, Helen Buchanan."

The woman was biting her lower lip, glowering impatiently at both of us. I tipped my hat in her direction, but my courtesy didn't change her demeanor for the better. "Why were you watching us at the house?" she snapped. "All we took was what belongs to me. If Trace called the police and told you something else, he's a damned liar and I can prove it."

I held up my hand in a placating gesture to let her know she was mistaken. "It's nothing like that, Mrs. Buchanan," I said gently.

"Not for long," she broke in.

"What?"

"It won't be Mrs. Buchanan for long," she said. "Not if I can help it."

"You're moving away, I take it," I said.

She looked at me as if I was a complete moron. Two people driving off in a loaded moving van. What did I think they were doing? Going to the prom? "Damned right I am, and divorcing that son of a bitch in the bargain," she said. "I was hoping to have all my stuff out of the house and be halfway back to Kansas by the time he got home. Nearly made it, too, but he arrived just as we were finishing up. Told me I couldn't take anything but my clothes." She chuckled wickedly. "Jack straightened him out about that. If that bastard thinks he can . . ."

"I don't think Mr. Starbranch wants to hear your life story," Jack broke in, teasing her gently, the way an older brother will. He smiled and patted her on the knee. "Not that it isn't a fascinating tale."

"Then what does the officer want?" she asked tightly.

Jack shrugged his shoulders good-naturedly. If she'd been in this mood all the way, I imagined the drive from Kansas had seemed like a billion miles.

"Five minutes of your time," I said. "I've been looking into the murder that Carl was accused of, and I just have a couple of questions if you don't mind."

At the mention of Carl's name, Helen Buchanan's body tensed. She took a final drag of her cigarette and ground it out in the ashtray, which was already full to overflowing. She pulled a fresh smoke from her pack and fired it up, inhaling deeply. She blew the smoke out in a long stream, and it clouded the cab of the vehicle, making Jack wince. A big, juicy gob of chew was one thing, but secondhand smoke was something else entirely. He waved it away from his face, but she just puffed out another noxious gust. "I don't want to get involved in that," she said. She grabbed her brother's arm. "Let's go, Jack."

Jack looked confused, reached for the keys in the ignition, but hesitated at the last second. "Why not answer the man's questions?" he asked. "What can it hurt?"

"Because it's over, that's why," she said. "That boy is dead, and there's nothing anybody can do about it, least of all me. All I want is out of here. Now let's go."

"Helen . . ." he began.

"Jack, goddamn it, I said let's go." She reached over and turned the keys in the ignition herself. The starter ground, but the old motor refused to catch.

Jack pulled her hand away from the keys, and reached to start the vehicle. He turned the ignition on, but the motor wouldn't go. Flooded. "Hell's bells," he said. "Now you see what you've done?"

It looked like I had a captive audience, for a while at least. I knew I'd better make the best of it. "Do you think Carl Buchanan killed Victoria Austin, like they say?" I asked.

Helen eyed Jack suspiciously, as if he might have flooded the motor on purpose. Then she narrowed her eyes and looked at me. "What does it matter what I think?" she asked.

"It matters to me," I said.

She pursed her lips in an expression that said she believed that as much as she believed in the tooth fairy. "Then hell no, he didn't kill her," Helen said. "He was screwed up beyond belief, but murder was not in that boy's character. Confession or none, I never thought he was guilty, but now it doesn't matter one way or another since he's beyond my help *and* yours."

To tell the truth, I was getting sick of Helen Buchanan and her attitude, but I bit my tongue and tried not to let it show on my face. It wasn't easy. "Could Trace have killed her?" I asked.

Helen snorted derisively and turned away, folded her arms across her chest.

"Maybe she's not the most objective person to ask about that," Jack said.

Helen was looking out the window, away from us both. "Trace is capable of anything," she said. "That man's soul is like the Red Desert, parched and brittle and empty. Did he kill her? I wouldn't put it past him, but I don't know one way or another." She looked back at me, and her green eyes flashed. "And to tell you the truth, Mr. Starbranch, I wouldn't tell you even if I could prove Trace did it. Like I said, I don't want to get involved. Now, if you don't mind, we've . . ."

"Was Trace home the night Vicky Austin disappeared?" I asked. Helen stared blankly at me for several seconds, then turned away from us again. I looked at Jack, my eyes pleading for his help.

He shook his head, his look telling me there was little he could do, but he'd try. I felt very sorry for Jack Staub. It was going to be a long ride back to Kansas. "Helen, listen to me," he said softly. "This man isn't your husband, so there's no reason to treat him like this. It can't hurt to tell him what he wants to know."

She turned back toward us, and I could see that her hard exterior had cracked. There were tears in her eyes, and she brushed them away roughly. "Of course, he wasn't at home," she said. "He hadn't been home at night for two months, and he didn't come home for months after that. Why do you think I finally I left him?"

"Do you know where he was?"

"I assume he was with that bitch," she said. "The redheaded university whore he'd been fucking while his children and I waited for him to come home."

"Do you know her name?" I asked. "I'd like to talk to her."

"Yes, Mr. Starbranch, I know her name," she said harshly, "and I know where she lives, because I followed them. The slut's name is Annie Quinn."

I smiled at the mention of Quinn's name and nodded as if that was the answer I'd been expecting all along. Now, I asked myself rhetorically, why wasn't I surprised?

Helen Buchanan shut down after that and refused to talk any more, so I let them go in relative peace after getting their home phone number from Jack and hanging around until he got the engine started. Then I hopped in the Jeep and hotfooted it back to the Buchanan house so I could catch Trace and Cassie before they left again.

The Wagoneer was still on the street, so I parked in the driveway and rang the bell. The door was open, and I could hear voices coming through the screen, so when no one answered after thirty seconds, I rang the bell a second time. Trace answered a couple of long minutes later, his face still as darkly clouded as a summer storm. When he saw me, there was a hitch in his step and a look of surprise on his face that quickly turned to annoyance. Maybe he was expecting something else, like his wife crawling back to him. Fat chance of that.

"What do *you* want?" he asked from the other side of the screen.

He didn't invite me in, so I took matters into my own hands. I opened the door and squeezed past him into the living room before he could stop me. "I was just driving by and thought I'd stop in to pay my condolences to you and your mother," I said.

I removed my hat and sunglasses and stood in the middle of the living room, waiting for my eyes to adjust to the change in light. When I could make out detail, I saw that there was a thick coating of dust on every flat surface and the coffee table was littered with pizza boxes, moldy TV dinner plates, and empty beer and soda cans. There were dirty clothes on the floor, shoes, and a huge stack of junk mail and newspapers still folded and held by rubber bands. There were a couple of empty spaces where it looked like pieces of furniture had been before Helen whisked them away, and several places on the wall where pictures had hung. The paint behind them was lighter and cleaner than the rest of the wall. The carpet looked like it could use a good vacuuming, and there was a funny smell in the air, sort of a combination of rotten potatoes and spoiled milk.

The place was a dump, in other words, the kind of place where your shins start itching the minute you walk in because you imagine crab lice and dust mites are crawling up your pants leg.

Trace, on the other hand, looked like he'd just stepped from the pages of Shepler's summer catalog. When I'd seen him at the university, he'd looked almost normal, but he'd undergone a change in the interim. Dressed in sharply creased black jeans, a burgundy polo shirt that emphasized his muscular biceps, and a pair of fancy ostrich-skin cowboy boots that probably cost more than my first house, he wore a wide belt with a phony rodeo trophy buckle the size of a saucer and a necklace of thick gold links. Even at a distance of several feet, I could smell his strong cologne, and his hair was slicked back with about a quart of gel. He'd also shaved off his beard, except for the bandito mustache that made him look like Pancho Villa with upscale pretentions.

I'm sure he thought he looked like a real lady-killer, but everything about him screamed freshly separated loser—the kind of man you find in the lounge of every Holiday Inn on the planet. Then again, I didn't like him much, so maybe I was just being uncharitable.

I was just about to make a mean comment about his housekeeping, or lack of same, when I saw Cassie standing in the doorway that separated the living room from the kitchen, where she'd obviously been working. She was holding a mop, and a kitchen towel was draped across her shoulder. The good mommy cleaning up after her little boy.

The last time I'd seen her, she'd blamed me for talking Carl into killing himself and told me she'd hate me forever. If I'd expected her to mellow over a little time, I'd been badly mistaken. If anything, her feelings were harder toward me than ever. "What is it you want from us, Harry?" she asked bitterly. "I just sent my son's body out to be cremated. Haven't you done enough?"

Both her words and her anger stung, but I knew there was

nothing I could do at that moment to change her mind. I'd just have to ride it out and hope for the best. "Listen, Cassie," I said, "I've been looking into Carl's case like I promised, and I've found some things you might be interested in."

"So what do you want?" Trace asked sarcastically. "A pat on the back?"

I ignored him, and Cassie shot him a glance to keep him from saying more. "I know you've been looking into it," she said. "But you can quit now, Harry, with my blessing. As a matter of fact, I'm going to insist."

"Cassie . . ." I began.

She held her hand up to stop me. "My boy's dead, Harry. He killed himself out of remorse. I think you had something to do with that, and I always will. But now, I just want to get past it. Me, Trace, maybe Carl most of all. It's time he rests in peace."

I sat down on the couch and started to rest my hat on top of a grease-stained pizza box, but thought better of it. I held my hat in my hands and looked Cassie in the eyes. "What if Carl wasn't guilty?" I asked her. "Would you still want me to stop, or would you want me to clear his name?"

"What are you talking about, Harry?" she asked angrily. "You never believed Carl was innocent, not for one second. How could you be so cruel as to . . ."

Her voice faltered then, and she held her hand over her mouth, in such pain she couldn't go on. Trace was at her side immediately, cradling her in his arms and murmuring words of comfort. He turned to me in absolute hatred. "I want you out of here, now!" he said. "Get out, or I'll call the police!"

Cassie pushed him away to arm's length. "No, Trace, don't," she said. She turned to me, and when she spoke, there was steel in her voice. "I want to know what he's talking about. Tell me, Harry, damn you."

I looked at them standing there and knew there was no way I could tell her what I'd learned in the last few days, or of my suspicions. Not with Trace in the same room. And there was no way I could question Trace in Cassie's presence without giving every-

156

thing away. I'd have to get them apart, but there was no way to accomplish that at the moment. The best thing to do was make a graceful exit. I stood up and jammed my hat on my head. "I'm sorry, Cassie, I didn't mean to upset you," I said. "I'll give you a call later, and we'll talk."

I started for the door, but she crossed the room, grabbed me by the shirtsleeve, and pulled me up short before I'd gone two steps. Her small hands seemed as strong as eagle talons, and her nails dug into the flesh of my arms. "What are you talking about? Tell me!" she demanded.

I didn't want to lie, but I couldn't tell her the truth either. "It's nothing definite. I've just found a few things that raise some questions," I told her. "I can't prove it yet, but I think there's a possibility Carl was innocent."

Trace had heard about enough. "Jesus Christ, you expect us to listen to this bullshit? Can't you see how much this is upsetting her?" He walked across the room, took me by the elbow, and began exerting pressure to move me in the direction of the door.

Cassie was pulling in the other direction, holding me in place. "Tell me, Harry!" she demanded yet again.

I pulled my arm loose from Trace's grip, the look on my face letting him know that if he touched me again, I'd put him on the floor—at least I'd try. At six-two and a hundred-ninety pounds, I was almost three inches taller than Trace Buchanan and twenty pounds heavier. But despite his tendency toward pudginess, he was at least ten years younger than I and fairly fit. I figured that if worst came to worst, twenty-five years of military and police training, street-fighting experience, and dirty tricks would give me the upper hand, but I also figured that when the dust settled, we'd both know we'd been in a scrap.

For his part, Trace didn't look particularly worried. As a matter of fact, he looked a lot like a pit bull right before it goes for a bigger dog's throat. Semicrazy, in other words.

I'd left my blackthorn walking stick at home that morning, and I was beginning to regret my decision. If I had it and Trace came at me, I could use it to bash his kneecaps. Without it, all I had was my fists—and my gun of course, if it came to that. I put my free hand on the butt of my Blackhawk .357, just so he'd get the message.

"I can't talk about it right now, Cassie," I said, although what was left unsaid told both of them plenty.

Her eyebrows raised at what my vagueness implied, but she shook the idea off as ridiculous. "You can talk in front of Trace," she said. "He has the right to hear anything I do."

I shook my head no. "I'd rather not, Cassie," I said. "I'd rather wait until later."

"But why . . ." she began.

If he had been a cartoon character, Trace Buchanan would have had steam coming from his ears and nostrils like a locomotive. His face flushed, and his ears turned bright red. I could almost feel the heat radiating from his skin, and I could hear his shallow breathing. The man was having a titanic adrenaline rush, lucky devil. "Because this son of a bitch thinks I had something to do with it, that's why," he spat. "He thinks I had something to do with Vicky Austin's murder."

I looked Trace in the eyes and gave him a thin smile. Bingo, it said. "You said it, not me," I told him softly, realizing even as I spoke that things were getting out of hand and my big mouth wasn't helping.

I don't know exactly what I expected to happen next, but it was most certainly not the thing that happened. Trace's hands clenched at my insult, and I expected him to take a swing. I did not expect Cassie to ball her own fists and deal me such a stinging right-cross to the cheek that it staggered me and brought tears to my eyes. She was shrieking, "Goddamn you, Harry! You won't take both of them!" and I turned to face her just in time to see her winding up for another punch. I brought my arms up to ward it off.

That's when Trace Buchanan hit me in the back of the head so hard I dropped to my knees and threw up all over his ostrich-skin boots.

"I told you to get out of here," he growled, "and now you're try-ing to hit my mother!" He cocked his leg and kicked me hard, the

158

pointy toe of his boot connecting with my collarbone with such force it threw me over backward. My head bounced off the cushion of the couch and crashed to the floor with a thump that brought stars to my eyes and softened the edges of my vision. I was going out, is what I was doing, and that simply wouldn't do. I shook my head, rolled over on my stomach, and pushed myself to my hands and knees, just as Trace was getting ready to put boots to me again, this time aiming for my face.

With as much strength and force as I could muster, I lunged toward him like a lineman coming off a three-point stance, buried my skull in his crotch, wrapped my arms around his legs, and drove him backward until he crashed into the wall with a little "Woof!" as the air rushed from his lungs. He started to bend over from the apparently considerable pain in his groin, and I stood up quickly and gave him two hard jabs to the side of the head that put him down on one knee, but only briefly. He came up bellowing, swinging wildly, and I deflected his blows easily. I stayed inside his punches and peppered his face with a flurry of quick punches that hurt nothing but my knuckles.

By that time, however, Cassie had joined the battle in earnest, and was hanging onto the collar of my shirt with one hand and whacking the back of my head with the other. She wasn't doing much damage, but her repeated blows did start my ears to ringing, and she was distracting me from a much more dangerous threat— namely Trace Buchanan, who had pulled himself together and was crouching in a boxer's stance, getting ready to do some serious damage to my handsome face. I threw her off harder than I'd intended, and she seemed to soar across the room until she came down in a bumpy landing on Trace's La-Z-Boy recliner.

The sight of his mother being tossed around like a doll was more than Trace could bear. He came in on the balls of his feet and threw a loopy roundhouse left that I deflected without any trouble. The straight right he followed with was another story. I caught a piece of it on my left forearm, but not enough. The rest of it caught me flush on the chin and would have rattled my dentures, had I been wearing any. As it was, it felt like he had dislocated my jaw,

159

and the tidal wave of pain that washed across my face brought back that going-out sensation. That's my trouble as a fighter, a glass jaw. Never could take a good crack on the chin.

In desperation, I sort of willed my body forward and lurched into him, wrapping my arms around his neck in a Muhammad Ali clinch, hoping to hold on until I could gather my wits. I suppose it worked well enough. With me hanging on like a limpet, Trace couldn't put any real power into the blows he was raining against my midsection. We stood there for several seconds, grunting like a couple of bulls, him whenever he threw another restricted punch and me when it landed.

Then I switched tactics on him. I let go of his neck with my left arm, held on with my right, and pivoted my body away from him until I was in a position to throw him in a combination judo/karate number that sent him crashing through the front door and down the porch steps. He landed at the bottom in a heap, and I was on him at once, my arm around his throat in the submission hold known in police circles as a sleeper. The hold cuts off the blood flow to the brain and rapidly causes unconsciousness. It can also be fatal if you don't let up in time, but killing the man wasn't what I had in mind. All I wanted was Trace Buchanan out of commission long enough for me to get the handcuffs on him.

The sleeper worked like a charm. Trace fought me forcefully for a few seconds, but I could feel him start to weaken almost immediately. Before I knew it, he was out, his limp body a dead weight in my arms. I laid him down, took out my cuffs, and started to close one side around his right wrist. It ratcheted into place with a satisfying click of metal.

The metallic click that followed almost simultaneously was not as satisfying. That click was the sound of a pistol hammer being cocked, and it wasn't far from my ear. Cassie jammed the barrel of the weapon into the side of my head so hard I was afraid she'd break the skin. "You stop it right now, Harry Starbranch," she commanded.

Later, I discovered she was using my own revolver, which she'd somehow managed to pull from my holster during the confusion of the fray. At that moment, however, it didn't matter whose gun it was. There are some people—and I tend to agree with them—who say a gun is a lot like a stiff Johnson. Neither has much of a conscience.

I'm no fool. I did exactly as she ordered—laid facedown on the grass, my hands clasped behind my head like a felony flier. It might have been my imagination, but the patch of grass where my face was pressed smelled suspiciously like dog shit.

Tell the truth, I was stunned by how quickly the whole situation had gone to hell. I'd come to ask a few questions and somehow wound up in a brawl with the old woman I was trying to help and her psychotic kid. I sure didn't have any answers. What I had was a sore jaw, an aching head, throbbing ribs, puke all over the front of my shirt, a face full of dog crap, the muzzle of my own weapon pointed at my brainpan, and no good way to explain any of it.

What else could go wrong, I wondered?

In the distance, I could hear the wail of sirens. Perfect, I thought unhappily—Trace's nosy neighbor must have called the cops.

TWELVE

Albany County prosecutor Walker Tisdale's red face was about an inch from mine as he asked a question for which I didn't really think he wanted an answer. "What are you, Harry?" he asked. "Some kind of flaming asshole?"

I spread my hands in a who-knows gesture. "Admittedly, things got a little out of control," I said. "But I don't think that qualifies me as a flaming asshole, Walker. Maybe a smoldering asshole, but flaming?"

My lame attempt at humor wasn't endearing me to the prosecutor, and I guess I wasn't surprised, since he's not exactly a charter member of the Harry Starbranch Fan Club.

The great-grandson of one of the biggest Wyoming cattle ranchers of the last century, Walker was the latest in a long line of Republican ranchers in this state who eventually turned their eye to politics. A tall, good-looking man in his early forties, Tisdale had a fifty-dollar haircut, a gold Rolex, and a blue pin-striped Brooks Brothers suit, none of which he would have been able to afford if it wasn't for his massive family trust fund. He also had the morals of a greedy, egg-sucking hound, a reptilian instinct for self-preservation, and almost limitless ambition, the realization of which usually exceeded his grasp.

Over the years, it had become common knowledge that Tisdale had aspirations for political office beyond the prosecutor's chair. He just wasn't having much luck.

162

He'd passed up a run for the state senate—a seat he probably could have won—to run for governor a couple of years previously. To his chagrin, he'd been eliminated early in the primary season because he pulled a Dan Quayle during the first and only debate, accusing his opponent—one of the party's most venerable but conservative elder statesmen and a highly decorated veteran of World War II—of being a communist sympathizer. Even though Walker later said that that was just an unfortunate slip of the tongue occasioned by his opponent's well-known love of travel in Russia, Walker was thumped so badly by the press for his blunder that he barely got out of the contest with his hide.

The very next year, Tisdale had been soundly trounced in his bid to replace one of the state's two U.S. senators, who was retiring due to prostate trouble and an embarrassing bladder-control problem. Naturally, he blamed me personally for *that* loss, and I'm proud to wear that blame like a badge of honor.

In the years since I came to Victory, Walker and I had wound up on opposite sides of the field on numerous occasions, and while we'd both won a few and lost a few, it's true that Walker's losses had been more public and humiliating. The year of his ill-fated Senate bid, he'd doggedly tried to put Curly Ahearn on death row for a murder he didn't commit, even though I tried to tell him all along that my friend was innocent. When I finally proved it, the bad publicity certainly cost Walker the election, and the man definitely held a grudge.

Now, here I was again, telling him that Carl Buchanan, whom Walker had personally prosecuted and put on death row, was very possibly innocent. And because he's fairly astute when it comes to that sort of thing, Walker knew full well what would happen if I was right. A prosecutor who tries to put two innocent people on death row in as many years has about as much chance of winning higher political office as Clarence Thomas has of getting a date with Anita Hill. He'd be finished, in other words, and that was a prospect Walker Tisdale did not even want to contemplate.

Still, I thought his current rage was maybe a bit of an overreaction. If the veins in his temples started throbbing any harder, I figured he'd probably have a stroke. "It isn't funny!" he shouted. "You've just been accused of enough crimes to put you in jail for thirty years—trespassing, harassment, damage to property, creating a public disturbance, two counts of aggravated assault, one of them on a woman old enough to be your mother, false imprisonment, attempted murder, assault with a deadly weapon . . ." He waved the police paperwork in my face. "And enough additional crimes to keep me busy for months if I so choose. Crimes I haven't even thought of yet. If all you can do is laugh, then get the hell out of my office and face the consequences."

I tried to suppress my chuckles, but they got stuck in my throat and made an amusing burbling sound. "I apologize, Walker, I truly do," I told him insincerely when I could finally speak clearly. "But if all you can do is insult me, maybe I *will* leave. You called me up here, remember? I didn't necessarily want to be here. I just came as a favor."

Which was the truth. The Laramie policemen who had arrested me in Trace Buchanan's yard took the three of us to the station and spent a couple of hours sorting out our stories. When it was all over, they didn't feel like they had enough to file formal charges against anyone due to our conflicting tales, but they'd let Cassie and Trace register complaints against me and put the legal system in motion to sort it all out. I couldn't file countercomplaints against Trace without filing against Cassie at the same time, which I had no intention of doing. But if the Buchanans stood by their guns, I'd eventually have to answer their charges in court. I figured Cassie would probably drop hers before it came to that. With any luck, I'd prove Trace had something to do with Vicky Austin's murder, and his would be dropped as well.

I wasn't particularly worried, in other words, which enabled me to see the humor in the present situation.

It hadn't taken long after the arrest for Walker to hear about the brawl at Trace Buchanan's house, and he tracked me down by phone while I was still at the police station. He'd demanded I come to his office as soon as I was released and explain what the hell I'd been doing.

164

So I did, even though I considered it a courtesy call. And as part of that professional courtesy, I'd told him everything I'd learned since I began my investigation, and I'd told him of my theories. I'd explained how my inquiries had led me to Buchanan's house that day, and how my attempted pursuit of information had led to the fight in Trace's living room. I also told him I planned to continue my investigation until I finally arrived at the truth, no matter how he felt about it.

Walker pretty much went ballistic at that point, and called me a number of coarse names, most of which made "flaming asshole" seem positively tame and benign by comparison.

"I know I called you, and you'll stay until I'm finished with you, Starbranch," Tisdale yelled. "You'll stay until we have a few things perfectly clear between us."

"Such as?" I asked innocently.

"Such as the fact that I think your whole theory sounds like you found it in the bottom of a bottle of Jack Daniel's," Walker said. "It's the most harebrained, half-baked piece of garbage I've ever heard, and you don't have one ounce of hard proof, do you? Do you have one little thing? Besides that circumstantial load of bullshit you've been spreading around here?"

I shrugged my shoulders sheepishly and gave him an impish grin. "I'll admit it hasn't exactly gelled yet," I said.

"Of course it hasn't, and it never will, because it's not true," he said. "Not only did the man who really killed Victoria Austin confess to the crime, he was convicted of it and took his own life because he couldn't live with what he'd done."

"*Non semper ea sunt quae videntur,*" I said.

"What?"

"It's Latin, Walker," I said. "I read it in a book and memorized it in case I ever had a chance to impress a lawyer. It means things aren't always what they seem."

"Fuck you and your Latin," he said. "I'll give it to you in plain English." Tisdale kept talking, ticking the points off on his fingers as he went. "First, this case is closed, and I will not reopen it. Second, I will not have the reputations of truly innocent people tar-

165

nished by the likes of you and your boozy theories. Third, if you continue to slander Trace Buchanan and Annie Quinn, I will personally convince them to sue you for everything you've got, and I'll leave public office so I can take the case myself. You will butt out of this, Harry. Do I make myself perfectly clear?" He pulled up a fourth finger, but he'd apparently run out of points.

"What if I get the proof, Walker? What then?"

The veins were really throbbing now. Pretty soon, I figured his eyeballs would roll up and the tilt sign would flash. "What if a meteor drops out of the sky and lands on your thick fucking skull?" he asked. "You think there's much chance of that?"

I looked in the general direction of the heavens and smiled, let him know I wouldn't be surprised if a hunk of space debris crashed through the ceiling. "Anything's possible," I observed.

"That's right, Starbranch, anything's possible," he said. "And it's just possible I'll press the charges against you and put your miserable ass in jail where you'll stay out of trouble. Stay away from those people, because if you don't, and you screw up, I will make it my life's work to see that you pay. I will make it a crusade, Harry. I will be fucking relentless. Do you understand what I'm trying to tell you?"

"I think so," I said meekly, which seemed to infuriate him all the more. "I think that in the interest of protecting your professional reputation and polishing your tarnished image, you've just told me you want to let a couple of possible murderers go scot-free. Is that about right?"

Walker slammed his fist on his desk, and the blow made all his papers jump in the air. It also spilled his coffee all over the top of his expensive walnut desk. He didn't even look for a paper towel, just swept it off the desk with his hand and wiped himself dry on his pants leg. It was going to leave a nasty stain.

"That is not what I'm talking about, and you damned well know it!" he shouted. "I've told you to leave this family alone!" He was almost sputtering now, he was so mad. "You do anything to hurt these innocent people, and I'll see you run out of law en-

166

forcement altogether. You'll never work in this goddamned state again."

"You sound like a Hollywood producer," I said. "And I've got to tell you that you ought to think about watching your language. I haven't heard such low-rent, trailer-trash vocabulary since Lenny Bruce died. Didn't anybody ever tell you that reliance on banal profanity to emphasize a point is the sign of an unimaginative and uncreative mind? If you want to insult somebody, call him something unusual—call him a "retromingent buffoon," for example. If I called you that, it'd mean I think you're a clown who pisses backward. Now that's a creative insult." I smiled hugely. "I got it from George Will."

Walker looked like he wanted to come across the desk and choke me to death, but I don't think he had the courage for physical confrontation. With him, it was words or nothing. "To hell with you, Harry," he said. "You just keep pushing on this, and you'll wind up one sorry son of a bitch."

Walker's an entertaining human being, but a little of him goes a long way. I stood up, brushed off my pants, and put my hat on at a rakish angle. I gave him a zillion-watt smile and a snappy military salute. "Nah, you're gonna be the one who's sorry, Walker," I told him as I turned toward the door. "And when the manure starts raining down on your head in great, big soggy clumps, just remember old Harry warned you."

I could still hear him barking and cursing through the closed door after I marched out of his office, down the stairs, and out of earshot. For all I know, he's bellowing still.

I felt so happy to know I had the full support of the prosecutor's office behind me that I decided to celebrate. I called Cindy and made a dress-up date for that evening—drinks, dinner, and dancing at the Trails End, followed by champagne, strawberries, and hanky-panky at her place. Then I pointed the nose of the Jeep toward Victory, my plan being to stop by the house and see how Robert was getting along in his covert attempt to breach the electronic walls at

Loveladies Pharmaceuticals and at the U.W. Department of Molecular Biology.

For about two seconds on the way out of Laramie, I toyed with the idea of stopping in at the university for a surprise visit with Annie Quinn, but I rapidly abandoned that notion, because I had no clear idea of what I'd ask her. I'd save that visit for a while, maybe until after I'd learned what new tidbits my son had filched from cyberspace.

As I passed the turnoff to Brees Field, I could see roiling thunderheads gathering to the west, rolling across the Snowy Range like iron-gray balls of raw cotton and spilling over the peaks of Bald and Corner Mountains on the outskirts of Victory. I noticed the change in the sunlight that goes before a big storm, the sunlight now a deep and almost living yellow, and I could feel the drop in barometric pressure in my bones. The parched prairie seemed to come alive in anticipation of rain. The air was thick and filled with the smell of native vegetation, the purple sage providing the base note to a symphony of aroma. I opened the windows of the Jeep and let it wash across me, savored the exotic nuances of smell—the heavy-scented rabbitbrush, the delightful fragrance of late-season Coulter's daisy, blueberry, and greasewood, and the earthy perfume of larkspur and Wyoming paintbrush.

At Hatton Reservoir, I pulled to the side of the road to watch a herd of pronghorn antelope, almost giddy with joy, racing full-out, forty miles an hour or better, along the banks of Victoria Ditch, whose water feeds the Little Laramie River. Overhead, a bald eagle rode the air currents along the leading edge of the storm, his sharp eyes scanning the ground below him for an unlucky rodent or snake. From the mouth of his burrow, a prairie dog chattered a warning to his family about the danger overhead, and a mother sage grouse and her brood skittered through the undergrowth, trusting their camouflage to make them blend in with the sagebrush and protect them from the hungry raptor. Outraged magpies, whose dinner of roadkill carrion had been disturbed by the passing of the great bird, squawked from their perches atop the fenceposts, and in the distance, I heard the lilting song of a meadowlark.

168

I watched the eagle until he was only a speck on the horizon, and then I took my binoculars from the glove box and watched the clouds roll across the flanks of the mountains, watched as their shadows swiftly moved across the landscape, drowning the rich yellow light and turning the prairie landscape into a tapestry of muted grays and subtle browns.

I stayed there, watching, until the first fat drops of rain began to spatter on the windshield; then I switched on the wipers and pulled back onto the blacktop. Before I had gone a mile, the storm was coming into its own, the wind-driven rain so heavy that visibility was reduced to thirty yards. The ground, baked and hardened by the sun, could not absorb it quickly enough, and already rivulets of water were cascading down gullies and washes, and flowing along the barrow pit at the side of the road. There was at least a quarter-inch of water on the asphalt, so I slowed down to keep from hydroplaning, and crept along at thirty miles an hour while the rain drummed an insistent tattoo on the cloth roof of the Jeep and my wipers fought a losing battle with the deluge.

By the time I crossed the Victory city line, the violent microburst was over, having dumped an inch of rain in under ten minutes. There was standing water on Main Street, and the gutters raged with runoff like miniature white-water rivers. Shopkeepers and tourists peeked out the front doors of Victory's businesses, bars, and restaurants, their eyes looking skyward as the late afternoon sunlight began to poke through the tattered remnants of the storm clouds. The air was sweet with the clean smell that follows a hard rain on the prairie, but that wouldn't last long. In another hour, the standing water would all be gone, and in two, the land would be dry and hard again, as if the whole thing had never happened.

The door to the office was closed and Frankie's cruiser was nowhere to be seen, so I didn't stop. Instead, I just drove on through town toward the farmhouse, where I found Robert on the front porch with a pitcher of sun-tea and that week's edition of *Sports Illustrated*. He was barechested and barefooted, dressed only in a ragged pair of cutoffs and a Mo Hotta Mo Betta baseball cap.

169

He looked up from his magazine and waved when I coasted to a gravel-crunching stop at the end of the driveway.

"Hey, Pop," he called as I was clomping up the steps. "I'm sure glad I didn't have to come to Laramie and bail you out of jail. I've only got about ten bucks in my wallet, so it's likely you'd have had to spend the night in the cooler."

"How'd you know I'd been arrested?" I asked. I sat down in the wooden chair beside him and helped myself to a glass of tea. It was an absolutely perfect afternoon in Victory Valley, the kind of day we live for in Wyoming. The rain had broken the back of the heat wave, and the landscape looked fresh and new and vibrant. It might have been my imagination, but I thought that even the dry buffalo grass and squirrel tail looked a little greener than they had that morning. Amazing what a ten-minute rainstorm can do. I knew it would be cool that evening, and if I didn't have other plans, I thought it would be nice to sit on the deck, sip coffee and brandy, and watch the moon rise over the peaks and listen to the coyotes howl as they hunted the piny banks of Gold Run Creek.

"Frankie heard about it and called here a while ago looking for you," Robert explained. "He wants you to call him at home this evening and give him the skinny."

"It was no big deal," I told him. "Just a misunderstanding."

"That's what they all say," he said, smiling, but the smile was short-lived. "I'm afraid I didn't have much luck hacking, Dad. I think they're onto me."

"What happened?" I asked, imagining all sorts of bad things, like computer cops showing up at my front door.

Robert shrugged and finished his glass of tea. "Nothing really," he said. "There's nothing interesting about Annie Quinn or her project on the university's servers, so if she has anything we might want, it's almost surely on one or more of the hard drives in her office, and that means I can't get at it with my modem. To get access to that stuff, I'd have to get it directly from her computer."

"So why do you think someone is onto you?"

"Because when I gave up on Quinn and decided to go back into the Loveladies system to explore it from that end, it looked to

170

me like they'd made some changes since I last visited. For one thing, the password and access procedures had been changed, which might not mean anything by itself, but the files I pulled yesterday and printed for you had been deleted."

"Which means?"

"Which means that someone got uncomfortable with those files being on their server and got rid of them," he said. "I have to assume they know they had a breach. They'd also cleaned out a lot of other files with proprietary information, so all that was left at their lower security level was completely innocuous. I think they know someone was snooping around, and don't want that snoop to find anything else if he or she comes back."

"Can they trace the break-in to you?" I asked, suddenly feeling very ignorant and frustrated at my lack of technological knowledge.

Robert shrugged again. "I don't know if Loveladies has anyone on staff who can do that, but it's certainly possible," he said. "I didn't do anything to cover my tracks when I broke in. I suppose I should have, Pop, but I'm kind of new at this."

"Should we be worried?" I asked.

"It depends on how paranoid you're feeling," he said. "When you come right down to it, I didn't find anything damaging when I pulled those tidbits from Loveladies' system—but it's certainly possible there were other more sensitive files available that I just didn't find. If there were, Loveladies wouldn't necessarily know I don't have them. They might think we learned more than we did. If that's the case, and they can track the system breach to me, you can probably expect an unfriendly call from their attorneys in the very near future."

"Could you be in trouble with the law?"

"I suppose I could, because what I did was illegal," he said.

"Don't worry. If they arrest you, I'll go the bail," I said.

Robert patted my knee, the way I used to do when he was a kid and needed comfort or reassurance. "I wouldn't worry about that much," he said. "I didn't do anything to sabotage their system or their company while I was browsing their servers. All I did was look around where I wasn't supposed to be—sort of like a guy who breaks into your house and doesn't steal anything, just peeks in all your drawers. The hackers who get in trouble with the law are usually the ones who create some malicious mischief once they get inside a system. I doubt I'd be prosecuted, because the people who try to punish crimes like this have bigger fish to fry. That wouldn't stop the company from filing a civil lawsuit, though, and that could be expensive."

"What's your best guess?" I asked. "What do you think will happen?"

Robert smiled confidently. "My best guess is we don't have anything to worry about," he said. "If we haven't heard from them in a day or two, that means they either couldn't trace me or aren't interested in pursuing their legal channels, and the whole thing will probably blow over."

That sounded good to me. "Let's hope it does," I told him. "And in the meantime, you and that computer of yours ought to lie low. Don't try to break into the Loveladies system anymore, or the university's either."

"I won't," he said. "But it's too bad I've got to mind my manners. I was having a good time."

"I know, and I appreciate it," I told him. Then I went into the house and got us each a beer, which we drank on the porch as we savored what was left of that glorious Rocky Mountain afternoon. Me and my kid, both of us crosswise with the law. A couple of modern-day desperadoes, kicking back under the eaves.

It was prime rib night at the Trails End, and Cindy and I had about as much fun there that evening as you can have in Victory with your clothes on.

I don't think I'd ever seen her looking more beautiful. Dressed in a clingy, knee-length black dress with spaghetti straps, heels, and a single strand of pearls, she smelled of Chanel, and her summer-tanned shoulders felt soft and warm on my fingertips when I touched them.

We took a dark booth at the rear of the restaurant and lingered over cocktails and appetizers, our heads close together as we laughed and talked and caught up on each other's lives. She was feeling particularly ebullient because she'd signed a contract on one of the expensive summer houses on the Little Laramie River south of town, and stood to make a handsome commission. She even suggested we order champagne to toast her success, so we did, drinking it with our arms entwined like newlyweds.

When our dinner came, I demolished my prime rib, but Cindy ate light, picking at her pasta and chicken. She commiserated when I described my day and my battles with the Buchanans and Walker Tisdale. It was her opinion that Cassie would eventually come around, and I shouldn't worry about Walker in the least.

"You have to remember that a man is judged by the caliber of his enemies, as well as by his friends," she said. "I wouldn't lose sleep because Walker Tisdale despises the ground you walk on. The time to worry is if he ever decides he likes you."

When we finished our meal, we shared an after-dinner coffee liberally laced with Bailey's Irish Cream, and by then the band was warming up, so we stayed around and danced to a few buckle-polishers. My bum leg prevents me from doing any of the modern line dances you see on those country western television programs, but I can hold my own with a two-step, especially if it's dark, the dance floor is crowded, and my partner is more interested in snuggling than cutting a rug, which Cindy most definitely was. The band played an eclectic mix of songs, so we stayed on the floor while they covered Jerry Jeff Walker's "Night Rider's Lament," Garth Brooks's "Beaches of Cheyenne," and a song by Aaron Neville called "Show Some Emotion," during which the feel of Cindy's lush body swaying against mine, the smell of her perfume, and the feel of her blond hair on my cheek almost caused total sensory overload and made me weak at the knees.

The band was halfway through a nice adaptation of James Taylor's "Sweet Baby James" when Cindy put her arms around my neck, pulled my head down, and whispered warmly in my ear that it was time to go home, a sentiment echoed by nearly every fiber of my body.

We raced to her house and spent the next two hours making love by candlelight. When we were sated and nearly exhausted, she led me by the hand to her hot tub for a long soak, then wrapped me in a thick robe and took me back to her bedroom, where she brought forth a cache of fragrant lotion and gave me a deep, full-body massage that relaxed me so completely I felt like I'd been drugged.

I fell asleep in her arms and dreamed of a summer from my youth when my father and I spent two weeks camping in Estes Park outside Denver. It was my first "grown-up" trip with the old man, and he bought me all the grown-up tools: a pocketknife, a canteen, my own fishing pole, and a straw hat that matched the one he wore. In my dream, the two of us were fishing a small pond near our campsite by moonlight, standing together on the bank as the moon's silvery light was reflected from the surface of the black water. My casts were clumsy and tentative, but his were perfect, a living testament to the fly-fisherman's art. I watched in awe as his line snaked gracefully through the air and as he laid the fly down on the water so gently it did not create a ripple. I watched as he played the fly across the surface, coaxing the fish below to rise and take it whole. I watched as the trout rose completely from the water in its lunge for the bait, watched as my father set the hook and his rod tip bent double.

The battle between man and fish was still raging when the ringing phone jarred me awake. For a moment, I didn't know where I was, but when I remembered, I reached across Cindy's sleeping form and pulled the receiver from the hook. She murmured at the sound of the phone and my movement, but did not awaken. "Starbranch," I said softly.

The voice on the other end of the line was Robert's, and even through the haze of sleep, I immediately heard the fear in his voice. He was speaking softly, in a rush, as if he didn't want to be overheard. "Pop, you gotta get home as soon as you can," he said tensely. "Someone was in the house, and he . . . I can't . . . oh, Jesus . . ."

174

His sentence was cut short by the horrendous clatter that must have been caused when the phone fell to the floor. Then he was gone, and I was left in the dark with nothing but the sound of my hammering heart to fill the sinister silence.

THIRTEEN

I stumbled into my clothes and raced home through the predawn darkness, but it was still better than twenty minutes between the time I got Robert's call and the time I crashed through the front door to find him crumpled on the floor of the kitchen, barely conscious and still holding the phone in his hand.

Dressed only in the sweatpants he sleeps in, the whole right side of his face was red from the blood of a head wound somewhere above his hairline, and more blood puddled on the white tile of the floor beneath him. I knelt down and rolled him over, took him in my arms, and brushed the bloody and matted strands of hair away from his face. Much of the blood came from the head wound, but just as much of it came from his earlobe, where one of his earrings had been ripped out. He moaned when I touched him, and his eyes opened briefly as he tried to focus on my face. Then he drifted out again as I checked his vital signs, relieved beyond words to find his heart beating strongly and his breathing normal. I laid him down gently and raced into the bathroom for some smelling salts, which I brought back and held beneath his nose. He came to quickly, coughing and gagging, and pushed the smelling salts away from his face. I cleaned him up with a dishtowel, and then folded another one and placed it under his head for a pillow. When I was finished, I stood up and unholstered my Blackhawk to do what I should have done when I first came in—check to see whether whoever had done this to my son was still in the house.

"You just stay here for a couple of minutes," I told Robert. "Don't get up, and don't make noise."

He gave me a grunt of affirmation, and I held the pistol in front of me in a two-handed combat stance as I went through the door of the kitchen into the darkened living room. I didn't sense another presence, and I couldn't see one in the bright moonlight streaming through the windows, so I quietly worked my way through the room toward the hallway leading to Robert's bedroom, from which yellow light from his night lamp poured. I inched my way down the hall and burst through the door of his room, sweeping it with the barrel of my .357. The bedroom was empty, but was even more of a disaster area than before. In addition to the usual detritus of my son's existence, the video monitor of his computer was smashed and thrown on the floor, and the box containing his hard drive looked like it had been broken open with a sledgehammer. His modem was also smashed, and the phone line was ripped from the wall. The plastic box where he keeps his various computer disks was also on the floor, but I saw none of the fifty or so discs he owns, containing everything from games to the collection of Pamela Anderson photos he pulled from the Internet. His office chair was lying on its side, and every drawer in his chest had been pulled out and the contents dumped. The printouts of the information he'd pulled from Loveladies' computer system, which had been in a plastic in-basket next to his terminal, were also gone, the basket smashed and on the floor.

I left his room and took a quick tour through the rest of the house, which I found untouched by the intruder. Whoever it was had only been interested in Robert's room, and it was plain to see why.

By the time I had holstered my weapon and rushed back to the kitchen, Robert was sitting up with his back resting against the cabinets, holding the dishtowel to the side of his head. The white towel was already pinkish from the blood it was absorbing.

"I could have saved you the trouble of looking around," Robert said. "He left long before you got home."

"Who left before I got home?" I asked. An old, familiar rage was building in my belly, black and insistent, and I had to choke it back. My son needed me now, but what I really wanted to do was find the person who had attacked him and beat him to death with my bare hands. Push my fist down his throat and pull his heart from his body while it was still beating. Show it to him before he died. Teach him what it means to hurt my family.

Robert shook his head as if to clear it. "I don't know who it was. I didn't see his face," he said.

"Then tell me what happened," I said. I took the towel from him and ran it under the faucet to wash away the blood. Then I took it back, knelt beside him, and started to dab away the rest of the blood on his face. I looked to see if there were other injuries, and he flinched when I ran the towel across his damaged ear. I imagined that one stung, but it was bleeding out of proportion to the seriousness of the wound. He wouldn't be wearing an earring for a while.

"I'd been up late working on the computer, but I suppose I went to bed around one-thirty. I didn't even lock the door," he said apologetically.

"We never lock the door," I reminded him. "Nobody in Victory does."

"Maybe we should start," he said. "Sometime later, something woke me up. Maybe it was a noise, but maybe I just sensed something. I lay there for a while, and I thought I heard a car driving up. I figured you wouldn't be home tonight, so I got up and went to the front door to see who it was. I couldn't see a car from the door, so I stepped out onto the porch, and that's when he whacked me."

"From behind?"

"On the side of the head," he said. "I went down on my knees and he hit me again on the back of the head; then he wrapped his arm around my neck and hit me once more for good measure. I blacked out then, and when I came to, I could hear him in the house. He was making a racket, and it sounded like it was coming from my bedroom, so I got up and went inside. I guess I wasn't thinking very clearly. I should have just tried to get away."

"He was still in there?"

"Yeah, he was destroying my computer," Robert said. "When he saw me come in, he stopped what he was doing and came at me again. He had one of those things in his hand that beat cops used to carry to thump people and make 'em more reasonable."

"A sap?"

Robert nodded. "It felt like it was filled with birdshot or something. Anyway, he hit me with it again, and the next time I came to, he was gone. That's when I called you."

"Was the light on in your room?" I asked.

"Yeah," Robert said.

"Then why didn't you see his face?" I asked.

"Because he was wearing a black ski mask that covered everything but his eyes," Robert said. "He wasn't a huge guy, Dad, but he was sturdy. A few inches shorter than you, and lighter. Big biceps. You know, like a weight lifter."

"How was he dressed?"

Robert leaned his head back while he thought. "Khaki pants, workboots. A light blue windbreaker zipped up to his chin."

"Anything else you can think of?"

"Nah," he said sadly. "And to tell you the truth, he popped me so hard, I'm not even sure about that."

When I had Robert resting comfortably on the living room couch, I called my physician, Fast Eddie Warnock, got him out of bed, and told him he needed to make a house call. He grumbled about the hour, but as soon as I told him what had happened, he said he'd be over in a half-hour. Then I dialed Frankie's number and let it ring until Frankie picked up. He knows that good news never comes in the middle of the night, so he listened while I told him what had happened and what I wanted him to do. I didn't know who we were looking for, and I didn't hold out much hope of finding him, since he could be back in Laramie by that time, or even across the Colorado line if he'd headed south. Still, I wanted Frankie to cruise town to see if there were any suspicious cars moving around driven by people who matched the physical description Robert had provided. I also wanted him to call the highway patrol, in case they stopped someone who looked like he might be our man.

When I was finished, I paced the kitchen until Fast Eddie pulled up in the driveway and rushed through the door still wearing his pajamas and bedroom slippers and carrying one of those black, old-time doctor's bags.

Fast Eddie had been in Victory nearly as long as I had, having come there on one of those programs the state runs to provide general practitioners to small, rural towns. In exchange for college tuition, the doctors must agree to spend at least three years in the boondocks, and at the end of their sentences, most of them can't wait to get away and move somewhere they can make real money. At the end of his contract, however, Eddie had surprised us all by declaring his intention to stay, but the decision seemed to have accelerated his natural aging process. In the last two years, the thirty-four-year-old sawbones had lost nearly all of his hair, gained twenty pounds, and gone from regular eyeglasses to bifocals. The man could use about a gallon of Annie Quinn's fountain of youth medicine, if it worked.

That night, as he examined Robert's wounds, he looked like a pudgy Kelsey Grammer having a very bad hair day. Comical, in other words, but he had patched me back together on more than one occasion, and I trusted his skill implicitly. He clucked to himself while he examined and dressed Robert's wounds, noting that none of them was severe enough to warrant stitches. When he was finished, I sat quietly while he asked Robert a series of questions like "Do you know what the date is?" and moved his fingers around in front of my son's face to see if he was responding properly to visual stimuli. When he was satisfied, Fast Eddie snapped his bag closed, gave Robert a pat on the knee, and stood up. "This is your lucky day, kiddo," he said. "Looks like you got your old man's hard head. One of these times, the bad guys are gonna figure out that if you want to hurt a Starbranch, you gotta hit him someplace besides the skull."

"He's all right?" I asked.

"He's fine. It just looked worse than it is on account of the blood," Eddie said.

I felt overwhelming relief that my son was not seriously hurt, but now that I knew he was all right, the fear gave way to a return of my anger. I was anxious to start getting some payback, and Eddie apparently didn't like what he saw on my face. He motioned me in the direction of the kitchen, and I followed him until we were out of Robert's hearing. He sat his bag on the counter, and spoke quietly. He had his lecture face on, the same one he wears when he berates me for not having enough fiber in my diet. "As I told you, I'm almost positive he's fine, but he's had a moderate to severe concussion, and it doesn't pay to take chances," Eddie said. "I want to get him into the hospital in Laramie tomorrow to make sure he doesn't have a small fracture, but tonight, you need to watch him closely. Put some ice packs on that head, give him some Tylenol, and if he goes to sleep, wake him up every two or three hours to check his alertness. Ask him specific questions, like his address or birthday. If he can't answer you, give me a call quick and get him to the hospital."

"Anything else?" I asked.

"Yeah, if he gets unusually drowsy or develops a stiff neck, vomits more than once, or starts acting abnormally, it's the same drill. I don't think there's any real danger, but you'll have to watch him for the next twenty-four hours, just to make sure."

"Thanks, Eddie," I said. "I can handle that."

"You'd better handle it," Eddie said seriously. "I know you, Harry, and what you're thinking is that you can't wait to get out there and catch the person who did this before he gets away." He poked me in the chest with a knobby finger. "But you can't leave Robert alone right now. If you want someone to come and stay with him tomorrow while you go about your business, fine. Right now, though, your son's your number one priority. Are you reading me, *compadré?*"

"Loud and clear," I said.

"Good," he said, picking up his bag. "Because if I find out

you've disobeyed doctor's orders, I'll come back here and thump *you* on the head. Only I won' use some wimpy sap filled with bird-shot. I'll use a lead-filled baseball bat."

Trace and Cassie Buchanan were eating breakfast on Trace's deck when I pulled to a stop in front of his house at eight-thirty the next morning.

Cassie hadn't answered her phone when I called, so I'd assumed she was still staying with her son, and I had wanted to catch them before they left for any errands they had planned. Cindy had gladly taken the morning off work to drive Robert to the hospital in Laramie for an X-ray, ferry him back to Victory, and stay with him until I returned. I felt guilty about going off on business, but there was no way to avoid it. It was clear to me that the break-in and beating were directly related to Robert's recent hacking activities, and there weren't that many people around who had a direct interest in what he might have found. There were two of them, to be exact—Annie Quinn and Trace Buchanan—and if they thought for one second I'd sit still while they invaded my home and attacked my flesh and blood, they were very badly mistaken.

The Buchanans looked up from their breakfast when I rolled to a stop, and watched with a sort of horrified awe as I stormed across the yard and up the steps, as if they couldn't believe I was really there. When he finally realized I wasn't some ghastly special-effects trick, like Godzilla invading Tokyo, Trace threw his napkin down and stood up. "You've got some goddamned nerve to . . ." he grumbled, but he never got a chance to finish because I shoved him back in his seat, leaned over, and grabbed him by the front of his shirt. "What the . . ."

I leaned close to his face and twisted the fabric of his shirt so tightly it must have hurt. Even in the fresh air, the smell of his aftershave was overpowering. "Guess you thought that just because Frankie or the highway patrol didn't pick you up last night, you'd gotten away," I growled. "Well, you didn't, asshole. You hurt my son, and that was the worst mistake you've ever made." I saw something in his eyes that might have been fear, but might also have

182

been confusion. He started to speak again, but I pulled him upright, grabbed his wrist, and spun him around so I had his arm locked behind him. I didn't put enough pressure on to break it, just enough so he couldn't stop me when I grabbed his hair with my free hand and slammed him forward, face-first onto the table so hard it spilled both of their coffees.

By that time, Cassie was on her feet, her skinny arms whirling like a windmill as she pummeled the side of my head. "What the hell do you think you're doing, Harry?" she shrieked. "Have you gone completely crazy? Let him go right now!"

Trace was grumbling loudly, but it was hard to tell what he was saying, because his face was smashed into the butter dish. I let go of his hair long enough to bat away Cassie's most recent blow and shove her back in the direction of her chair, where she landed with a thump. "I'm crazy all right, but not the way you think, Cassie," I told her. "Your little boy here broke into my house last night and beat my son. He's at the hospital right now with a concussion."

The look on her face said she thought she was in the company of a certified, and very dangerous, lunatic. "What?" she asked.

"You heard me, Cassie," I said. Trace was struggling in my grasp, but I levered his arm upward until he became more compliant. "It's a good thing I didn't catch him in the act, or he'd be dead by now instead of on his way to jail."

"Why would Trace want to break into your house?" she asked.

"To get Robert's computer records and find out how much he knew," I said. "Trace was involved in Victoria Austin's murder up to his neck. Hell, he probably did it himself—and now he's scared someone's gonna find out about it. He's too late, though, Cassie, because I already know."

Cassie's face softened a bit then, and she stood up and moved toward me. This time, however, instead of hitting me, she laid her hand on my shoulder, softly, they way you'd gentle a stallion that won't take the bit. "I'm sorry about your son, Harry," she said. "But you're making a big mistake here. What time did all this happen?"

Trace wriggled again and spat butter. I gave his arm another nudge. Much more pressure, and I'd break it at the elbow. I could only see one of his eyes, but a little tear of pain was growing at the corner. He whimpered as it rolled across the bridge of his nose and spattered on the table. "Between two and two-thirty," I said.

She nodded, as if that was exactly the answer she'd been expecting. "Then Trace had nothing to do with it," she said. "He and I watched movies together until two, and then we made ourselves hot cocoa and sat out here and drank it until we finally felt like we could sleep. It was almost three by the time we were finished. Then he went to bed, and I stayed up for another hour to read. Trace was here with me all night."

I believed her, and when my mind processed what she'd said, and what it meant, I felt like one of those blow-up punching bags about five seconds after someone pulls the stopper and starts letting out the air. There was a sick feeling in the pit of my stomach, and all the strength seemed to go out of my arms. I let go of Trace's arm and his hair, and backed away from him. He stood up, rubbing his shoulder and glaring at me like I was a rabid dog. There was a huge smear of butter on his cheek, and more of it packed inside his ear. "You're gonna pay for . . ."

"Shut up, Trace!" Cassie commanded, and her son did so sullenly. He began wiping the butter off his face with a napkin.

Cassie crossed over to me and took me by the arm. "Walk with me," she said, although it wasn't a request, but a command. She guided me off the deck and across the lawn toward my vehicle, and when we were out of Trace's hearing, she stopped and looked into my eyes. "You're in a lot of trouble," she said. "After what you did yesterday, this doesn't look very good at all. I suppose I should call the police." She paused a beat. "But I won't if you'll just tell me what's going on. You owe me that much, Harry."

I knew full well how much she'd be hurt by what I'd learned, and what I suspected. She'd already lost one son. If I could prove my theories, she was going to lose another. Still, she'd have to learn the horrible truth sooner or later. I just hoped she was strong enough to take it. "I don't think Carl killed Victoria Austin," I told her. "I think Trace and Annie Quinn set him up to take the blame. Did you know Trace and Quinn were having an affair?"

She shook her head uncertainly.

"Well, they were," I said. "That's why Trace's wife left him. I think they either killed Austin, or had her killed, to keep the truth about Quinn's research from getting out. I think they let Carl take the blame because Trace wanted to get his hands on the ranch, and there was no way that was going to happen if Carl was free. Trace wanted him out of the way permanently, and he succeeded. You blamed me for Carl's suicide, Cassie, but it wasn't me." I pointed at Trace, who was standing on the deck, watching us intently. "It was him. He was involved in Austin's murder. He sat by and watched while they handed Carl a death sentence. When that was too slow for his purposes, he talked Carl into taking his own life. He had something to do with the break-in at my house and the beating of my son. And I'm not going to let him get away with it, Cassie, any of it. I'm gonna take him down."

Cassie's eyes grew wider as I talked, and she was breathing through her mouth. It looked like it was a struggle for her to remain standing. She grabbed onto my arm for support, and looked down, emphatically shaking her head no. "Can you prove any of this, Harry?" she asked.

"Not yet, but I will," I told her. "I'm sorry about this, Cassie, but there's nothing I can do about it. I have to see it through to the end."

It took her a moment, but she gathered her strength, willed her breathing back to normal. Then she looked me full in the face, and set her jaw. When she spoke, there was sadness in her voice, but also grim determination. "I never believed Carl killed that young girl, but I *know* Trace didn't have anything to do with it," she said. "If you've got no proof, then I want you to leave us alone, Harry. I don't ever want to see you around us again. When you leave here, I'm going downtown and apply for a restraining order against you. If you bother us again, I'll see you in jail."

With that, she rejoined Trace on the deck, took him by the arm, and led him toward the house. He held the door for Cassie while she went inside, but before he went in himself, he looked at me for a moment, put his fist to his groin, and pumped it a few

185

times like he was whipping his skippy. He watched my face impassively until he was sure I understood the insult, smiled, and then casually went inside and let the screen door slam behind him. Shimmering heat tendrils seemed to rise from the concrete sidewalk where I was standing, like translucent cobras dancing in the sunlight.

I had one more stop to make before I returned to Victory, but I felt considerably less confident about it. After all, Cassie had sucked the wind from my sails by providing Trace with an airtight alibi.

Because Robert's physical description of his assailant had matched Trace Buchanan in terms of dress and size, I had naturally assumed he was responsible for the break-in and Robert's beating. If Trace had been home with Cassie, however, that meant someone else was to blame. I didn't know who that might be, but I still believed that Trace and Annie Quinn were behind it. I couldn't prove a thing, and almost nobody in the world would have believed me had I gone public with my suspicions. But if nothing else, I wanted to let Quinn know there'd be violent consequences if it happened again.

I parked the Jeep on Lewis Street and steamed up the stairs leading to the Department of Molecular Biology on the fourth floor of the College of Agriculture building, my bad leg throbbing with nearly every step and the tip of my blackthorn walking stick clicking on the tiles. I didn't even slow down at the department secretary's desk because I had no intention of announcing my arrival, but just kept going until I came to Annie Quinn's office.

The professor was at her desk, her eyes glued to a computer monitor. When she saw me come through the door, her initial facial reaction was one of surprise, maybe shock, but that was fleeting and was almost immediately replaced by a warm and welcoming smile, as if of all the people in the world, I was the person she'd most hoped to see that morning. "Why, Mr. Starbranch, what brings you here?" she asked cheerfully. She was dressed in a yellow sundress that showed off her tanned, freckled shoulders and in open-toed sandals with no hose, and her dark red hair was pulled back and held in place with a tortoiseshell barrette. She looked like she could be on her way to a church picnic at the park, and she'd undoubtedly be the most beautiful woman there. So I wouldn't see what she'd been working on, she poked a button on the keyboard that turned off the monitor, and then stood and held out her hand.

I didn't take it, and I could feel my jaw muscles clenching with anger. I leaned my walking stick against her desk and rested my hand on the butt of the .357. I felt curiously tongue-tied, and I didn't trust my ability to keep my emotions in check. Every time I looked at her face, I saw Robert's bloody one, and it took almost all my self-control to keep from lashing out at her, woman or not. I'm not a particularly rational man when my family is threatened, never have been.

"Is something wrong?" she asked. Her face showed real concern. The professor, I noted, was a hell of an actress.

"I think you know perfectly well what's wrong," I said.

She shook her head no, and then sat on the edge of her desk facing me. Her position caused the hem of her skirt to ride up to mid-thigh, giving me a good look at her long, slim legs and inviting me to inspect the merchandise. "I'm sure I have no idea what you're talking about," she said. "But from the look on your face, it appears to be serious." She gestured toward one of the comfortable black leather chairs facing her desk. "Why don't you have a seat and tell me about it?" She checked her watch quickly. "I don't have to be anywhere right away, so you've got my full attention."

"I don't need to sit down, Miss Quinn," I said tersely. "I just thought I'd come and tell you that my son is going to be all right, which is a lucky thing for you."

She looked startled by my unexpected aggression, but she regained her composure quickly, thrust her chin forward. "What?" she asked.

"He was beaten last night by someone who broke into my house," I said. "Someone who was very interested in his computer and what he'd been doing with it the last few days."

She licked her full lips, straightened her skirt. "I'm very sorry to hear about your son, and I'm glad his injuries weren't serious," she said calmly. "But I don't understand what it has to do with me."

"It has everything to do with you, and you know it," I told her. "He'd been helping me look into the abduction and murder of Victoria Austin, and as part of that, he'd been poking into your research project with Loveladies Pharmaceuticals. That's what got him beaten up, Miss Quinn. And if that's what got him beaten up, then you had to be behind it."

Quinn contemplated my face like someone studying a caged gorilla at the zoo for signs of human intellect, a little nervous because she was not protected by a set of heavy-gauge steel bars. It was a look I'd been getting a lot lately. "You think I had something to do with what happened at your house last night?" she asked incredulously. "You think I had something to do with Vicky's awful murder?"

I nodded my head. "That I do, ma'am," I said. "I think you and Trace Buchanan have been in this thing together from the start." I gave her a grim smile. "I'm going to prove that eventually, but in the meantime I just want you to know that if you come after my family again, you'll have to go through me first."

Quinn stood up from the edge of the desk and looked over my shoulder, as if judging the odds of running past me and out of the office before I could stop her. There was no way she could do it, so she apparently decided the best defense is a good offense. There was no fear in her eyes or her voice when she spoke. "That sounds very much like a threat," she said.

I shrugged my shoulders. Take it any way you want, the gesture said.

Quinn gave a short, hard laugh that let me know she wasn't afraid of the likes of me. Beneath the designer clothing, this was one tough woman. "You're going to get yourself in a great deal of hot water, Mr. Starbranch," she said. She wasn't making a threat of her own. Her inflection said she was just stating fact. "But maybe I can save you some trouble. Would it help if I told you that on the night Vicky Austin disappeared, I was out of town?"

I didn't answer, just stared at her blankly and waited for her to go on.

"Well, I *was* out of town," she said. "I drove to the airport in Denver early that morning to pick up several people—reporters and scientists intent on inspecting my research project—who were coming in on flights throughout the day. My guests started arriving at nine in the morning, and the last one didn't arrive until seven at night. After that, I treated them all to dinner at the Broker downtown, and then we all stayed overnight at the Brown Palace. You can check the records, Mr. Starbranch. We didn't leave Denver for the drive home until the next morning, long after Vicky Austin had been abducted." She walked to the seat at her desk, sat down, and scribbled for a few minutes on a piece of paper. "Here," she said, handing the paper to me. "These are the names of the people I was with until very late that night. Call them. Call the hotel, too, while you're at it. I'm a hell of a woman, Harry, but it would even be impossible for me to be in two places at the same time. Somebody killed Vicky Austin, but it wasn't me."

I looked at the paper she'd given me, which even included the phone numbers of the people who could confirm her alibi. It would take about ten minutes to check it out, and because she was so confident, I had no doubt she'd been exactly where she claimed. Still, that didn't clear her of involvement in the young woman's murder. It only meant she hadn't done it herself. I believed she'd been in the background, pulling strings, the same way she'd pulled them in the break-in at my house. "Maybe you didn't do any of this yourself," I told her. "But the last time I looked, conspiracy to commit murder was still one of the big-league felonies in Wyoming. When I prove it, you might not get the death penalty, but you'll still do hard time."

She laughed again. "Well, proving it, that's the rub, isn't it, Mr. Starbranch?" she asked. "You can't find the proof that would tie me to anything, and you never will. Why? Because I'm not guilty. I had nothing to do with it."

"You benefited from Austin's death," I said. "You and your

lover, Trace, both came out ahead. The pair of you certainly had motive."

She shrugged her shoulders. "Maybe, maybe not," she said calmly. "But I'm afraid that's irrelevant to the question at hand, even if I agreed with you for the sake of argument, which, by the way, I most emphatically do not."

"Were you and Trace having an affair?" I asked. Might as well go for the gold, I thought, but her reaction was as neutral as it had been to everything I'd said so far.

"I'm afraid that's none of your business," she said. "Even if we are, or were, however, there is no law against sex between two consenting adults, even if one of them is married." She gave me another of her award-winning smiles. "If there were such a law, even someone as upstanding as yourself might have trouble staying out of jail."

Her conspiratorial tone—one sexual juggernaut to another—was insulting, but I didn't let her get to me. "I'm not interested in whether you're having sex without benefit of marriage, Miss Quinn," I told her. "It's just a piece of the puzzle is all."

"Perhaps, but it still looks like you're lacking the most important pieces," she said. She stood up and leaned forward, the palms of her hands resting on her desktop. The sexy coquette was gone, replaced by someone hard and aggressive—the real Annie Quinn, I suspected. Her tone and body language were all business. "Now, Harry, I've cooperated with you, even though I didn't have to. I suggest you check out what I've said, and then I have some very important advice: You may suspect I was involved with Victoria Austin's murder and with everything else leading up to that unfortunate business at your house last night, but you have no proof. Even so, if a word of those suspicions leaked out, you could cause some serious damage to my reputation and my career." She waited a beat for that to sink in, leaning even closer to me. I had the distinct impression she wanted to leap across the desktop and go straight for my throat. She didn't do that. Instead, she attacked me with words that came fast and direct, like jabs to the midsection. "If that happens, I promise you that I will personally sue you for everything you have. I'll have your job. I'll have your house. I'll have your car and all your money. I'll have every dime you earn for the rest of your career. I will own you, Mr. Starbranch. I will be your worst nightmare, and I will be unmerciful. Do we understand each other?"

First Cassie and now this. I'd been threatened enough for one day. Time to get out of there while the gettin' was good, before she decided to call the campus cops and have me forcibly removed. I nodded that I understood her perfectly, stood up, and put my hat on my head. "Here's a promise for *you*," I growled. "I promise I'm not going to give up. I'm going to keep digging until I get to the truth. But if anything happens to anyone in my family again while I'm digging, anything at all, I promise I will hold you personally responsible. And then, Miss Quinn, you'll know firsthand what the word *unmerciful* really means."

For emphasis, I picked up my blackthorn stick and rapped it loudly on her desktop, the knobby end landing right between her hands. She flinched, but didn't move, the steady cold look in her dark eyes a direct challenge, one gunfighter to another.

That wasn't quite the reaction I'd wanted. I'd wanted to get her attention, maybe even scare her a little. Let her know I was serious. Annie Quinn apparently didn't scare easily, but at least she was quiet as I spun on my heels and marched out of her office and the building.

First time a woman ever gave me the last word.

FOURTEEN

It took longer than I'd estimated to check Annie Quinn's alibi when I returned to the office in Victory. Instead of ten minutes, it took nearly an hour, because the switchboard operator at the *Wall Street Journal* kept me on hold for fifteen minutes while she tracked down Bruce Tegner, the reporter who'd written one of the stories that put Quinn's research project, and Loveladies' stock prices, back on track. Like the other three people on the list, Tegner confirmed Quinn's story that she'd been out of town and busy the day Victoria Austin was abducted and murdered. He was with Quinn, he said, from the time she picked him up at Denver International Airport at a little after nine until well after midnight when he saw her to her room at the Brown Palace. He met her in the coffee shop next morning at 6 A.M. for the drive back to Laramie. At the time of Austin's death, Quinn was over a hundred-fifty miles away with plenty of witnesses. No way she could have taken part in the actual kidnapping and murder.

I was in a foul mood when I pulled into the driveway at my house at about twelve-thirty, a mood which only deteriorated when I saw that Cindy's car was parked in front of the garage, right next to the black Mercedes with TORT ACE vanity plates owned by my ex-wife's boyfriend, Howard Stokes. I knew what that meant, and my first instinct was to put the Jeep in reverse, head back to the blacktop, and keep driving until I got to Mexico. It took almost all of my intestinal fortitude to fight off that urge and clomp up the stairs, across the deck, and into the house, feeling every bit as apprehensive as Braveheart William Wallace must have felt on his way to being castrated, disemboweled, and finally—humanely—beheaded.

The four of them were in the kitchen, where they'd apparently been awaiting my arrival. Howard, looking as doughy and hair-challenged as ever, but dressed in a color-coordinated leisure ensemble that would have made Robert Goulet green with envy, was sitting at my kitchen table sipping iced tea from one of the mason jars I keep around so company won't have to drink from jelly glasses. At the table with him was Nicole, who for some reason had cut her long, auburn hair and gotten a tight perm that made her look like she was wearing poodle fur. Robert and Cindy stood at opposite ends of the kitchen counter. Robert, bruised about the face and tired-looking, but otherwise no worse for wear, had his fists balled like he wanted to take a swing at someone. Cindy was wearing the "I've got a Miss Manners smile on my face, but I'd really like to cut your heart out" look I'd only seen once before—the day we'd stopped for breakfast at the Village Inn and run into the woman she'd caught her husband screwing in his office before their divorce. A very cheery bunch, indeed, if your tastes run to the Addams Family.

There was only one thing to do. I nodded to them all and made a beeline for the refrigerator, where I liberated a cold Coors and drank half of it in a single gulp. When I was fortified, I wiped beer from my lips with the back of my hand and belched good-naturedly. Mr. Hospitality. "Nicole, Howard," I said cheerfully, "I see you've met Cindy Thompson."

Cindy glared, Howard nodded stupidly, Robert grunted, and Nicole's eyes shot daggers straight at my miserable heart. "We introduced ourselves, Harry, while we were waiting for you to get home."

I looked at Cindy for help, but she ignored me completely. "I'm sorry I wasn't here," I said. "I had some business in town that wouldn't keep."

Nicole gave me one of her patented "I can't believe what an asshole you are" smirks. "That's how it always goes, doesn't it, Harry?" she asked. "I can't believe . . ." She paused briefly, as if what she were about to say were almost incomprehensible, even to someone with as much Harry Starbranch experience as herself. She pointed a lacquered red fingernail at Cindy. "I can't believe you couldn't even take your own son to the hospital. That you left it to *her.*" The way she said *her* made it sound like she meant "redneck, Spam-eating, trailer-trash harlot," and Cindy was not amused. If nasty looks were laser beams, Cindy's would have burned Nicole to black and smoking cinders.

"Mom," Robert broke in desperately, "it wasn't that way at all. Dad and I have been working together on this case, and he . . ."

Nicole didn't let him finish. "He almost got you killed," she said. She looked back at me, and I could almost feel myself shrinking. "Jesus, Harry, what were you thinking?"

There was no answer, of course, so I didn't give her one. I felt like a soldier in the middle of a minefield, one false move in any direction and ka-boom! I took another pull of my beer. "You didn't have to come up here, Nicole," I said defensively. "He wasn't hurt badly, and everything is under control."

"Yeah, right," she said. "Then why did Robert have to call me at eight-thirty this morning to get his health insurance information? They wouldn't even look at him without proof he had coverage."

Cindy shrugged her shoulders. What could I do?

"So instead of just giving him his health insurance group number and talking to me about it later, the two of you hopped in Howard's German land boat and drove here as fast as you could," I said. "Just to make sure old dipshit Harry didn't . . ."

"Precisely," she broke in. "Just to make sure you didn't run off and put him in more danger. We came to take Robert home, Harry."

"I already told you, Mom, I'm not going anywhere," Robert said. "None of this was Dad's fault and . . ."

I held a finger to my lips to silence him. "You're right, Nicole, I put him in danger—but I didn't mean to," I said. Might as well

194

try a little reasonable conciliation. Give a little, get a little. "And I've been out this morning making sure it won't happen again."

Nicole wasn't in a conciliatory mood. "You're damned right it won't happen again," she spat. "Robert is still my child, and I'm going to do whatever it takes to . . ."

"He's old enough to make his own decisions," I said.

Howard, who'd been quiet up to that point, took that opportunity to chime in. "Well, technically, he is old enough. But since Nicole raised him alone after you left, I'd say she has every right to . . ."

"Shut up, Howard," I told him, and to my surprise, he did. "You don't have a dog in this fight. It's none of your business what . . ."

"I'm not exactly a disinterested observer," he said petulantly.

"Then what the hell are you?" I asked.

"Her husband," Robert said, looking at his mother as if she were Benedict Arnold in drag. "They flew off to Las Vegas last weekend and got married. Isn't that cute?"

My beer bottle actually slipped from my fingers at that news and rolled across the floor, spilling the dregs of my brew. "What?"

Howard, looking nervously at the .357 Blackhawk strapped to my hip, was twisting something nervously on his finger that looked suspiciously like . . . yes, it was . . . a wedding ring . . . the twin of the one I now noticed on Nicole's hand.

Nicole reached over and patted his arm, the way you'd comfort a hound dog who's afraid of thunder. "It was just one of those spur-of-the-moment things," she said. "I was going to tell you, but I just hadn't found the right moment."

"For that kind of news, there would never be a right moment," Robert said angrily.

Howard looked like he'd been sucker punched by my son's outburst, but Nicole glowered at me as if this, too, was my fault. To her credit, Cindy crossed to Robert and patted his cheek. "Why don't we go outside and get some air?" she asked. She took my son by the arm and led him to the door. When he was outside, she turned back toward us. "Howard, Nicole, it was a pleasure to meet you. Feel free to drop by any time."

The three of us waited until Cindy and Robert were off the deck and walking, arm in arm, down the dusty driveway in the general direction of Edna Cook's grave on Antelope Creek. I picked my empty beer bottle up from the floor and tossed it in the trash. Then I got myself a fresh one and sat down at the table across from Nicole and her new husband. I was feeling shock, disbelief, betrayal, all rolled into one, and the combination was enough to make me feel like I was outside myself, watching the whole thing happen to someone who just happened to look a lot like me. Despite her strange new hairdo, it occurred to me that my ex-wife looked more beautiful than ever. Much too good for the pompous, overweight, wimpy-dressing, shiny-headed, ambulance-chasing, German car–driving, bottom-feeding *pendejo* beside her—Howard Fucking Stokes. I had been a terrible husband to Nicole, and no great shakes in the father department, but I didn't want this . . . *this fat, bald-headed attorney* . . . sleeping with her. I was jealous, is what I was. Was that rational? Should I begrudge Nicole when my own lover was within calling distance? I don't know, but it made perfect sense to me at the moment. I wanted to lash out in eloquent rage, like King Lear in the face of the storm, reduce them to quivering lumps of remorse and regret. Instead, my lips seemed to move independently of my brain. "Holy shit," I said, apropos of nothing. "You got married, huh?"

Nicole, the only one of us who seemed to retain the capacity for coherent speech, nodded, acknowledging that it was indeed true. "I'm sorry you had to find out about it like this," she said. "But all that is beside the point. The point is that I won't have you putting our son in danger when you obviously can't protect him. He's going home with us this afternoon."

"I can protect him," I said. "Nothing's going to happen to the boy."

Nicole was never one to fight fair in a marital spat, and she lived up to her reputation. "Sure, Harry, like you protected Edna Cook? She died right in front of your house, didn't she? Did your protection keep her from being beaten to death? Maybe you'll protect him like you did me the night that child-killer Jerry Slaymaker shot me in the head, right in your own living room."

Nicole's low blow hurt. The woman always knew how to poke me in my most vulnerable spot. She knew I felt incredible guilt about both of those incidents, and always would. She also knew there was nothing reasonable I could say in my own defense, since it was all true. That didn't stop me from trying, however. "The bullet bounced off, Nicole," I said. "You didn't even have to spend a day in the hospital."

"So what does that have to do with anything?" she asked, fuming now. "The point is someone, someone you don't know and certainly haven't caught, walked right into your house and attacked my child. You didn't protect him from that, Harry, and you might not be able to protect him if this man comes back. You might not think it's a big deal, but I'm telling you I won't take that chance. Until this case you're working on is finished, the safest place for Robert is with Howard and me in Denver."

Although there is a plethora of evidence to the contrary, I usually recognize the truth when someone rolls it up like a newspaper and slaps me upside the head. And although I hated to admit it, Nicole was right. I couldn't protect Robert twenty-four hours a day, and until the person who broke into my house was caught, my son was in some danger. The best place for him to be was with his mother and brothers and Howard, although I didn't think Howard could protect anyone from anything. Maybe I was just being petty. I thought about what she'd said for several long minutes before I answered. "All right," I told her. "But he's not gonna like it. You go ahead and take him back with you this afternoon. I'll put his things together and ship them down in a day or so."

"Fine," she said, putting an end to the discussion. She stood and motioned for Howard to come along.

I stopped him with a hand gesture before he could unwind his long, but pudgy frame from the chair. "Why don't you two wait here for a few minutes?" I asked. "I'll go and talk to Robert. He might take this better coming from me."

Nicole looked like she wanted to argue that point, too, but she finally acquiesced grudgingly, got her own mason jar from the cupboard, and helped herself to a glass of iced tea. Howard just looked relieved.

Robert's initial reaction to the news that I wanted him to go home with his mother was exactly what I'd expected: he cursed and hollered and told me he'd been wrong to think our relationship was worth rebuilding, that I was still the same cold son of a bitch I'd always been and would never change. But the more we talked, the more he came to understand my perspective and my fears, even though he didn't agree with them. We'd come that far in the weeks he'd been with me. We could now at least listen to each other without shutting down.

In the end, he grudgingly agreed to go back to Colorado for two weeks, although he assured me he planned to spend the entire time camping in Estes Park so he wouldn't have to pass a single night under the same roof with Howard Stokes. I told him that two weeks would likely be plenty of time for me to wrap up the case, and that he was welcome to come back early if I finished it sooner.

Cindy, pleading a pressing appointment, had taken off, leaving Robert and me to pack a few of his things while Nicole and Howard waited impatiently on the deck. When we were done, we threw his duffel bags in the trunk of Howard's Mercedes, and the two of us stood for a few awkward moments, shuffling dirt with the toes of our boots, while we said our goodbyes. Before he opened the door and folded himself into the backseat, he surprised me by embracing me in the kind of hug he hadn't given me for ten years. "I love you, Dad," he said. "I'm sorry for what I said earlier. It's worth rebuilding."

For several seconds, the lump in my throat prevented me from answering with anything more than a grunt and a smile. My cheeks felt hot, and I knew that in a few seconds, I'd probably start to cry. "I love you too, Robert," I told him. I hugged him again, hard, drawing him to me as if I was afraid to let go. When I was finished,

198

I held him at arm's length, my hands resting on his broad shoulders. "Catch a lot of fish for me," I said. "This time of year, you might try a grasshopper. You have any? If you don't, I tied a few extras I could part with. It'd only take a minute to . . ."

I was stalling, and he knew it. "Don't worry, Pop," he said, winking. "I've got a few left over from the last time we went fishing. As I remember, they didn't work that well anyway. I'll just buy some worms."

I laughed in spite of myself. "You turn into a worm fisherman, then don't bother coming back," I said, but I don't think he heard me. He was already inside the car with the door closed, waving at me through the lightly tinted glass.

When they drove away, I stood in my driveway watching the Mercedes until it was only a black speck on the horizon; then I went inside and walked around my empty house. Suddenly, the place seemed too big, too sterile, too impersonal. I'd lived by myself for a long time, but having Robert around had reminded me how much I missed the clutter and chaos of children. How much I missed regular and routine human contact. How much I missed being part of a family. I consoled myself with the knowledge that he'd be back in two weeks, but it wouldn't be long until fall when he planned to enlist in the service, and then I'd be alone again.

Suddenly, my whole life seemed shallow, empty, without positive direction and without a clear vision of the future. A large part of it, naturally, was the fact of Nicole's marriage. For years, I'd nursed the hope that eventually we'd work through our differences and get back together. Since I'd become involved with Cindy, that hope had been in the background, but it was still there, whether I consciously acknowledged it or not. Now it was dashed. Nicole was out of my reach, no longer a possibility. She'd taken a definitive step in her own life, and from now on, that life would not include me.

I knew I had no right to be angry with her, and considering the kind of husband I'd been, I shouldn't have expected her to want me in her life, maintaining our on-again, off-again romance for as many years as she had. Still, it stung that she had chosen Howard

Stokes over me, even though the rational part of my brain told me we would likely never have been able to reach a comfortable compromise in the issues that had divided us since the early years of our marriage. I still loved Nicole, I always would—and I suspected that at some level, she felt the same about me. But our definitions of success and our notions of how we should live our lives were so incompatible that we both knew that love was not enough to enable us to live together happily over the long haul.

That's what the rational part of my brain said, anyway. The emotional, irrational, knuckle-dragging side said I ought to hop in the Jeep, chase the Mercedes down, and haul her back, forcibly if necessary, to the place she really belonged. Tell Howard, Mr. Tort Ace, Stokes that if he ever showed his face again, I'd trim what was left of his hair with a weed wacker.

Luckily for Howard—and his hair—my rational brain won the debate.

I wandered my house for another half-hour, then spent a few minutes tidying the kitchen. Then, feeling incredibly sorry for myself and with my mood darkening by the second, I decided to take decisive action.

I locked the doors, jumped in my vehicle, and with Travis Tritt blasting from the radio, pointed its nose toward Victory and the Silver Dollar Saloon.

The lunch rush was over by the time I pulled up in front of the Silver Dollar and took the parking space next to Mayor Curly Ahearn's current clunker, a dilapidated Chevy four-wheel-drive pickup. A bumper sticker in the rear window read, "I didn't fight my way to the top of the food chain to be a vegetarian," and another on the actual dented bumper said, "Wyoming—at least our cows are sane." One of Curly's several dogs, an Australian shepherd named Axl Rose, waited patiently in the bed, enjoying the sunshine.

Curly was on the sidewalk in front of the bar, scraping his huge barbecue grill clean of the blackened sauce and grease that had dripped from the baby-back pork ribs, hamburgers, and hot dogs he'd served to that day's crop of tourists. When he saw me, he gave me a friendly wave with his industrial-sized spatula. Then he tossed Axl a meaty rib bone, which the dog caught in midair and commenced chewing before all four feet came down to roost. "Harry, you're almost late for lunch," he called happily. "There's one more rack of ribs left, and they're yours if you want 'em." Before I could answer, he shoveled the remaining ribs off the back of the grill onto a paper plate, and closed the cover.

If there are smells in heaven, I figure the predominant one will be the heady aroma of barbecued ribs cooking on a charcoal fire. As I breathed in, my mouth began to water, reminding me that with all the hubbub, I'd missed both breakfast and lunch. A full stomach won't cure a broken heart, but in my experience, it goes a long way in dulling the ache. I took the plate gratefully and held the door open for Curly to go inside.

The Silver Dollar was dark and nearly deserted that afternoon, the only customers a couple of old-time cowboys throwing darts by the pool table and a lumberjack in a cast that came up to his left knee. The cowboys were arguing about the joint decision of the Montana Department of Livestock, the U.S. Forest Service, and officials from Yellowstone National Park to shoot some of the buffalo migrating from the park onto other public and private lands and to send others off for slaughter. It was one of the current hot buttons in the state, and you couldn't get two people to agree about it, certainly not the two old codgers at the dart board. The lumberjack was sitting morosely by himself at one of the tables, listening to Faith Hill on the jukebox and watching a soap opera with the sound off on the big-screen television.

Lou McGrew, wearing a red pair of skintight shorts, a white peasant blouse scooped low in front to reveal plenty of extraordinary cleavage, and high heels, was wiping down a vacant table. She smiled and blew me a kiss when she saw us come in.

I gave her an air kiss back, carried my lunch to the bar, climbed onto a stool, and started eating while the mayor went behind the counter to draw me a cold draft beer. He smiled when he set it in front of me. "I heard Nicole was in town," he said. "So I naturally wondered how long it would take for you to show up here to lick your wounds."

I stopped in mid-gnaw and licked some of the sticky barbecue sauce from the tips of my fingers. "How'd you know Nicole was in town?" I asked.

Curly gestured vaguely in the general direction of Victory outside his door. "Gossip pipeline," he said. "News like that moves so fast around here, I probably knew she was in town before you did."

"You probably did," I said. "She'd been there a while before I got home."

"And not alone, either," Curly said. "I hear she brought that attorney with her."

I nodded miserably. "Her husband," I told him, a statement that froze Lou McGrew in her tracks. That was one bit of gossip even she hadn't heard, and if she strained much harder to eavesdrop on our conversation, I imagined her eardrums would pop. "They got married in Vegas last weekend," I said.

Curly looked as if I'd just told him the president of the United States was outside, walking down Main Street in a leather S&M costume and a studded dog collar. "Well, I'll be a blue-balled coyote," he muttered. He drew himself a beer and sat it beside mine, rested his elbows on the bar, settling in. "You'd better tell me all about it," he said.

So I did. The entire, depressing story. I brought him up to date on the progress of my investigation, and my suspicions, and how I thought the whole thing related to the break-in at my house and the attack on Robert. I told him about Nicole's anger and the reason she and Howard Stokes had made an emergency trip to my house. I told him it was my intention to keep pushing until I had enough to put Trace Buchanan and Annie Quinn behind bars.

When I was finished, he whistled through his teeth, threw the remains of my lunch in the garbage, and poured us both a fresh beer. He grabbed a bottle of Jack Daniel's from the back bar and held it in my direction. Did I want a shot to go with my Coors? I shook my head no, but he poured one for himself and tipped it back, draining it in a single gulp, and then wiped his mouth with a paper napkin. "Well, I guess that explains one thing," he said.

"What?"

"The call I got from Cassie Buchanan this morning."

"The last time I saw her she wasn't very happy with me," I said. "She even threatened to get a restraining order."

"It looks like she talked herself out of that notion," Curly said. "But she's still plenty pissed off. She said she'd asked you to leave her and Trace alone, but it hadn't done a damned bit of good, so she thought I might have better luck. She wanted me to order you to back off."

"What did you tell her?"

"I told her I'd have a talk with you, which it looks like I'm doing right now," he said. He smiled faintly. "I don't suppose it would do any good even if I ordered you to do what she wants, would it, Harry?"

"Do you want me to quit?" I asked. "Seems to me, you're one of the people who talked me into getting involved in this sucking swamp of a case in the first place."

"I think I remember that conversation myself," he said. He fumbled around behind the bar until he came up with a box of highly illegal Cuban Cohiba cigars, removed one for himself, and handed another to me. He waited until we'd trimmed the ends and fired the delicious stogies up. "What's your take on this, pardner?" he asked through a haze of blue smoke. "You think Carl was innocent and that Trace and this Quinn woman were the real culprits?"

I nodded yes. "I'm almost convinced of it," I said. "I think they set that boy up to take the rap."

Curly scowled in obvious disgust. "That's a damned shame," he said. "That kid was nothing but a heartbreak to his poor momma, but he didn't deserve that. I agree with you. You should stick with this until you see it through. I'll tell Cassie something or other to keep her off our backs." He smoked in contemplative silence for a few minutes while I finished my beer. "Still, Harry, it sounds to me like you've still got a couple of major problems to solve, starting with the fact Carl confessed and killed himself out of guilt. You got any idea why he did that if he was innocent?"

I shrugged. "He said he couldn't remember much of anything that happened the night Austin was abducted and murdered. Said he was in some kind of drug haze he didn't come out of 'til he woke up in some fleabag motel in Fort Collins several days later. In his suicide note, he said he could no longer bear the thought he might have had something to do with the murder after all."

"And you believe that?" Curly asked.

"I don't know," I said. "He was a major-league drug user. I've heard of alcoholics going on weeklong benders and not remembering much of what they've done after they got themselves sober. Maybe heroin addicts have the same kind of blackouts. Hell, Carl told me that if the smack didn't get him high enough, he mixed and matched drugs according to what he had on hand. Maybe he cooked up some god-awful chemical stew that just knocked his brain offline for a while."

"Like a self-induced Mickey Finn," Curly said doubtfully.

"Something like that," I said, thinking back to the veritable pharmacopia, taken from Carl's home, that I'd sifted through in the evidence room of the sheriff's department, all of the drugs bad enough by themselves and likely devastating in combination or in large doses—diet pills, antidepressants, pain pills.

And Rohypnol, I remembered, suddenly coming to attention. Along with the law officers who initially investigated the case, I'd assumed Carl had the roofies in his possession for the same reason they're popular with the college date-rape crowd. I'd figured he intended to use them on some unsuspecting woman, maybe even Victoria Austin, so he could put her out of commission, rape her, and have her remember nothing about the incident except perhaps murky bits and pieces.

But what if he'd been taking them himself? That would certainly explain the memory gap.

I dismissed that thought almost immediately. I'd read a lot about Rohypnol in the last few years, and I couldn't recall a single instance of anyone taking it as a recreational drug. What's the point of getting high if you can't remember the euphoria?

And that's when it hit me like the proverbial bolt of prairie lightning—the quantum, intuitive leap you see so often in detective movies and so rarely in real life: What if someone gave him the roofies? Someone who, for their own reasons, wanted Carl to have a large and unexplainable gap in his memory? Someone like Trace Buchanan?

"Jesus, Mary, and Joseph!" I said out loud as I jumped off the bar stool and hotfooted it toward the front door in such a hurry I left the best cigar I'd had in months smoldering in an ashtray.

"Hold on, Harry!" Curly yelled. "Where are you going?"

"Colorado," I hollered over my shoulder on the way out. I was fumbling with my keys, my blackthorn stick, and my hat, hoping I didn't drop anything important in my mad dash. "I think I just found the answer!"

FIFTEEN

If I hurried, I figured I could be in Fort Collins, not far across the Colorado border, by late afternoon. But first I had to make a quick stop in Laramie to pick up a copy of Carl Buchanan's booking photo at the Albany County Jail and then a brief visit to the University of Wyoming Coe Library to get a decent photo of Trace copied from the faculty section of the school's most recent yearbook.

With those in hand, I stopped by a pay phone on the way out of town and dialed Ken Keegan's number at the Department of Criminal Investigation in Cheyenne. Keegan was at his desk and answered on the second ring, sounding tired and irritable. He said he was late to another one of his department's endless round of budget meetings, but he had time to check his notes and give me the name of the motel where Carl said he'd been staying when he finally came out of his chemical fog five days after Austin's disappearance, a place on the edge of Fort Collins called the Arapaho Motor Lodge.

I knew the place well, not because I'd ever stayed there but because every time I passed it, I promised myself I never would. The kind of down-at-the-heels place favored by long-haul truckers, hookers, and businessmen knocking off a nooner with someone other than their wives, its marquee promised adult movies on cable twenty-four hours a day, waterbeds, and "honeymoon" suites with heart-shaped hot tubs and "genuine Victorian furnishings," whatever that meant. Probably four-poster beds, always popular with the bondage crowd.

Keegan was curious about what I was up to, but I gave him a vague answer and promised to get back to him later in the week. If I found what I was looking for in Colorado, we'd have to have a serious, and probably unpleasant, conversation about Carl Buchanan, but I didn't want to tip my hand and run the risk of making him angry, just in case I was wrong.

When I hung up, I stopped at a convenience store for an extra-large iced tea and some beef jerky for the road, and then I headed south on Highway 287 for the sixty-odd-mile hop to Fort Collins. I usually enjoy the ride across the barren, high plains country between the towns, both of them small, vibrant college communities, but that afternoon I was distracted and in such a hurry I didn't even make my usual stop at Tie Siding to shoot the breeze with the postmistress. A gabby old woman named Hollis Jansen, she just happens to be an artist with a fly rod and ties the most effective Golden Ribbed Hare's Ear I've ever used. Usually, I swap a few Starbranch Special Stonefly Nymphs for a few of her specialties, but that day, I didn't even slow down.

There wasn't much traffic on the highway between Laramie and the Colorado line, but it started picking up when I got to the foothills of the Roosevelt National Forest near Livermore—ranchers, college kids out for an afternoon drive, and tourists who were probably heading up to do some camping and fishing on the Cache la Poudre or any of a number of small, productive lakes north of Highway 34. As usual, I felt a twinge of jealousy that they were going fishing on a workday and I wasn't, and just a touch of the haughty disdain that locals in this part of the world always feel for outsiders who come in to enjoy our spectacular scenery, catch our trout, shoot our wildlife, litter our campgrounds, complain about how the West is becoming "Californicated," and give us advice about how things really ought to be run. These people, I've found, are usually from New Jersey, a state whose idea of a wildlife refuge is a landfill, because garbage attracts gulls. Like the man said, "There's no snob like an I'm-from-Colorado snob, unless it's an

I'm-from-Colorado snob who was actually born in Colorado," and as someone born and raised in La Junta, that describes me to the collar buttons. It's not my most attractive quality, but I've learned to live with it.

It was almost four o'clock when I pulled into the parking lot of the Arapaho Lodge, early enough in the day that the parking lot was almost empty and no one was using the outdoor pool. I wheeled into a space near the double glass doors leading to the lobby, went inside to the registration desk, rang the bell, and waited for several minutes before the manager emerged from whatever he'd been doing in the partitioned room behind the desk. Maybe he had a bed back there and I'd awakened him, because his shirt-tail was hanging out of his pants, his eyes were red and puffy, and his thin fringe of greasy brown hair looked like he'd styled it in a wind tunnel. He did a double take when he saw the badge pinned to my shirt—it probably wasn't the first time his siesta had been in-terrupted by a cop—but he relaxed when he read it and learned I was out-of-state heat. He picked up a pad of registration forms and slid them across the counter to me. "Room?" he asked.

I shook my head no. "Just information," I told him. "I'd like to see your guest logs from October second of last year until October seventh or eighth."

"You looking for anything special?"

"Yeah," I said, "I'm interested in a person who said he was stay-ing here during that period, and I want to know anything I can about his visit. Who he checked in with, if anyone was with him, how he paid, how he acted, what he did while he was here. Any-thing you can tell me would be a big help."

"This person got a name?"

"Carl Buchanan," I said. Then I waited while he pawed around under the counter for the record book he was looking for, turned to the October entries, and scanned them with the tip of a dirty fin-ger until he found what he was looking for. He closed the book with his finger marking his place and looked up. He was obvi-ously having second thoughts—or at least pretending that he was.

"I don't know if I ought to show you this," he said. "You got some kinda warrant?"

I understood what was going on now. He knew full well I didn't have a warrant, and he hoped there might be something in this for him if he cooperated. I pulled out my wallet, took out a twenty, and dropped it on the counter. "No warrant, just cash," I said. He stared at it blankly until I added another ten. When he picked up the money, it disappeared into his pants pocket so quickly it was as if it had never existed. He opened the book and spun it around so I could read the entries. According to the records, Carl Buchanan had checked into the Arapaho Lodge at 5 A.M. on the morning of October third—plenty of time to have driven to Fort Collins after Austin's abduction and murder—and hadn't checked out until five days later. The book said he'd paid his tab in cash.

I took Carl's photograph out of my shirt pocket and held it in my fingers where he could see it. "This the guy?" I asked.

He shrugged his shoulders. "I wouldn't know, 'cause I never saw him," he said.

"What do you mean?"

"Just what I said," he said petulantly. "If he checked in at 5 A.M., that would have been on Billy Hogan's shift. He's the night manager. I don't recall ever seeing that guy out of his room, and he kept the 'Do Not Disturb' sign on his door, so we didn't even bother to clean. I wasn't here when he checked out, either, but I heard the place was a damned mess. Puke everywhere. Probably should have fumigated."

I took another twenty out of my wallet. "Would this jog your memory a little further?"

The manager stared at the bill greedily and then, sadly, shook his head no. He leaned across the counter close enough to give me a whiff of his breath—bad teeth and onions with a sour top-note of cheap bourbon. "Look pal, as much as I'd like to help you spend your money, I told you I never saw the guy," he said. "I can't help you, and more's the pity. I can always use the bread."

I put the money away and copied the information from the log-book onto my notepad. When I was finished, I looked at my watch. Not yet four-thirty. "Billy Hogan still work here?" I asked.

The manager nodded yes and tucked the book back under the counter. "He comes on at eight," he said. "You want to talk to him, come back then."

I indeed wanted to talk to Billy Hogan, but I had a few hours to kill until his shift started and I didn't particularly want to spend it in the lobby of the Arapaho Lodge—I thought I could sense crab lice in every corner, just waiting for the chance to scurry up my pants leg and start raising a family in my groin.

The beef jerky was sitting uneasily in my stomach, so I decided to settle it with some real food. I drove a couple of miles to a restaurant called the Moot House on College Avenue and was shown to a table immediately. There are lots of fine eating establishments in Fort Collins, including a good one called the Sundance Steak House where the urban cowboys and cowgirls go to dance, but that afternoon, I was in the mood for a dark restaurant and a good rib eye. The Moot House, with its Elizabethan motif, pewter serving ware, and pretty coed waitresses, satisfied both of those requirements.

When I was done, I found a bookstore and bought the latest James Lee Burke in hardback. I took it to a small, shady park near the campus of Colorado State University and read Dave Ro-bicheaux's latest adventure until the sun started going down. Then I lay back on the grass, put my hat over my eyes, and napped until the little alarm on my wristwatch started beeping to let me know it was almost eight.

By the time I got back to the Arapaho Lodge, the place had started to fill up for the night. The parking lot was more than half-full and a couple of middle-aged women in one-piece bathing suits were splashing around the pool. Two men, who might or might not have been their husbands, still wearing their business suits but with their collars unbuttoned and their ties at half-mast, sat in lounge chairs on the deck, one of them drinking a beer and the other sipping one of those premixed margaritas that comes in a can. The sound of a television game show came through the opened window of one of the rooms, and the sound of a woman's laughter came through another. On the second floor, a big-haired blond woman wearing white hot pants, a metallic-silver halter top, and sandals with criss-cross laces that came almost to the middle of her calves was filling a bucket at the ice machine. She gave me a friendly wave when I got out of the Jeep, an energetic motion that made her halter slip low enough to give me a look at her full breast in the neon glow of the motel's sign. She giggled and tugged the silver halter back into place before carrying the full bucket to the door of a nearby room, where a well-built, shirtless man wearing Levis met her at the door. He glared at me as he held it open for her to enter and then slammed it closed with a thud.

The manager I'd spoken to before was not behind the reception desk, but in his place was a scrawny, gum-popping stoner with a buzz cut, two little tears tattooed under his left eye, a stud through his nostril shaped like a death's-head, a half-dozen earrings, and a "Porno for Pyros" T-shirt with a pack of cigarettes rolled up in the sleeve—a demented James Dean. He was reading what I assumed was the latest issue of *Leg Tease* magazine when I came into the lobby, and didn't even bother looking up when my entrance made the little bell over the door jingle. Without taking his watery blue eyes away from his literature, he nudged the registration pad across the counter and was so surprised when I shoved it back that he jumped a little.

"You Billy Hogan?" I asked.

I towered over him in my Stetson, and his eyes grew wide when he saw me, my badge, and my gun and his brain registered the two most frightening words in a diminutive punk's vocabulary: "redneck cop."

"Maybe," he said, but the words came out in a croak. "What is it you think I did?"

"I think you did it *all*, Billy," I said, smiling my most evil smile. "But that's not what I'm here for. This evening, all I want to do is talk." I didn't have to come on that strong, I suppose, but because of the money I'd given the day manager and the cost of dinner and the book, I was running low on cash. With limited resources for bribery, I'd have to economize and get the information I still needed some other way. I figured intimidation was as good a way as any.

He closed the magazine and rolled it up, as if that might serve as a sort of truncheon if I decided to lunge across the counter and go for his throat. "So talk," he said. He gave me a goofy grin, a submissive gesture like a dog rolling over to show you its belly. "I got no pressing appointments for at least an hour."

I took Carl's photo out of my pocket and flopped it on the counter. "This guy stayed here for almost a week early last October," I said. "You remember him?"

Billy Hogan bent over and studied the photo as if it were the answer to the final question on the old game show "You Bet Your Life." When he'd committed it to memory, he nodded energetically. "Sure," he said. "I saw him the day he checked out. Guy who looked as bad as he did is hard to forget."

"What about when he checked in?" I asked. "Didn't you see him then?"

"Nah," he said. "It was almost morning and a woman checked in for him. She paid cash for a week in advance and stayed with him in his room most of the time. She went out to get his meals and such. Used his truck."

"A woman?"

"Yeah, a local girl name of Missy Poteet," he said. "She's a workin' girl, if you know what I mean. I see her around here sometimes."

"He didn't go out? Make any calls?" I asked.

"Nope," Hogan said. "Like I said, he kept to himself. I'm glad he left when he did though, 'cause I remember thinkin' he looked real sickly, like he was fixin' to die, and I didn't want him kickin' off here at the Arapaho. He made an awful mess up there, too. Took me almost four hours to clean up after him when he took off. The dude was on some bad drugs, if you ask me. I seen that look in people's eyes before, you know what I mean? Besides that, he left some paraphernalia behind. A whole set of heroin works. I threw that crap in the trash."

"Did the woman leave with him?" I asked.

"Nah," Hogan said. "She was gone by then. That last day, I went out to talk to him as he was getting in his truck, and he acted real funny. Said he didn't have the money to pay me, but he'd send me a check as soon as he got home. He was real surprised to find out Missy had already paid. He left alone. I don't know where Missy was." He looked at me sheepishly. "With all I found up there, I probably should have called the cops, huh?"

I didn't answer, and I didn't mention that Billy had apparently failed to refund Carl the two days' rent he had coming if he'd only stayed for five days. I just fished around in my pocket until I came up with Trace's photo. Then I laid it on top of Carl's. "How about this guy?" I asked. "You ever seen him?"

Although I think Hogan would have probably loved to have recognized Trace just to keep me off his back, this time he drew a blank. He looked at the picture, scratching his head, until he was absolutely positive. "Sorry, mister," he said. "If that guy's ever been a customer here, I don't recall him."

I put the photos back in my pocket. "Thanks, Billy. You've been very helpful."

"That's all then?" he asked suspiciously.

"Not quite," I told him. "I need to know how to get in touch with Missy Poteet."

He gave me an exaggerated shrug of his bony shoulders. "That I couldn't tell you. Like I said, I see her around here sometimes, but that's all. I don't know where she hangs out."

That was a lie, and we both knew it. He was wringing the rolled-up magazine in his hands, so I leaned across the counter and took it away from him. "That is absolute bullshit, Billy," I said. "If I was just some out-of-town businessman looking for a little action, I'll bet you could get in touch with her soon enough. Now, I've had a very long day, and I'm in no mood to screw around. I'll ask you nicely one more time. How would I get in touch with Missy Poteet?"

Billy Hogan obviously had no stomach for confrontation, and he scared easily. Sweat was gathering on his upper lip, his cheeks were flushed, and I could see the big arteries in his neck pounding. "All right," he said. "I'm pretty sure she works for an escort service called The Gentlemen's Club. If you want her, you call the service and leave your request. They track her down and send her over."

I smiled and handed him his magazine. "Then do it," I said.

"What?"

"Call her escort service and get her over here."

Billy was really sweating now, nearly hyperventilating. "Look, mister, if I call her and they find out I've called her for a cop, they'll . . ."

"They'll what?"

The prospect was too frightening for Hogan to contemplate. The boy had seen too many movies about vengeful pimps with box-cutters and forty-fives. "I don't know, and I don't want to find out," he said.

I sat down on the lumpy couch and put my feet up on a coffee table littered with old travel magazines and back issues of the *Rocky Mountain News*. "Let me ask you a question, Billy," I said. "Do I look like the kind of person you want to piss off?"

He shook his head no. I could tell by the look on his sallow face that the kid hated me and everything I stood for. Most of all, he hated me for making him afraid. Still, I figured I was safe as long as I didn't turn my back on him in a dark room. He wasn't the kind who'd ever come at you head on.

I gave him a predatory grin, the kind I never use around small children. "Well, I'm here, and the people Missy works for aren't," I said simply. "If you know what's good for you, I suggest you get that hooker over here before I run out of patience."

It was over an hour before Missy Poteet turned up, during which time three more hormonally charged couples and a few seedy-looking single men, most likely attracted by the twenty-four-hour porno movies, stopped by the registration desk to check in for the night.

214

Missy entered the lobby on a breeze of floral-scented perfume, a slender woman in her late twenties with shoulder-length hair a uniform, rich black you'd never find in nature. Dressed in a black leather skirt so short she'd have been arrested for indecent exposure in any of the Bible Belt states, black hose, and a red top that looked like some sort of Victorian corset and made her breasts look like Cadillac-bumper bullets, Missy wore stiletto heels that clacked on the tile floor as she tottered her way up to the desk. If she saw me, she didn't pay the least bit of attention, and she gave Billy a playful pinch on the cheek. "Hey, sport," she said happily. "Buster says you've got a hot one for me. Thanks for the referral."

Billy nodded stupidly, looking at me nervously over her shoulder. "Don't thank me yet, Missy," he said.

She didn't catch his meaning. "All right, I won't," she laughed, made a playful money-counting gesture with her fingers. "But if the guy's a good tipper, I'll come back and thank you later. Might even be worth twenty bucks. You wanta point me toward his room?"

Billy looked so miserable I'm sure he was trying to will himself into invisibility. "He doesn't have a room, Missy," he said.

"What? Then where is . . ."

Billy pointed at me, and when Missy turned around to see what he was pointing at, the smile melted from her carefully applied face. I'd seen that look on hookers' faces before, back when I pulled a short stint in vice. It was the look they had about three seconds after they named their price and you pulled a badge out of your pocket instead of a money roll. "Oh fuck, Billy, what did you . . ."

"Don't blame Billy. I made him do it," I broke in. "I wanted to see you."

She didn't understand what was going on, and misread the situation. She figured I was there to bust her, or coerce her into free sex in exchange for letting her stay in business. As much as we hate to admit it, that's a common arrangement between policemen and whores. "Well, I don't do cops," she said. "As a matter of fact, I don't do anyone the way you're thinkin'. I'm an escort, and that's what I do. I get paid to escort people places. What I'm paid for is company and conversation, so if you want . . ."

I cut her off with a dismissive wave of my hand. "I guess you're in luck then, because that's *all* I want," I said. "Conversation."

She snorted as if that was the best joke she'd heard all day. "Sure you do," she said. "As long as you can talk with your di . . ."

Billy didn't let her finish. "He wants to talk about that strange guy you had last fall," he told her helpfully. "That stoner who stayed in his room all the time."

"His name was Carl Buchanan," I said. I stood up and crossed the floor toward her. She folded her arms across her chest defensively, but she looked at Carl's photo when I held it in front of her face. "You remember this man?" I asked.

There was immediate recognition in her eyes, but she didn't say a word, playing it close to the vest. "It looks like you remember him well enough," I said. "I want you to think back and tell me everything you remember about the time he was here."

"Why do you want to . . ."

"You let me worry about that," I broke in. "You just tell me what I want to know and I'll be out of here." I decided to sweeten the pot. I dug out my wallet and removed my last fifty-dollar bill. "I'll even pay you for your time."

Missy eyed the money covetously, but she didn't snatch it away like the day manager had. For all she knew, that money was just the bait on a trap that would spring closed as soon as she reached for it and cut her hand off at the wrist. "You're sure that's all you want?" she asked suspiciously. "No strings?"

I took her hand, folded the money into her palm, and closed her fingers around it. "No strings," I agreed, even though I knew that was not technically true. If she told me anything worthwhile, she might eventually have to testify, but I decided that like Teddy Kennedy, we'd drive off that bridge when we came to it.

It took her a couple of minutes, but she eventually concluded her safest bet was to go along and hope for the best. Anything was better than handcuffs and a night with the dykes in the local lockup. "Then yeah, I remember him," she said. "Who could forget?"

"Tell me about it," I said. "How did you wind up in his room?"

Missy bit her lower lip, thinking back. She must have applied fresh lipstick before she came in, because there was a cherry-red smear of it on her front teeth. Sensing it, she scrubbed it off with her tongue. "It was real weird," she said. "A guy I'd trick . . ." She corrected herself in midsentence. "A guy I'd escorted a couple of times called me about four o'clock in the morning and arranged it. Said he had a friend he was worried about and needed someone to stay with for a few days because he couldn't do it himself. Said he had to get back to work. The two of them met me a few blocks from here in a pickup truck. The guy you say is named Carl was slumped over and passed out on the passenger side. This guy paid me for a week in advance, along with enough money to pay for a week here at the Arapaho. He told me I didn't have to do anything sexual, just stay with this poor sick puppy, make sure he could fix when he needed to, and make sure he took his medicine twice a day. Then he made us hang around while he called a cab at the pay phone. As soon as it came to pick him up, he left me with Carl and took off."

"What kind of medicine?"

"I didn't know, but he said it was for some kind of heart problem," she said. "I got pretty worried, because the guy was also a heroin addict. I was supposed to help him fix when he needed it, and this guy needed all the help he could get. He was completely out of it most of the time, drifting in and out, like he was kind of there, but not all the way. He wouldn't eat, and he just kept getting sicker and sicker, throwing up all the time, even though I gave him his pills. I figured he was gonna pull a John Belushi on me, and I started getting scared."

She paused in her story, and it looked like she was reluctant to go on. "You're sure this won't get me in some kinda trouble?" she asked.

"Not if you tell the truth," I assured her.

217

I don't think she believed me, but she pressed forward. "After a few days, I finally told Buster what was going on, and he asked to see the pills," she said.

"Did you show them to him?"

She nodded yes, remembering. "Buster said it was no wonder the guy was so out of it," she said, "since I wasn't giving him heart medicine."

"What were you giving him?"

"Roofies," she said. "You know, date-rape pills. Between them and the heroin, it knocked that poor boy for a hell of a loop. I didn't know what they were, I swear it. If I had known, I never would have . . ."

"What did you do then?" I broke in.

Missy looked at me as if I were a bona fide idiot. "I put those pills back in his pants pocket, along with the keys to his pickup, and hit the road," she said. "I was afraid he was gonna die, but he must have come to real early the next morning. Billy said he looked awful when he checked out."

Billy nodded to confirm her story. "I never saw anybody look like that except in a hospital," he said. "Looked like he'd puked up a lung."

I thought I'd heard the truth, or at least a good bit of it. "The man who set it all up . . . what was his name?" I asked.

"The times we'd been together, he said his name was Robert Mitchum," she said. "I didn't believe him though. Wasn't Robert Mitchum some kind of country western singer?"

"An actor," I told her. "But don't worry, he was popular before your time." I pulled Trace's yearbook photo from my pocket and held it up so she could get a good look. "Recognize this fellow?" I asked.

Missy's eyes locked on the photo and flashed a spark of anger. "That's Robert, or whatever the hell his name is," she said. "That's the bastard stuck me with that damned druggie and got me in this jam in the first place."

* * *

I was feeling pretty full of myself when I left the Arapaho Lodge and pointed the Jeep north into the darkness and the highway home, a full cup of coffee balanced on my knee, a Bonnie Raitt tape blasting in the tape player, and the cool evening air washing across my face through the open window.

What I'd learned didn't prove Trace Buchanan's direct involvement in the abduction and murder of Victoria Austin, but at least it nailed him for aiding and abetting after the fact. It also put some meat on the bones of the theory I was trying to prove. If Carl had been under the influence of Rohypnol, which, according to my theory, was administered by his brother, it was entirely possible he was telling the truth when he said he remembered nothing about the day of the crime, and nothing for the next five days. It was even possible he could have been along when it took place, semiconscious and not taking an active part.

If Trace was setting him up for the fall, using Carl's vehicle during the crime, that would help to explain a lot, including the strands of Carl's hair found on Austin's body, the victim's blood in his pickup, and the tire prints found at the place where her body had been dumped. Although an exact time of death had not been established, it was possible Trace had enough time after the murder to drive Carl to Fort Collins, dump him with Missy Poteet, hop a cab to the bus station, and be back in Laramie in time for work the next morning—although if he'd paid cash for his ticket, that might be difficult to prove.

If Carl had died in the hooker's care as a result of the chemical cocktail Trace prescribed, so much the better. Then, Carl would have taken the blame for the murder, Quinn's project would have been protected, and Trace would have inherited the ranch, all without the messy complications of a trial.

With a few notable exceptions, a nice tidy ending for everyone concerned.

What none of it did explain was Carl's subsequent confession, the major stumbling block in my whole complicated hypothesis. To explain that, I needed Ken Keegan to confirm a dark suspicion that had been lurking in the back of my mind for several days, a suspicion so personally disturbing I had been unwilling to confront it openly. Now, it looked like I had no choice.

I planned to be at Keegan's office in Cheyenne when it opened at nine the next morning, but I didn't know if our friendship would survive the encounter.

SIXTEEN

I couldn't sleep that night when I got back to Victory, so I killed a six-pack just to watch it die. Since a low-level hangover usually brings out the worst in me, I was in generally ill humor when I arrived at the Wyoming Department of Criminal Investigation at precisely 9 A.M. the next morning. Of course, the fact I suspected my conversation with Ken Keegan would be as pleasant as visualizing whirled peas did little to improve my outlook.

Keegan had not yet arrived for work, so I spent a few minutes shooting the breeze with the receptionist. She told me she moonlighted as a therapeutic masseuse, but lost interest in the conversation when I admitted I'd never been folded, and had no intention of ever doing so. Dismissed from her attentions, I settled in on the institutional couch with a year-old copy of *Guns & Ammo* magazine until my friend finally turned up forty-five minutes later.

Visitors to the DCI have to be escorted to the offices upstairs, so when the receptionist announced my arrival, I waited for a few minutes until Keegan came down in the elevator. When he got off, it looked like he'd aged ten years in the short time since I'd seen him last. His wrinkled suit hung limply on his stocky, square frame, and his crew cut was in need of a trim, spiky on top where it was usually two-by-four flat. There were bags under his bloodshot eyes, and his broad shoulders had developed a pronounced slump. He looked as if it was all he could do to stand up without support scaffolding.

As usual, he didn't bother coming over to say hello, just stopped at the receptionist's desk and wagged a finger indicating I should follow him to the elevator. When the doors closed, he leaned back against the wall to hold himself upright. "You should have called first, Harry," he said, not bothering to hide the annoyance in his voice. "I'm up to my ass in crocodiles, and I don't have a hell of a lot of time."

"It's nice to see you too," I chuckled. "I'm sorry if I caught you at a bad moment, but it's important and I won't take long. You still swamped with budgets? You look like you've been burning all the midnight oil and most of the three-in-the-morning oil at the same time."

"Budgets and a case," he said. He punched the button for the third floor, and the car creaked into motion. "Did you hear about the body of that woman the Platte County sheriff's department found up by Split Rock last weekend?"

"Only what I heard on the radio," I told him. If I recalled correctly, some picnickers had found the body in a campground and called the sheriff, who confirmed that the corpse belonged to a Wheatland schoolteacher who'd been reported missing by her husband ten days before, after she'd left home to go to Baskin-Robbins for ice cream and never came back. The death was immediately ruled a homicide because whoever killed her had cut her throat so deeply she was nearly decapitated, and then tried to get rid of the body by dousing it with gasoline and setting it afire. The killer had made a common mistake in not realizing it takes a lot more than a couple of gallons of gas to reduce a human body to ashes and destroy the forensic evidence. What's left is pretty charred and grisly, but still definitely human and capable of telling a capable coroner plenty. "Were you working that with the sheriff's department?"

Keegan nodded. "They initially called us in to help with the crime scene, but one thing led to another, and I ended up doing some investigatory consultation," he said. "I was here working on budgets yesterday afternoon when I got a call from the Platte County sheriff saying he finally had enough for an arrest warrant and asking if I wanted to drive up and ride along for the collar. He thought he owed me that little treat, since I'd helped him out with the evidence. I said sure, but when I got there, the perp wasn't around. We set up a surveillance and popped him about four o'clock this morning when the dumb asshole tried to sneak into his house for some clean clothes. Couldn't leave town without his toothbrush and his favorite bathrobe. Turns out the victim was his lover, although she was married to someone else at the time. Apparently, she tried to break it off, but this bastard couldn't handle rejection." He made a throat-cutting gesture with his index finger. "Decided to teach the schoolmarm a lesson she wouldn't forget."

He winced, rubbed his red-rimmed, bleary eyes with his fingertips. "I was up all night, and didn't get back to Cheyenne until just a few minutes ago. Didn't even have time to go home for a shower."

The world's slowest elevator groaned against the cables, and we rode the rest of the way to Keegan's floor in silence. Then I followed him down the institutional green hallway to his office. He closed the door, and I made myself comfortable while he got his coffeemaker going. When it was bubbling away, he sat down at his desk, folded his hands on top, and leaned forward wearily. "Now, why don't you tell me what I can do for you this morning?" he said. "Considering our last conversation, I assume your visit has something to do with Carl Buchanan?"

"That it does, Ken," I said, and then I spent the next fifteen minutes bringing him up to date on my investigation. I told him everything, and I knew he was listening closely, even though his eyes were half-closed, as if he were about to fall asleep. He perked up considerably when I got to the part about my trip to Fort Collins and what I'd learned from Missy Poteet—that she fed Carl Rohypnol like popcorn on Trace Buchanan's orders beginning the night of Austin's murder and continuing for the next several days. I told him Carl's wild stories were sounding more and more like they could be true. I told him that at the very least, I could now prove Trace guilty of criminal behavior, even if I couldn't prove him guilty of murder. I told him it was only a matter of time until I would nail him for that as well.

Keegan's shoulders slumped even further as he began to realize what Poteet's testimony meant. For the first time, I imagined he was considering the possibility that he'd screwed up, that Carl was just another victim, and he was both frightened and disgusted by that prospect. "Goddamn it, Harry, I never even talked to that woman," he said. "How could I have missed something like that?"

I shrugged my shoulders. Cops get tunnel vision like almost every other hunting mammal. They get a likely suspect firmly in their sights, and their focus becomes so intense they sometimes fail to notice other important clues right in front of their noses, especially if they're working a slam-dunk investigation, as the case against Carl appeared to be. "Why would you have tracked her down?" I asked. "The trail of evidence you were following didn't lead you to her. It led you to Carl, and once you had him, he even confessed."

It was out in the open now. I knew it. He knew it. Keegan looked into my eyes, searching for something he didn't find. Understanding? Forgiveness? When he spoke again, there was resignation in his raspy voice. "And that's why you're here, isn't it, Harry?" he asked. "You're here to talk about that confession."

I sighed and looked down, searching for the words to go on. When I found them, I nodded sadly. "I'm afraid so, pardner," I said. "There's no way around this, so I've gotta ask you plain. Carl told me you coerced that confession, that the only reason he signed it was because you kept him locked up in the interview room without his dope. He told me you beat him. He told me the only way he could get you to stop and get himself a fix was to sign on the dotted line." I stopped, trying to read my friend's face, and then asked him the sixty-four-thousand-dollar question flat out. "Was he telling the truth, Ken?"

Keegan looked as if there were a battle of demons raging inside him. He didn't answer for several minutes, stood up, and went to look out the window with his back to me. When he turned around, his square face was flushed. He was angry, taking it out on me. For the moment, I'd let him. "Maybe I did cut a few corners," he said. "But don't you come in here and act self-righteous about it. I've known you a long time, Harry, and I know for a fact that you don't even hesitate to bend the law if that's the only way you can close a case. It's gotten you in trouble more than once, hasn't it, friend?"

I nodded agreement because, of course, he was right. During the course of my police career, I've broken and entered, taken evidence without a warrant, manipulated evidence, and lied to suspects and my superiors. Although I've never beaten a suspect during interrogation, I've threatened to if I thought it would help. I've abused my authority and taken the law into my own hands more times than I cared to count. Over the years, my actions have indeed gotten me in trouble and have nearly cost me my livelihood and, on a few occasions, my life.

I'm not proud of it—any of it—but I live with my dark side by telling myself that because the legal system is so unfairly weighted toward the criminal, there are times when a cop can't protect the innocent people he's sworn to defend any other way. If it's a question of bending the law or letting a killer go free, saving another life down the road, I'll bend that sucker nearly every time. The crooks never play fair, and neither do I. Sometimes, the good guys have to fight dirty if they want to win.

"I'm not trying to be self-righteous," I told Keegan. "I think I understand what happened between you and Buchanan. You truly believed he was guilty. He wouldn't admit it, so you did what you thought you had to do to close the case and get a little justice for Vicky Austin." I stood up and put my hand on his shoulder, looked into his eyes, let him see I was sincere. "I honestly don't know if I would have done it any differently. The problem is, Ken, I'm pretty sure you were wrong. I think Carl Buchanan was innocent, but right now, that damned confession is keeping anyone from believing me when I say it. That's why you've got to tell me how you got it. You've got to tell me the truth."

Keegan seemed to deflate. If a strong wind came through the window, I'm sure it would have blown him away. "And what will you do with the truth?" he asked softly. "If it turns out you're right, it'll be the end of my . . ."

I shook my head no. "I'm not going to tell anyone now," I said.

"If worst comes to worst and I need your testimony, you'll have to look inside your conscience and decide what's right. Until then, it's just between us, but I have to know—was Buchanan's confession legitimate?"

Keegan sat down at his desk and lit an unfiltered Camel pulled from a battered pack in his shirt pocket. He smoked half of it and then ground it out in his overflowing ashtray. He'd made his decision. He couldn't lie to a friend, not that I ever expected him to. "I beat it out of him, Harry. Is that what you want to hear?" He picked up a wooden pencil, held it between his hands, and bent it until it snapped. "Every bit of evidence I had pointed to that little prick, and when I got him in the room he looked and sounded like such a guilty little weasel I didn't believe a word he said. I'd hoped he'd give me a quick confession, but he stuck to this cockamamy tale about not even knowing Austin and conveniently blacking out, waking up in that motel room. We went through the story a thousand times, but he wouldn't budge. I knew he was afraid of me and that he needed to fix, so I finally decided to play hardball until he came around. Eventually, it worked."

That's what I thought. "Then you wrote out a confession for him," I said.

"I wrote it," Keegan said miserably. "Held the poor son of a bitch by the hair until he signed." He leaned forward and held his head in his hands.

I didn't say a word, because I didn't know what to say. I had what I'd come for, but I didn't feel like celebrating. Keegan had just told me that the most damning evidence against Carl Buchanan was bogus, but if I used that information with abandon, I'd end my friend's career for doing something I might well have done myself in the same circumstances. A world-class headache was beginning to build right behind my eyes, and my stomach was rolling. I needed to get out of there, needed time to think. I stood up and jammed my Stetson into place.

Keegan looked up. "What now?" he asked.

"I don't know," I told him honestly.

He stared into the middle distance for several minutes, and

when he spoke, his words reminded me why I respected him so much. "I do," he said. He stood up and took me by the arm, his big hand clamped just above my elbow. I saw the old Ken Keegan in his hard face. "If Carl Buchanan was innocent and my actions put him on death row, then I'll have to answer for that. It's not your problem, Harry, and I don't want you to try to protect me."

I started to protest, but he cut me off. "I mean it," he said angrily. "I'm a big boy. I make my own choices, and the consequences are on my head. All you have to worry about is proving your theory. If Carl was innocent and somehow Trace and Annie Quinn were behind the murder, then they have to pay." He gripped my arm harder. "They have to pay! Do you understand me, Harry?"

"I'll do my best," I said uncertainly.

"We'll do it together," he said. "If that boy was innocent, I'll never be able to make up for what I did to him. I can't bring him back to life. All I can do is help to clear his name and make sure the truly guilty suffer—but by God, I can help to do that, even if it's the last thing I do as a cop."

There was a note of desperation in his voice, but also determined strength. Despite the hell he'd brought down on Carl Buchanan, I was proud of my friend for standing up, taking responsibility for what he'd done no matter what it might cost him. Although I could never convince—or even explain it to—anyone outside the profession, I knew that at root, he was a good man, an honest man, and a good officer. I wanted to tell him that.

"Ken . . ." I began, but he didn't let me finish. He already knew what I was going to say. After all, we'd been friends a long time.

"Call it atonement, Harry," he said. "Call it saving my sorry soul."

With Keegan back in the game and the investigation into Victoria Austin's death officially reopened, I left the DCI feeling pretty good, despite the headache that was proving itself amazingly resistant to the aspirin I had taken in such massive quantities that my ears were ringing.

At some point, my friend would have to deal both psychologically and professionally with the enormity of his blunder, but at least for now he was focused on reexamining the initial evidence in the crime. For starters, he told me he'd never ordered Carl's pickup checked for any prints but Austin's because he hadn't seen a need to do so. Luckily, the vehicle was still in the county impound lot in Laramie, so that afternoon, he planned to send a couple of technicians to go over it bumper to bumper. If Trace's prints turned up, as we suspected they would, we'd have another piece of circumstantial evidence linking him to the murder.

In addition, Keegan would order the techs to go over Carl's cellular phone for prints while they were at it. If Trace had been setting his brother up to take the blame in Austin's homicide, it was likely that Carl was also telling the truth when he claimed he had not made any of the harassing phone calls to her in the six weeks prior to the crime. When I visited him in prison, Carl told me his cellular phone had disappeared several months before the murder, and claimed he didn't know how it came to be in his house when investigators found it there. If you accepted his story, then it was entirely possible that Trace had taken the phone, made the calls, and put it back where it would be found and used as evidence against Carl. We both remembered that Trace had been the one to bring Carl's history of telephone harassment and his suspicions that his little brother had been making similar calls to Austin to Keegan's attention in the first place.

If we made any headway with those two avenues of inquiry, Keegan thought he could probably talk his way into a warrant to search Buchanan's house on the chance that the rope used to strangle Austin or the shovel handle used in the sexual assault were still on the premises.

He'd also ask the court to order Trace to provide blood and hair samples to match against additional hair specimens found on Austin's corpse. A human being wearing clothing collects a cornucopia of fibers, hair, and assorted gunk over the course of a normal day, so of course the forensics team had discovered lots of fibers and hair on the victim when they examined her and her clothing in minute detail. Because Carl was the primary, and at that time only, suspect, however, they'd only been looking for hair that matched his. They found it, and that evidence was used against Carl during the trial.

Keegan predicted that a reexamination of the fiber and hair evidence would establish Trace's presence at the crime scene as well. "After that, we'll bring the gold-plated son of a bitch in and charge him," Keegan said.

Which was fine, as far as it went, but even if we could make a case against Trace Buchanan, we still didn't have a scintilla of evidence to use against the second person I believed was involved in the murder, as well as in the break-in at my house and the beating of my son: Professor Annie Quinn. I voiced that frustration to Keegan, and he scoffed.

"We get Trace and we'll get her," Keegan said confidently. "My bet is, we bring Trace in, and in no time he'll be offering to trade a kidney for any deal that will keep him off death row. If we can convince Walker Tisdale to make it part of a plea package—and I think we can, considering the political ramifications of what he did to Carl—Trace will give up Professor Quinn like a bad habit." He made a motion like shutting a book. "Case closed."

I left him with the telephone receiver to his ear, making the first of the calls that would put our plan into motion. Then I spent the entire drive back to Victory wondering how I was going to complete my current part of the investigation, which was to do absolutely nothing in the next couple of days that would spook Trace before the fingerprint results came back and the wheels of justice were poised to squash him flat.

Because Frankie Bull had been running the police department single-handedly while I worked the Buchanan case, it was my design to stop by and send him home for the rest of the day, and all the next day too. That's the only way I figured I could do what Keegan wanted and maintain a low profile for a couple of days. I'm not good at waiting around, doing nothing, when I've got my teeth in an investigation, so I needed to keep myself busy and distracted.

When I got to the department, however, there was a note from Frankie on my desk telling me that he was at Carl Buchanan's memorial service and would be back a little after noon.

I spent twenty minutes piddling around the office, reading incident reports, and returning phone calls. Then I locked the door, got back in the Jeep, and drove two blocks to the white First Christian Church on Main Street.

Like many rural towns the size of an Oreo cookie, Victory is served by what seems a disproportionate number of bars and churches. To make sure the spiritual needs of our six hundred and fifty residents are met, there are five churches. To make sure their need for spirits are met, there are an equal number of saloons. While I'm more or less a regular in all of the watering holes, I don't attend any of the churches on a frequent basis. When I do—say, on Christmas Eve or Easter—I go to the First Christian because I like the imported pipe organ and because Reverend Phil Sottile has the best collection of bootlegged Ry Cooder concert tapes in the western United States and sometimes slips me a copy of his better specimens—like the one of Cooder and David Lindley at the Royal Festival Hall in London—as a reward for attendance. If there's music playing in heaven, I'm sure those guys will be in the band, playing "Jesus on the Mainline" for the celestial host. Stadium seating. Great acoustics. Bobby King and Chaka Khan singing backup. Jim Keltner on drums, Flaco Jimenez on accordion. Ry's hot licks on slide-guitar. No prissy harps allowed.

The church parking lot was nearly full, and both Cassie's and Trace's vehicles were tucked in among the throng. I was too late for the start of the service, but since I didn't have anything better to do, I backed the Jeep into a a shady spot at the back of the lot, killed the engine, and listened to the sweet sounds of "Amazing Grace" coming through the opened doors and windows of the meeting-house.

I sat there for the better part of an hour, watching the tourist traffic on the main drag and dozing occasionally until the first of the people who'd attended the service began leaking out into the bright sunshine. I recognized lots of locals, friends of Cassie's, and at least two reporters, Sally Sheridan from the *Casper Star-Tribune* and Ron Franklin, editor of the *Victory Victor*. Sally's flag-red hair blazed in the shimmering light, and Ron looked as if he had actually wilted and was being dragged down by the weight of the camera around his neck. The two of them leaned up against the side of the building and lit cigarettes, apparently waiting to talk to some of the people still inside.

I got out, crossed my arms, and leaned against the hot fender. After about five minutes, the congregation milling around the front door had grown to over a hundred including Cindy Thompson, Curly Ahearn, and Frankie Tall Bull, who's so lofty his head and shoulders stood well above the crowd. Sottile, dressed in a lightweight blue suit, white shirt, and tie, was standing on the top step consoling the last of the mourners to come out, Trace and Cassie Buchanan.

Since Carl had been cremated, there was no casket, no hearse waiting around for the body, and no rite at the cemetery to follow the church observance. Still, nobody was in a big hurry to leave, seemingly content to hang around in the stifling warmth and pass the time of day.

Eventually, some people left for their cars, and the crowd began to thin out. That's when I noticed Annie Quinn among the mourners, standing in a group that looked like the university crowd. Dressed in a black sheath dress, hose, heels, and a black tailored jacket, she was even wearing black designer sunglasses in keeping with the somber occasion. From what I could see, however, her mood was anything but gloomy. She was chatting happily with her colleagues, laughing whenever someone said something particularly witty.

When Trace had finished his visit with Reverend Sottile, he whispered something in Cassie's ear and left her standing on the steps of the church while he joined Quinn and the assembled academics. There were handshaking and condolences all around as his friends expressed their sorrow at his loss, but when he came to Quinn, he got more than a handshake. The good professor wrapped her arms around his neck and pressed her body against his in a bear hug that ended with a tender kiss on the cheek. I don't think anybody else in the group saw it, but when their little grope was over, Trace dropped his left hand down to squeeze her fanny, the kind of intimate gesture that's common between lovers, but not standard practice between platonic colleagues. She responded with a radiant smile and returned the intimacy by dabbing her lipstick from his cheek with a handkerchief.

They still had their arms around each other when a thick-bodied man with long brown hair and wearing an ill-fitting black suit went to Quinn's side and said something to her that caused all of them to look in my direction. I could see the hatred in Trace's eyes all the way across the parking lot when he recognized me, and his whole body seemed to tense. Quinn said something to Trace and the heavy man, and then stalked away angrily in the direction of the parking lot. When she'd found her car and was opening the door, Trace and his companion began walking quickly toward me, their fists balled like they were getting ready to fight.

I stood my ground and waited for them, but I took a better hold on my blackthorn stick, just in case. It took them about five seconds to cover the tarmac between us. Trace's cheeks were flushed, and I could tell his adrenaline was pumping, but the other guy was a cool customer. He came to a halt at Trace's side, standing loose, his dark, empty eyes watching me like a rattlesnake regarding a mouse.

"What the hell are you doing here?" Trace growled. "What makes you think you're welcome?"

I didn't look at Trace when I answered him, but just stared into the eyes of the other man, taking his measure. In his early thirties, he might have started out as handsome, but he hadn't ended up that way. His nose was lumpy from being broken repeatedly, and his face was webbed by small fine scars that stood out against his sun-browned skin. His fists were large with the kind of knobby knuckles you get from hitting things. He looked like a former boxer, maybe a practitioner of some other martial art. Whatever it was, judging from his nose and the scars on his face, he'd taken his share of punishment. He was breathing through an open mouth, and I could see a gold canine tooth in his maw. Had someone knocked the original out, or was that just his idea of manly jewelry? "I didn't think I'd be welcome, and that's why I stayed out here," I said calmly. "As to what I'm doing here, Trace, I'm the chief of police in this town. I can be anywhere I damned well please." I nodded toward the other man. "This a friend of yours? I don't think we've been introduced."

"My cousin," Trace answered grudgingly. "Bandy Dowd."

I nodded, but didn't offer to shake hands. "Pleased, I'm sure," I said. "At times like this, it's important for families to come together." I smiled at Trace, pointedly dismissing Bandy Dowd as inconsequential, letting him know I thought he was no great shakes. "Where'd your girlfriend go? She leave already?"

"Fuck you, Starbranch," he said. "She's not my girlfriend."

"Oh?" I asked, surprised. "She let everybody grab her tush like that?"

I don't know for sure what I thought I was doing, but a voice in the back of my head was arguing fairly strenuously that provoking Trace into a confrontation at his brother's memorial service was a very bad idea. Trouble was, once again my mouth seemed to be acting without input from my brain, an unfortunate affliction that's gotten me whipped on more than one occasion. Unless I could think of a way out quickly, it was looking like it might happen again. I already knew I was more than a match for Trace, but Bandy Dowd looked like a different breed of cat. And even if I got lucky with Dowd, I wouldn't last long against the two of them.

"Seems to me like you could use some manners," Bandy Dowd said, his face as expressionless as a hunk of granite. He began moving slowly to his left, forcing me to turn my body to follow him. Pretty soon, I'd have my back to Trace, and that wasn't a good position to be in at all. "Maybe I could teach you."

Say what you want about Harry Starbranch, at least he talks a good game when he's cornered. "I don't know how it is where you live, but in Victory we frown on people who assault police officers," I told him. "You want to go to jail? Because if you do, I'll put you there." Mr. Big Shot. I brought the blackthorn up like a staff. If he came at me, I might be able to whack him on the temple with the knob. Then again, he might take it away and beat me to death with it.

I don't know what he found so amusing, but his smile was the only real expression I'd seen on his face so far. "Chief, when I get through with you, you won't be in any condition to do anything," he said. "By the time you come to, I'll already be back in Montana." He brought his fists up and began to square off, still circling, but now on the balls of his feet. "Trace says you think you're pretty tough. Why don't we see if you're right?"

I could sense Trace moving behind me as I circled slowly with Bandy Dowd, and I expected a blow to the back of the head at any second. I didn't watch Dowd's hands, because I learned a long time ago that if a man is going to telegraph a punch, the message won't be in his fists but in his eyes. I didn't see anything in those eyes as he moved, but I saw surprise registered in them when Trace Buchanan came flying across my peripheral field of vision and crashed into the fender of the Jeep. Air whooshed from his lungs, and he bounced off the fender and landed on his butt in the dirt. Before he could get up under his own power, Frankie Bull picked him up by the back of his suit coat and stood him up, one-handed. "Stay there," he said. Then my enormous second-in-command calmly removed his hat and set it on the hood of the vehicle, removed his coat, folded it, and laid it gently beside the hat, like he was getting ready for bed. He came to my side, his arms hanging limply, no worries in the world. I noticed that despite his casual demeanor, his legs were in a classic karate T-stance, from which he could launch his huge body into a hundred offensive or defensive maneuvers. I couldn't be sure, but I'd swear Bandy noticed it too. "You have a problem, Harry?" Frankie asked softly, his eyes locked on Bandy Dowd's.

"Not anymore," I said. I nodded toward Dowd. "I think this gentleman was just leaving. Going home to Montana."

Bandy Dowd looked for about two seconds as if he thought he might try his luck against Frankie Bull after all, but he saw something in Frankie's face he didn't like—like the end of the world—

and his common sense prevailed. He dropped his fists and nodded to Frankie, one junkyard dog to another. Not today, his look said. Maybe never. Then he walked to Trace, took him firmly by the elbow. "Come on," he said. "Your mom's waitin'."

Trace looked as if he couldn't believe what he was hearing. Maybe he thought Bandy was invincible. Maybe he'd never seen him back down from anything. Then again, maybe he'd never seen him face to face with anyone like Frankie Tall Bull. Someone who looked as if he could rip your spine out and use your tailbone to pick his teeth. It's easy to be brave when somebody else's ass is on the line. Trace glared at his cousin, who ignored him completely. Bandy started to lead him away, but before they'd gone five steps, Trace wrenched himself loose and turned back to where Frankie and I were standing beside the Jeep. His face was contorted with rage and humiliation. "I'll see you again," he hissed.

He started to say something else, but the very sensible Bandy Dowd grabbed him and dragged him away, Trace grunting with every painful step.

If he twisted Trace's arm any harder, I imagined it would snap like a twig.

SEVENTEEN

If you calculated the time in dog years, the next forty-eight hours seemed to last around eleven months, and the waiting for Keegan almost drove me crazy.

Frankie had been more than happy to take me up on my offer of a couple of days off and had spirited his wife off to see an exhibit called "Season of the Buffalo" at the Plains Indians Museum in Cody, leaving me to man the fort by my lonesome. I spent the first morning catching up on every bit of paperwork I'd been putting off for the last six weeks, and after that I did something I rarely do, went out and wrote a few traffic tickets to the tourists passing through that day. Then, satisfied that I had made my personal contribution to Victory's municipal coffers for the entire quarter, I spent some time working an investigation that had been plaguing us for months—the regular slaughter of Ernesto Varga's roosters.

Ernesto, who lives within the city limits, had been in direct violation of local ordinances for years by keeping a henhouse on his property and raising goats in his backyard. Most of his neighbors didn't complain about the chickens, because they appreciated the eggs he sold them every week, but a few had drawn the line when his goats started slipping out a hole in the fence and devouring their decorative flowers (the goats seemed to have a special appetite for tulips). As a compromise, Ernesto agreed to give up the voracious goats as long as he could keep the chickens, and that had apparently smoothed everyone's feathers.

236

The previous spring, however, Ernesto came outside one morning to feed his birds, and while the hens were perfectly happy and laying according to schedule, every one of his three roosters had recently died from a broken neck. He put the roosters in the stew pot and replaced them immediately, only to have the whole thing happen again a month later, and again a month after that. To date, he'd replaced the birds five times, always with the same result, and he was getting sick of it. His most recent batch of cocks had been in the coop for almost a week, and he was getting tired of staying up all night in the hope of catching the rooster slayer in the act.

"I'm gonna fall asleep one of these nights, and that's when they'll come," he told me when he called that afternoon. "Maybe I ought to buy a Rottweiler."

"Don't buy one yet," I told him. "Dog like that'll kill *all* your chickens, not just the roosters. Why don't you give me another crack at solving this thing, so you can get some sleep?"

I should point out that this wasn't the first time Ernesto's birds had come under attack. A couple of years before, some racist, right-wing morons trying to scare him into leaving town had poisoned all of his chickens. I didn't think that was the case this time, however. In the first place, the right-wingers who'd caused the problem before were dead. In the second, whoever was terminating his birds with extreme prejudice was being very selective in executing only the males, which suggested a motive unrelated to the fact that Ernesto is Hispanic. Over the months, either Frankie or I had talked to most of his neighbors and various other usual suspects, but had failed to turn up a promising lead.

It was a mystery, is what it was, right up my alley.

Ernesto agreed to hold off on buying a dog for the time being, and between us, we came up with a sting operation I thought I'd put into action that night. As the sun was setting, Ernesto and his wife, Mercedes, made a very big deal of piling all of their kids into his geriatric Chevy Suburban and driving off for an evening of entertainment at Cheyenne's Frontier Days. Before they left, Ernesto and the kids mentioned their plans to as many of their neighbors as they could without seeming too obvious, as well as their intention to stay until the place shut down for the night. They wouldn't be home until well after midnight, maybe later.

I watched them drive past the office on the way out of town, and then I read an Elmore Leonard novel until it was fully dark. When I was sure the night would cover my movements, I turned off the lights at the office, locked the door, and then made my way down the street to Ernesto's backyard, keeping to the shadows like an old-time spy.

There's an old saying that one man's junk is another man's treasure, so I guess you could say Ernesto's backyard is absolutely full of booty. Because he makes his living as what used to be known as a jack-of-all-trades, fixing everything from washing machines and leaky plumbing to chain saws and antique motorcycles, he acquires a lot of stuff that people he works for no longer want but he figures might be worth fixing. He drags most of the refuse home and parks it in his yard to await rehabilitation, so there was no problem finding a place to hide once I got to his house. I just tucked myself between a rusty Maytag washing machine and the hulk of an orange Volkswagen Beetle resting on concrete blocks, made myself a little pillow of my jacket, and leaned back with my hands behind my head to look at the stars.

It was a nice evening, the ground was still warm from the scorching afternoon sun, and it wasn't long before I drifted off, dreaming of an afternoon on the farm in La Junta when I was a kid, the smell of fresh-cut hay in my nostrils and a girl named Pickle who lived on the place next door and rode an Appaloosa mare named Zanona. Some of my favorite memories of childhood are of riding bareback with her through emerald-green fields of alfalfa high enough to graze her horse's belly, her legs long and brown in shorts, her blond hair flowing behind her like a mane. I haven't seen her in over twenty years, but she still visits me regularly in my dreams. Unlike me, she hasn't aged a day.

I don't think I've ever solved a case in my sleep before, but that's what happened a couple of hours later when I was awakened by the sound of chickens squawking and someone thumping around inside Ernesto's coop. Through the windows I could see the slim beam of the intruder's flashlight playing against the walls of the coop, and I could hear him cursing as he banged around inside the small building. I sat up, rubbed the sleep from my eyes, unsnapped the safety catch on my Blackhawk, and picked up my own flashlight, one of those industrial-sized things that can either be used to light airport runways or as a club more devastating than a medieval war mallet. Then I tiptoed to the gate of the chain-link fence that encloses the coop, slipped through as quietly as possible, and eased through the opened door of the shack.

The intruder, who was holding his flashlight in his mouth, had his back to me. He was apparently having trouble controlling the agitated rooster he was holding under one arm while he tried to ring its neck with his free hand. I snapped on my light and shined it in his face before he could complete his act of mayhem, however, and I've got to say I was surprised to see the squinting, wrinkled face of Hugo Krassner at the end of my beam. Hugo, a toothless, octagenarian retiree from the Union Pacific Railroad, is Ernesto's next-door neighbor, and as far as I knew, he and his wife, Hortense, had been on the best of terms with the Vargas for years. My sudden appearance startled him so badly he dropped the struggling rooster, which flapped off in an indignant huff. "Hugo," I sputtered. "What the hell are you doing here?"

Although I'm sure he couldn't see my face behind the bright beam of my light, he certainly recognized my voice. "Oh, crap," he muttered. "Now I suppose I'm gonna get arrested. That'd be the perfect end to a perfect day."

He looked so dejected and pitiful I almost laughed. "You know, Hugo, sometimes you get up in the mornin' and it's just not worth the effort of puttin' in your teeth to eat your breakfast," I told him. "I guess I probably am gonna arrest you, unless you have a damned good explanation for all this. You care to tell me why you've turned to murdering chickens in your golden years?"

Hugo snorted and sat down on a crate. He pulled a can of chew from the pocket of his overalls and tucked a wad in his cheek. "Golden years, my ass," he said when his tobacco was situated.

239

"I'm eighty-five years old, Harry. I got a pacemaker, my pizzle don't work proper, my feet got bunions, I go through Preparation H like water, and the only thing I'm ever hungry for is mashed potatoes. I didn't complain, though, because at least I could always get a good night's sleep."

He stopped talking, as if that explained everything. "The roosters," I reminded him. "What does that have to do with the roosters?"

He shook his head, apparently unable to believe my stupidity. "Everything," he said. "About three, four months ago, my rhythms changed for some reason, and I suddenly couldn't sleep at night. I could only sleep during the day. That's when I started noticing it."

I was becoming more and more confused. "What?"

"The noise," he said. "At night, these birds are asleep, nice and quiet, but once the sun comes up they get real sprightly. You ever heard a bunch of roosters and chickens in a love frenzy, Harry? That's all they do is screw, all day long, and the squawkin' and screechin' and carryin' on is unbelievable. So damned noisy it makes a John Philip Sousa march seem celestial by comparison, and I don't care for tuba music. Nobody can sleep through that. Even them fancy swimmer's earplugs didn't help."

"Why didn't you complain to Ernesto?" I asked.

Hugo shrugged his sloping shoulders. " 'Cause I like him, that's why," he said. "He's been good to me and the wife, and I didn't want no hard feelings. I like Ernesto. It's his roosters I can't stand."

There was a rooster sitting on the only other crate inside the coop, eyeing us both suspiciously. I shooed him off and sat down. "So you've been sneaking over here at night to ring their necks?"

Hugo's ancient head bobbed, his shriveled face so sad he looked like a beagle. "Yeah, I guess so, but I didn't figure it was all that wrong," he said. "I wouldn't take food out of those kids' mouths, so I didn't steal them birds. I just killed 'em. Got myself a little peace and quiet 'til he bought himself a new batch." He stood up and held his hands toward me so I could slap the handcuffs on, like he'd seen bad guys do in the movies. "Eighty-five years, and the only time I ever got arrested was in nineteen-thirty-two when

I whacked a railroad bull on the head with a pair of pliers. That old boy dropped the charges, but I guess I'll have a record now, huh? Hortense is gonna kill me."

I stood up and shook my head. I'd made a wise and compassionate command decision, which as chief of police I had the authority to do. It's good to be the boss. "I'm not gonna arrest you, Hugo," I told him.

What passed for a hopeful look crossed his wizened face. "You're not?"

"Nope," I said. "But you are gonna pay Ernesto for all those roosters you killed, and you are gonna promise not to do it again. My guess is, the Vargas won't want to press charges, and if you tell 'em the truth, they might even do something about the noise. That way, maybe both you and Ernesto can get your beauty rest."

That was what he needed to hear. From a second pocket he pulled a half-pint of cheap bourbon, unscrewed the cap, and took a pull. He grimaced as it burned its way down. Then he offered the bottle to me to seal the deal. He looked almost grateful when I declined. "I hope so," he said, giving me a toothless grin. "I'm too damned old for a life of crime."

Ken Keegan's call came about nine the next evening, just as Cindy and I were settling in at my place for a Kevin Costner double feature on video. I'd lobbied for "Dances with Wolves," even though I've seen it around a billion times, and she'd agreed, as long as we could follow it up with "The Bodyguard." We were just at the point in the movie where Kicking Bird tries to steal Dunbar's smart horse when the phone rang. "Shit," I grumbled. I extricated my arm from around Cindy, hit the mute button on the remote, and padded to the phone wearing nothing but my bathrobe and a scowl. "Starbranch," I said.

"Harry," Keegan said, and even in that single word I could hear crushing fatigue and excitement at the same time. "Hope I didn't catch you at a bad time."

"No, I'm not doing anything important," I said. I looked at Cindy in time to see her roll her eyes.

"Good," he said. "I'm just on my way to pick up Trace Buchanan for questioning and thought you probably deserved to come along. Meet me at the police station in forty-five minutes?"

"Make it thirty," I said, but I don't know if he heard me because I had slammed the receiver down and was dashing for my clothes before he could answer.

On the drive to Laramie, my heart raced almost as fast as my engine, but I made the trip in record time, speedometer buried and passing everything in sight. Keegan was waiting in the parking lot of the police department, leaning against the fender of his government-issue Ford and smoking a cigarette, his squat body foreshortened in the light of the mercury-vapor lamp illuminating the lot. I started talking before I was even out of the Jeep.

"Trace's prints . . . ," I said.

He flipped his cigarette to the asphalt and ground the butt under the sole of his wingtip. "Were all over everything," he said. "The steering wheel of Carl's pickup, all over the rest of the truck, the cellular phone. The whole deal. I got the results back this morning."

"This morning? Then why didn't you call sooner?"

He laughed. "Easy, Sherlock," he said. "I had to go down to Fort Collins and take a statement from that prostitute, Missy Poteet, and she isn't an easy woman to find." He patted the pocket of his suit coat. "After that, I had to get a search warrant for his house and another one to take physical samples from his person. The team will show up at his place in a while, and go through it while Trace is downtown for questioning. With any luck, this murdering bastard has spent his last night as a free man for a very long time."

We didn't talk much on the way to Buchanan's house, both of us a little uncomfortable about the way we'd left it the last time we met and not quite willing to bring our feelings out in the open. Plenty of time for that later.

Although the afternoon had been hot and dry, a storm was moving in from the north, and high clouds scudded across the face of the quarter moon. The wind was loud in the leaves of the poplar and willow trees along the streets, and the air already smelled like rain.

Trace's car was in the driveway, and we parked on the street in front of his house. It looked like he'd finally cut his grass, but he'd done it in uneven rows, and long tufts stuck up in the places he'd missed. His porch light was off, and the house was dark, except for the flickering light of a television coming through the open front door. We climbed the porch and could see him sitting in a recliner, watching a sitcom. He looked up when we knocked. "Jesus, don't you ever give up?" he asked when he recognized my face. He was clad in blue jeans, sneakers, and a T-shirt with a picture of Albert Einstein wearing a beanie and a mathematical equation below his face in large letters saying, "2+2=5, for extremely large values of 2." University professor humor, apparently. He had an opened can of Coors between his legs. Three empties sat on the coffee table beside his chair.

Keegan didn't wait for an invitation, just let himself in through the screen door with me following in his wake. My square friend came to a stop in the middle of the room and put his hands on his hips, a movement that exposed both the sweat stains on his shirt and his shoulder holster. "We're here to have a little talk about the murder of Victoria Austin," Keegan said.

Trace took a long drink of his beer, finished it, and crushed the can. He threw the empty on top of the table with the others, and it landed with a tinny clank. "That case is closed," he said angrily.

"Not anymore," Keegan told him flatly, his voice like a buzz saw tearing through a pine plank. "I officially reopened it two days ago."

Trace looked guardedly back and forth from Keegan to me. "And now you're another one thinks I had something to do with it?" he asked. He nodded in my direction. "You been listening to Tweedledum? That must make you Tweedledumber."

Keegan didn't laugh at Trace's beery humor, and neither did I. Keegan, in fact, looked as serious as cancer. "That's exactly what I think," he said. "And unless you have a very good explanation of how your prints turned up all over your brother's pickup and how you ended up in Fort Collins with him the morning after the murder, you're coming downtown with me until we get to the bottom of it." He pulled a sheaf of folded papers from his pocket and threw them in Trace's lap. "While we're at it, those papers are a search warrant for your house, and one for your person. We'll be executing them tonight, as well."

Trace opened the warrants and tried to read them in the weak light of the television, but he gave up inside of ten seconds. He made a big production of wadding the warrants in a ball and tossing them at Keegan's feet. "Fuck that," he snarled. "I'm not going anywhere."

"I don't think you have a choice," Keegan growled.

What happened next was completely unexpected and over in less time than it takes to tell it.

Keegan smiled thinly and began to pull his handcuffs from the leather pouch on the back of his belt. Trace dropped his hand to his side, reaching for something hidden between his body and the arm of the recliner. When his hand came back up, it was full of chrome-plated .380 automatic. Buchanan thumbed the hammer back and began to raise the pistol.

My mind and Keegan's registered danger at the same instant, and we both went for our weapons. We were both too late.

I dove for the floor, frantically grabbing for the safety strap on the Blackhawk. Still standing above me, Keegan was reaching for his nine-millimeter, but his hand had barely touched the butt of the automatic when the muzzle blast of Trace's .380 leapt toward him, seeming to link the men with bright yellow flame. The first slug took him high in the left shoulder, staggering Keegan backward. The second, which followed so closely the report sounded like an extension of the first, hit him in the right eye, exited the back of his head, and splattered hunks of brain matter all over the white living room wall.

As my friend fell to the floor, Trace flew up from his recliner, screaming incoherently as he swung the weapon toward me, firing as he came. The first shot hit the wall well above me, but the second whizzed past my head so closely I could hear the buzzing whine of the bullet above the roar of the blast. The third grazed the skin of my neck. It burned, like a long gash from a white hot razor.

By then, the Blackhawk was in my hand, but by the time I had it cocked and pointed in Trace's general direction, he was already running. I fired blindly, and the bullet knocked a hole in the wall a good three feet behind him as he scurried out of the living room through the kitchen door. I could hear his footsteps pounding on the kitchen tile, so I fired a second shot through the wall, hoping the slug would tear through the sheetrock and find him in the next room. It didn't. A split second later, I heard him hit the back door and crash through into the cloudy night.

Then he was gone.

I knew I should chase him, bring him down, but my hands were shaking so badly I couldn't get my weapon back in the holster. When I finally had it seated, I stood up. My legs were trembling as badly as my hands. I could barely walk. There was no way I could run. Blood was flowing from the wound on my neck, and it made a dark stain around the collar of my shirt. I was hardly aware of it, paid it no attention.

On television, Al and Peg Bundy were arguing because he never took her to bed. The studio audience laughed hysterically. On his back in the middle of the floor with his remaining eye wide open, Keegan seemed to be watching. He wasn't laughing. He was moaning. Still alive, if only barely.

I found a phone on the kitchen wall, dialed 911, and told the dispatcher to send an ambulance and backup. Then I came back into the living room and knelt at Keegan's side. I picked him up and cradled his ruined head in my lap. I could feel the wetness of his warm blood as it soaked through the denim of my jeans. His breath was coming in ragged gasps, and when he exhaled, blood bubbled from his mouth and nostrils. I turned his head until his staring, unfocused eye looked into my own, and then I tried to hold his brains in gently with the tips of my fingers. I used my free hand to grasp Keegan's, and even though I'm not sure he was aware of my presence, I swear he returned the pressure of my grip. There was a tear in the corner of his eye, whether from pain or involuntary reaction, I didn't know. It rolled slowly down his cheek, mixing with his blood.

Tears of rage, frustration, and gut-wrenching sadness were leaking from my eyes as well. There was nothing I could do but make him comfortable. Make sure he didn't cross the river alone. A day that began so perfectly had gone horribly wrong. "You just lie quiet," I told him softly. "Help'll be here before you know it. You're gonna be all right."

But of course, that was a lie. He would never be all right.

Ken Keegan died in my arms before the first paramedics arrived.

EIGHTEEN

The paramedics tried to revive my friend, but it was a pointless effort. When his big heart stopped beating, it stopped forever. I rode in the ambulance with Keegan's body and sat with him at the hospital until James Bowen, the mortician who serves as the county coroner, sent a hearse to pick him up. Only then would I let the emergency-room doctor dress the wound on my neck. It was no big deal and looked a lot worse than it was, so I turned down the doc's offer of a mild painkiller because I wanted a clear head when I went to meet the small army of cops from the Department of Criminal Investigation, the Laramie police, and the sheriff's department who were waiting in the lobby to talk to me.

There's nothing quite as determined as a group of heavily armed law officers eager for some payback, but despite their bloody resolve to bring the cop killer in, it looked like he'd slipped through their nets for the time being.

The first officers on the scene put out an all-points bulletin within minutes of arriving, but a thorough search of the neighborhood came up empty. About an hour after the manhunt began, a homeowner four blocks from where Trace lived called in to report that his four-wheel-drive Toyota had been stolen from his driveway. Since Trace had escaped on foot after the murder without his own vehicle, everyone believed he'd stolen the missing Toyota.

Which meant he could be almost anywhere. There are 4,392 square miles of ground in Albany County, and only about thirty thousand people to fill them. Since about twenty-seven thousand of those live within the nine or so square miles occupied by Laramie, you're pretty much alone once you get past the city limits. And that's only if he stayed in Albany County and didn't run for any of the other twenty thousand square miles of virtually empty real estate in southeastern Wyoming.

There was also a good chance he was already out of state. The highway patrol had put up roadblocks on the major highways leading out of Laramie in all four directions, but since they didn't get them in place for a good sixty minutes after the shooting, Trace would have had more than enough time to cross the border into Colorado by heading due south and nearly enough time to get to the Nebraska line heading east.

If he was still in town, the search would turn him up sooner or later, but if he'd gotten out of Laramie, it would take more than a small army of cops to find him. It would take a division and a lot of luck.

Naturally, I wanted to be out looking for Buchanan along with everyone else, but there was not much chance of that. As soon as the doctor kicked me loose with instructions to change the bandage that covered the entire left side of my neck regularly and to apply the antibiotic salve he'd given me twice a day, Derrick Bell, Keegan's taciturn boss at the DCI, bundled me into his car and sped me to an interrogation room at the police department, where I spent the next four hours going over the details of Keegan's death about a thousand times.

Because Keegan had filled his superiors in on his reasons for reopening the investigation into Victoria Austin's death, I didn't have to cover that well-trodden ground. But they wanted to know exactly how and why my friend had died while the images were still fresh in my mind. They also wanted to pick my brain clean of anything I might know about Trace and his life that would help them make an arrest.

There wasn't much I could give them, but as a result of our talks, officers were dispatched to Cassie's house in Victory and to speak with Annie Quinn.

Cassie, who was asleep and alone, said she hadn't spoken to Trace all day. Two officers were left to watch her house and wait, in case Trace sought refuge with his mother.

When the cops rousted Quinn out of bed at around three in the morning, she was also alone and assured everyone she hadn't seen or spoken to Trace since his brother's memorial service. Bell's investigators told her not to leave town and that she should present herself at the police department the next morning at ten for questioning.

Although Quinn and Cassie were no help, the search team working Trace's house while I was at the hospital turned up some very interesting evidence. Tucked away in a shoe box in his attic, behind boxes of Christmas decorations, were a three-foot piece of bloody clothesline rope, a pair of women's panties, and a brassiere. Bell rushed those off to the DCI crime lab in Cheyenne for testing, but he and everyone else believed the blood on the rope and the trace evidence on the underwear would be linked to Victoria Austin. Bell reminded another of the DCI investigators with us in the interrogation room of a detail I'd overlooked in the reams of investigative and forensic reports: although the killer had dressed Austin in pants and blouse after the murder, no undergarments were found on her corpse.

"My guess is he kept 'em as souvenirs," Bell said.

Keeping trophies or reminders is fairly common among killers—even those who aren't serial killers. I realized that the fact that the evidence would almost certainly have been found in the search may have been the reason why Trace reacted so violently when Keegan and I went to take him in for questioning. Like a cornered animal, Trace knew that if he didn't make his escape at that moment, he might never have another chance.

I also realized that Keegan and I both should have been prepared for that reaction. The fact that we weren't, that we'd underestimated Trace Buchanan and let him get the drop on us, was lethally sloppy police procedure. A couple of tough law-enforcement professionals, ten feet tall and bulletproof, we'd apparently started believing our own press. We'd been so arrogant, so self-confident, that we hadn't been ready, and we'd let a university professor outgun us. We'd made a rookie blunder, and Keegan had paid for it with his life. I figured I'd be paying for it the rest of mine.

I was bone-weary and emotionally numb when the DCI contingent finally decided they'd pumped my mental bank dry and told me I was free to stay or go as I pleased. I was tired but I wasn't about to take myself out of the action. All I needed was a refresher. I figured I'd go to the house, grab a quick shower and a gallon of black coffee, and be back in time to join the search for Buchanan a little after daybreak.

When I left the interrogation room, however, I almost ran into Margie Keegan, who was being comforted in the hallway by Derrick Bell, who had his arms around Ken's widow while she cried into his shoulder. A stout, earthy woman who loves dark beer and a good dirty joke, Margie teaches pottery classes at Laramie County Community College in Cheyenne and owns a small boutique near the state capitol building, where she sells her own work. She was dressed in baggy denim pants, a U.W. sweatshirt, and white sneakers with no laces, and her long, salt-and-pepper hair looked like she'd just gotten out of bed, which was probably the truth. Knowing Margie, nothing could have stopped her from racing over the mountain between Cheyenne and Laramie as soon as she'd gotten the news. When she saw me, she whispered something in Bell's ear, kissed him on the cheek, turned, and held her arms open for me. We wrapped each other in a comforting embrace, and when she finally pulled away, she touched the bandages on my neck gently. "Is it bad?" she asked softly.

"Just a scratch," I told her.

"Thank God," she said. She took my hands in her own. "I don't think I could stand to lose both of you." She led me to a wooden bench at the side of the hall, and we sat facing each other.

I had so much to say to her I didn't know where to start. "I'm so sorry, Margie. This is all my fault. If only I had . . ."

She didn't let me finish, but held a finger to my lips to quiet me. "Ken told me everything," she said. "I know why he had to be there, and I know you would have kept him from getting shot if

250

you could. I know you, and you've probably been wishing you could have taken that bullet yourself."

I hung my head and didn't answer. Words would not pass the growing lump in my throat. I felt as if I couldn't breathe.

"I want you to listen to me, Harry, because what I have to say is very important," she said. I looked into her sad, red-rimmed eyes, waited silently for her to continue. "I've been the wife of a policeman for most of my life, and I know that what happened to Ken was *not* your fault. I don't believe it was your fault. Nobody else in this room believes it. And if I ever hear you say that again, I'll slap you so hard your ears ring. I need you strong, Harry. I need your shoulder to lean on. I don't need you so filled with self-pity you can't function."

"I can function," I told her. "I'm gonna catch this bastard, Margie. You can count on it."

Margie's eyes sparked. She gestured toward the cops crowding the small police department. "That's their job," she said. "You're in no condition for a manhunt. You'll just get yourself hurt."

"But I need to be . . ."

She caressed my cheek. "You need to be with me, Harry," she said. "When I leave here, I've got to go to the mortuary and make a formal identification of my husband, and then I've got to find a way to get through the rest of the day. I've got to start making funeral arrangements, I've got to talk to reporters, and I've got to call our kids at college and find a way to tell them what happened to their father. I've got to talk to Ken's family, to my family. I've got to do a thousand things I haven't even thought of yet, and unless you stay with me, I've got to do it all alone. I know it's a lot to ask, Harry, but I need you to lean on, just for this one day."

As much as I wanted to be in on the hunt for Trace Buchanan, I knew I couldn't refuse her request. I owed Ken, and her, at least that much. I put my arm around her and helped her up. She leaned into me for support. "I'm here for as long as you want," I told her. "Just tell me where you want to start."

Margie took my arm and held on, began leading me toward the door. The hum of conversation stopped as we passed, the cops paying their respects. "I want to start by getting you a clean shirt," she said. "That one's covered in blood."

Late that afternoon, I'd done as much as I could for Margie for the time being, and I was running out of gas. I was so tired that everything around me seemed almost surreal. Margie and I had made funeral arrangements for her husband, called every relative in her Rolodex, and stalled a half-dozen reporters who were after interviews. Keegan's death was too late for the morning papers, but it was the top story on all the local radio and television stations. The network affiliates in Denver had even picked it up and used it to lead their noon broadcasts.

Margie and Ken's two children were flying home from college that evening, but I didn't need to hang around to pick them up. A couple of Margie's friends from the community college dropped by around four and offered to stay with her and drive her to the airport. I saw Margie down for a rest and waited until I was sure she was comfortable. Then I hopped in the Jeep and hit the highway for the ride back over the mountain to Laramie.

It had rained off and on all the previous night and all day, and the sky was still choked with low-hanging, pewter clouds that seemed to suck the color from the landscape, turning the foothills and Medicine Bow National Forest into a muted palette of browns, coppery reds, and greens so deep they were almost black. The air seemed thick and oppressive, and even the ubiquitous scents of pine and sagebrush, usually so comforting, were heavy and cloying. I was so tired that I was almost hallucinating, and I knew I should probably pull over in a rest area before I dozed off at the wheel. I couldn't afford the indulgence of sleep, however, so I slowed down to about forty-five and crept along with both hands clamped on the steering wheel and an old Commander Cody album I'd found in the tape box blasting so loudly I was afraid my ears would start to bleed.

The technique got me to the Laramie Police Department in one piece, and when I went inside, I found the crowd had thinned considerably since morning. As a matter of fact, the only people in the bullpen were the dispatcher, two patrolmen doing paperwork, and Chief Tommy Carroll, who was at the front desk, deep in conversation with county prosecutor Walker Tisdale.

The last time I'd talked to Walker, he'd threatened to put me in jail and run me out of office if I continued to "slander" and harass Trace Buchanan. He'd refused to reopen Austin's murder investigation himself, claiming there was as much chance of my finding proof against Trace as there was of a meteor falling out of the sky to crush my skull. Once again, he'd proven himself to be a negligent bumbler, and I couldn't help reminding him of that fact. If he'd listened when I came to him, Keegan might still be alive. "Hello, Walker," I said, my voice dripping with antagonistic sarcasm. I looked heavenward, as if waiting for a stony deluge from outer space. "You think I ought to buy a hard hat?"

If I expected one of his profane comebacks, I was mistaken. As the man who had sent Carl to death row, Walker was in deep trouble and he knew it. The knowledge seemed to have humbled him considerably. "Harry, I'm glad you're here," he said. "We need to have a talk."

I shook my head no. "This isn't a good time, Walker," I said. "Give me three or four days, and I'll see how my schedule looks."

"Five minutes?" he asked hopefully, but I ignored him.

I turned to Carroll—a lanky Texan with sandy brush-cut hair, leathery skin, and smile lines around his eyes—who'd been listening with some amusement. "Any luck?"

"Not a bit," he said. "The highway patrol and the sheriff still have people on all the highways, but Trace hasn't come through and we haven't found him in town, either. I don't know where he got to, but it's like he dropped off the face of the earth. Don't worry though, we'll get him sooner or later."

"Mind if I hang out with some of your people?" I asked. "Maybe later I'll go out and help man one of the roadblocks."

Carroll looked me up and down. "You look like hell, Harry," he said. "Why don't you go home and get some rest? I'll call you if anything happens."

I smiled weakly. "There'll be plenty of time for sleep later," I said. "For now, I need to be a part of things. You understand, don't you?"

Tommy Carroll, who got his start as a patrol officer on the violent streets of Houston and who, like me, worked homicide before moving to Wyoming, had been a cop long enough that he understood very well. "Suit yourself," Carroll said. "Wait here, and I'll radio in one of the detectives for you to ride with."

When Tommy went off to make the call, Walker hooked a thumb over his shoulder toward a small, empty interview room off the lobby. "Come on, Harry," he said. "Five minutes in private. Please?"

The last place I wanted to be was a closed room with Walker Tisdale, because I was afraid I might be overcome with the urge to strangle him with my bare hands. Still, he wasn't the sort to go away if he was ignored. I scowled and followed him to the interview room, sat in one of the metal chairs, and waited while he closed the door. The room was hot and smelled like a combination of sweat, dust, and old gym socks. One tattered poster on the wall, a holdover from the Reagan era, encouraged kids to "Just Say No" to drugs. Another, featuring Officer McGruff, the dog detective, exhorted us to "Take a Bite Out of Crime." Some miscreant had scratched out most of the word "Crime" and substituted "my ass" in scrawled magic marker.

Walker made sure the door was locked and sat in the other chair, his face the picture of concern and sympathy, the hypocrite. "I'm very sorry about your friend," he said. "But how are you holding up?"

As if the smarmy weasel cared. "Just about how you'd expect, Walker," I said. "I haven't slept in over twenty-four hours, and I might not sleep for another twenty-four. I've been shot at and wounded. My friend was murdered right in front of my eyes, and I couldn't do a damned thing about it. I'll see that scene in my nightmares for the rest of my natural life. So I guess you could say I'm not holding up very well at all, but thanks so much for asking."

If Walker was stung by my tone or my attitude, he didn't let it show, which I imagined was a supreme effort. Like a professional boxer, Walker doesn't let many verbal punches go unanswered unless he's on the ropes and ready for the standing count. "Listen, Harry," he said, "I know we haven't always gotten along very well, and the last time we talked I'm sure you could have interpreted some of the things I said to be . . ."

"Moronic?" I broke in. "Insulting? I seem to remember the words 'flaming asshole' featuring pretty prominently in that conversation, Walker. Where I come from, that's pretty hard to misinterpret."

Even a trained equivocator like Walker couldn't dispute that. He could only hope to mitigate. "I was out of line, I'll admit it," he said. "But we're both on the same team, here. I just hope you won't let the past come between . . ."

"Oh, give me a break," I groaned. "We might be on the same team, if you insist on using sports metaphors, but the fact is I don't like you. I've never liked you, and I doubt I ever will. You might have a rich daddy, a fancy law degree, and enough money to eventually buy yourself a political office, but I think you're a pompous, amoral, greedy, self-serving, no-talent, feloniously incompetent dilettante. You're a charlatan, counselor. A fraud, a fake, a counterfeit, liar, pretender. You are a disgusting, putrid imitation of a human being, and standing this close to you is making me physically ill." I stood up and reached for the door. "So if you don't mind, I think I'll go somewhere else before I puke."

He reached out and grabbed my wrist to stop me before I could turn the knob, and the look I gave him let him know that if he didn't let go, I'd yank his arm out at the socket. He released his grip as if my wrist was covered in acid and held his hands up, palms outward, in apology and surrender. "Come on, Harry, calm down," he said placatingly. "I know you've been through a lot, but that's no reason to . . ."

"Exactly what is it you want, Walker?" I asked brusquely. "You've got five seconds."

Walker sat down heavily in the chair, the starch completely

gone from his spine. It looked as if it actually pained him to come to the point. "The press," he said. "Have you talked to them yet?"

The urge to reach down and throttle him was stronger than ever, almost irresistible, but I whipped it into submission. I just didn't know how long that hungry tiger would sit obediently on its stool. "I can't believe you," I said. "Two innocent people are dead because of you, at least one stone killer is on the loose, and the thing you're most worried about is how this is all going to play in the news? Or are you just worried about how your miserable part will play?" I shook my head disgustedly. "No, Walker, I haven't talked to the media yet. Why do you ask?"

"You'll have to talk to them eventually, and we both know it," Walker said.

I looked at my watch. "Make your point, Walker. You're ten seconds into overtime."

Walker took a deep breath. "OK, here it is, no sugar coating," he said. "You're going to come out of this looking like a hero again, but some of us won't be so lucky. You could make it easier on us, though. When you talk to the reporters, I won't ask you to lie, but you don't have to talk about everything you know."

I had a feeling I knew where he was going. "And the part of my memory you'd like me to ignore?"

"Look, Harry, you're gonna have a choice," he said. "You can stand up there and quietly take the credit for solving this case, and let it go at that—or you can use the pulpit to dump on everyone who didn't listen to you. It all depends on your spin. You can blame me for Carl's death and for Keegan's. You can tell everyone you came to me and I refused to listen. You can do it, but it will ruin me, Harry. I'm asking you not to do that. I promise I'll make it worth your while."

I decided to take him at his word. See if he was serious. "Will you resign?" I asked.

"What?"

"You heard me. Will you resign if I let you off the hook?"

"But why would I . . ."

I poked Walker so hard in the chest with my index finger it

staggered him backward. "Because that's the only thing you can offer me that has any value," I said.

I turned the knob, opened the door, and started walking out. At the last second, I turned back. Walker looked pasty white, and frightened. "You revolt me," I said. "You think I'm interested in taking credit for breaking this case? Considering all that's happened, you think the fact I'll get my face on the front page makes it all worthwhile? God, do you think I'm like *you?*"

"No!" Walker sputtered. "That's not what I meant at all. All I meant was . . ."

"Bullshit! That's exactly what you meant, but you're wrong! I'm not like you!" I shouted. I was losing it, barely in control. "And forget what I said about resigning voluntarily, Walker. When I get through with you this time, you won't have a choice."

I rode with Detective Danny King until almost midnight, but when I fell asleep in the front seat of his unmarked car and a particularly spectacular burst of snoring startled him so badly he almost crashed into a telephone pole, he insisted I go home and pick it up the next morning.

In the previous hours, we'd been in every bar and restaurant in Laramie, we'd been at the movie theaters, and we'd driven the university campus a dozen times. We'd sat watch with the cops who were staking out Trace's house and with the pair who were watching Quinn's. We'd driven every back road within ten miles of town, and we'd checked in with several of Trace's friends and neighbors.

All we'd gotten for our efforts were sore butts and aching feet. If Trace Buchanan was still in Laramie, it looked as if he'd figured a way to make himself invisible.

When King pulled into the rear entrance of the police department parking lot where I'd left my Jeep, I saw Sally Sheridan, the flame-haired, unrelentingly aggressive reporter for the *Casper-Star Tribune* standing on the front steps gabbing with a reporter for the *Laramie Boomerang* and a trio of other rumpled newspaper types I didn't recognize. A couple of their colleagues from the electronic media were leaning against the fenders of a van sporting the logo of the CBS affiliate in Cheyenne.

I knew why they were waiting around, and I also knew I'd be mobbed if they spotted me. I'd have to bolt, like a raccoon running from a pack of redbone hounds. Thankfully, I'd left my ride at the back of the lot, so I scrunched down in the seat and had King pull up right next to my vehicle, so I could jump out, start it up, and be off before they saw me.

The plan worked like a charm, and thirty minutes later I was back in Victory, which looked so quiet I would have sworn it was a ghost town if I hadn't known otherwise. The parking lots of the Trails End and Gus Alzonakis's steak house were almost empty, there was no traffic on the streets, and the neon lights in the windows of the bars looked lonely and forlorn. Frankie Bull's cruiser was still parked in front of the police department though, so I stopped by to check in before I called it a day.

Frankie had his feet up on the desk and was reading one of his "wife's" florid romance novels when I came in. He tried to hide it when he saw me, stuffed it in his desk drawer, and tried to pretend he'd been studying the day's incident reports instead of the steamy bodice-ripper.

"You're working late," I said, smiling to let him know I was onto him.

I think he was blushing, but on his burnished skin, it was impossible to tell for sure. "Actually, I was waiting around on the off-chance you'd stop by, and here you are," he said. "I've been listening to the radio. Still no luck with Trace?"

"No," I said, and I spent the next few minutes telling him everything that had happened in the last twenty-four hours. He nodded sympathetically at the appropriate moments, but he didn't offer any condolences. I realized that was because he knew there was nothing he could say that would ease the pain I was feeling. All he could do was be there, let me know I could call on him if I needed to. At that moment, his presence and his quiet strength were plenty.

"I'm sorry I got you into this," he said softly when I finished.

I put my hand on his shoulder. "Nothing for you to be sorry about," I said. "I'm only sorry about how it turned out."

"So is Cassie," he said.

That took me by surprise. "You talked to her?"

He nodded yes. "She called for you several times this afternoon and stopped by once," he said. "She's on the edge, Harry. I'm real worried about her."

"Me too," I said. "What does she want to talk about?"

"Well, first off, she feels horrible about what happened to Ken Keegan, and all the things she said to you," he told me. "She's had to face the truth about Trace and the enormity of what he's done to her family, and I think that may be more than she can bear. Still, she doesn't want to see him killed."

"If he won't give himself up, I don't know what I can do about that," I said.

"She's aware of that, too," Frankie said. "She wanted to know whether you'll make sure Trace isn't hurt if she can find him and talk him into giving up. She wanted to know if you'd take him in— she says you and I are the only policemen she trusts."

"Does she know where he is?" I asked.

"I don't think so," he said. "But she figures he'll eventually contact her."

"Should I call her? Stop by?" I asked.

Frankie chuckled and shook his head no. "It looks like you've had enough excitement for one day," he said. "I'm sure tomorrow will be all right. Besides, I already told her not to worry, that if she could talk Trace into surrendering, we'd make sure he got to jail in one piece."

I nodded gratefully. "Did she say anything else."

"Yeah, Harry, she said for you to be careful," he said somberly. "Says she's had a bad feeling all day."

"Not to worry," I said. I stood up, adjusted my hat, and jangled my keys. My legs were so tired I could barely support my own weight, and I leaned on the blackthorn like an ancient pensioner. My brain felt slow and mushy, and my eyes burned as if they were full of Red Desert sand. Like Rip Van Winkle, I figured I could sleep for forty years. If I didn't leave immediately, I'd end up collapsing on the office floor. "I'll go straight home, and I promise to look under the bed before I shut off the lights," I said.

Turns out, I didn't have to look that far.

NINETEEN

The lights were on, and Cindy's car was parked in the driveway when I finally arrived at the house about twenty minutes later. Although I was glad she was waiting, I hoped she didn't have anything more strenuous in mind than a hot bath, a shot of Rebel Yell, and a chaste peck on the cheek before she tucked me in.

The two old quarter horses and the Shetland pony I'd adopted after Edna Cook died were snorting and pacing in the corral the way they sometimes do before a big storm. I fed and watered them before I went inside, but instead of trooping over to see if I happened to have a couple of apples tucked in my pants pocket as they usually do, they stayed on the opposite side of the enclosure, eyeing me suspiciously, their big ears peaked, and their rear hooves cocked so they could kick out at any attack from behind. I didn't know what had spooked them; maybe a coyote down from the hills and looking for dinner had come close enough for the horses to get his scent. Tomorrow, when I had better light to work with, I'd go looking for tracks. If I found them, I'd have to set some traps.

The door was unlocked, and the lights were on when I went into the kitchen. The clock on the wall said it was two-ten, and I could hear the television going in the living room. Cindy didn't answer when I called, and I imagined she'd probably fallen asleep waiting for me to get home. I hung my hat and my Blackhawk on the peg by the door. I hadn't eaten all day, so I thought briefly

261

about making a sandwich or even a bowl of cereal, but I was just too pooped. Exhausted as I was, however, my nerves were jangling from all that had happened. To calm them a bit, I filled a glass with a double shot of Rebel Yell, and padded out of the kitchen to join her.

I suppose the behavior of the animals and the fact that my door was unlocked should have tripped my early-warning radar and alerted me that something was terribly wrong, but perhaps I was just too tired to pay attention to the signs. That's why I was unprepared for what I saw when I entered the living room.

The television was on and tuned to an old John Wayne western, but that was about the only thing that was normal. The big Navajo-print throw rug was bunched, and one of the table lamps had been tipped over and was lying on the floor beside a couple of cushions from the couch and a spilled bottle of wine. Cindy, wearing a bathrobe that had come loose to reveal the fact she was wearing nothing underneath, was facedown on the floor in front of the television, hog-tied with silver duct tape. Her wrists were bound behind her back, and her legs were bent upward at a harsh and painful angle so whoever tied her could fasten her ankles to her wrists. One of my old denim shirts was wrapped around her head and fastened at the neck with more tape. A leather belt was coiled around her throat.

Despite the horribly uncomfortable position, she was not moving, but even from across the room I could see that she was still breathing. I suppose I should have gone for the Blackhawk before I did another thing, but I was too frightened. I dropped the bourbon glass and sprinted to her side, my pulse racing from a sudden burst of adrenaline and my mind filled with images of Victoria Austin's corpse, her head covered in a jacket.

Cindy's muscles stiffened at my touch, and she began to strain against her bindings, but I spoke to her gently and rolled her on her side while I removed the shirt from her head. Her eyes were wide and frightened, and I saw that there was another length of tape across her mouth. She was trying to talk, but the words were muffled and garbled. I pulled the tape free, and as I did, it began

262

to register that whoever tied her had roughed her up first. Her right eye was purple and swollen, and there was crusted blood around her nostrils. The red imprint of a man-sized palm was outlined on one cheek, and there was another on her shoulder. Two of her fingers were raw and bloody, the nails broken off below the quick.

I gathered her in my arms and held her close. Her heart was pounding, and I could feel it against my chest. She held me as if I were her only anchor to planet Earth. "Are you all right?" I asked urgently.

"I'm fine," she said. Her eyes darted fearfully around the room. "He's still here, Harry!" she said.

I knew immediately who she was talking about. "Trace," I said. It wasn't a question. No wonder we hadn't been able to find him in Laramie.

She nodded enthusiastically. "He came about two hours ago. Must have just walked in while I was sleeping. I know you told me to lock the doors when I was here alone, but I forgot," she said. She closed her eyes, remembering. "I fought him as best I could, but it was no use," she said, almost apologetically.

My own heart skipped a beat as I remembered his brutal sexual assault on Victoria Austin before he strangled her. "Did he . . ."

"No, thank God," she said. "He tied me up and then just sat there on the couch waiting for you to come home. He didn't even talk much, except to say you had ruined his life and he was going to kill you. A few minutes ago, he got tired of waiting and wrapped that shirt around my head and the belt around my neck. I know he was going to strangle me."

"Where is he now?"

"I don't know," she said. "He ran out the back door when he heard your car pull up in the driveway. Maybe he changed his mind."

"I doubt that," I said. "Did he have a weapon?"

"A pistol. Kept it tucked in his waistband."

If Trace was outside under cover of darkness, Cindy and I were sitting ducks in the well-lighted living room with nothing to protect us but the plateglass picture window. I didn't know what kind of marksman Trace was, but it wouldn't take much skill to take a shot at us. I had to even the odds. "Stay here," I whispered. I crawled to the side of the couch and turned the lamp off. I stood and raced to the kitchen in a crouching run, pulled the Blackhawk from the peg, doused the lights, and locked the front door. I ran to the back door and locked it as well, but before I came back to Cindy I stopped in my bedroom and took one of my backup weapons from the nightstand—a World War II–vintage Colt .45 military sidearm I'd confiscated from one of Victory's residents a few years before. I racked the slide to put a fat round in the chamber and set the safety. Then, with the house secure, I scrambled back to the living room where Cindy was waiting, sitting on the floor with her back to a wall.

Cautiously, my eyes trying to see something, anything, in the inky blackness beyond the window, I fumbled for the telephone on the end table beside the couch. We were safe enough for the time being. If Trace tried to break in, I'd certainly hear him. All I had to do was call Frankie Bull, the sheriff's department, and anyone else I could think of, and then just hunker down and wait for reinforcements. When I put the receiver to my ear, however, instead of a welcoming dial tone there was nothing.

"Shit," I muttered. I edged along the living room wall until I came to the kitchen door, slipped through, and grabbed the receiver of the kitchen wall phone from its hook. That phone was dead too.

Trace must have cut the lines.

I went back to the living room, knelt beside Cindy, and put the forty-five in her hand.

"What's this for?" she asked.

"The phone lines are out," I told her. "That means we've got to try something else. I'm going outside to look for Trace, but if he comes back while I'm gone, shoot him."

"Absolutely not!" she said vehemently. She grabbed my arm hard, and I could feel her remaining fingernails digging into my flesh. "You're not leaving me alone in here!"

264

"Cindy, I have to . . ."

"I said no, damn it!" she broke in. "You think you're so goddamned tough, Harry, but what if something happens to you out there? What do I do then? Do I just sit here and wait for him to come back and kill me? Christ, I've never even fired one of these things. I don't know if I could do it."

I placed her thumb on the safety lever of the forty-five. "All you have to do is flick the safety off, cock the hammer, and fire," I said. "It's semiautomatic, so you just keep shooting until he goes down. It won't come to that anyway. I'm better at this sort of thing than Trace Buchanan."

She wasn't about to change her mind. "You're not going anywhere without me," she said flatly. "Think of something else."

"All right," I said, but the trouble was, there weren't that many options. If we stayed in the relative safety of the house until daylight, four hours away, Trace would have plenty of time to escape again, if that was his intention. Which left only one choice. We had to get away ourselves, get to a phone, and call for backup while I still had a good idea where he was. If we could get between him and Victory, then he was as good as caught, since there are only two main routes out of town, Highway 130 to Laramie and the two-lane mountain road over the Snowy Range to Saratoga.

I told Cindy what she had to do, and then kept watch while she went to the bedroom and pulled on her clothes—blue jeans, a sweatshirt, and sturdy boots. When she was dressed, we crept into the kitchen and opened the door. I went through first and stood on the porch with the Blackhawk in a two-handed combat stance, my ears straining for any sound or movement in the shadows that would give Trace away. I heard the whinny of the horses in the corral, the breeze through the branches of the trees, the chirp of crickets, and further up the flanks of the mountain, the hoot of a night-hunting owl. In the distance, I could hear the screeching jake-brake of a big diesel rig, probably a timber hauler, coming down the steep grade into Victory. Nothing out of the ordinary.

"Go!" I told Cindy, and she ran past me, down the steps.

Her feet flew as she crossed the twenty feet between the porch and the Jeep. She opened the door and threw herself in, and I heard the metallic click as she inserted the ignition key. Then she crouched down in the seat so she wouldn't be visible through the window. "Come on, Harry! Hurry!" she said.

I followed her as fast as I could go, and lunged into the driver's seat. I turned the ignition, and the engine roared to life. I threw the transmission into reverse, cramped the wheel and hit the gas, and turned around in a tight spin so that the nose of the Jeep was pointed toward the highway. Then I dropped it into second, popped the clutch, and tried to keep us from fishtailing as the big rear tires kicked up a storm of gravel that pinged off the porch and the side of the house.

I knew the quarter mile of dirt road that serves as my driveway as well as I know my own face. There are a couple of sharp turns and a narrow wooden bridge over Antelope Creek before it reaches the blacktop leading into town, but nothing I couldn't navigate by feel alone if I had to. I didn't even bother with the headlights because I didn't want to draw more attention to our escape than I had to—I just pushed the pedal to the metal and kept a tight grip on the wheel.

Cindy, who was feeling safer now that we were in motion, began to sit up as we passed the end of the barn. I was distracted by the motion and glanced at her quickly, and I suppose that's why I didn't see the dark blur of the Toyota roaring toward us from the building's shadow until it was too late to prevent Trace from ramming us broadside. Cindy saw it before I did, and screamed, but by the time I turned to see what had frightened her, the Toyota was so close that all that registered was the heavy metal bull bar on the front.

I instinctively braced for the collision that came a split second later in a banging crash of steel on steel. The force of the impact rammed my head against the driver-side window and threw Cindy sideways in her seat. Cindy was almost lying in my lap, and her body hindered my ability to respond. The Jeep spun crazily out of control, and I had the sensation that I was on the Tilt-a-Whirl ride at the county fair. I heard the screaming whine of the Toyota's

266

motor, the shriek of agonized metal, and the scraping of my own tires as they fought for traction and were pushed across the hard-packed roadbed. And then I was rising, being lifted, and I realized with a sickening clarity that we were going over. I held fast to the wheel to keep from being thrown, and when the Jeep reached the top of its arc, I looked down at Cindy. She'd been whipsawed by the momentum of the roll completely across the interior compartment until her head smacked the passenger-side door with a sickening thud, like a ripe melon dropped on concrete. Her eyes were closed tightly, her mouth was open, and her lips were pulled back in a piercing wail. She looked like something from my nightmares.

When the Jeep rolled onto its top, my face was stung by hunks of broken glass from the exploding windshield, and I felt like a rodeo cowboy six seconds into an eight-second ride on a twelve-hundred-pound bull. For another terrifying moment, I thought the force of the impact was sufficient to send us into a second tumble. The Jeep didn't roll again, however. It threatened to, then rocked back down with a heavy thump and a cloud of dust.

I shook my head and tried to clear it to take stock of the damage. I could feel Cindy's body tangled with mine. I'd banged my knee and shoulder in the wreck, and they both throbbed with intense pain. "Cindy? Can you hear me?"

She didn't answer, but simply moaned instead. Already, I could smell gasoline leaking from the tank, so I untangled our arms and legs and began looking for a way out before the volatile accelerant found something hot enough to ignite it.

The soft-top door of the Jeep hadn't come open during the roll, so I kicked at the plastic window as hard as I could with my uninjured leg and punched through easily. Fortunately, the roll bar had done its job and prevented us from being squashed by the weight of the Jeep. Although the rear of the vehicle was higher than the nose on account of the roll bar and the way we'd come to rest, there was still about eighteen inches of clearance between the front seat and the ground, enough to wriggle out through the opening. I scrambled around and pulled myself out headfirst. Bits of broken glass cut through the thick skin of my palms.

When I had finally pulled myself through, I pushed my bruised body upward onto my hands and knees. My head was reeling, my knee and shoulder were afire, and I could not seem to get my breath. The smell of gasoline was overpowering. I thought I might pass out. With every bit of strength I could muster, I tried to stand.

I didn't get far before I felt the cold muzzle of Trace's pistol against the skin of my neck. "Don't even think of moving," he said. I froze in place as he took the Blackhawk from my holster and threw it into the brush at the side of the driveway. "Smells like gasoline," he said. "You have a match?"

I couldn't seem to focus on the danger I was in. In fact, Trace didn't seem real—he was more like a bad hallucination. All I could think about was Cindy still trapped, perhaps unconscious, under the Jeep. I was single-minded in my urgency. "I've got to get her out of there," I said. I tried to stand again, but he pushed me down roughly to my hands and knees.

"You don't have to do anything but die," he said. "I'll worry about the bitch later." He grabbed me by the hair and jerked me upward until I was kneeling in front of him. I heard a dry click as he thumbed the hammer of his pistol into firing position, and I could almost feel his finger tightening on the trigger. I knew that in a few seconds I would probably die, and there was little I could do about it. I didn't know if my bum leg was broken again, or only twisted and bruised, but it didn't matter. Even if I could stand, my leg wouldn't carry me fast enough to turn around and take the pistol from his hand before he fired. I certainly couldn't outrun his bullet if I tried to flee.

Which left my mouth as my last line of defense. "You don't have to do this, Trace," I said.

"Of course I have to kill you," he said, as if that was the most reasonable thing in the world. "What other choice do I have? I had it all—the girl, the ranch, the whole thing. And then you stuck your nose in and took it all away. It's over, Starbranch. Completely, utterly, irrevocably over. If they take me alive, even Gerry Spence couldn't keep me off death row, so I'm not gonna let them take me alive. I'm gonna die because of you, and the best I can hope for is to make sure you go first."

I knew he meant exactly what he said. He had thought it through and come to that insane conclusion. His instability, desperation, and hatred made him exceedingly dangerous. "You could make a deal," I said. I was grasping at smoke, but I knew that the longer I could keep him talking, the better chance I had of coming up with a way to turn the tables. I shook my head to clear it, tried to focus, to concentrate. My head felt as if I were swimming underwater, my thoughts trapped in sticky gauze. "You weren't in this alone. The prosecutor will bargain in return for what you know."

Buchanan laughed out loud. "You'd like that, wouldn't you?" he asked. "You'd like me to say that Annie Quinn was behind this whole thing, that she thought it all up, and dumb-assed Trace was just the piss boy who carried it out."

Trace was on a roll. "I'm not gonna do that," he said. "I'm not gonna give you that satisfaction. I'm gonna kill you, and you're gonna die without ever knowing what really happened to Vicky Austin, or why. And I will never, ever, bargain with anyone. I love that woman, Starbranch, and I won't allow anything to happen to her. When the dust clears from all this, she goes free, because not a single one of you has any proof against her, and you never will."

"That ought to make her happy," I said. "But tell me one thing. If Annie Quinn had no part in any of this, who broke into my house and beat my son? We both know the only reason that happened was because he'd been investigating Quinn and Loveladies Pharmaceuticals."

I didn't expect him to answer. I was just stalling for time. I used it to center myself, while I tried to ignore the pain and marshal my energies for one last desperate act if the opportunity arose.

Buchanan snorted. "If you knew ten times as much as you think you know, you'd still be a moron," he said. "My cousin Bandy broke into your house and beat your kid because I asked him to drive out and knock the shit out of you. You weren't there, and I guess he didn't want to go home skunked. He did your kid because he felt like it, and it was fun. End of story."

"I don't believe you," I said, and I truly didn't. Bandy Dowd may have been the man who beat Robert and trashed his computer, but the reason behind the attack was more complex than the horse manure Trace was spreading. I believed Robert had been beaten because he was getting too close to Quinn and Loveladies, and they wanted to get their hands on his information and scare him off. If Dowd had provided the muscle, he'd used it because Trace had asked him to in order to protect Quinn. Nobody could convince me otherwise, but there was no percentage in arguing. I couldn't force Trace to tell me the truth, and he was in no mood for confession.

"This may come as a surprise to you, but I don't give a damn what you believe," Trace said. "It's irrelevant." He poked me in the neck again with the muzzle of the pistol. "Take your shirt off," he said.

"What?"

"You heard me, take it off!"

I did what he ordered, unsnapped the buttons of my shirt, and shrugged out of it. The night breeze felt good on my skin and raised goosebumps on my arms.

"Put it over your head," he commanded.

I knew what was coming. I looked up and saw a sliver of moon poking over the crest of the mountains. The cloud cover was almost completely broken, and the sky glittered with a million stars. I wondered if that was the last time I'd ever look at that great western sky, and the feeling that it was made me incredibly sad. It also made me angry. If Trace was going to kill me, I'd cross over with my eyes open. I wadded the shirt in a ball and threw it as far away from me as I could. "Screw you," I said with all the authority I could call into service. "You're such a fucking coward you're getting ready to shoot a man in the back of the head. I'll be damned if I'll make it easier for you. Ken Keegan didn't, and neither will I. Our faces will haunt you through eternity."

"Your call, Starbranch," he said.

I knew I was out of time, and I also knew I would never go without a fight. I lunged forward as far as I could and rolled to the left, hoping that he'd be so surprised he wouldn't shoot straight. Maybe if he missed me with the first shot, and the second, and the third, I'd have time to hobble up on my one good leg and rush him, take the gun away, and beat him to death with it. The odds of success were about a billion to one, but it was the only chance I had. And if I failed . . . well, as Frankie's people said in similar circumstances, it was a good day to die. At least I would have tried.

His first bullet smacked the earth about two inches from my face before I'd even stopped rolling, and it kicked up a storm of dirt that stung my eyes. I couldn't see, and I rubbed at my eyes frantically, trying to clear them so I could go on. I could sense him taking aim again, and I gritted my teeth, waiting for the bullet that would tear through my cranium.

The report came almost immediately, but instead of the searing moment of pain I'd been expecting, I heard Trace cough and begin to gag. I opened my tortured eyes and saw him falling to the ground. There was a huge exit wound in the right side of his throat, and pulsing streams of blood spurted from his carotid artery and jugular vein, saturating the stupid Albert Einstein T-shirt. He dropped the pistol and tried to stanch the torrent with his hands, but it was no use. It leaked out through the spaces between his fingers, covering the backs of his hands and the front of his shirt with a dark and spreading stain.

Behind him, Cindy, fighting to stand on unsteady legs, held the huge forty-five in shaking hands. She was bruised and battered, her hair wild, her face a puffy mask of dirt and blood. Somehow, she'd managed to free herself from the Jeep. Somehow, she'd managed to come up behind Trace without him hearing her. Somehow, she'd found the courage and determination to save my life.

I stood and crow-hopped to her, and she was passive as I removed the forty-five from her grip. I put myself between her and Trace, so she wouldn't have to look at what she'd done. Then I led her away from the overturned Jeep, away from the stink of gasoline and cordite to a safe place between a tall sagebrush and one of the granite boulders that line my driveway. I sat her down and caressed her cheek. She gave no sign that she felt my touch. "Thank you," I said.

She hugged her knees to her chest. She was shivering and so ghostly pale in the darkness she seemed to shimmer. I didn't know the extent of her injuries, but when she looked into my face, she was a thousand miles away. I'd seen that look on people's faces before, after they'd had a severely traumatic experience. She was in shock, and I knew I had to get her to a hospital as soon as possible. "Did I kill him?" she asked. There was agony in her voice, and I knew that a raw part of her psyche wanted to hear that of course she hadn't killed him, that this was nothing but a bad dream.

I didn't answer her heartbreaking question. I left her sitting there and hobbled back to Buchanan's side. He wasn't dead, but it was clear his wound was mortal. He was thirty miles from the nearest medical attention, and already I could hear the death rattle. His eyes were open, staring into mine. He was bleeding profusely, choking in his own blood. He had bare minutes to live, maybe seconds.

I knew what I had to do. Cindy had saved my life, but she'd taken one in the process. I knew from the tenacity of my own ghosts that the act would change her forever, weigh on her spirit like a stone. There would not be a single day when she didn't think of Trace Buchanan and wonder if she could have done it differently, wonder if something in her was so evil that she wanted to snuff out his life.

Even though she'd had no choice, hers was a gentle soul, and I feared the self-doubt and guilt might eventually crush her. I couldn't let that happen.

I raised the forty-five and shot Buchanan in the face. His body jerked at the impact of the heavy slug, and his eyeballs bulged in their sockets from the pressure explosion in his brain and skull. His arms waved like a spastic marionette, and his heels drummed the ground. Even though I'd seen it before, the macabre dance was a horrible thing to watch. It seemed to go on forever, but gradually his convulsions subsided and he was quiet, the last of his lifeblood gurgling from his body, soaking the dark, rich earth.

"Harry?" Cindy asked.

"You didn't kill him, honey" I told her. "He was still alive, going for his gun."

I tucked the forty-five in the waistband of my jeans. I'd made bones so many times, one more skeleton would hardly matter. If I could bear that burden for her, I'd do it gladly. "*I* killed him," I said.

And using the most literal interpretation of the phrase, I believe that was the truth.

TWENTY

I had walked almost four miles down Antelope Creek with my fly rod in my hand, not really fishing but just enjoying the September scenery. It was eight-thirty in the morning, and the season's first veil of frost still sparkled from the leaves of the willows and aspens on the stream bank. The old horses, invigorated by the brisk morning air, were frisky in the pasture, chasing each other through the banks of purple sage, their manes and tails flying and their big hooves pounding the ground, sending up tiny explosions of white alkali dust with each step. I ambled along, stopping occasionally to cast a dry fly into one of the larger pools, stopping even more often to watch the small herds of deer in the foothills, the pronghorns on the flats, and a pair of bald eagles riding the thermals above the granite face of Corner Mountain. The trout weren't biting, but I didn't care. That's why they call it fishing, not catching. It was enough to be alive on that gorgeous morning and in the place I loved the most.

I was halfway back to the house when Frankie Bull pulled his cruiser to the side of the rutted jeep trail that follows the stream and killed the engine. Frankie's luxurious hair, which had always been so black it was almost blue, was now showing signs of gray. It was carefully braided, and the ends of the braids were wrapped with strips of red cloth and otter fur, which the Sioux believe imparts swiftness and cleverness to the man who wears it. He honked the horn and rolled his window down. "Crawl in, Harry," he said.

I hopped over an ice-crusted puddle and stepped around some deadfall timber that had come down in the last big blow. The cruiser's big Detroit engine was rumbling, and a white cloud of exhaust spewed from the tailpipe and hung around the vehicle in the still air. Frankie leaned across the front seat and opened the passenger door impatiently. "Come on, get in," he said.

"It's Sunday morning, and this is my church," I told him. "I don't know why you think you need to interrupt me, but it had better be important."

Frankie laughed. "It's Monday, Harry, and it is important," he said. "The state attorney general is waiting to see you at the office."

I walked to the side of the cruiser, then paused and took one last look over Victory Valley and the violent rise of the mountains in the distance, the sun reflecting off the snowcapped peaks. Then I got inside and closed the door. Frankie smelled like wood smoke with a top note of Old Spice aftershave. There was Native American music playing in the tape deck, heavy on the flutes, whistles, and rattles. It sounded comforting, like water burbling over rocks. "What does he want?" I asked. "I wasn't supposed to go and see him in Cheyenne until tomorrow."

"Maybe he couldn't wait," Frankie said. He dropped the transmission into drive, and we lurched forward toward town.

I thought I knew why the attorney general had decided to pay me a personal visit.

It had been almost three weeks since Trace Buchanan's death, but nobody was any closer to proving Annie Quinn's involvement in the whole affair than they had ever been. Not for lack of trying. Two days after the shooting at my house—while Cindy and I were still recuperating from our wounds, none of which were particularly serious—Walker Tisdale surprised everyone but me by resigning from office. That left the mopping up and any additional prosecutions resulting from the case in the hands of the state attorney general, a hard-nosed former county prosecutor named Tim Keller who'd made his reputation by winning the highest conviction rate Natrona County had seen in over forty years. Keller threw every investigator the DCI could spare into the search for evidence that would tie Annie Quinn to the murder of Victoria Austin, and they worked around the clock.

Trouble was, the evidence trail had dried up and disappeared when Trace Buchanan died.

Bandy Dowd had been pulled in for questioning, but everyone knew there was not enough evidence to charge him with Robert's beating, and he was in no mood to volunteer any information concerning the real reason for the attack. As a means of tying Trace and Quinn together in the murder of Austin, he was a washout—which left the investigators with nothing.

If Trace and Quinn had conspired to kill Austin and frame Carl Buchanan, which I believed with every fiber of my being, there was no way to prove it. Ken Keegan predicted that Trace would eventually give his lover up, but in that my friend had been wrong. Buchanan had taken what he knew to the grave, and to no one's surprise, Quinn denied everything. Her attorneys were threatening lawsuits against everyone from me to the governor himself if suspicion against her became public.

Under Keller's direct orders, I had taken no part in the protracted investigation, but the scuttlebutt was that the attorney general—who'd been under constant pressure from the media, something he could scarcely afford since it was an election year and his boss, the governor, was facing an uphill battle to retain his job—was ready to call it quits. Word was he wanted to close the case once and for all and blame the whole thing on Trace. I figured he was there to give me the bad news before I heard it somewhere else.

As we came into Victory and stopped at the lone traffic light, I could see Keller's black Lincoln parked in front of the office. The plainclothes highway patrolman who serves as his chauffeur was leaning on the front fender, reading that morning's edition of the *Laramie Boomerang*. Frankie pulled into the parking space beside the Lincoln and cut the engine.

I nodded to Keller's driver as I got out of the cruiser, my old knees crackling with the effort. Then I clomped into the office, where the attorney general had his black wingtips propped on my desk while he read through a stack of incident reports and call sheets that had been awaiting my attention. He looked up and smiled his wide, politician's smile when I came in, dropped the reports back in the basket, and stood up to shake my hand. About my height, I guessed Keller probably outweighed me by forty pounds, most of it in his substantial trencherman's belly. The Windsor knot in his red silk tie looked like it was cutting into the flesh of his thick neck. His haircut was expensive, and the gray suit he was wearing had obviously been custom-tailored to fit his bulky frame. He looked doughy, out of shape and weak, but I knew of lots of people who had underestimated Tim Keller and paid dearly for their mistake. Underneath the middle-aged flab and behind his horn-rimmed glasses, the man was as mean and deadly as a pit bull. A good man to have on your side, but not a man to cross. "Hello, Harry," he said. "Sorry to drag you off the stream."

I shrugged. "They weren't biting anyway," I said. I filled myself a cup of coffee and sat down on the old railroad bench we keep around for visitors. "If you want to hang around, though, you can come with me and we'll try again this evening when they're hungry."

Keller chuckled. "I'm afraid I didn't drive out today for the fishing, and more's the pity," he said.

"I didn't think you did," I told him. He looked uncomfortable in our small, cramped office. I didn't imagine he went slumming in the boondocks very often, preferring the rarefied, august air of the state capitol. I didn't feel all that comfortable with him being there, either, particularly since he was sitting at my desk as if he owned the place, letting me know who was boss. I didn't imagine he'd take very kindly if I tried that in his office. "I figure you're here to soften the blow about Annie Quinn, so why don't you do us both a favor and cut to the chase?"

I thought he might be offended by my brusque tone, but he wasn't. In fact, he looked as if he appreciated the opportunity to get the unpleasantness over with. He smiled at Frankie. "Mind if the chief and I talk in private?" he asked.

Frankie left and closed the door. Keller waited until he could see him talking to the driver through the window, then he leaned forward and supported his considerable weight on his arms atop my desk. "Here's the way it is, Harry," he said. "I know you think we ought to charge Annie Quinn with conspiracy to commit murder and a host of other charges, but I'm afraid it isn't gonna happen. My people have spent all the time I can afford to spend on this investigation, and they've come up with nothing I can take to court. I agree your Loveladies Pharmaceuticals angle is an interesting theory, but it looks like that's all it is, a theory, kind of like the possibility of life on another planet. We all agree it's highly possible, but nobody's gonna prove it in our lifetimes. That's why I'm going to announce that the case is officially closed at a press conference in Cheyenne tomorrow afternoon."

That's pretty much what I'd been expecting, but anticipation didn't make it easier to swallow. "Come on, Keller, you can do better than that," I said angrily. "If you . . ."

"Could *you* do better than that?" he broke in. "How would you solve this, Harry? You tell me, and I'll get right on it."

He had me there. "I don't know," I admitted. "But that doesn't mean I'd stop trying until I had the killer."

"And you'd never get any closer than you are right now," he said hotly. "You'd have an open, unsolvable investigation going for the next twenty years. I'm not gonna have that hanging fire, Starbranch. I *have* the killer. As a matter of fact, I have the whole thing tied up with a pretty little bow."

"But Trace and Quinn . . ."

"Forget Quinn!" he said. "Forget Loveladies and this whole fountain-of-youth goose chase! It's a red herring, Harry. As far as my office and the state are concerned, Trace killed Victoria Austin because he wanted to frame his brother for murder and get hold of the mineral rights to that ranch. That's all there is to it. It's over."

"Maybe," I said sullenly. "But you know what, Keller, you're sounding more and more like Walker Tisdale, taking the politically expedient way out and ignoring what you know to be true. Down deep, I think you know Annie Quinn is guilty, and you're gonna let her go free. How do you feel about that? How do you think the voters would feel about that, if they knew?"

Keller's eyes narrowed. "Is that a threat? Are you threatening to go public?"

I shrugged noncommittally and sat back on the bench. Keller knew I had plenty of contacts in the press. I figured I'd let him sweat.

Keller didn't look particularly worried, just angry and foreboding. "I wouldn't do that if I were you, because in this case there is more than one thing I know that I've chosen not to act on," he said. "You feel like playing with fire, Starbranch, just go ahead and start running your mouth to the press. You'll be one sorry son of a bitch."

"And why is that?" I asked. "What else have you chosen not to act on?"

Keller looked like a diamondback rattler who'd just spotted a slow mouse. "Let's talk about the shooting of Trace Buchanan," he said. "Let's talk trajectory, angle of entry. The first bullet came from behind, and I can buy that it was fired by Cindy Thompson to save your life. But the second shot, that one came while the man was flat on his back, incapacitated, and dying. Who knows? He might have lived if it hadn't been for your coup de grace. You wanted to make sure he was dead. You executed him, Starbranch. You know it, I know it, and the coroner knows it, but none of us has acted on that knowledge. You think that second shot was legal? In case you have any doubt, let me tell you it was not." He paused, letting it sink in. "How far down that road do you want to travel?" he asked.

I didn't answer, but just looked him in the eyes. My silence was answer enough.

He smiled. "That's what I thought," he said. "Now, here's what I suggest. You're a hero right now. You proved Walker Tisdale and the whole county justice system incompetent. You solved a difficult case and cleared an innocent man's name. You caught the bad guy, brought down a perverted rapist, murderer, and cop-killer. You won the gratitude of your state, your governor, and myself. I suggest you just sit back, keep your theories to yourself, and bask in the glow of victory." He stood up and put his hands in his pants pockets. "That's what I suggest, Harry, because let me assure you, as far as you're concerned, the alternative truly sucks."

With the summer term ended and the fall semester in session, the University of Wyoming campus was considerably more lively than it had been the last time I was there. Instead of a relatively small number of people enjoying the sunshine on Prexy's Pasture, the grassy promenade was crowded with earnest-looking students wearing backpacks and coveys of tweed-jacketed professorial types arguing the fine points of academic debate. A couple who looked old enough to be grad students were sitting on the steps of the College of Agriculture, disputing the symbolic meaning of the wilderness in Nathaniel Hawthorne's *Scarlet Letter,* and a trio of younger men who sounded like exchange students from somewhere in the Middle East were puzzling over mathematical equations in an open notebook spread on one of the student's knees.

Fascinating stuff. Unfortunately, I didn't have time to participate in any of the discussions. I trudged up the stairs to the Department of Molecular Biology on the fourth floor, past the department secretary's office, and down the hall to Annie Quinn's office. Her door was closed and locked, so I made my way to the laboratory, where I found Quinn with a model of a molecule in her hands, lecturing to a group of graduate assistants in white lab coats, none of whom I recognized from my last visit.

I stood with my face in the door window until she looked up from her dissertation and saw me. A look of anxious surprise crossed her pretty face when she recognized me, but that was quickly replaced by one of annoyance. She said something I couldn't hear to the students and walked through the doors to where I was waiting in the hall. "What is it you want, Mr. Starbranch?" she asked. "As you can see, I'm in the middle of a class."

Not quite the pleasant reception she'd given me before, but I'd put a bullet through her lover's head, so what did I expect? "Five minutes of your time," I said. "I promise I'll never interrupt another of your classes again."

Quinn thought it over for a few seconds and then stalked off in a rustle of elegant black skirt in the direction of her office, leaving me to follow as best I could. She waited at the door until I was inside, and then she closed and locked it behind us. She didn't sit down, and she didn't invite me to, either.

"I didn't see Marsha Jackson out there with your other assistants," I said by way of introduction. "Is she still around?"

"Is that why you're here?" she asked.

I shook my head no. "Just curious."

"Well then, I'll satisfy your curiosity," Quinn said. "Miss Jackson's assistantship was not renewed for the fall term, and neither, I might add, were the stipends of any of my other assistants. I've got a whole new crop."

None of whom know the first thing about the pitiful state of your programmed cell-death research project, I thought. None of whom can cause problems or raise questions. "How convenient for you," I said.

If she got my sarcasm she didn't let on. "It's not convenient at all," she said tautly. "I've got a lot of work to do because I'm having to train these kids from scratch." She paused, looked pointedly at her watch. I figured I was at least two minutes into my time. "But I suspect the expertise of my research team is not the reason for your visit. Would you mind getting to the point?"

No problem. "The point is Trace Buchanan," I said.

Quinn didn't flinch at the mention of the name. "I can't believe what he did," she said. "The investigators tell me there's no doubt he killed Vicky Austin and set poor Carl up to take the blame." She seemed to shudder. "I had no idea," she said. "If I had known . . ."

"Of course you knew," I broke in. "You were lovers. The two of you planned it together. You probably put him up to the whole thing, and I just want you to know that I . . ."

"We were dating!" she broke in, the color rising in her cheeks. "That's all it was. It doesn't mean I knew about his other side. It doesn't mean I knew about what he was planning or the despicable things he did. It doesn't mean I helped him in any way. If I had known what he was doing, I can promise you I would have stopped him. Your friend Keegan would still be alive and that horrible business at your house would have never happened." Her whole body was wire-tight, and her hands were clamped in small fists. "I hate him for what he did! I'm glad he's dead, and you and Cindy Thompson deserve medals for killing him!"

She opened the door and held it for me. Her outburst seemed to have taken something out of her. She looked tired, emotionally spent. Acting again, and putting on a hell of a performance. "Now, I'd like you to leave so I can go back to work," she said.

I didn't move, just looked her up and down, taking her measure. "You're a cold woman, Annie," I said. "I hope you can live with what you've done."

She sighed, the weight of my words just one more of the many burdens she was forced to bear. Annie Quinn, martyr. "I'm just fine, because I've done nothing to be guilty about," she said. "Trace Buchanan victimized me, the same way he victimized everyone else he touched. I hope you'll eventually understand that and have some compassion. Until then, I'll just be glad this is over and we can all get on with our lives."

She tapped her foot impatiently, letting me know the interview was over. "I don't want to talk to you any more, and I don't have to," she said. She sounded as if she was disappointed in me. "Either you go now, or I'll call campus security."

I walked out into the hall and took a couple steps in the direction of the exit. I turned back as she was closing the door behind us. "There are lots of victims in this business, but you're not one of them," I said. "There'll come a reckoning, depend on it."

The martyr's mask dropped, and her expression changed. There was arctic tundra in her smile. Showing her real face. The face of a she-wolf on the prowl. "Don't hold your breath, Harry," she said. Her switch to the familiar use of my given name sent a shiver down my spine. "I don't want you to turn blue and die."

She brushed past me and walked away without looking back. Nothing on her back trail. Not a worry in the world.

*   *   *

Cassie Buchanan was waiting at the office when I got back to Victory around three-thirty that afternoon. I was not exactly anxious to see her.

Two days after Trace died in a hail of lead at my house, Cassie left town to spend some time on Carl's ranch and had been out of touch. Although I knew I'd eventually have to see her and confront all that had happened, I'd hoped that meeting would come later rather than sooner. Now she was back, and I didn't have a choice. I braced myself for the meeting.

She was sitting on the railroad bench when I came in, and she looked much better than she had when I'd seen her last, the day after her eldest son's death. We'd passed in the hallway of the hospital, and she'd looked a hundred and ten years old, stooped and beaten and barely able to walk under her own power. Now, she looked tired and world-weary, but healthy and more sure of herself. Her hair was neat and held back from her narrow face by a stylish Navajo silver clasp, and she was dressed in sturdy, well-kept working attire—khaki pants, a blue denim shirt rolled up crisply to the elbows, and serviceable Timberline workboots. For the first time in months, she was even wearing makeup.

I hung my Stetson on the peg and sat on the edge of my desk, facing her. "Cassie, how have you been?" I asked.

She carefully marked her place in the book, closed it, and tucked it away in a canvas bag at her feet. She smiled at me, and that smile almost broke my heart. "About like you'd expect," she said. "It's been very hard. I loved those boys, no matter what they did, and now they're both gone. I just can't seem to get used to the idea that I'll never see either one of them again. A mother shouldn't have to bury her children, Harry. It ought to be the other way around."

I didn't know what to say, but I knew I had to make some kind of peace with her, at least try to explain why Trace had died. "Cassie, I am sorrier than you'll ever know about what happened. All I can hope is that someday you find it in your heart to forgive me. I'll understand it if you can't, but . . ."

Cassie got up from the bench and came to me before I could finish, wrapped her slender arms around me, and pulled me close. She buried her face in my neck, and I could feel the tears on her cheeks. We stayed like that for a long while, and then she broke the embrace and stepped back, her hands resting on my shoulders while she looked into my face. "You have to know that I hated you after Trace died," she said softly. "I couldn't help myself, and that's why I had to go away. I've had a lot of time to think in the last few weeks, and I understand some things now that were impossible before."

She paused and looked down, gathering her thoughts. I waited patiently for her to go on. When she spoke again, she was sure of herself, her words strong and comforting. "It wasn't your fault I asked you to help Carl, and it wasn't your fault the facts you uncovered led you to Trace," she said. "It wasn't your fault Trace killed Ken Keegan and tried to kill you and Cindy. It wasn't your fault the two of you killed him. You were just defending yourselves. It was all *his* fault, Harry, not yours. I understand that now. You don't have to ask for my forgiveness, because it's already been given."

Her grip tightened on my shoulders. "I've come to ask for your forgiveness for all I put you through. I feel horrible, and I don't know how I can ever make it up to you."

I was almost overcome with a wave of tenderness and relief. I didn't know how to start, but if things were ever going to be right between us again, I had to clear the air and tell her the truth. "I was just doing my job, Cassie," I said. "And there is something about the shooting I think you should know. Cindy fired the shot that brought Trace down, but I . . ."

She held a finger to my lips to silence me before I could finish. "I don't want to know," she said. "But I want you to know this. It wasn't your job to be there. You were just doing a favor for an old friend. I owe you, and it's time to repay the kindness." She smiled again. "I'm here today to offer you a proposition, Harry, and I hope you'll listen."

I shook my head. "You don't owe me anything, Cassie," I said.

"You let me be the judge of that," she said. "Will you listen?"
I nodded to let her know I would.

"Good," she said. "You know about the sixteen hundred acres Carl owned, and I know you also suspected that Jules Black at Black Mesa Petroleum was interested in drilling some exploration wells up there?"

"I did indeed," I said.

"Well, your suspicions were right," she said. "I've talked to Jules a couple of times in the last weeks, and he is interested. That ranch is mine now, and all we have to do is negotiate a price for the drilling rights and the royalty percentage if they hit crude. I don't know if I'm up to that, Harry. I want you to handle it for me, and be around to watch things while they drill. If we hit oil, I want you to manage our investment."

I was so surprised that I laughed out loud. "I'm sure you can handle Jules Black," I said. "You don't need me for that."

"Maybe not," she said. "But I want you, and that's what's important. And don't worry, you'll be paid for your time. If we make money on this deal, I'm going to take part of it and endow a scholarship in Carl's name at the university for students studying substance abuse counseling. I'm also gonna build a new library here in Victory. I'll use the rest of my half to live on, and you can use your half for whatever you want. I figure we'll split the profits fifty-fifty. Absent the value of the land itself if we ever decide to sell, we'll be equal partners."

"I can't do that, Cassie," I said. "You're talking a lot of money here, maybe millions."

"I hope so," she said. "Do we have a deal?"

I leaned forward and kissed her cheek. "No, we don't have a deal," I said. "I'll help you negotiate with Jules Black if you want, and you can even pay any expenses I incur. But I won't take your money from the drilling rights, and I won't take the oil royalties. You can think of better things to do with that money than give it to me."

She chuckled. "And what would I do with it, Harry?" she

asked. "How much money do you think it takes for an old woman with no vices to live on? You, on the other hand, have vices to spare, and I'll just bet they're expensive."

"Cassie, I . . ."

Her voice was very serious when she broke in. "I've got no one else to give that money to, Mr. Starbranch," she said. "I've given this a lot of thought, and there's no one I'd rather have for a partner than you. I'm not crazy, and this is no joke. Will you do it?"

She held her small hand out for me to shake, and I let it hang in the air between us while I thought it over. I didn't have to think long. What did I have to lose? I took her hand and pumped it heartily. "You've got yourself a partner," I said. "When do we start?"

"As soon as you fulfill the only condition," she said.

Oh, oh. "What condition?"

Cassie set her jaw and drew herself up. "I want you to make that woman pay for what she did to my boys," she said. "I don't want her going unpunished."

My face fell. I was disappointed in her, and in myself. I should have known there'd be strings. "I don't know if I can ever prove she did anything, Cassie," I said. "And I won't do anything illegal. I'm afraid our deal is off."

Cassie smiled again. "I'm not asking you to kill her, Harry," she said. "I'm not even asking you to do anything illegal. All I'm asking is that you get us a little bit of justice. If you can't do it, it's not a deal breaker. We're still partners. I just want you to try."

"There's nothing I can do," I said.

Cassie patted my cheek. "Don't be so negative," she said. "I know you, Harry. You'll think of something."

Two hours, a double shot of Jack Daniel's, and a good cigar later, I did.

I knew I might not ever be able to put Annie Quinn in jail. I knew the law might never make her pay for her crimes. But despite her belief to the contrary, she wasn't invulnerable. I could still hit her where she lived, and I knew exactly how to do it. Marsha Jackson had given me the silver bullet.

286

I was filled with a sense of devilish elation as I picked up the phone and dialed the number. On account of the time difference, it was after nine in the evening in New York, but Bruce Tegner was still at his desk. He answered on the second ring. *"Wall Street Journal,* Tegner speaking," he said.

"Mr. Tegner, this is Harry Starbranch," I said. "We spoke a while back about your visit to Wyoming to do a story on Professor Annie Quinn's programmed cell-death research."

"Yeah," he said, his voice cautious. "What can I do for you?"

"Are you still interested in the story?"

"It depends," he said. "Is there anything new?"

I laughed. "No, old," I said. "So old they died of old age."

Tegner was not amused. "Look, Mr. Starbranch, I'm on deadline here, and I don't have time to play games. Why don't I call you back later, and you can tell me what you want." His voice let me know that call would never come.

"That won't be necessary," I said. "I'll get right to the point. Do you know an expert in molecular biology you can trust?"

"Of course I do," he said. "That's my beat. I've got a whole Rolodex full of 'em. Why do you ask?" His brusqueness failed to hide the fact that I'd piqued his interest.

"If you want a story that will knock Wall Street on its ass, here's what I recommend," I said. "I recommend you get hold of your expert and see if he's got a couple of days to spare. Meanwhile, I'll call my travel agent and reserve you two tickets to Laramie, Wyoming, all expenses paid. I'll meet you at the airport."

I listened to the long-distance wires crackle while he ruminated. "And what will we find there?" he asked. "Another spoon-fed public relations tour?"

I smiled to myself. I had him. All I needed to do was set the hook and reel him in.

"Plants," I said smugly. "I've got some dead plants in my freezer you guys are absolutely gonna love."

EPILOGUE

The person who said money can't buy happiness was obviously too poor to fly the Concorde to London and stay in an eight-hundred-dollar-a-night suite at the Mayfair Hotel on Park Lane, where you can have soufflé suissesse and homard à l'escargot served in your room twenty-four hours a day. Not that I'd ever eat either of those things, especially the snails, but they also serve a very decent Angus beefsteak and wine so expensive it ought to come with its own armed guard, just to make sure no one hijacks it on the way to your room.

It was two-thirty in the morning, and I was lying in our cozy four-poster bed, looking up at the high Victorian ceilings, and listening to the traffic on Park Lane and Oxford Street leading to Marble Arch Station outside the big double windows. Cindy was snuggled beside me in a jumble of pink sheets, one bare leg peeking out and draped across my midsection, her head nestled on my shoulder, and her hand resting comfortably on my manly organ, which—thanks to an interesting experiment she'd dreamed up involving some very minty lotion—was as content as an old hound dog with a hambone and a patch of warm sunshine to lie in.

It took a while, but I finally untangled my various limbs from Cindy's without waking her. Then I slipped into the black silk robe I'd draped over the back of the overstuffed wing chair beside the bed and padded out to the bar in the sitting room. They don't have those cheesy honor bars at the Mayfair. Instead, they have a full bar

288

stocked with just about everything a dedicated tippler could ask for and Waterford crystal glasses to drink it from. I poured myself a deep snifter of brandy and warmed it between the palms of my hands. Then I took my middle-of-the-nightcap and sank down in the leather chair beside the window facing Hyde Park, where Cindy and I had spent almost three hours walking in the gentle April rain that afternoon.

We'd been in England for almost a week, and had seen just about everything that had been on our agendas—all the touristy stuff in London and Bath and Billy Shakespeare's house in Stratford-on-Avon, a once-quaint town overrun by travelers in tour buses, where we also saw a production of one of the best detective stories ever written, *Macbeth*. One day, we'd rented a car and driven up to the lake country so I could see the region that had inspired William Wordsworth and Samuel Coleridge and all those other romantic English poets I occasionally read when no one is looking. Next afternoon, we were off for a week touring the medieval castles of Scotland and to see if I could find Rob Roy's bloody spirit wandering the Highlands. And after that, a week in Van Morrison country, Ireland, sampling Guinness and scones.

When we finished, I thought we might as well see Paris in the springtime, and as long as we were already on the Continent, take a little train ride through the wine region in Germany and try on some liederhosen. After that, maybe Italy or Greece. Maybe stop in Monte Carlo to check out those beaches where the women go topless. I'd tucked an extra bottle of suntan lotion away in my bag, just in case Cindy decided to join in.

We'd just see what we felt like, play it by ear. I felt like a kid on the last day of school, with an endless, bright summer stretching before me, except now it was better because I was mature enough to appreciate it. For the first time in my adult life, no one was expecting me back to work, and we had all the time in the world and plenty of money to enjoy it.

I owed it all to Cassie Buchanan.

Five months before, I'd negotiated a good deal with Jules Black for the drilling rights to Cassie's Pumpkin Buttes ranch that put just under a million dollars in my bank account as my share of the proceeds. Not one to mess around, Jules started sinking his first well within three weeks of signing the papers, and to everyone's happy surprise, the driller struck oil—not a gusher, but a steady four hundred barrels of crude a day. His second well came up dry, but the third proved out and was bringing up two hundred and fifty barrels. Jules thought he might drill another fifteen or sixteen wells on Cassie's property before it was all over, and he was confident they'd hit crude on a good number of them.

I was rich, is what I was, with more oil royalties piling up every day, so I celebrated by resigning my job as chief of police, leaving Victory in Frankie Tall Bull's more than capable hands.

I didn't intend to retire, however.

Watching over the drilling operation and investing our profits took up some of my time, but not enough, and I got antsy sitting around over the course of the long winter. I'd talked Cindy into this six-week vacation beginning the first of April, and when we got back, I planned to open a fly-fishing business on a few acres of land I bought along the Little Laramie. I figured I'd stay open during the warm months of the year, sell obscenely expensive rods and flies and tackle, and guide a few of the out-of-state tourists who want a quality experience on a blue-ribbon stream and have the money to afford it. That might sound pretty boring to some people, but to me, getting paid for fishing every day is the realization of an ideal. I was lucky beyond my wildest imagination, and the skeptical part of me kept looking over my shoulder to spot the hand reaching out to snatch it all away.

Cindy told me to relax and enjoy it, but I could never take my good fortune for granted. I knew how quickly fate can reverse the tables. I'd seen it happen often enough.

Take Annie Quinn, for example. One minute she's got the world by the tail—power, prestige, a fat grant, the possibility of millions of dollars in profits if any of her research ever pans out, and a lover dumb enough to keep his mouth closed and die so she could keep it.

The next minute, she's got reporters camped on her doorstep, her face on the cover of the nation's largest newspapers and on the network news, agents from a half-dozen federal agencies including the Securities and Exchange Commission jamming subpoenas down her throat, her very pissed-off benefactors at Loveladies Pharmaceuticals (whose stock was at the lowest mark in the company's history) making dark threats to her continued well-being, and a department chairman so embarrassed he hired a moving crew to clear her university office in the middle of the night.

I don't know where she is now, since she left Laramie and went into hiding in an effort to evade prosecution, but wherever she is, I'll bet she'll never take a good day for granted again.

If she ever has another good day, which I pray she does not. I wasn't able to see that she received the punishment she deserved, but I did the best I could with the materials at hand. She wasn't in jail—yet—but she was discredited, broke, hunted, and plenty miserable. Considering the way it might have turned out, that wasn't a bad outcome. She should have been looking over her shoulder when she walked away from me that last day in her office, but she wasn't. She never saw it coming.

When they finally catch up with her and bring her to trial for fraud, I plan on attending every day, just so she can look at my face and be reminded who it was who brought her down. I'm sure Cassie will want to be there too.

Through the window, I could see that the rain had returned, a steady drizzle, and with it a heavy fog moving in from the Thames began to cloak the darkened park in an impenetrable shroud. In minutes, it was so thick that it was impossible to see more than a few feet, except when bolts of lightning scorched the London skyline with bright, momentary fire.

I didn't hear Cindy as she came from the bedroom, the sounds of her bare feet muted by the thick Indian carpet on the sitting-room floor. Naked, her pale skin seemed to glow in the dim light of the room. She sat on the arm of the chair and laid her arm comfortably across my shoulders. "Nightmares again?" she asked.

I shook my head. "No, I was just thinking," I said. "I was thinking how lucky I am to be here with you."

She was quiet for a moment. She took the brandy snifter from my hands and helped herself to a sip. "I've been thinking, too," she said. "With Robert out of basic training and off sailing the Mediterranean, I think you ought to invite Sam and Tommy to come up and spend the summer with you. You need to spend more time with your boys, Harry. Time has a tendency of slipping away, and before you know it, they're all grown and it's too late."

"They'd probably enjoy it," I said. "But what brings that up at this hour?"

She shrugged her shoulders. "I don't know," she said. "I've just been thinking about your kids lately is all. I feel like I've taken you away from them, and I don't mean to."

"You don't need to feel that way," I said. "But I appreciate your concern."

Although she was quiet then, I knew Cindy well enough to know there was more she wanted to say, something that had been on her mind for several days. We sat in companionable silence, watching the lightning flashing like a strobe light through the fog, until she was ready to talk. "You know, I never thought I could have children of my own," she said finally. Her voice was quiet, thoughtful, and serious. I listened closely. "Harv and I tried, but the doctors told me there wasn't much chance, and that I ought to get used to the idea. Harv wasn't interested in fertility drugs or in-vitro fertilization or any of that, not even adoption. He said it was just meant to be and we could have a good life without kids. That attitude made me very unhappy for several years, but I guess I finally learned to live with it. I have a rich life, and I have you, but I've always felt incomplete. I want children, a family, more than anything else. Do you understand what I'm saying?"

"I understand," I said. "And I'm sorry."

She bent over and kissed my cheek, held my face in her hands. "There's nothing to be sorry about, cowboy," she said. "As long as you're sitting down, I might as well tell you the rest of the story." She paused and then smiled. "I'm pregnant, Harry. Either it's a miracle, or you're a hell of a man. For argument's sake, I'm betting on the latter."

292

I heard her words well enough, but when comprehension of what they meant began to wash over me like iron-gray waves in a heavy surf, I was too stunned to respond. A thousand conflicting emotions battled for dominance as I struggled for equilibrium. I was tongue-tied, and she misinterpreted my silence as the stall tactic of a gun-shy bachelor trying to think his way out of a commitment trap that doesn't involve biting his own leg off.

"You ought to see the look on your face," she said. "Like someone just hit you over the head with a sledgehammer." She kissed me again. "Don't worry, though, and please don't be angry. I want this baby more than I've ever wanted anything, but my choice doesn't have to affect you or your life. When the child is born, it will be my responsibility. I'd like it if you accepted it as your own and took some time to know it, but I won't ask any more than that." She looked out the window for a long moment. "I'm sorry to spring it on you like this," she said quietly. "I've been waiting for the right time to tell you, but it just never came."

I asked a stupid question. "Are you sure you're pregnant?"

She nodded. "A little more than two months. That's why I spend so much time in the bathroom every morning, not that you've noticed," she said. "The baby should come sometime next October."

She was quiet then, and so was I, lost in thought as I finished the brandy. I put the empty glass on the bar and crossed the room to where she was still sitting on the arm of the chair. I knew what I had to do. I knew what I wanted to do. I guess I'd known for a while. I only had one provision. I knelt on the floor in front of her and took her hands in mine. "As long as it isn't October fifteenth," I said.

"Why not the fifteenth?"

"First day of deer season," I said.

Of all the possible responses from a middle-aged man who'd already raised a family and just learned that his new girlfriend was in the family way, that's the one she expected least. Incomprehension was written on her pretty face. "What does that have to do with anything?" she asked tartly. "You don't even hunt anymore."

293

I grinned and drew her closer until her face was inches from mine. "I might have to take it up again," I said. "Even a contented family man needs to get out of the house once in a while, away from the wife and kids."

She looked into my eyes, and a sweet smile grew on her lips as she began to understand what I was saying. "Is that your demented idea of a marriage proposal?" she asked.

I gulped and nodded. My emotions were in free fall, as if I'd just leaped from the observation deck of the Empire State Building. "Yeah, I guess it is," I said.

She didn't hesitate. "Then I guess I accept."

I bowed my head, waiting for the beat of my joyous heart to return to normal. Then we stood, and I carried her to the bedroom, her arms wrapped around my neck. We made sweet and tender love until the first rays of morning sun began to burn through the fog, the dawning of our future, and then we slept in each other's arms until Big Ben chimed noon.

For the first time in months, the ghosts did not come to trouble my dreams.